Simon Spurrier was born in 1981. A graduate from S.I.A.D.'s Film and Television degree course, he .... aries at both the National Academy .... ol, and has worked with the BBC a .... me an award-winning graphic novel .... 00AD – and has penned several lic .... book, Contract, was published by H ....

Simon lives in North London and is active in online and new-media communities. Visit *www.simonspurrier.blogspot.com* for more, or follow Twitter's **@sispurrier**.

Praise for *A Serpent Uncoiled*:

'An elaborately tooled razor of a book' Warren Ellis

'A unique protagonist, a unique voice, and a plot that sucks you in from the first page. Spurrier's sharp, brilliant prose is addictive' Mike Carey, author of the Felix Castor novels

'*A Serpent Uncoiled* is a great book, but not for the faint hearted . . . Spurrier has created a novel that will I hope become a classic' *Shots*

'The most original book of the year' *Bookgeeks*

'Spurrier's writing is intricate and deliberate . . . In this manner he weaves not just a classic noir crime novel, but a tale of a man twisting free of his past which is as memorable as it is dryly funny' *A Fantastical Librarian*

'[*A Serpent Uncoiled*] has everything: action, suspense, humour and passion. Don't miss it' *I Will Read Books*

'If you love crime with an urban fantasy twist, a flawed lead character and a twisted plotline that will keep you guessing then you've come to the right author' *Falcata Times*

'*A Serpent Uncoiled* is a book about a man on the edge – of society, of self-destruction and of reality – but not over it. With it, Mr Spurrier proves he's on the edge as well, taking the step from a promising talent to a great writer' *PornoKitsch*

By Simon Spurrier and available from Headline

Contract
A Serpent Uncoiled

coiled

SIMON SPURRIER

headline

First published in 2011 by
HEADLINE PUBLISHING GROUP

First published in paperback in 2012 by
HEADLINE PUBLISHING GROUP

1

Cataloguing in Publication Data is available from the British Library

ISBN 978 0 7553 3593 0

Typeset in Garamond by Avon DataSet Ltd,
Bidford-on-Avon, Warwickshire

Printed in the UK by CPI Group (UK) Ltd, Croydon, CR0 4YY

Headline's policy is to use papers that are natural, renewable and
recyclable products and made from wood grown in sustainable forests.
The logging and manufacturing processes are expected to conform
to the environmental regulations of the country of origin.

HEADLINE PUBLISHING GROUP
An Hachette UK Company
338 Euston Road
London NW1 3BH

www.headline.co.uk
www.hachette.co.uk

To Ciz
(*mine*)

Acknowledgements

I owe a great many people a great many thanks. Without their help, support and friendship this novel would never have been started, let alone completed. Special mention must go to Ian and Sherrie Spurrier, Tracey and David Couch, Stephen Dow, the unconquerable quaffhounds of the UK comics-scene, Ant and Winnie Whitehead, Jason Godfrey, Pedro Tudurí Pons (and all the other friendly, fascinating folk of San Lluis in Minorca), the sage philosophers of the Monday Club, Mike Donachie (whose superbly 'Scottished-up' sections went sadly unused), Ariana Osborne, William Christensen and the guys at Avatar (for being as understanding about deadlines as they are wrongheaded), the excellent grindslingers of the Sacred Cafe in Holloway, and those inestimable Sherpas among the peaks of publishing: Rachel Calder and Ali Hope.

I owe particular gratitude to Warren Ellis, to the gestalt intelligence of T.W.S., and above all others to my wife Chiara. Without her support, patience and insight I'm worth precisely nothing.

—S.

Chapter One

London hacked up its lungs and glistened.

The November drizzle had held off for the first time in three nights, but the air seemed choked regardless: a clammy ambient moisture caressing slick bricks and grey, leafless trees. On ledges through Soho, pigeons sulked in moronic bedragglement, while brave smokers lurked in smoggy palls outside steaming pubs, muttering at the indignity. In doorways along Oxford Street tramps clutched at dreaming dogs for warmth, and in Camden even the dealers – initially optimistic at the break in the rain – took to lurking near kebab shops and club queues, leeching excess heat, to mumble their mantras:

'Skunk, hash, pills . . . skunk, hash, pills . . .'

Out east, surly below a jaundiced sky, fog-windowed buses roared like dying lions through old puddles, dodging limping foxes and indifferent cats.

And in Hackney a girl screamed until her voice gave out.

The buses drove on. The foxes barely twitched.

The shriek surrendered to a ragged silence, then spiralled in a tangle of yelps to a single, shell-shocked moan. The neighbours turned up their TVs.

Only one man listened carefully, and he did so with a sigh, pulling his many-pocketed coat tighter. Even inside his grimy van – alone beneath a piss-toned street light – his breath steamed with every huff.

He was listening to sex and bemoaning his lack of arousal.

Not a twitch.

The girl rapidfired a series of gasps, like a train shunting through water, then groaned in a register reserved for wolves and whales. She yapped like a chihuahua, she babbled in a foreign language; and all along the *fapfapfap* noises never slowed.

The listening man rubbed his brows. With a pair of expensive headphones knuckling his brain it was easy to imagine the woman was speaking in tongues, and he smirked at the idea.

The Holy Spirit came upon her, he thought.

Right on her tits, I bet – the dirty old sod.

The man's name was Dan Shaper. Anticipating a headache, he adjusted the headphones and flicked a switch on the matte-black receiver in his lap: Channel B. Another exquisitely hidden audio bug, another eavesdropped room, another eardrum assault. This one, he judged (with a connoisseur's confidence), was only just getting started. For now, the male participant was the more enthusiastic.

'Oh bitch,' the voice rasped, syrupy with a forty-a-day wheeze. 'Oh bitch, *yeah*, oh bitch, *yeah* . . .'

Shaper felt distinctly as though he was being rogered in the ear.

He sighed again and rummaged through endless pockets for the zipped edge of his medication file. On the outside it looked for all the world like a chunky personal organiser: a relic of the eighties fossilised in faux leather and nylon. But inside, replacing neat pages, it clutched at dozens of tinny tablet sachets, each in its own elastic loop. Pic'n'mix for the brain.

He ran fingers along coloured rows like an artist hunting shades, and turned down the volume on the receiver. Soon, he knew – after tonight, with a little luck – he'd need to take some time out: a detox holiday to reset and recharge. Even after years of practice, judiciously self-medicating to keep his brain at bay, his mental diet was a constant flirtation with disaster. The blood could only be polluted so far, and the psyche dammed so high, before the first turned irretrievably toxic and the other burst its banks.

All under control.

Two Phenotropils this time – fat Russian stims – to dissolve the glimmers of incipient paranoia. And perhaps half a benzo – Zoloft, for choice, net-bought with US decals – to see off the amphetamine shadows. Taking it easy.

He swallowed them with the dregs of his coffee and flicked onwards to Channel C.

'*Oh god, oh god, oh god, oh goddddd . . .*'

He sighed again, profoundly unstirred. Melanie in Room 3 always feigned the most devout of climaxes.

At any other time, he supposed, he might have found this sad, grubby little gig a source of guilty arousal. But after a week of morosely flicking between squelches, shrieks, grunts, holy invocations and the occasional unprofessional fanny fart, he'd reached the unhappy state of desensitisation.

Besides, tonight there was a further impediment to his libido. At that moment it was sprawling across the passenger seat in a fog of fag smoke, helping itself to another beer and squinting at the bland terrace across the street.

'Don't look like a proper brothel to me,' it slurred.

Shaper, a lifelong avoider of unenclosed urinals, was not the type to be comfortably horny in male company. Particularly when said company was six foot six, sweated pure testosterone, and was rumoured to be hung like a planet.

'Don't be an idiot, Vince,' he muttered. 'What's a brothel supposed to look like?'

Vince – too tall, too wide, too pissed to do much but flap an enormous set of skinned knuckles out the window – stifled a belch. 'Just thought it'd be . . . y'know. More obvious.'

'Red lights, neon signs, tits in windows?'

'Well . . .'

'It's not bloody Amsterdam, mate. You've got to be discreet.'

Melanie, with exquisite timing, chose that moment to go supernova: a pterodactyl shrill counted out in bedspring squeaks. Shaper loosened the headphones and ignored Vince's smirk.

'Discreet,' the brute said. 'Yeah.'

Vince was Shaper's best friend – in the sense they could stand each other's company longer than most – and despite first impressions, one of the more fundamentally interesting people he knew. True, the man worked in a variety of interrelated professions on an ad hoc, cash-in-hand basis, all of which tended to involve hitting people until someone told him to stop. And yet – for instance – he somehow knew a great deal about fine wines. He read literature by dead people Shaper had never heard of. He was avowedly homosexual, but technically (and secretly, since picking up his latest boyfriend) bi. He had a peculiar phobia about tomatoes, claiming their texture reminded him of baby skin. He was a human being with more surprising, inexplicable facets than anyone had any right to; he just also happened to be hired muscle who'd snap a leg for five hundred quid. He'd probably even apologise afterwards.

Vince, in his chaotic and contradictory way, stood as a perfect representative of the muddled world Shaper had occupied as long as he could remember. The man was also, Shaper could tell, insufferably bored.

Which meant, by automatic association, he was drunk, burpy, farty and irritating. There was a reason Shaper had never brought him on a job before.

Across the street a pair of figures – balding heads catching the lamplight like sickly eggs – slunk from the glow of a doorway and hurried off. A third was just arriving: a frail man bent over a stick, creaking into the house and out of sight. Little Mrs Swanson shuffled into view to close the door, thick-rimmed specs misting in the cold, and visibly had to restrain herself from waving across the street at Shaper. It had taken her three nights of delivering tea and cake to the van to fully grasp the concept of 'undercover' surveillance, and she still laid out biscuits in case he got cold and came inside. She was the least Madam-like Madam he'd ever met.

Good biscuits, too.

'So how come the neighbours don't complain?' Vince grunted, derailing Shaper's thoughts. He rubbed the bridge of his nose with a sigh, noting that the headache was now in full swing. As, in his ears, was Melanie.

'They're paid not to.'

'How'd you know?'

He shot the brute a look. ''Cos it's my bloody job to know, ain't it?'

Watcher. Perve.

Troubleshooter. Issue wrangler.

Fixer.

The way Shaper saw it, all the men and women who grubbed about in his patch of dirt – all these broadly decent folk getting by with a few odd quid from a few odd sources – they needed someone to call in tricky times, same as anyone.

For Shaper's people, the cops weren't an option.

Take Mrs Swanson. As sweet an old lady as one could meet, who just happened to run the most successful knocking shop west of Stratford. For her, when certain 'valuable products' had started disappearing from the premises, a call to Shaper was as natural as a thrice-dialled '9' was to a more conventional business owner.

'Is this,' she'd querulously asked, 'the sort of thing you do?'

Oh yes.

Another eager customer knocked at the front door, sucking on his gums. Shaper caught Vince watching with narrowed eyes and could almost hear his inner cogs meshing.

'Is it just me,' the big man said, 'or are these punters a bit . . . y'know?'

'Long in the tooth?'

'Like a bloody tyrannosaur, yeah.'

Shaper slow-clapped the observation. 'Specialist establishment.'

Mrs Swanson's genius, which had elevated her business from one among hundreds of unconvincing massage parlours into a coffin-dodgers-only cash cow, had been to realise that punters of a certain age were not only far less trouble than their younger counterparts, but far more prepared to divest themselves of their – as she'd put it – 'ripened' savings.

'Used to be,' Shaper explained, 'she'd get the occasional old duffer showing up at the door who couldn't bring himself to . . . fully commit.'

Vince, to prove his comprehension, straightened a curled finger with a cartoon squeak. Shaper nodded, bitterly aware of his own moribund tackle.

'Exactly. And nobody wants to get sent home with a sympathetic refund, do they? So old Mr Droopy starts asking "Have you got anything for it . . . ?" and Mrs Swanson thinks, well, maybe I should.'

Vince smiled hugely, getting it. 'So she starts shilling Viagra?'

'To start with, yeah. Cialis, Revatio, Levitra. Healthy mark-up. Easy money.'

'Genius!'

'No, disaster.'

Vince scowled. 'How come?'

Shaper loosened the headphones another notch, brain ache still growing. ''Cos Mr Droopy's got a grandkid knows how to order it online for half the price. And the regulars compare notes in the changing room. Before you know it, they start showing up pre-primed.'

Vince raised a foaming toast to pensioner kind. 'Cocktastrophe!'

Between them, shrilling from the headphones, Melanie's voice ramped up for a second climax. Shaper knew from too many nights sitting just here, concentration creaking at narcotic extremes, that she allowed two orgasms per customer – no more, no less – timed with eerie precision. Each of the girls had their own little routines and he'd come to know them all. Ruth with her post-coital analysis, persuading the john that – *really, I don't often say this, I mean it, that was great.* Ksenia, she of the speaking-in-tongues, whose ecstasy (the customer was given to believe) was so profound that only her mother language could express it. Or Vicky, who made determined pleas that the punter blow raspberries in her cleavage then howled like a freight train. Compared to most, Melanie's breathless little appeals to the Ultimate were preferable by far.

'*Oh god, oh god . . .*'

He rolled his eyes and turned down the volume again.

And abruptly frowned. One of his hands had started to shake.

'So?' Vince prompted, oblivious to Shaper's sudden trickle of fear. 'What did the boss lady do?'

'What? When?'

Not now, not now, not now.

Probably, he told himself – dismissing the dry mouth, clenching his fist, ignoring the way one of his feet had started tapping a silent rhythm in the footwell – it was just the cold. Nothing to worry about.

Or . . .

Or a warning. A klaxon shriek to announce the stims had failed in their mission and his brain was tilting off its axis.

Relax, idiot . . .

Vince, of course, had no inkling, beered-up and impatient. 'C'mon,' he prompted. 'What did she do? When they stopped buying the Viagra?'

'Oh, *that*.' Shaper rubbed his temples, focusing. 'What could she do? She went looking for an alternative.'

Briefing him at the start, the old lady had delicately explained the establishment had taken a bold step into more exotic territory. Feelers had been gently extended, and after a month or two the very shadiest of supply routes began to deliver.

'What, then?' said Vince.

Shaper looked away. 'Powdered tiger cock,' he muttered.

'You *what*?'

He sighed. 'Look, it's a . . . a traditional Eastern medicine. The punters can't get it themselves and it costs a bloody fortune. It's a smart move.'

'Powdered t— But . . . You *what*?'

'I know.'

'But that's—'

'I *know*, Vince, all right? The point is, they keep coming back.' He gave a resigned shrug, feeling stupid. 'And now someone's stealing it. And I'm here to find out who.'

'Tiger's cock,' Vince muttered, slumping into head-shaking silence. 'Shit.'

It was, Shaper confessed, odd.

The merchandise arrived in exciting little tubs with intricate paper wrappings and ink drawings of tigers and naked women. Distributed by the girls themselves at the 'point of sale' – another Swansonism – the stuff fair *crackled* with arcane promise. All part, as Shaper had firmly opined, of the placebo effect. He doubted the stuff had been within a million miles of an actual tiger.

Mrs Swanson had put paid to that when she'd confessed, with an air of mortal guilt, that when 'the product' first started going missing she'd topped up stocks with a concoction of burnt sugar and flour. 'We had to refund everyone,' she'd mumbled. 'None of the poor dears could perform *at all*.'

Using the powder, the punters never failed to get their money's worth. Whole gaggles of shy old men achieved not only the means but the mindset: lousy with charisma and confidence.

It was, yes, odd.

Vince, massive chin jutting, didn't do odd.

'That's why we're here? To guard magic cat dick?' He sniffed through the lumpy remains of what had once been a nose. 'So why can't we just sit inside and watch the bloody stuff?'

'House rules. The stuff gets sold by the girls direct. "Intimate transaction" – nobody else in the room to keep an eye. Nobody dishing it out beforehand. Only chance is to work out who's taking it and catch 'em purple-palmed.' He worked his jaw. The shivers, he noted, had spread to the other hand. 'And it's got to be tonight.'

Vince flicked ash, muttering. 'Tiger pizzle . . . It's not fuckin' *Columbo*, mate. How hard can it be?'

'Lot sodding harder than I thought, all right?' Shaper tried to knead the spasm out of his hands. 'Look, it's a brothel, OK? Whole thing's about discretion and trust. Repeat buyers, like. The old dear almost croaked when I suggested cameras. And no customer searches either. Even the girls were arsey about me going through their bags, to start with.'

'Not now?'

'No, 'cos less product means less tips. Couple of days with an "out of stock" sign on the door and they were queuing up to help.'

'Did it?'

'Did it bollocks.'

Vince shrugged: case closed. 'So it's one of the punters.'

'Uh-uh. I sat in that changing room every day for a week. Went through every bloody pocket there was. Watched 'em in the shower, even.'

Vince smirked. 'Hot.'

'Not remotely. And I'll tell you this, mate, not a single one carried anything out of the bedrooms.' He discreetly breathed a gust of stolen smoke. 'In the same week five grand of the product went missing.'

Vince choked. 'You what?'

'Exactly.'

'Five grand?'

'Yeah.'

'But it's . . . it's cat dick!'

The brute pitched an empty can into the van's compartment and slumped into disgusted silence. Shaper had given up telling him not to.

'Anyway,' he said, as much to reassure himself as Vince, 'tonight's the night. You wouldn't be bloody here otherwise. Simple case of cross-referencing, when you get down to it. Girls on duty, vanishing stocks. Connect the dots.' He tapped the receiver kit with a confidence he didn't feel. 'It's one of these three. I worked it out.'

It has to be tonight.

The shaking hands. The pins and needles in his toes. The sticky shadows of nausea. He recognised them all too well.

After two weeks on the job, after seven nights in the van, after too many hours straining to hear anything unusual among shrieks of fake ecstasy, it could hardly come as a shock. No sleep, no rest, no peace; just a twanging narcotic plateau of high focus, fraying with every breath.

Detox or detonate, mate.

By the end of the week before, already sensing the onrushing burnout, he'd said fuck it to doing things the hard way and broken into the brothel one morning, laying audio bugs in smoke detectors and plug sockets while Mrs Swanson napped. Silent and secret – skills he'd learned long ago in the pursuit of less honourable goals. Client respect and staff trust were all well and good, he'd decided, but what Mrs Swanson didn't know couldn't hurt her.

Or his fee.

'It's one of these three,' he muttered again. 'Definite.'

Almost convincing.

'Fine. Great.' Vince nodded at the receiver with a fresh upsurge of impatience. 'Which one, then? 'Cos the quicker you get on with it, the quicker I can make with the Judge Dredd bit,' he mimed a door-smashing kick, leg thumping off the windscreen, 'and the quicker we can sod off down the pub. How'll you tell?'

Shaper felt the shakes creep up his arms and pretended he didn't.

'By listening carefully.'

'For?'

'I don't know. Anything out of the ordinary.'

Vince's eyes bugged out. 'Mate, there's a houseful of geriatrics snocking back the powdered phallus of an apex-fucking-predator over there. Exactly what part of this is *inside* the ordinary?'

Shaper ignored him and cycled gloomily through the channels. Room 1 was silent now; Ksenia's transaction over and done with. In Room 2 a guttural bellow suggested Vicky had finally persuaded her john to plant that raspberry, and – moving swiftly on – Room 3 brought him back to pious little Melanie, rising up the scale to yet another climax.

Nothing.

It *had* to be tonight. Already he could feel the narcotic swaddling dissolving like salt in a stream; his tolerance to the drugs growing stronger. Already he could sense the Sickness beneath the meds, quivering at the scent of freedom . . .

'Mate,' Vince rumbled, blind to the gathering panic. 'I'll tell you what, your job's a lot more interesting than mine.'

'Yeah?'

'Different every day, innit? Tiger cock . . . Jesus.' The brute tossed his dog-end out the window and tried not to slur. 'I mean – me? You hit a bloke once, you hit him twice, might as well've hit him a thousand times. And don't even get me started on bouncing outside clubs, *there's* an exercise in monotony, Kerist . . .'

Shaper had stopped listening. Breath catching in his throat, something hot behind his eyes.

'Hit a bloke once . . .'

Once, twice, thr—

'Fuck!' His hand scrabbled for the van door.

Vince, glancing up through the alcoholic fug, became aware only slowly that he was sitting alone, registering just an impression of something scruffy hurtling across the street.

'Mate?' he said.

By the time Shaper had pushed past Mrs Swanson, bewildered in the doorway, things were starting to fray in his brain.

Fuck.

The brothel was a fish-eyed ribbon of pink gloss, like a wet mouth beneath froth and fire. The shakes were in his shoulders now, fed by adrenaline, and as he blundered through the changing room he became convinced his skull was spitting with tesla-coil sparks, his feet crumpling through static frequencies. No wonder everyone was staring.

Narcotic meltdown in ten, nine, eight . . .

'Coming through!' he hollered. Then smirked.

Coming. Fnar.

Keep it together, keep it together . . .

Somewhere behind him he could hear Mrs Swanson administering apologies, chasing after him. Probably with her hands over her eyes – bless. He ignored her and aimed for Room 3.

'Got you,' he kept muttering. 'Bloody got you.'

At the door he paused to pull himself together, brain testing the walls of its amphetamine prison, warping the world with every hammer-heart throb. He held his breath to quieten the din and pressed his ear to the wood.

Inside someone shrieked and gasped, bedsprings creaking, a male voice grunting in time. Clockwork fucking.

Fapfapfapfapfap.

Melanie's voice rose in a new chorus – '*Oh god, oh god . . .*' – and above it all, superimposed like a special secret, came the ghostly tolling of church bells, the stink of rotten meat, and a swarm of blood-red flies below the door.

The broken sensations of a broken brain, Shaper knew; invisible and silent to anyone else. His own unspoken suspicions, dressed in sensory drama.

The Sickness: fucking with him.

The door was locked. Shaper grinned as he backed up a step and lowered his shoulder, only distantly aware of the inner voice reminding him he'd brought someone with him for precisely this moment.

Fuck it.

He tensed for the charge.

And—

'Stop this *at once*.' Mrs Swanson darted into view, sprightlier than she looked. All trace of cheerful indulgence gone now, fishbowl eyes shooting razors. 'This is a *discreet* establishment, Mr Shaper. I won't have you barging into the—'

'Three orgasms.'

She faltered. 'P-pardon me?'

'Three orgasms, Mrs S! Melanie only does two!'

Over the Madam's shoulder, muffled through the door, the

oh gods returned to joyous cries, staccato blasts broken by gasps. The bedsprings didn't miss a beat.

'She's stalling, see?'

Mrs Swanson actually blushed at the melody, recoiling from the door. At a safer distance she regained her poise, waggling a finger. 'Now see here—'

But Shaper was already moving.

The lock ripped open with a disappointing lack of splinters and screws. The door flopped aside as if embarrassed, and for just a second – before the shock of intrusion froze both occupants – the action continued unabated.

Shaper gawped.

Melanie, lingerie-clad, tight little body flushed with exertion, was bouncing on the bed like a schoolkid on E-numbers. *Creak, creak, creak.* Her hands, gently pinching her own face, were quivering the wet interiors of her cheeks against her gums, and all the while she moaned, grunted, shrieked.

Fapfapfapfap.

Convincing.

The girl stopped. For a second she simply stood and stared – at him, at Mrs Swanson, at the other customers peering from the changing room behind. And then she looked down, guilty, at the floor beside the bed.

Where a naked eighty-year-old with psoriasis was daintily shoving a double-bagged condom stuffed with powdered tiger cock up his arse.

Grunting in time.

Melanie crumpled cross-legged on to the bed, as if she'd been switched off. The old man creaked to his feet, jaw set. The offending package, interrupted in its patient insertion, bounced off his thighs like the shimmering turd of a wild haggis.

Behind him Mrs Swanson made a delicate little noise like a sleeping baby. '*Oom.*'

Shaper fought the urge to retch. 'Right, then,' he croaked. 'You're nicked.'

The room seemed to be filling with water, pooling against all physical sense across the ceiling. He felt the shakes work up into his throat. *Just keep breathing*.

'You a cop, then?' said the old man, voice unexpectedly deep.

The room hazed. A buzzing built in Shaper's ears, somehow infecting him with a growing panic that it had always been there, and now that he'd noticed, it would never go away.

Paranoia. *Brilliant*.

'Not exactly.'

'Right, then.' And the geriatric hit him.

Later, when his nose stopped bleeding, Shaper explained with some conviction that he hadn't wanted to raise his fists against a potentially frail man, and had felt it the more honourable option to roll with the punch. Mrs Swanson and the girls, gathered to feed him restorative biscuits, nodded dutifully.

Fortunately, Vince – who had finally caught up – suffered no such reservations, and as Shaper went down like a sack of spuds, the big lug deftly stepped past and nutted the pensioner between the eyes. Vince was still carrying his beer.

Shaper enjoyed a moment or two of blissful unconsciousness, and when he darted back upright – too late – with a ninja-like grace that convinced nobody, he noticed with slight surprise that the shakes were gone.

Job's a goodun.

Chapter Two

Alice Colquhoun, always a sharp one, deduced she was going to die long before the killer's blade punctured her skin. Like a death-row inmate thoughtlessly salivating at the distant scent of a favourite meal, she'd decoded her impending assassination before fully realising what she was doing, and even enjoyed a perverse shiver of satisfaction at her own cleverness.

Alone in a darkness of glossy plastic and rural odours – restrained, jaw aching at a rubber ball gag – she calculated her doom with the same detached logic that had built and sustained a career almost as high-flying as she liked to boast. Her entire life had been a mercenary thrust of self-confidence so iron-bound that her third husband had joked she could deter a bullet with a glare, yet here she was, trussed in a pink leotard, shivering through the rubble of her annihilated dignity.

Knowing, now, that she was going to die.

Through an iron door, barely visible in the gloom, a stereo whined with a poorly recorded sitar, its mosquito shrill increasingly punctured by the soft-flesh thumps of a tabla. Now and then, lost in the pulse, she could hear a gentle rustle, a wet-tongued *cluck* of anticipation from the next room.

Her killer, she knew: preparing for murder.

It was the restraints, in the end, that had settled the matter. Before she'd given them serious thought, through all the traumas of the evening – all the shocks and terrors and indignities – she'd maintained a façade of resilience, a characteristic refusal to despair. The hooded man breaking into her home, the waggled blade, the silent gestures compelling her to dress in her lurid jogging gear . . . And then the cowl on her head, the ride in a padded van, the endless jolts and shoves and terrors. At every stage she'd sustained herself against anguish by focusing on the breadth of possibilities that might yet underpin the mystery. The chance, say, that ransom notes were winging their way towards exes and major shareholders, or that unheard sirens were whooping closer even now. The hope, even, in the hateful pit of her soul, that her captor would prove to be merely some degenerate, some uncomplicated rapist whose appetites could be sated, or at least drawn out.

But no. The restraints had put paid to all that. In the context of all that had happened tonight, they glowed to Alice like beacons in the mire of confusion, the final shards of data to complete the equation. The restraints had doomed her as surely as the blade that would – without question – kill her.

Each of her hands was encased in a boxing glove, modified with soft laces and nappy foam, enveloping both arms to the elbow. Leather straps hooked into the knuckles, securing them to the cushioned seat behind her back. Similarly, duvet strips with straitjacket cords were fitted round each ankle, rising to the knee, fastened with rubber-coated chains to the chair's frame. All of it immaculately sewn and sealed, clean and unpatched.

That the rig was built to prevent escape was obvious from the outset (though Alice had methodically tested each seam any-way), but what had occurred only slowly was the obsessive *gentleness* of it all. There were no hard edges at the wrists, no chafing cords cutting ruddy lines round ankles and knees. Here was a soft sort of domination, a thing of care and padded pressure, and its sheer kinky inoffensiveness had hidden its true meaning all too long.

She had it now.

Her restraints had been designed solely and specifically to leave no marks on her skin. No signs of captivity, no trace of the evening's terror.

Why take such fastidious care if a captivity was purely temporary – a prisoner awaiting ransom? Why such obsessive coddling if violence and rape were the only goals?

No. No, she was too clever to cling to empty hope. The restraints had assured her that, whatever happened next, the only thing that would ever prove she'd been taken from her home, that she'd suffered in terror and trauma, was her own testimony. It stood to reason she wouldn't be given the opportunity to present it.

She blinked back incipient tears with a cold growl, refusing to succumb, and re-examined her prison. On hanging frames to either side, dimly perceptible beneath the plastic sheets which covered every surface, crude paintings of blue-faced figures thrust hips and tangled their many arms, waggling red tongues. Beneath their manic gaze a wooden table bore a rank of foggy jam jars and a single sputtering candle, its feeble glow the only illumination. Strangest of all, on the ground around her, a dozen chrome dog bowls stood arranged like a flotilla of UFOs, faint traces of straw and sawdust glimpsed through the membrane beneath.

In the light of Alice's murderous predictions, even they fitted this place.

It would look like an accident, she supposed. Perhaps a mugging. Something ugly and senseless – an impersonal, chaotic end – to justify the killer's insistence she wear her jogging gear. She found she could imagine the scene with a hideous clarity: her own body left to bleed out among the nettles of the Queen's Park nature trail, where she ran every evening without fail.

It was only then, with her own death scene so perfectly

rendered, with every ghost of an outside chance exorcised – as the tabla gathered pace – that Alice Colquhoun surrendered and began softly to weep. Unable to cry out intelligibly past the ball gag, she restrained from any dribble-flecked moans or discordant grunts. Those old boardroom habits – suffer in silence, show no weakness – died far harder than—

Well, than she was about to.

Nonetheless, when the door opened and the sitar swelled inwards, a groan detonated from some secret place inside her: involuntary, unbidden. She hated herself for it, and the scalding flare of anger came close to purging her misery.

Until the killer drifted across the light. Until the hooded shape melted into the room and began slowly, in measured steps, head tilted in animal query, to dance.

Arms dead at its sides like broken wings, whispering a private chant in time to the beat.

The sitar raced, the drum rose to its hectic climax, and as its gyrations grew more crazed, the figure turned to face her and eased back its hood.

In that moment what little courage Alice still retained flooded out of her. The breath she'd been saving escaped with a hiss, and it was only her inner anger – *how dare her body betray her?* – that kept her bladder clenched tight.

The face beneath the hood was a thing of primary blue and distorted hate. It bobbed through shadows and light: a vision of sapphire, gold and glossy red. In the pits of its black sockets Alice could see white eyes rolled back, moist and exultant behind the mask.

The killer leaned close, warping through the mist of her tears, and raised a gloved hand for inspection. In its latex grip, the knife that would kill her poured with reflected light.

The mask whispered, *'Ram.'*

And Alice understood.

And so, as the knife first entered her, as it slid into the cavity of her stomach then slowly – *lovingly* – cut sideways, as her blood rattled into the waiting dog bowls like a perverted percussion, Alice Colquhoun had the feeble satisfaction of answering the one riddle she'd thus far failed to solve: *why*.

Chapter Three

When, Shaper wondered, chewing a pillow, did the universe turn evil?

It wasn't that his bed was roughly as comfortable as a barbed-wire rack – though it was – nor that he felt the makers of his 'blackout' curtains should be prosecuted under the Trade Descriptions Act. Though he did. No, with a cushion squeezed round his ears, his current preoccupation lay with silently hating any creature winged, beaked or twittery.

Fucking birds.

Wallowing in the tetchiness of the morning after, failing to ignore the avian chorus outside, he lay on a foldout futon and tried, entirely without success, to sleep. His flat festered in the Victorian abyss between Camden and Kentish Town – an area celebrated for its colourfulness, which nonetheless suffered an ironic lack of greenery – and he simply couldn't understand what business the feathery little bastards could have in the vicinity of his window.

Sometimes squadrons of parakeets – day-tripping down from Hampstead Heath, where they'd established a stranglehold over indigenous species like Mardi Gras gangsters – would go out of their way to accumulate in his gutters, exchanging ear-piercing bleeps like a gaggle of kids comparing mobile ringtones.

They were clearly doing it on purpose.

He sighed and rolled over, flicking on the TV in despair. It took him just two channel hops – via a slick-haired provocateur (*wanker*) leading an in-studio discussion titled 'My Wife Hates My Husband', then a clammy regional show about an experimental artist called Merlin (*wanker*) using London's skyline to generate 'Echolocation Dioramas' – before the disgust overboiled and he gave up. The world, he concluded, loathed him, and the feeling was seethingly mutual.

Three days of this.

Shit.

The shakes had stayed away since last night's adventure. His brain had gifted him with an uncharacteristic let-off and he didn't intend to abuse its generosity. He'd been keeping the rotten thing stretched taut with his narcotic regime since the last detox intermission a couple of months ago, and knew from bitter experience it took several days of hermit-like dullness to let the compacted layers of psychoactive sediment leech from his skull. His blood and body demanded the break, partly to stave off the risk of overdose, partly to stage a hollow protest against dependency; mostly to assuage the threat of an ever-building tolerance. If all went well, by the end of the detox, the meds would be back to working at full effect and the Sickness – the memories, the guilt, *the past* – could be locked away where it belonged.

The trade-off, of course, was that for the duration of these cleansing bouts the horror was permitted to shuffle from its cage and flex its muscles. Shaper knew all too well that when that happened – perhaps later today, perhaps tomorrow – he'd *wish* for preoccupations as harmless as birds and broadcast bullshit.

He surrendered to sleeplessness and got up, pretending not to notice the head rush, and flapped for something to eat while his guts still worked. The coming miseries could only be tolerated, he knew, by refusing to leave the flat – by mitigating the traumas with a torrent of inactivity and solitude – and his cupboards were therefore packed with enough canned goods to shame the nuttiest of nuclear survivalists. Simple, bland, and utterly undesirable.

His intestines bubbled.

Probably just as well.

It wasn't that he enjoyed the drugs, particularly. As a day-to-day motive there was little recreational about it, and in the rare moments when one effect or another rose above the clamour (a shiver of speedbomb confidence, say, or a languid moment of potheaded introspection), it was more a warning flag than any opportunity to enjoy himself; a signal that he'd tilted off centre, that the delusions and distortions might trickle back at any second, and that another adjustment was required. Or, as now, that he needed a fucking holiday from the whole thing, and would just have to put up with any ugliness that that entailed.

As if testing him – *bastards* – a couple of unnecessarily loud sirens dopplered past outside, making his head pound. He caught himself reaching for the pill file without thinking and restrained himself with a scowl.

The more you take, the less it achieves.

It didn't seem fair.

He pushed the file away and looked for something else to do: staying busy while his brain hit freefall.

The flat was a tip – albeit in a highly organised way – there was no disguising it. For every drift of paperwork, stack of unpaid bills or heap of Internet-purchased surveillance gear, there was, theoretically, a perfectly shaped void in some drawer or cupboard somewhere, so it could all be scooped away at a moment's notice. Not that he'd ever tried.

Home.

He hated it, mostly. It wore its Young Professional Couple credentials on its sleeve – one among a dozen clones above the terraced shops and bars of Kentish Town Road – and as time passed he'd felt a compulsion to explode his detritus all across it, as if reclaiming it from the ghost possibility of a non-existent cohabitee.

He'd stopped sleeping in the bedroom long ago. He'd told himself he was keeping it for one-nighters or guests – not that either were in especially rich supply – but knew deep down he was simply uncomfortable sleeping there. A big double bed in a big double room, designed for big double things.

Bit too close to the nerve, that.

In his eyes the whole flat stank of functionality and embarrassed solitude, and it was there, in the pits of past sins and the loneliness that had followed, that the Sickness lurked at its most potent.

Three bloody days.

He picked up the phone and dialled Vince on instinct, desperate for distraction.

'I'm asleep or in prison,' said what was probably an answerphone. 'Fuck off and die.'

No bleep.

Vince, Shaper reflected with a sigh, typified the circles of society he'd graduated towards all his life: a world of shades of grey, driven by the chugging engine of back-alley capitalism. A world populated by people who were *technically* but not *psychologically* 'criminals'. Vince, Mrs Swanson, her girls, even the punters at the brothel: all normal, everyday people – broadly speaking. You could slice them into quantum nuggets, Shaper knew, and not find a single echo of black-hearted criminality, yet still they spent a goodly portion of their time flirting or fucking with matters extralegal.

Little wonder he felt so often that he'd prolapsed all moral certainty.

He reached for the pill file again, and this time didn't catch himself until the zip was opened and his fingers were tracing along colourful little rows. He snapped it shut with a growl and chucked it across the room, not watching where it fell.

'Piss off!' he shouted. Then felt ridiculous.

The alternative to all this, he knew – to keep going, medicating, working, *living* – was terrifying. Yesterday's incipient shakes, and those first ghosts of hallucination in the brothel were a clear sign that his chemical barriers were failing. Far better to take down the walls himself, to manage the resulting trauma here – temporarily, and on his own terms – than to let them irretrievably crumble out in the real world.

His eyes dropped on to a small baggie of brown powder on a tower of Final Demand envelopes. Mrs Swanson had thrust it into his hands with a mischievous grin last night, along with his pay. 'Your tip,' she'd twinkled. Her turn to make him blush.

He drummed his fingers and tried to gauge if he was already bored enough to experiment with freebie penis powder, or if he should try and save it for when things got desperate. Or at least when in company. Eventually he decided with a self-punishing sigh that any substance abuse – mystical or otherwise – violated the spirit of detox, and sulkily pushed it away.

It was going to be a very, very tough few days.

He'd tried doing things the conventional way, of course. Five years before, while the Sickness was still young, while the parade of criminal horrors and guilty abhorrence that had caused his mind to collapse was still fresh, there'd been doctors, prescriptions, 'medications' in the truest sense. He'd crawled up from the darkness of – he now knew – a breakdown, to find himself incapacitated, locked in a fugue of anodyne sensation, yet still haunted by the—

Well.

By her.

By the Corams.

By betrayal and bullets and blood. By hospitals and ultrasounds and warm hands going limp and lies and lies and lies . . .

So no. The doctors had tried to fix him and made him a

zombie in the course of failing. It had taken him just a month to find his own solution. Not quite a cure, but a dodge, a second stability. A high-wire amphetamine plateau, teetering above and beyond the jaws of the past, allowing him to operate with every appearance of normality and package the secret slime at the back of his brain, like a tumour packed in gristle.

It allowed him to function – to focus and think and feel; an occasional few days easing the pressure seemed a small price to pay.

Over the next few nights, he knew, as the stimulants left his system, he'd catch his mind beginning to wander. He'd trip on razorblade memories. He'd choke on a sob and not know why. He'd see smoke and hear screams. The delusions would uncoil from his hindbrain like a punishment, muddling and infecting everything he saw or heard. Excitement or stimulation would only make it worse, so he'd try and sleep through as much as he could. The rest could be blunted, at least, through sensory deprivation.

Dark rooms, lukewarm baths, tasteless food . . .

And then on the third or fourth day he'd hear her voice. See her sad little smile.

And in that second, before it dragged him down into the pit of his sins, he'd knock back the first Dexedrine tab and start the whole process again. Hopping between the frying pan and the fire, two months at a time.

So far it was working.

On the tabletop, a few envelopes cascaded from the pile to reveal a prehistoric face with a profoundly disinterested expression.

'Ziggy!' Shaper declared, overjoyed at the distraction. 'How's it going, old son?'

The creature blinked with theatrical slowness and shat on the bills. Even that seemed an act of existential apathy.

Shaper had been resistant, at first, to the notion of pets. One night at the pub Vince had garrulously diagnosed 'his problem' (a perennial favourite among topics) as a desire for affection and structure. *Bollocks*, he'd said – only vaguely convincing – while a loose confederacy of regulars mimed cuddly kittens and speculated whether a puppy would give his worthless life any meaning. He'd forgotten all about the incident until he was hired several weeks later to find the missing daughter of a reptile smuggler from Leyton (shacked up with a prominent dealer of snakeskin footwear, it turned out), and in a moment of inspiration asked for payment in kind. He'd always liked dinosaurs.

Ziggy was a green iguana with the magical ability to make people feel like shit. His eternal aspect of heavy-lidded disinterest contrived to suggest he regarded humans as inconvenient natural hazards rather than living things, and he was – in general – fractionally less lovable than an ice sculpture or a corpse. Shaper had installed an incubator light in one corner shortly after bringing him home – supposedly to provide the energy Ziggy needed to survive – but it quickly became clear that the scaly sod preferred his signature state of dormant irritability and never went near it. So much, Shaper had quickly reflected, for affection and structure.

On cue, the critter scuttled into a listing stack of receipts and left him alone.

'Three days,' he muttered. 'Piece of piss.'

And then the door buzzer went.

Shaper was out of his chair and at the intercom before the first metallic growl had died away. He had at least a few hours, he judged, before the lonely suffer-in-darkness shtick properly kicked in.

'Yeah?' he said, face to the microphone. 'Hello?'

'Mr Shaper?'

'Yes! Who's that? Actually, doesn't matter, just come up.'

Even a bible botherer, he recklessly decided, would make a worthy distraction.

He pressed a button. The LED marked 'door unlocked' twinkled green. The one marked 'door open' remained resolutely unlit.

'I'm sorry, Mr Shaper. I'm in a hurry.' It was a woman's voice, thick with Scandinavian inflection. 'I cannot stay. I was hoping you maybe come down.'

His hand reached for his jacket without consulting his brain. He pocketed his keys in the same move and groped for the door.

Then stopped. Caught up with himself.

He leaned back into the microphone. 'Um. *Why?*'

'I have job for you.'

Shaper deflated like a balloon.

'I'm . . . It's . . . it's sort of my day off.' He coughed into a fist. 'I need a holiday.'

'Oh.' The voice punched straight through disappointment and deep into bloody betrayal. 'It is just . . . It may be important. Not for long. Few hours only.'

'Yeah, sorry . . . It's just not a good time.' Every word hurt.

'Mr Shaper?'

'Mm?'

'You get one thousand pounds. Very short talk. Second opinion only.'

Shaper sniffed.

Final demands, he reasoned. Plus poor Ziggy's got to eat.

Priorities.

'On my way,' he said, halfway out the door.

He could delay the detox an hour or two. No problem.

Her name was Tova Isberg. Tall, blonde, dainty of feature and spectacular of chest, she'd lingered over their oh-so-chaste handshake as if expecting Shaper to recognise her. He hadn't, and hoped it was only his imagination that she seemed relieved.

Driving her to work like a dutiful husband (who knew exactly how lucky he was), Shaper kept snatching sideways glances, partly trying to place her face, mostly just ogling. Every shift of his van's increasingly decrepit gears – dipping a hand close to her legs – was an exercise in guilty restraint.

He'd spent all week eavesdropping on bonking couples. It was too much to hope that his inner super perv had faded already.

'West,' she said, glancing at her watch. 'Go west. Already I'm late.'

For all that she was undeniably beautiful, she had about her a manner of studied non-flirtatiousness – a polite null zone where a pheromone crackle might have been – which firmly dissuaded Shaper from trying a self-diagnostic on his malfunctioning crotch. Her mannerisms put him in mind of Mrs Swanson's girls: shorn of any daffy expectations regarding the romantic importance of sex or sexuality. Clattering past the roundabout at Swiss Cottage, the thoughts of working girls flipped a switch somewhere in the murkier realms of his memory.

'Got it,' he said. '*Tova, The Valkyrie Virgin*. Your phone-box flyer had the pointy helmet and everything. Swedish, right? Came over in oh-three.'

She stared out of the window and failed to be excited by memory lane. 'Oh-two.'

'You were one of their first, weren't you? The Corams, I mean. They'd only just started the agency . . . "EsCort Red-Handed", for fuck's sake. Tacky as you like, but a good little earner.'

'Good little earner,' Tova said. Quiet. Cold.

Shaper squinted and tried to remember. The period in question occupied a nebulous realm of his memory beginning shortly after his schooldays and ending at the cataclysm which had scabbed over all that had gone before. The past was still visible to him – with a little patience and a lot of interpretation – but the drugs had cut it mercifully loose from any sense of personal connection, and sealed it in amber. Looking back now was more like glancing sideways of flicking through someone else's sordid biography. And for every memory worth reconnecting to, there were a dozen brimming with violence and venom, carefully frozen under years of chemical winter.

These days, he didn't dig too far.

A thought sleazed itself up from the ice.

'Did we ever . . . uh . . .' He flapped a hand.

Tova shook her head, unembarrassed. 'You were with Anna.'

Shaper's turn to go cold, now. He concentrated on driving, smile fixed. 'Ah,' he said. Almost no quaver at all.

The name alone shot frosty nails up his shoulders and throbbed in the domes behind his ears. He bit on the insides of his cheeks and thought of everything that wasn't her. Right on time, one of his hands began to shake.

Five minutes passed in silence. Belsize Road, Kilburn, Queen's Park. A gaggle of neon jackets stood at the roped-off entrance to the kids' playground; an ambulance pulled up by the road. The kind painted black.

Another stabbing, Shaper supposed. Youths knifing youths.

The ugly notion came complete with an only-in-London inner shrug, and a perverse relief at the mental diversion. (Maybe he'd imagined the shakes after all. He couldn't feel them now.)

'South from here,' said Tova, when they hit Kensal Rise. 'Holland Park.'

'Very posh.'

'He's rich. My client.'

Ah.

'So you're still, y'know . . .' He flapped his hand again. 'For the Corams?'

'Not working for them any more. I got out.'

'Very smart, very smart.' He cleared his throat. 'I did something similar mys—'

'I heard.'

The path that had brought Shaper to this most difficult-to-define niche had rarely strayed into the strip-lit sterility of 'legal'. He'd dabbled comfortably with dodginess since the age of sixteen: a snotty little East Ender with a broken nose, beating up posh kids to survive the school he'd been sent to when his dad died. In the years since then he'd seen more of the secret bruises beneath London's tourist-tattooed skin than almost anyone – most of them in the employ of the self-same Coram family who'd once salaried Tova – and nowadays spent a good portion of his time trying to forget all those he'd caused himself. Even now, approaching the whole thing from an opposite and less destructive direction, his success depended on his clients being assured – via whichever ethereal process brought them to him – that he still knew the score.

A reputation, he'd gloomily accepted, clings a lot harder than a career.

Another troubling idea shifted him in his seat. 'This is . . . nothing to do with them, right? The Corams?'

'Nothing.'

''Cos I'm . . . I'm well out of all that.'

And I won't go back. Not to them.

Not to that vicious family fraud. Not to Maude and her kids, and the turbulent stink of betrayal that surrounded them like a nuclear cloud.

Never go back.

God, I miss them . . .

'Nothing to do with them,' Tova said.

'Right then.' He gave a professional little sniff and eased the van down Ladbroke Grove, stuck behind a bus. An advert on its rear window read 'Overdoing It?', above a cartoon tortoise outpacing a startled-looking hare: a tub of energy tablets clutched in one claw. On instinct, Shaper's hand dipped to his pocket to brush lightly across the zip of the pill file . . .

Which, of course, wasn't there. Thrown, blindly, across his flat.

No big deal. (Trying not to panic.) *Just a couple of hours. Back to the detox.*

'Where are we going, Tova?'

'I told. Holland P—'

'Not what I meant.'

She shrugged. 'My patient, he calls me. Ten a.m. I am still in shower – is very early, for him.'

Shaper tried not to imagine her in the shower. Gave up.

'He was very agitated. Wanted to speak with somebody who is . . . finding things out, yes? I suggest you. He's very wealthy – talk only.'

'A "patient"?' Shaper repeated. Then broke into a grin as realisation dawned. 'You mean, like . . . naughty nurse?'

Tova threw him a look of deafening neutrality. 'No. I mean like *real* nurse.' She twitched aside her jacket. All whites and medical blues.

'Oh.' He coughed into a fist. 'Sorry.'

They drove in silence after that.

It cost four pounds twenty to park for the minimum term – a metered bay half a mile from their destination – and the atmospheric hum of wealth didn't diminish thereafter. Tova led Shaper along a leafy street lined with four-by-fours and phallus cars, and up the steps of a white marble mansion terrace which, he guessed, had been dumped through a time warp from ancient

Rome. He noted with irritation that, despite the abundance of neatly pruned trees, not a single bird chirped.

Hate, hate, hate.

Tova let herself in with a private keycard (he'd half expected a retinal scan or a doorman with a rifle), and up an ox-blood staircase to a carved oak door. Another key.

Shaper clenched and unclenched his fists in his pockets while she opened up, an inexplicable paranoia prickling in the small of his back. He tried to focus on the kaleidoscope of expensive clutter rather than his own sweaty state, and realised that, London being London, he could name three crack dens in crumbling local authority blocks within two streets. If you looked from far enough away, he knew, squeezed in side by side, the city's class divides merged into a single, average-income blur.

Seen from a distance, monstrous wealth was almost invisible.

Seen from the inside, on the other hand, it looked a lot like a mahogany-lined palace of over-indulgence and drear. Far gloomier than it should have been, with dark rugs aligned meticulously along parquet hallways and maroon blinds stifling the light.

Too quiet.

Tova began bustling in a cupboard just inside the door, dragging out a torpedo-like oxygen bottle and loading it, deftly, on to a trolley. 'Third door at the right,' she said, nodding up. 'Walk noisy, yes? He doesn't like to be startled.'

Shaper nodded, feigning confidence, and began clattering up the hallway as clumsily as he could manage.

'He's very lovely,' Tova called out, like an afterthought. 'Only wants you to listen. See what you say at end.'

'Right. Thanks.' He reached for the relevant door, noting that his fingers shook – unmistakably this time – as they tightened. A clammy nausea climbed in his belly.

The chemicals, leaving his blood. Or the tension baiting the Sickness like a caged lion. Either way – *shit*.

'Oh, one thing.' From the gloom he could just discern Tova's face, peering over a tangle of nebulisers and tubes. 'He can be . . . how do you say . . . Eccentric? Confused, yes? Is best if you just let it go. Big stories, he tells. Just smile, I think. Not argue.'

'Not argue. Check. Has he got a name?'

She shrugged. 'He is Mr Glass.'

Shaper stepped through the door. He was instantly bathed in an electric ripple of darkness and light: coruscating blue tones in cold angular coffins, suspended in pitch blackness. And, as if taking its cue from the unexpected surreality around him, his vision began to blur.

Crap.

He blinked and battened it down, muttering to himself. 'Aquariums . . .' Lots and lots of aquariums.

He walked between the aisles as if compelled, absorbed in the gentle sputtering of filters and halide-lit bubbles. A sterile taste of life in the womb: muffled, liquid, all-enclosing. To one side a phalanx of bright fish, yellow and red, hung in formation above a punctured coral like a brain, he thought, rotten with ulcers, and over his shoulder a gorgeous shrimp waved frond-like claws across a circulatory jet. In the tank above it an anemone beckoned sensuously, then caressed erotic tendrils across the bellies of three striped fish.

Shaper shook his head, sensing the honey-like sludge of reality oozing from his grip, and swore at himself for leaving the meds at home. No, worse: for even *coming* here.

He blinked and tried to bullshit his way through the weirdness, marching further along the neon sepulchre, but it was too late. The Sickness had found a crack among the fading drugs and the simple weirdness of the bubbling room, and the distortions were taking hold.

The tanks became serried rows of angelic tombstones, epitaphs inscribed in alien letters of living light: gulping water and flicking fins. As the pulse of the filters unified to a single frog-like warble, he became convinced he could see the souls of every living thing. Each fish a beacon of light, each roiling sea plant a lattice of lasers, given perfect purity by their ignorance. No lies, here. No treachery or falsehood. No synaesthetic swarms of ruby flies or pestilent smells – like those haunting the doorway to the brothel – only the clean simplicity of dumb existence.

This, at least, was a familiar delusion. One that gripped him at some stage during each of his detox episodes, rendered harmless in the dull sanctuary of his own home.

But here . . .

He found himself raising a hand for his own inspection, already knowing what he'd see. On the jag of his third knuckle, the skin *bubbled*. Spots appeared around the quivering pustule, strobing from bloodless white to rotten black. A red tinge smeared itself through the nearby veins: a disease gurgling wider. In this dream his body was dying, necrotising from the inside out, infected by the pestilence hiding deep in the vile coil he laughably called a soul.

His own guilt. The things he did, the people he hurt, the lives he broke.

His own filth, trying to get out.

His eyes widened. In the heart of the decaying skin a lesion stretched under pressure. Something white and wet heaved up from below, tiny body throbbing with peristaltic life.

Maggot.

Pale and mindless, it snapped through the blister and writhed free, bringing a low groan from inside him, and oozed across the back of his hand. He felt his knees weaken.

'Here!' said a voice, rippling across the sky. 'Don't knock on the tanks.'

Shaper tried to explain he wasn't, tried to hold up the hand to show whoever was there – whatever oddity was creeping up in the dark – that *look, see, can't you tell I'm dying?* But what left his mouth was just sound, and when he finally persuaded his head to turn to look, all thoughts of his own horrific state flooded away.

There was a man made of light, staring at him.

Radiating. Crackling with whiteness every bit as pure – every bit as simple – as those feckless, flawless little fish dotting the darkness. At the edges of the corona the glow prickled with a violent tinge, and as this divine absurdity reached out a hand towards him, Shaper felt his own filth retreat, his pestilence submerge.

The maggot dissolved like ash on a nuclear wind.

'You must be this Shaper fellow, then?' the vision said. 'Nice to meet you.'

'Who . . . ?' he squeezed from empty lungs.

'I'm George Glass,' said the light, taking his hand. 'And I'm three thousand years old.'

Which is when Shaper passed out.

Chapter Four

He awoke to find himself – broadly speaking – back in the real world.

The distortions were gone, and when he'd blinked back from the blackness, the buzzing in his ears had died away. Only the endless bubbling and the glitterball of light through water remained, disorientating and distracting even as it soothed.

He stood gingerly and waited for the headache to settle.

An old man was staring at him, leaning shakily on a stick with a set of bramble brows curled in confusion.

'Are you quite all right?' he said.

His eyes were an almost transparent brown, bringing to Shaper's mind nothing so much as twin pools of whisky, which lit up abruptly above a smile so preternaturally guileless that Shaper caught himself grinning back, mumbling, 'Fine, fine.'

The headache, against all historical precedent, faded like the end of a bad song.

'I have this condition,' he explained. 'Sometimes it flares up. I— it's fine now.'

Condition.

Now *there* was a joke.

Oh, the doctors had shot names at it, he remembered, as if a label were the same as a cure. The Capgras Syndrome of Existential Uncertainty; Somatoparaphrenic Disconnections from parts of his own body; Monothematic Delusions of corruption and decay, *blah-blah-blah*. But none of the hats was a perfect fit, and a simple name couldn't alter the underlying truth.

Shaper's past had branded his present like a coloured lens over his senses.

His 'condition', if it had a name, was 'Fucked By Guilt'.

But the old man didn't know any of that, and merely waggled his brows in concern. 'You're sure you're feeling better? Best sit down anyway, eh? This way!'

And off he hobbled.

Optionless, Shaper trailed him – patient at the creaking progress – to a bright living room, mercifully free of psychedelic triggers. 'Fish,' the man muttered, as if hearing his thoughts. 'Either very relaxing or terribly dull – depends how you feel. I find they help me remember.' He tapped his head. 'Do you know, I spent a summer diving for pearls? Got a soft spot for the little sods while I was down there. It's all nostalgia.'

'Pearls,' Shaper mumbled. 'When . . . when was that, then?'

The old man shrugged. 'Buggered if I know.'

He settled himself into a colossal armchair and took a moment to catch his breath. Shaper sank on to an artfully distressed leather settee and contemplated his host.

A resilient fringe of white hair clung to the slopes of the old boy's skull like a treeline, from which the dome of his scalp – pointier than seemed sensible – emerged like an olive-toned iceberg. To Shaper, his complexion suggested the Mediterranean, but he had no trace of an accent and, where the wool of his hair met his temples, there was a distinct hint of sandy blond. He wore baggy lounging clothes: linen trousers and a crinkled shirt, one step above pyjamas, one step below formal. He folded his slender hands – constantly shaking, Shaper noted – across the head of his stick, and smiled the smile of everyone's dream grandfather.

'So then,' he said. 'Mr Shaper, Private Eye.'

'Sort of. Yeah.' Shaper hated the title, but for some reason couldn't bring himself to say so. 'And it's . . . it's Mr Glass, isn't it?'

'These days, *ha*. These days!'

Rrrright.

Above all else, beyond the obvious eccentricity and manic smiles, the man radiated a sense of extraordinary warmth – genuine interest, genuine care – which in spite of all his instinctive suspicion, Shaper couldn't bring himself to doubt. He found himself haunted by that final vision from next door's wig-out: the ghost of a pure, cleansing aura of white and violet.

Mess-i-bloody-anic, as Vince would've put it.

Shaper knew all too well that his lunatic brain farts couldn't be trusted, but they were tough impressions to shake. He'd been stumbling over such hallucinatory nonsense for the past half-decade – whenever the drugs were out of synch or the situation became overwhelming – but they rarely took his breath away as profoundly as today's, and had never before described an image of such focused incandescence. On the contrary, vague psychedelics and blurred associations were the usual stock-in-trade of his Sickness, mundane fantasies he'd long since rationalised as manifestations of his own subconscious – gut feelings and first impressions given form and colour. At best they were an unwelcome obfuscation of his senses; at worst – as with this last episode – an incapacitating crash of the meat computer in his skull.

He avoided them as much as possible.

Nonetheless, soothed by the memory of that purifying halo, he found himself bizarrely calm in Glass's presence. Even when he found the brown eyes inspecting him with the same quizzical interest he'd been applying himself, he felt no awkwardness, no desire to look away or bristle.

Tova broke the silence by bustling in with a tray, balancing a glass of water and a small pot loaded with colourful tablets.

'Pill time,' she said, setting it down. Glass rolled his eyes with a twinkle – for Shaper's benefit – and began diligently swallowing the stash, water sloshing in his trembling hand. Shaper watched the tablets vanish with a tiny twinge of envy.

'Sandra called,' Tova declared. 'They're almost here. I have set up for Freddie in guest room.'

The old man paused between sips. 'My daughter and her son,' he explained to Shaper. 'They visit every week.'

'Very nice.'

'He's a bit . . . how do they put it now? "Special needs." The boy. Lovely little chap, though.'

'Right.'

'That's why I got Tova, y'see? She looks after him, mostly. But she can do me too.'

Arf arf, Shaper successfully didn't say.

Tova demonstrated more accurately what was meant by 'doing' by shushing the old man and rattling the remaining pills. He sighed and kept swallowing.

'Most days,' she explained to Shaper, 'I come here, then go see Freddie at other house.'

'Other house?'

'I told you, Mr Glass very rich. Big house outside town. Is where Sandra lives. Have to get train, let myself in, very boring. Thursdays they come here instead. Much more easy for me. More time.'

Glass handed back the empty pill pot with a smile. 'Enough to make us a cuppa, d'you suppose?'

Evidently even frosty little Tova wasn't immune to Glass's charm, smirking with fake irritation and asking both men how they took it.

'White,' Shaper said, strangling innuendos. 'Three sugars.'

'So,' said Glass when they were alone. 'Sandra's coming. I'm afraid this'll have to be rather quick, then. I don't want her fussing.'

Quick? Shaper panicked. *As in less than £1,000?*

'Fussing about what?'

'Well, that's it, isn't it? That's why you're here.' The old man opened a drawer and removed a white oblong, cut across its top edge. 'It arrived before I even woke up. I want to know what you think.'

Shaper took it from the shaking hand. It was an ordinary enough envelope, self-sealing with a sticky strip, address written in chunky, disconnected letters. No stamp, no postmark.

'Sloppy,' he muttered. 'Someone's in a hurry.'

'How's that?'

Glass, he found, was watching him closely.

He shrugged. 'Sender wanted it to be untraceable. No lickable strip for DNA, no freeform handwriting. But, actually, that's a bit of a cock-up right there. He's done these big nursery-school letters to try and disguise the cursive, but a decent expert could still tell you all sorts. Cops these days can d—'

'No police,' said Glass.

Shaper glanced up, quietly surprised at the conviction in the voice. It wasn't that a desire to avoid Her Majesty's finest was unusual among his clients, simply that it somehow didn't tally with the world of George Glass he'd seen so far.

Hm.

'No police,' he said, oddly disappointed. 'Right.' He turned back to the envelope. 'Anyway, something happened, didn't it? He's written out the address, all ready to post, but he never goes through with it. No stamp. Decides to do it by hand instead – much bigger risk. So something changed. Something happened this morning.'

'Very good.' Glass almost clapped. 'See for yourself.'

Inside were four folded sheets of paper. Shaper fished them

out one by one, opening them with care. The first two had been cut from consecutive issues of the *Evening Standard*, each a small article with a connecting strip to the page-top date: one from the previous day, one from the edition before that.

The earliest dealt in simple, matter-of-fact terms with the death of one Heidi Meyer (63), whose entire existence was summarised in a textual splat so dreary that a typo in the second line seemed the most interesting thing about her. She had been, Shaper read, 'a keen gardener' and 'frequent exhibitor at the Chelsea Plower Show' – uh-huh – who'd slipped while pruning in her rooftop garden near Richmond. 'Police were alerted when a neighbour spotted the body at the foot of a communal light well.' Shaper scanned the rest with a guilty stab of impatience: terrible accident, lovely old lady, never a harsh word, *yadda yadda*, '... and are not treating the death as suspicious.'

The small photo showed a dowdy little woman in tie-dyed overalls with bird's nest hair, posing with a trowel for some long-past appearance at the Chelsea 'Plower' Show.

The second article, from yesterday's edition, wasn't much bigger. This one used the discovery of a badly damaged body, beside train tracks in Clapham, as a lead-in to a wider declamation on the area's use as a dogging spot for homosexuals. It described a bridge with an overhang offering perfect shelter for nocturnal goings-on, and thoughtfully reassured readers that 'local officers are aware of the problem'. The article even wheeled out a councillor to wobble his jowls and condemn the immoral, illegal, and above all dangerous practice of fucking by train light. Except he didn't call it that.

In all this, Shaper noticed, the unfortunate sod whose body had prompted it all got remarkably little mention. It was clear he'd been hit by a train, and given the darkness of the tunnel it perhaps wasn't a surprise that no driver had reported an incident.

The article suggested – what with the reputation of the area – that the man probably hadn't been alone ('appeal for anyone who witnessed the incident to contact police') but, as with the first article, surmised it was a terrible accident and nothing more. It added, almost as an afterthought, that the police believed the casualty was a well-known 'local sex worker' known as 'Kingsley', and were seeking relatives to confirm his identity.

The name, at least, caught Shaper's eye. Nothing like familiarity to make an ugly, trivial little death seem important.

Kingsley the Cocker, minor celebrity of the extralegal world, boyish of face and (so they said) goddish of everywhere else . . .

Rest in pieces, old son.

Tova brought the tea as he flicked to the third sheet. 'Is he any good?' she asked Glass, hooking a thumb.

'I'll let you know.' The old man smiled.

The third sheet was a printout from the BBC News website. A two-paragraph tangle of uncertainty regarding the reported discovery of a body in Queen's Park, NW6. Shaper scowled and thought back to the police cordon he'd passed on his way here.

Still fresh.

Details were sketchily unhelpful. The body, the article suggested (with all the cunning inaccuracy indemnity it could muster – *alleged, believed to be, unconfirmed reports*) belonged to a 49-year-old local businesswoman. She'd been stabbed multiple times, probably while jogging, possibly in a botched mugging. Shaper caught himself getting annoyed at the severe drought of fact, which somehow transformed the tragedy of death into an irritating spuff of non-committal nonsense. Only the date – today's – and the time signature – 0615 (one of the Beeb's copywriters on an early shift, no doubt) – seemed noteworthy.

Across the room, Glass slurped noisily at his tea and nodded at the printout.

'There's your "something happened this morning",' he said.

'Yeah. Except . . . he was waiting.'

'Who?'

'Your mystery poster. He was waiting for the story to break. There's too little detail here for it to have just caught his eye at random.'

Glass shrugged as if this were academic. 'I rather assumed he knew what to look for because he was responsible for it.'

'Why?'

Glass waggled his brows at the envelope.

Shaper gently withdrew the final sheet. And stared.

Four words. Another computer printout, landscape orientation: the text expanded to fill the page.

YOU'RE ON a LIST

'I see,' said Shaper.

Bugger, said Shaper's brain.

The merest whiff of that word – *murder* – pitched him well beyond his depth. It was true that in the armpit of his past he'd occasionally been involved, peripherally at least, in the art of making people disappear. But in the wake of the tumultuous episode that had so changed him five years ago, he'd self-consciously burrowed a new niche into an old territory, and tried to build a career out of fixing things instead. Dead bodies, by definition, didn't feature highly.

'So what do you think?' Glass watched him intently.

He puffed out his cheeks. It contravened every instinct he possessed, but the course seemed unavoidable.

'I think you should go to the cops.'

Glass opened his mouth to protest, but Shaper cut him off with a teacherly finger. 'Listen, it's probably nothing. My bet is you'll get another one in a day or two, fishing for money. Wealthy bloke like you, there's always some nutter. But . . . This ain't my sort of gig, Mr Glass. Dead bodies and that. *You're* not my sort of employer.'

You're too nice.

The old man knotted his hands together, hiding the shakes. 'All I want to know is if I've anything to worry about.' He looked like a kicked puppy, all confusion and watery eyes, and in the face of his anxiety Shaper's cobwebbed heartstrings chimed. It had been a while.

He flicked back through the papers with a sigh. 'Did you know any of these people?'

'I can't remember.'

'What do you mean?'

'I mean I can't remember. I told you, I'm three thousand years old. One's mind does rather fill up.'

Shaper stared for a moment, then sat back on the sofa and steepled his fingers.

'I see,' he said, mentally reordering priorities. 'I think I'd like to have a look at my payment, if it's all the same.'

Glass smiled as if he'd been expecting it, and rummaged again in the drawer. He removed two objects. The first was a block of twenty-pound notes, messily bound with a strained elastic band, which he placed on the table beside him. It held Shaper's concentration so firmly that he hadn't noticed what the second object was – a notebook, bound in red leather – until Glass raised it in trembling hands and started to read.

'*Paris,*' he said. '*Late 1757 or early 1758.*'

He paused and glanced up, checking Shaper was listening.

'*Probably after Christmas. Exquisite dinner with Madame de Gergi. Fine company. Met the famed Giacomo Casanova. Shorter than I expected, very feminine voice. Conversation developed into a duel of anecdotes. Believe I settled the matter with the news of my pigmentation laboratory at Versailles, and His Majesty's delight at my work. Spent all night flirting with petite wife of Hungarian Ambassador. Brief fuck before cigars. Casanova very poor loser.'*

Glass blushed as he glanced up. 'Sorry – language.'

Shaper said nothing. It took all his effort.

The old man flicked forwards a few pages and cleared his throat. 'Ah, here. *1420s – maybe earlier. A summer's day. Vienna? Met Heinrich Khunrath at coaching house to discuss the Rosenkreuz manuscript. Fellow unusually preoccupied with John Dee's Universal Symbol; attempted to explain its application. Grew inebriated and produced grotesque artefact from baggage: the "severed limb of a villain", transformed into a rudimentary lantern. Claimed it possessed "Magikal Properties", but grew belligerent at demand for evidence. Argument with landlord ensued. Some violence.'*

Another flicker of the pages, another glance to check Shaper still listened.

'*1886,*' he read, '*New York. Publishing reception for first edition of* America Heraldica. *Laudanum circulating. Astute bibliographer mentions* La Très Sainte Trinosophie; *asks if an ancestor is responsible. In inebriated state I explain I authored that too; 100 years before. Much hilarity.'*

He looked up and started to flick pages again. Shaper finally stopped him with an outstretched hand, hunting the right words.

'This,' he said, settling on an old favourite, 'is bollocks.'

Glass tried not to look hurt. He closed the book and placed it down, sparing his hands.

'My name is the Count of St Germain,' he said, with a simple, almost apologetic, shrug. 'I'm an Unascended Master of Theosophical Doctrine. I once held the knowledge of the Universal Medicine; have melted diamonds without loss of brilliance; am an occultist, a thaumaturge and a necromancer; and have lived a little over three thousand years. I've been Ahasuerus and Saint Alban, was called Proclus in Athens, and went by the name Bacon twice – two hundred and fifty years apart. I am the Chohan of the Seventh Ray, have been called Master Rakoczi and the Hierarch of the Age of Aquarius, and except for the odd flash of memory,' he pointed at the notebook, 'I can't remember a bloody thing about any of it.'

The words flowed with such deadpan conviction that, had he not been listening carefully, Shaper would have sworn the old man was simply working his way through a shopping list. These, Glass contrived to suggest, were not extraordinary or insane claims, but the undeniable and mundane realities of an entirely average life.

Shaper stood up and cleared his throat. 'This is a wind-up,' he said. 'You can't believe all that.'

'I'm afraid I do.'

'Then you're deranged. Sorry.' He turned for the door.

'Mr Shaper, please . . .' Glass smiled sadly. 'Look at it like this. Deranged or not, I really am remarkably wealthy. That's the fruit of some very, very long-term investments. *Ha*. Now, someone's threatened my life and I'd like you to look into it. You come very highly recommended. Everything else is basically irrelevant, isn't it?'

He picked up the money and tossed it over.

Shaper fumbled the catch and stooped to retrieve the wad, resisting the urge to count through it. 'A grand don't go far,' he lied, hunting a way out. 'Just . . . go to the cops, yeah?' He prepared to toss it back.

'Oh, that's not for the job. That's the consultation fee. An investigation would be worth rather more, I think.'

Shaper paced. 'Get a bodyguard.'

'If that's what you think's best.' Glass settled back with an air of gracious victory, as if the matter were settled. 'I'll leave the details to you. Though I have to say I'd rather like to know who's after me *before* they show up with a knife.'

'Want another three thousand years, do you?'

The old man didn't rise to it. Shaper felt weirdly cruel.

Somewhere, in the muffled bowels of the building, the front door clumped open and closed. He thought he could hear voices.

'The timing's all wrong,' he spat, down to his last – and truest – excuse. 'I need a holiday.'

The old man squished the objection with a smile and a quiet mental *splat*. 'Shall we say fifteen thousand? That's five a week for three weeks, or the full whack for a decisive result. Whichever comes first.'

Sweat itched on Shaper's head.

'A . . . a decisive result being what, exactly?'

Glass shrugged. 'A culprit. Perhaps just a demonstration that there's no threat after all. A reason to stop worrying, d'you understand? I can't abide it.'

Shaper worked his jaw.

I need a break. I can't do it. My brain. My bloody brain!

Except . . .

Fifteen grand, mate.

Fuck.

He opened his mouth, not entirely sure what he was to going to say, and—

'Who's this?'

A woman strode into the room, jerking a thumb at Shaper even as she pecked at Glass's cheek. Quietly appending, 'Hello, Dad.'

For the second time Shaper envied Glass the quality of his female company. Even with fifteen grand bouncing in his head like a spiky-headed jester, it was difficult to focus on anything else. The man's daughter shared his olive complexion, but where his tended to leathery rumpledness, hers spoke of curves and softness, evoking the term 'ripe' without word or gesture.

She wore clothes of such galloping frumpiness that Shaper suspected a deliberate attempt to conceal her attractiveness, but she moved with the sort of bullshit-ye-not self-confidence that substituted for the missing allure. The grand impression was of a person acutely uncomfortable at appreciative stares but – accepting she'd always get them – more than willing to scowl them down.

Woe betide the builder, Shaper thought, who wolf-whistles this one.

'Mr Shaper,' said Glass, 'this is Sandra. San, this is Mr Shaper. He's doing a little job for me.'

She glowered at him, distrustful. He held the stare, curiously transfixed, until the old man prompted his attention like a well-timed boot to the bollocks. '*Aren't* you, Mr Shaper?'

He pocketed the cash with Judas-like haste and fled for the door. 'I'll be in touch, yeah? I need to think about it.'

'Think about what?' Sandra spat.

'Nice to meet you,' he said, trying not to stare at her chest. He glanced back at Glass but found him so utterly focused on his daughter that the farewell nod went ignored. Quietly relieved at the inattention, Shaper slipped from the room in silence.

Chapter Five

Hunting an exit among gloomy halls, Shaper caught an echo of a strange voice – a nymph-like singsong – and checked his progress. It took him a moment to recognise Tova's clipped tone, miraculously shorn of all frosty inflections, and as he passed the side door at its source he paused to peek inside.

She was singing nursery rhymes to a teenage boy. The lad nested among pillows in a bright bedroom, sunlight drenching his face, with a grin of almost divine bliss. To Shaper he looked fifteen or thereabouts, though from the first sight of him – naked but for a slim nappy and baby's bib – it was clear he was no regular youth. His skin, olive like his mother's, was mottled in yellow and brown, and his whole body shivered with sharp, electric spasms. His eyes – each brown pool set in an orb of margarine yellow – rolled constantly, straining to linger on Tova before tumbling on a fresh orbit. His hands were crooked at the wrist and his toes seemed fused like warm candles, but he flexed and waggled the deformities in time to the lullaby, gurgling in delight. Strangest of all were the growths jutting from his legs – huge cones of gristle straining the skin at his knees – and the flabby bulge above his abdomen. It looked at first glance like a pregnancy mound, but as the boy writhed, Shaper saw it was off-centre, its opposite flank pitifully emaciated.

The overall effect should have been monstrous. It should have roused a wince of pity or sympathetic pain, or at least the polite paranoia of Thou Shalt Not Stare. But the boy giggled with such tangible glee that Shaper felt no such embarrassment, experiencing instead a fading variant of his own recent seizure: non-turbulent this time, non-incapacitating. It surrounded the boy with the hazy ghosts of golden grass and the scent of thyme, and the ringing of distorted cowbells. He even caught himself quietly humming along to Tova's song.

. . . which was an error, frankly, amidst the business of eavesdropping.

Tova's head snapped up as fast as she fell silent, expression cycling through shock and shame on its way to dagger-like annoyance. The boy, for his part, kept on grinning, and Shaper inched the door open – *busted* – to return his best smile.

'Hi. I'm Dan.'

'He doesn't talk,' Tova monotoned.

'Right.'

'He is Freddie, anyway.'

'Sandra's son?'

'Yes.'

'Glass's grandson?'

She nodded, heavy-lidded. *Any other stupid questions, genius?*

Shaper drummed fingers on the door frame and wondered what to say. It rose, eventually, from nowhere. 'Um . . . Tova? What's wrong with him?'

Her eyes almost blazed. 'Nothing *wrong* with him,' she hissed. 'Is not *wrong*. Is not his fault.' She stroked Freddie's wrist, a fresh wave of spasms working along the arm. 'Is called Gaucher's Disease. Can't process types of fat. Spleen, brain, blood. Very bad, but not *wrong*.'

'Actually, um.' Shaper mimed an embarrassed cough, cheeks reddening. 'I meant the old man. What's wrong with him?'

Tova simmered down. 'Oh. Him.'

'The . . . the things he says. He's got to be a bit . . . y'know?'

She placed an oxygen mask over the child's face, shrugging. 'He is sweet old man. Confused is all – very old. You want my opinion, OK: maybe he had stroke sometime. I'm not his doctor, don't know. Messed his memories, is all. He is still happy.' She trickled a smile across Freddie. 'Is all that matters, in the end.'

Shaper nodded, a gatecrasher in a world he neither recognised nor understood.

'Gaucher's, eh? Sounds rare.'

'Very. Is why he hired me. You heard of Norrbotten?'

'Er.'

'Is place in Sweden. Is where I trained for nursing, before come to England and fuck fat men for money.' No shame in her voice, just the distasteful tremor of someone remembering a bad meal. Shaper avoided her eyes. 'In Norrbotten,' she said, 'many small communities. Insular. Small . . . what is the word? Pond for genes, yes? High incidence of Type Three Gaucher. Very bad. I looked after several.'

'And do you, uh,' Shaper flapped his hands. 'Do you . . . get better from it?'

Tova gave him a long, crystal-clear stare.

'Ah,' he said.

A hand fell on his shoulder. He yelped like a puppy and spun in his spot. *Super cool.*

'I thought you were leaving,' said Sandra, arms folded.

'Y-yeah, I was just . . . yeah.' He scuttled along the hall.

At the door, Sandra's voice caught him, suddenly shorn of all suspicion and accusation. She sounded tired and anxious, and he glanced back to find the force fields had somehow peeled away from around her. What lay beneath – in a lingering spectrum of headachey hints and half-seen impressions – was small, helpless and frightened.

'Is he in trouble?' she murmured. 'My dad?'

Shaper shook his head to clear the vision, shrugging lightly. 'Personally? I doubt it. But he's worried, yeah.'

'About what?'

'Can't say. He doesn't want you worrying too.'

She nodded, glum. Then, with a note of hope, 'Are you helping him, Mr Shaper?'

The fifteen-thousand-quid question.

Say no, say no, say no.

'I don't know yet. Probably not.'

She fidgeted. He could see there was something she wanted to say, but she scowled it off with a sudden flicker of petulance. 'I'll get him to tell me, you know. Whatever it is.'

Shaper opened the door. 'Good for you,' he said. 'Let me know what you think.'

He was barely halfway down the stairs when she spat it out.

'Mr Shaper? No police – *please*. For his sake.'

And when he turned to ask why, the door was shut.

He went home.

By the time he decided to actually do something, the world of drizzle and drear beyond his flat's grimy windows was already darkening.

He'd spent the afternoon pacing, failing to eat; drumming obsessive fingers on the retrieved pill file.

If he was going to take the gig, he'd need to start dosing up soon – before the detox got too far under way and the sweaty, controlled crash rendered him useless. But to jump from one intensive job to another . . . to keep on climbing towards narcotic tolerance . . . to risk overdose or collapse . . . It was a huge risk.

Fifteen grand.

Fuck.

And so, tormented by so much money being earmarked but uncollected, he'd decided to put himself out of the misery of indecision. Instead he would test the case for its relative complexity. He would weigh the money against the mental involvement required, and the associated risks of serious and lasting Brainfuckery. And he would do so by taking just one small, insignificant step.

He would break into the house of Kingsley the Cocker – 'accidental death' number two – and have a snoop.

By seven thirty he'd already run the van along the middle-tier road off Clapham High Street twice, convinced it would be an easy in. He'd found the address in an old notebook, buried under antique paper and mummified lizard shit, flicking through crumpled pages with an odd mix of reverence and dread. All those names and numbers, marked out in a spidery hand he no longer recognised as his own: relics of a life he'd long since surrendered.

There was no point hiding from it, he supposed. Once upon a time he'd been more accurately known as Dan 'that vicious shit' Shaper, and his role in the nebulous criminal underworld had been less a matter of resolving problems, more of generating them – with infamous creativity – for the enemies of his taskmasters. That notebook, concisely listing details of anyone who'd had dealings with the Coram family's operation, was one of the few tendrils remaining to link past to present. Inside, Kingsley the Cocker shared page space with launderers, people-smugglers, dope-growers, and a bloke from Balham with an illegal foie gras factory in his basement. At one time or another Shaper had violated, menaced, extorted or employed them all. He supposed it was little wonder that the likes of Tova – another of the family's cast-offs – were less than warm in his company.

Back then, he'd been the bogeyman who kept people like her in line.

He cruised Kingsley's street one last time. For a man re-nowned across the disorganised crime fraternity as a high-tier gigolo and tantric superstar, Kingsley certainly lived in a bland area. Three-storeyed Victorian terraces of respectable, mind-your-own-business middle-class mundanity, all of which suited Shaper's purposes perfectly. No twitching curtains, no inconveniently poised cameras, and above all no bored cops slurping coffee outside. Whatever the faults of the newspaper article that had reported Kingsley's death, it was accurate on one point: his dive beneath a nocturnal train was not being treated as murder.

Shaper parked next to a souped-up kid car – 'On A Mission' stencilled across tinted windows – and shook his head at the youth of today. Too busy lusting after alloy spinners and illusion bodykits to learn anything truly useful about the world.

(*E.g. breaking-and-entering.*)

He went over the wall of a small church a hundred yards further down the street, and worked his way back through scrubby garden patches, vaulting damp wooden fences and redstone walls. In the early gloom, blinds were already pulled, and nobody cared to peer out as he ninja'd by, happily oblivious in TV-lit bubbles of triple-glazed comfort.

Kingsley's back door was an irritatingly modern affair with a self-sealing latch and a fuck-you-burglars tumbler lock, which took Shaper ten agonising minutes to crack, delicately positioning foils along a flimsy tin pick. The gear was a recent acquisition from China – a supremely cunning piece of low-tech scallywaggery in which a soft metal strip was minutely wiggled within the lock, literally moulding itself into shape – but the fragility of the foils meant four out of five attempts ended with the inserts snapping off before fully impressioned. Clucking his teeth as yet another proto-key dissolved, Shaper mentally scowled at every shitty Hollywood movie that ever made it look easy.

A neighbour's cat paused to stare. It blinked with Ziggyesque disinterest and yawned massively. 'Know how you feel, mate,'

Shaper muttered – down to his last two foils – just as the lock crackled open.

An easy in. Uh-huh.

Kingsley's home was as meticulously modern as Shaper might have expected from a try-hard exec. He'd barely known the man himself, of course – even in the dark days Shaper sketchily recalled meeting him just once or twice – but he had heard enough tall tales of Kingsley's extroverted adventures to be quietly surprised at the pastel-and-silver blandscape. The only discordant notes among the clear-glass tables and inoffensive art prints were flourishes of what an adherent might call 'New Age esoteria', but which Shaper thoughtlessly dismissed as Hippy Bollocks. Here a tie-dyed sheet hung like a tapestry, a brushstroke glyph in a blazing orange disc; there a pair of carved dancers bent back sharp fingers and leered from the mantelpiece, while incense holders dotted odd surfaces. Some, he noticed, had been allowed to burn right down, ash flecking the sideboards. In a palace of such conspicuous precision, it was an oddly messy oversight.

Not that they were alone in that respect. Brandishing a small torch – careful not to lift the beam near the windows – Shaper noted a thin layer of dust across the stair's metal banister, whorled smudges dotting its surface like fossils locked in chrome.

Fingerprints.

So the cops *had* been here.

Strange, then, that the place was so unwatched. The merest whiff of foul play, Shaper knew, could generally guarantee at least a yellow-tape cordon, or an unlucky rookie on guard.

Hmm.

A motorbike howled past the front, shockingly loud, and he came close to grabbing the powdered rail to steady himself. Every now and then the detox sent an unhelpful patina of clamminess up his spine – *get on with it, mate* – and his nerves were already at full twang. He took a few deep breaths and hustled upstairs.

The bedroom was as painstakingly characterless as everywhere else. The cupboards – gingerly eased open with jacket sleeve over fingers – revealed nothing but sensible shirts, trendy trousers and polished shoes. Only a bedside drawer, crammed with condoms, satisfied Shaper's gigolo-based preconceptions.

No family photos. No paperwork. No convenient link to George Glass and his envelope of odd. Just more forensic cast-offs: ninhydrin prints on pale walls, gaps in cupboards where cops had taken who knew what, and the bland innards of a home every bit as unloved – though admittedly not as grubby – as Shaper's own.

In the bathroom he paused. The bath was full – water long since cooled, a slick of perfumed potions floating on the surface – and a burnt-out tealight nestled in a corner. He was still staring at it, as if personally insulted by what it implied, when he heard a noise downstairs.

And froze.

It was almost nothing. The sort of gentle scuff sound that might have been a sneezing neighbour or a pedestrian dragging heels outside, or simply his own cretinous imagination tricking him. It wasn't as if there was no precedent.

Or someone trying to be silent.

He crept to the top of the stairs and held his breath, extending his hearing into the silence like the tendrils of some questing jellyfish, probing for movement. *Nothing.*

He was midway down when it happened again – *chft* – and this time he didn't freeze. This time the adrenal explosion bypassed all else, and compelled him – shadows tickling the corners of his eyes – to hug every corner, to stay low, and to *get out, get out, get out.*

Nothing moved.

He was within feet of the rear door – left ajar: *rookie error* – reaching like a drowning man for a raft, eyes scanning the garden for movement—

When something slicked past his shins like bony liquid.

His chest almost popped.

The cat.

The fucking cat.

It looked up at him, still insultingly bored – *the little shit* – and miaowed.

He let his breath out in a great ragged burst, relief slumping his shoulders, and bent down to scratch the vile little fucker behind the ear.

And only then did the man who'd been lurking behind the door thump into his midriff like a wrecking ball.

Shaper snarled and didn't stop, throwing a startled punch, clawing at hair and skin, until an expertly applied pressure between his shoulders and the chilly clink of handcuffs told him everything he needed to know.

The cat, he discovered, was staring at him from the doorway, indecently smug.

'You Judas,' he croaked.

'That's enough out of you,' said the cop, straddling him like a novelty beach ride and beginning to pat him down. 'I'm arresting you on suspicion of burglary and assault on a police officer—'

Wait . . .

'Hang on,' he grunted.

'You do not have to say anything, but it may harm your defence if you do not mention when questioned something which you—'

'Wait, wait, wait.' Shaper tried to waggle a hand. 'Canton?'

The drone faltered away. A hand gripped his shoulder and flipped him over. A torch beam nuked his eyes.

Something groaned.

'Shaper,' said DI Canton, reaching for the cuff keys. 'Bollocks.'

Canton made coffee using Kingsley's stuff, clattering and slamming with many a dark glare. 'Forensics are all done,' he muttered, rinsing purple prints from a pair of mugs, then scowled as if he had no need to justify himself, least of all to Shaper, and stepped up his china-rattling sulk another notch.

Shaper ignored it, with just a hint of sadistic serenity.

Tall and thin, with a brushback haircut so immaculate Shaper had often fancied he could see the moulding joints, Canton's bony features weren't so much severe as *stark*. At first glance he put people in mind of a prim neurotic – the exquisitely clipped chin tuft, the slit-like specs, the death-before-scuffing shoes . . . But there was more to the man than that, and Shaper had recognised it long ago.

Canton moved with a curious confidence, a calculated grace which belied the gangly stereotype and hinted instead at secret – but dynamic – passions; like a machine concealing its reservoir of sultry angers. The man evoked something distinctly reptilian in Shaper's skewed senses: forever watching, contemplating, giving nothing away, and then blazing to unpredictable life at the critical moment.

They had history, the cop and him: a seedy co-mingling of favours and a grudging balance of respect. Shaper knew things about Canton that his polished-brass superiors would be oh-so-interested to hear, while Canton was party to things that could lock Shaper away for a long, long time. Murky truths engulfed them both, smoggy pollutants from a past each had done everything in their power to escape. It was in that simple shared desire – to be a better person – that they'd found a touchstone far stronger than their many differences, one which had led to more than a few reluctant collaborations.

The way Shaper saw it, Canton brought to the table a host of useful resources in the shape of equipment, files, sciences, and the all-conquering brand of officialdom. He, on the other hand, provided the invaluable skill of Talking To Shady Bastards Who'd Rather Eat Their Own Bollocks Than Speak To A Cop.

Symbiosis.

Right now the principle of the shared greater good didn't appear to hold much water with Canton. Shaper watched him scratch savagely at his goatee and awaited the explosion.

'I was having dinner,' the man finally snarled. 'Natasha from the lab. She's fucking *stunning*, Shaper.'

'Good for you.'

'Not good for me! Do you have any idea how long it's taken me to ask her out?'

Shaper shook his head, enjoying the performance. Once he'd shucked off his shell, Canton was magnificently dramatic.

'Fucking mmmmmonths! Months! Expensive fucking restaurant in Chelsea, dearest fizz on the list, and halfway through the starter, what happens? Ding-a-bloody-ling on the phone, and, "Sir, there's a bloke just snuck in the Kingsley place."' He stabbed a finger like launching the nukes. 'You've cost me the best bonk of my life, you little fuck. I should run you in on principle.'

'Sorry, mate.' Shaper's apology face was overthrown by a treacherous chuckle, which he dutifully drowned in coffee. A sly thought occurred mid-slurp. 'Vauxhall Nova with the tinted windows? "On A Mission"?'

Canton nodded, calming. 'PC Morgan. Volunteered for stakeout as long as he didn't have to put up with the shitty speakers in the patrol car.'

'Clever little sod. I parked right behind him.'

They sipped in unison, watching each other.

Canton drew first.

'What you doing here, Shaper?'

'I heard Kingsley was dead, didn't I? Just looking into it. Concerned friend.'

'Bollocks.'

'Well, I could ask the same question, couldn't I? Common little rent boy like him, terrible accident . . . Why all the interest? And why does the golden boy of the SOCA turn down his only whiff of a shag in decades –' (Canton flicked him a V) – 'to come running at the first sign of . . . what? A "development in the case"?'

The cop carefully placed down the mug, theatrically tight-lipped. Shaper waited him out. Canton could never keep quiet for long.

'Because you know as well as I do,' the man spat, folding his arms, 'a bloke doesn't run a nice relaxing bath and light all his fairy fucking incense if he's seconds away from sodding off down the dogging spot to assume the position.'

'Colourfully put. So? Did they find anything? Forensics?'

'Nuh-uh, bollocks.' Canton waggled a petulant finger. 'You first. What's in it for me?'

'Client confidentiality. Sorry.'

'So someone *has* hired you.'

'Sharp as a pin, you.'

'Spill, you scruffy little arse.'

'Y'know, it's terrible, the way we flirt.'

Canton turned up the glare.

'All right, all right – Jesus.' Shaper flapped a hand round the house. 'You know what Kingsley did for a living, right?'

'Like you said, rent boy. Local plods had him on file for years.'

'Well, yeah, but . . . There are *grades*, mate. Look, you've got your cracker, right, who'll sell his arse for thirty quid. You've got your specialist – he gets paid to give as well as receive. Maybe a couple of hundred a pop. And then you've got the likes of Kingsley.'

'So?'

'So this guy's charging a grand a night, Canton. Select clientele. And not just the blokes either; he'll fuck anything. And whatever or whoever it is will enjoy it like they've never enjoyed it before. That's the reputation talking there. He was sort of a hero. Best of the best.'

'The point being?'

'Point being, mate, even if he *had* got a job that night, and even if he *had* gone sprinting out and not even stopped to snuff his hippysticks, then the last place he's going to go is a grotty little free-for-all down by the tracks. He's a class or seven above that.' Shaper swilled his mug. 'My thinking is, he was moved there.'

Canton sat back. Digesting. 'What else?'

'Nothing else. Unless you can tell me if you've got cops parked outside a couple of other houses tonight . . .'

'I don't follow.'

Shaper chewed a cheek, remembering Sandra's quiet entreaty. '*No police – please.*'

Canton, he decided, didn't count. Besides, no need to mention Glass.

'Little old lady fell off her roof in Chelsea. Two nights back.'

Canton shook his head.

'Or that mugging last night? Queen's Park way?'

The cop shrugged, 'Yeah, think I heard about that one. So?'

Shaper's turn to wax theatrical. 'Oh, *nothing* . . .'

Canton swore and scribbled a note.

'Anyway,' Shaper grinned, 'I've showed you mine. Flap it out.'

Canton gave him a long and thoughtful stare, drumming

fingers against his mug. Shaper watched him closely, chasing away a spectral hint of pompous purple and the sound of typewriters.

Something juicy.

'Forensics did find something here,' the cop conceded. 'A print. Fresh, they reckoned, just outside the door. Marked out in wax, of all things.'

'From the candle upstairs?'

Canton shook his head. 'Thought of that. No, it's different: pure tallow – they're still testing it. Anyway, that's not why it's weird. They ran it through the system and got a match, and you know how fucking rare *that* is.'

'Who?'

Canton laughed, as if he couldn't believe it himself.

'Boyle,' he said, pouring coffee down the sink. 'It's Tommy Boyle.'

'Oh,' said Shaper. Goosebumps paraded along his arms. 'Shit.'

Half an hour later, festering in traffic on Euston Road, burning with the desire to hide under a blanket, Shaper's impatience got the better of him.

He called Vince, and was entirely unsurprised that the answering voice was already softened by a beery slur.

'Where are you?' he asked.

'Mutt's Nut. 'S karaoke night, innit? Tal just did "Unchained Melody" right at me – bloody heart-warming, it was. C'mere, you . . .'

A series of moist noises violated the phone. Shaper winced.

Tal – Talvir – was Vince's new boyfriend, a second-generation Indian whose parents would have been miffed to know he slid off his Sikh bracelet whenever he left the house, and positively gutted to see him slip the tongue to a six-foot-six ex-Special

Forces lug called Vincent. Shaper, gingerly listening, knew how they felt. He'd had enough wet sounds in his earhole over the past week to last a lifetime.

'Vince,' he shouted. 'Put him down. Stop it!'

The offending slurpage gave no sign of petering out, and Shaper bit down a growl.

'Tommy Boyle,' he said, dropping the bomb.

The noises stopped.

'Vince? You hear me? You know that name?'

A thick silence sang out, followed by the sulky grunt of Tal being pushed away.

'Yeah,' Vince said. Too serious. 'Yeah, I know the name. Sam Coram's old mate. He's dead.'

Shaper sweated and steered. '*Is* he?'

'Well . . . I mean . . .' The voice went quiet. In the Dog and Ball – better known as the Mutt's Nut – the walls had knuckles as well as ears. 'He done a runner, didn't he? There was some trouble. Ages ago, this was. Before your time, even.'

'What makes you so sure he's dead?'

'*Ha*. Because . . . because the Corams wanted a word with him, but never found him.'

'So?'

Vince adopted a tone reserved for idiots. 'So if the Corams are lookin' for you, mate, but can't fucking find you, it's on account of you not bein' available.' He sniffed. 'You know that.'

Most of the time, Shaper silently added, it was me doing the finding.

He adroitly steered clear of the memories and focused on more prosaic traffic: heading north. The truth was that Tommy Boyle occupied a niche in the nebulous history of the underworld not dissimilar to his own, but where Shaper had resurfaced in this new, ostensibly honourable role – in the process becoming a living joke to those who once feared him – Boyle's enigma had lingered far darker, mentioned these days only in whispered tones by old sluggers in tough pubs.

'Do me a favour, Vince, ask around, eh? See what people are saying.'

'Like what?'

'Like . . . I don't know. Like maybe Boyle's back.'

The silence stretched out.

'Dunno, mate,' the phone finally grumbled. 'Might be a bit . . . dodgy.'

Shaper rolled his eyes. 'Buy you four pints.'

'Ten.'

'Five.'

'Eight. And a Jaegerbomb.'

'Six and a shooter.'

'And some nuts.'

'Fine, and some nuts.'

'Deal.'

The phone went dead.

Shaper went home.

Chapter Six

He spent another hour judiciously self-distracting in the flat. His skull had started to ache alarmingly quickly, followed first by a fresh bout of the sweats, second by an unshakeable sensation of being watched, and finally by a series of longing stares at the pill file: all sure signs that the detox was inexorably advancing. Soon, he knew, the Sickness would be fully emerged from its cell and it would be too late to abort the cleansing period even if he wanted to.

Make a decision, arsehole.

Somewhere, he imagined, George Glass was staring at his death notice and awaiting a phone call, equally impatient.

Fifteen thousand quid . . .

Tommy Boyle . . .

Ziggy, staring from the top of a bookshelf at a bowl of chopped plums on the floor, implied through expression alone that Shaper's concerns – murders, mobsters, memories and all – didn't amount to a single reptilian crap pellet compared to his own suffering. Eventually Shaper grew sick of the glares and lifted the bowl up to the little bastard's shelf, where he promptly ignored it and went to sleep.

At eight thirty, switching off the TV in revulsion (another segment on 'urban artist' Merlin and his echo masterpiece), Shaper's nerves hit the no-more-putting-it-off point and succumbed to the only sensible choice.

No.

No no no no no. It's impossible.

Tell him no.

He lifted the phone with his jaw clenched.

Tova answered at the second ring.

'Put Glass on,' he demanded, forgoing pleasantries.

'But . . . h-he's not here.' She sounded flustered.

'Where then?'

'Why you want hi—'

'Tova, *where?*'

She rummaged briefly nearby then read out an address, frightened by the urgency.

Or maybe just frightened by me.

She remembers.

When he'd copied down the details, she seemed to gather herself, blurting, 'But is not to be disturbed! Is very impor—'

He had the phone back in its cradle before she could finish.

Dalston, then. He eyed the address. East. Eastwards, to get this thing tidied away and out of his brain for good. To untangle himself from the mess; to get back to his routine. Bollocks to the money.

Right?

Right.

He grabbed his coat and left. Then came back, dumped the pill file in a pocket, mumbled *just in case* to the judgemental universe, and slammed the door behind him.

Off to tell a scared old man he was on his own.

The address, cowering at the foot of a bunker-like apartment block, belonged to The Samadhi Alternative Therapy Clinic, a shop whose windows – festooned with colourful posters – gave Shaper the impression that a guided missile packed with nuclear rainbows had been blasted into a confined space. On closer inspection the prints resolved into technicolour diagrams, Sanskrit symbols, artists' impressions of human auras and – tucked discreetly among the collage – a laminated price guide. The list opened with the ominously titled Inner Interrogation (Tarot), at a very competitive £149.99. A handwritten sheet had been pinned beside it – all felt-tip stars and fireworks – to announce: Tonight: Audience With The Unascended Master.

Aha.

Shaper braced himself and pushed inside.

Within, when his eyes had accustomed to the sputtering cave light of candles and lanterns, was a broad space, stroked by a rumour of ambiguous music and packed with an incense pall of such density he almost choked. Almost instantly his senses warped – vision flexing like rubber – as if the Sickness were mischievously testing his ability to cling to the real in this clogged, choking sweatlodge. Desperate to refocus, he concentrated on the room's visible contents: a few items of vaguely medical-looking apparatus among a slew of dreamcatchers, palmistry charts, scrying stones and (in abundance) tissue boxes. A couple of spin-racks of books and charms had been pushed back for the evening's show, the foggy space now packed with fold-out chairs and soggy brown beanbags.

A man's voice, shorn of all expression, droned through the gloom.

'. . . and the Governor began at last to chant the seed vowels, by whose subtle names he penetrated the penultimate gateway; which is the chakra of the brow, which is Ajna, which is Shakti and Shiva, which is the twin-lobed lotus in white. There he lingered, constrained by thoughtless inequity, willing yet unable to progress, until by the touch of my hands his kundalini was invoked onwards, and . . .'

And so on.

Ignoring Shaper's arrival utterly, twenty or so people sat

listening to the monotone. At first glance they seemed a profoundly ordinary bunch, though on closer inspection Shaper noticed each had nervously dared to hint at some inner spark of esotericism. One woman, conservatively dressed, wore her hair in a rock-like bun above a single, brightly coloured dreadlock. A middle-aged man with headmaster specs and a stop-pretending-it-ain't-there bald patch had smudged a red-clay bindi above his eyes, while beside him a girl – obviously direct from work – had paused to shrug a saffron-dyed waistcoat over her severe jacket.

To his eye each self-conscious idiosyncrasy smacked of shame, flickers of individualism buried deep beneath the expectation of ridicule. The group reminded him abstractly of Kingsley's home, with its little flashes of colour, albeit here drenched in something far needier, far less contented. These people, he recognised, were the incomplete, the perpetually dissatisfied, minds so hungry for something *more* – for answers, for progress, for wings to lift them beyond the mundane – that they'd sacrificed sense for credulity and slowly, by grudging degrees, found their way here.

Hippies in denial.

Shaper tripped on a ceramic phrenology head being used as a doorstop and swore under his breath. Nobody seemed to notice.

'. . . in this fashion,' the voice intoned, 'I brought him to that final plateau, or *nirvikalpa*, and waited as his heart ceased to beat. There at last was the unchanging reality. There he encountered a divine condition – a transcendence accessible to all of us, all of *you* – which united his manifold selves and delivered him unto the Universe. In an instant every cell of his crude biology was flooded with the ocean of divine love and bliss.'

There was a joke in there somewhere. Shaper was too unnerved to find it.

The speaker was Glass. Seated on a huge cushion in his proto-pyjamas, eyes closed, hands clasped in his lap to arrest the shakes, he seemed asleep, locked in some weird trance. At the sight of him Shaper felt his own perceptions slipping slyly off their rails, that same blaze of white and violet coalescing like a double exposure. Even when he looked away with a silent growl – more determined than ever to get this over with – it remained somehow impossible to listen to Glass's robotic monotone without a thoughtless acceptance of its authority, and Shaper found himself regretting his mockery of the audience's gullibility. The old voice glimmered with hints of salvation and meaning, and better still wafted the promise of *practical* strategies to achieve them.

Shaper found himself hanging on every stupid, rambling word.

Hunting distraction, he forced himself to focus instead on the woman beside Glass, scribbling notes like a secretary taking dictation. He recognised the red-leather journal in her hands: the same one the old man had produced earlier. Glass's 'memories', recorded in biro and bullshit.

The girl glanced up for an instant, catching his eye with an indiscriminate smile, and like a stormcloud parting – like choirs of seraphim singing the rapture – something twitched in his crotch.

Hallelujah!

Hallelujah, Lord!

'Via the correct application of this method,' Glass droned, oblivious to the erectile revelation, 'all attachment to karma dissolves from the mind; as then occurred to that unhappy statesman. As he approached the divinity of *mahasamadhi*, I – who had guided him to that secret place – returned alone to corporeality, for I am not permitted to Ascend until the Seventh Ray is consolidated upon this Earth.'

The girl was stunning. Compact and lithe, with long fingers and perfect ears, she sat curled into the beanbag, with her legs tucked back and her bare feet jutting below her thighs. She put

Shaper in mind of a panther – a svelte paradox of straight lines and liquid curves – and to his eye she radiated a peculiarly *surly* beauty: pale and serious, cyan eyes sharp with suspicion. And yet what made her so disarming, what somehow heightened the allure to levels beyond the merely lovely, was that she'd attempted to annihilate every trace of that sultry, sexual creature from public view.

She wore not black leather – as seemed appropriate – but a heap of tie-dyed frumpage, complete with seashell beads and carved bangles. Her hair – so dark it was almost blue, like a comic-book murderess – was backcombed with a disregard for grace and pinned with a few brightly coloured clips which couldn't hope to contain its straggling sprawl. Her lips were a little too thin to support their soppy smile of choice, her eyes a little too cold for their puppy-dog air of good intentions and watery friendship. In Shaper's off-tilt senses she became a tainted masterpiece, a nihilistic coil of snake-like sleaze, bundled in a psychedelic babushka doll, unaware that the inner creature was by far the more interesting of the two.

At least, it was to him.

Like attracts like, he thought.

Or maybe, shit attracts flies.

'When the spirit was gone,' said Glass, snapping him back to reality, 'I served as the Governor of Chengalaput in his stead. The year was seventeen fifty-one. His was the four hundred and forty-second soul that had sought my aid in achieving the Allbliss.'

The crowd politely applauded. The girl stopped writing in the notebook, placed it theatrically down, and with a rodent-fast peek to check everyone was watching, shut her eyes. And began to sway.

The room held its collective breath. She rolled her body in tight little circles, face tilted upwards, and slowly raised her arms above her head. Shaper watched her wobble like a drunkard and welcomed the blood back to his crotch like an old friend.

Into the silence she suddenly groaned out loud, snapping open her eyes and lowering the monstrous gaze on to Glass.

As one the crowd shifted its attention to his old, bowed head.

Shaper alone lingered on the girl.

'I see you in rags,' she said, voice heavy with an overblown resonance thieved direct from a schlocky séance. 'You're arguing with a priest. He's refusing to bless you. Why is he so angry with you, teacher?'

Glass nodded. A small smile.

'Mm,' he said. 'Oh yes. It's coming back . . . Yes. An important lesson.'

The crowd murmured its soft anticipation. No longer centre stage, the girl settled back to narrow-eyed normality and retrieved the notebook. She threw Shaper another glance, smile still fixed, and poised her pen to write.

Faker! he silently screamed.

And wanted her all the more.

'Fifteen fifty-two,' said Glass, flat-toned, a crinkled shadow in the smoke. 'I was in Hamburg to preside at a secret tutorial upon the nine stages of involutive transmutation. Upon arrival I was confronted with rumours that I was the Wandering Jew of legend. The Bishop of Hamburg struck me with a splinter from his sceptred crucifix, and among the stalls of the Rathausmarkt I was set upon by the mob. Only when I refused to retaliate, recounting instead the *siddhi* by which they might free themselves of corporeal concern, did they become transfixed and relent. My lesson began thus: to be united as one w . . . w-with . . .'

The drone abruptly stopped.

Shaper, preoccupied with his groinal reawakening, tuned back just as Glass's eyes flickered open. The man's mouth gaped twice, teeth snapping with an audible crack, and then slowly, like a lazy tree, he toppled sideways.

For a second there was silence.

And then chaos.

The listeners surged forward, hands reaching for the old man, some trying to help, most – Shaper noticed – simply taking the opportunity to touch him. Above it all the girl – that wonderful liar, that beautiful fraud – raised her voice and screamed for silence.

'Give him some fucking space!' she howled, façade briefly cracking. The others recoiled as if electrocuted. She appeared to remember who she was – or at least who she was pretending to be – and switched the smile back on.

'I'm very sorry but the audience is over. The teacher needs to rest now. Would somebody help me move him, please?'

Every hand in the room shot up. A forest of finger-twitching enthusiasm, which wobbled and collapsed in a chorus of startled grunts as Shaper, smirking his best smirk, elbowed his way to the front.

He grabbed Glass's feet before anyone could stop him.

'Off we go, then,' he said.

The girl's home, linked to the clinic through a beaded curtain, was the evil twin of Kingsley the Cocker's. Where his had thrown up an impenetrable wall of tidiness and impersonality – attempting to eclipse its quiet esoteria – this cluttered blitzkrieg of a bedsit did the opposite: repeatedly punching the viewer with a brass knuckle of New Age nonsense, spiritualist screenprints and hand-dyed hemp, which collectively overexposed the eye and rendered almost invisible the few off-notes among the harmony.

Shaper wasn't so easily fooled. For every Turkish eye-charm at the window he noted a packet of fags and a vodka bottle by the bed – where Glass snored even now. For every wall chart marked Tarot: Major and Minor Arcana, or The Chakras and Their Roles, a small stack of grim paperbacks lined the sill: *Catch 22, Slaughterhouse-Five, Scepticism Inc.* For every CD rack crammed with *Whalesong Wellness* Vols 1–4, a buried smattering of Soundgarden, Alice in Chains, Bill Hicks . . .

Inside every hippy, he thought, is an angry grunge chick gagging for a pint.

'Beg your pardon?' said the girl, bustling back into the room with her smile at wide beam. Shaper realised he'd been think-muttering.

'Nothing.'

'Well, the others have gone,' she said, nodding at the door and girlishly touching her palms together. Oh-so-politely telling him to fuck off.

'Dan Shaper, by the way.' He extended a hand and resolutely failed to go anywhere. She took it with only a flicker of impatience – *smile, smile* – and avoided his eye.

'Mary Devon. Lovely to meet you. I can tell you're a . . . a warm, caring person. You have a very bright energy. Thank you so much for the help. But perhaps now you'd better—'

'So what's wrong with him?'

He could almost see her mentally change gears. The smile barely flickered.

'He's . . . just tired. Regressing takes it out of him. Remembering it all, you know.'

'Mm,' said Shaper. 'Right.'

Smile, smile. Best of pals.

'Don't you think it's a bit shit, though?' he said, pulling the trigger with a cheery tone. 'Exploiting an old man? I mean, how much did they pay, those incense junkies back there, to come and truffle for the salvation?'

Mary's face fell a mile. Shaper's groin didn't.

'They . . . there was no charge,' she said, dumping a desperate, all-concealing smile across the indignation. 'B-but . . . if people want to make voluntary contributions to the upkeep of the clinic – it *is* an expensive part of London – then I won't say no.' She glanced at the sleeping geriatric. 'And you can hardly call it exploitative, really. I mean, I understand why you'd say so.' *Smile, smile.* 'You're concerned. It's beautiful. But really, it's OK. It's *all* OK. He wants to do it. He knows how important it is. He knows what people *need*.'

Shaper gave her an encouraging nod, taking the opportunity to stare at her legs.

'He's the only Unascended Master we've ever found,' she burbled, moving to fuss over Glass. 'The things he can teach us! The wisdom he holds!' She artfully transformed the smile into a worthy, martyred sadness. 'Yes, he suffers a little but only because he chooses to. He knows that by using *my* gift – to see the invisible truth, to unlock the doors of his past – he can remember lessons relevant to the *present*. He can bestow his *own* gift on mankind, and change us all for the better.'

Shaper grinned. Nodded, nodded, nodded. And said, 'You're an extraordinary liar and you should be ashamed of yourself, love. You're hoodwinking a bunch of credulous dickwits into shelling out for some fake fucking meaning, and you're using a vulnerable shit-flinging nutcase in pyjamas to provide it. Would you like to have dinner with me?'

Mary just stared, mouth hanging.

And on the bed, with consummately inappropriate timing, Glass's whole body began to shudder. He groaned – quiet and weird – like creaking wood.

'He needs a doctor,' Shaper spat, annoyed – and guilty about it – at the interruption.

'No, no, it's just the trance. It's normal.'

The old man gurgled. A rolling spasm worked up from his

feet, rattling through his chest and drawing another deep, painful moan. Shaper almost snarled.

'He's having a fucking heart attack or something! I don't know CPR! Do you know fucking CPR?'

'It's normal. It's *normal*, OK?' She didn't sound convinced.

Glass suddenly went rigid. His eyes snapped open as if a switch had flipped, chin tilting back and jaw hanging open: an airless, strangled scream.

'Fuck normal! He needs a fucking ambulance!' Shaper scrabbled for his phone, strangely unable to look away from Mary even as he rummaged. A peculiar kaleidoscope of expressions was cycling across her face: the fake smile, a stab of irritation, a glut of panic. Around and around.

Glass went limp with a sigh.

The turntable jarred to a halt.

'Stop,' Mary barked, chin jutting. 'Stop it!'

Shaper's thumb froze over the '9'.

'We'll get him a doctor, OK? *OK?* There's only one he'll see, a . . . a private one. He's known him for years. He made me promise. Nobody else!'

And here, Shaper knew, was the *real* Mary. Here was the true her, calmly wading through seas of anger. Even lovelier than the fake one.

'What doctor?' he demanded. Thumb still hovering.

She dived into a cupboard, paddling through paperwork. 'I've got his card. Dr Nashkin. Or something. Where did I . . . I'll call him, OK? Here, look, I've got it. I'll call him now and—'

'No you won't.'

They both froze.

The old man gingerly sat up and blinked, smiling weakly.

Shaper recovered first. 'Mr Glass?'

'I'm fine, I'm fine. Just tired. Don't need a damn doctor.' He flapped a dismissive hand at Mary, still gripping the business card like a lifeline. She frowned, slowly placing it down on the table. And then switched on the smile.

Shaper rolled his eyes.

'Mr Shaper!' Glass abruptly declared, face alight with sudden recognition. 'How marvellous to see you!'

'You shouldn't be here, sir. This is . . . it's . . .' He struggled for the right words, uncomfortable at the depth of his own concern for the odd little man whose employment he'd come to decline. 'It's not good for you. You're being exploited, and—'

'Exploited?' Glass waved it away, still beaming. 'Nonsense, lad!'

Opposite them, Mary dropped the charm just long enough to shoot Shaper a *Ha, fucko* look.

'Mind you,' Glass added, 'I'm jolly pleased to see you so concerned for my welfare. Am I to assume you've come to accept the case?'

'What case?' Mary cut in, scowling.

Shaper ignored her, slouching as if by chance against the tabletop.

'I'm sorry,' he said, something stabbing him in the heart. 'I can't help you.'

'But why not?'

'Because it's . . . it's complicated.'

The drugs, sure. The return to detox. The simple, workable, manageable routine he yearned to resume. *Don't rock the boat, Dannyboy.*

But even more than that . . .

Tommy Boyle.

An unexpected name. A link to the Corams and the past they infected like a disease. A link to the seven years he'd spent being their weapon, and the five years he'd spent trying to forget it.

A Big. Fucking. Can of worms.

'Complicated,' he repeated, mouth dry. 'But . . . I mean . . . Your envelope, all that. I still don't think it's worth worrying about, all right? Somebody fucking around. Just . . . go to the cops, eh? And go to a bloody doctor, while you're at it. Stop trusting fucking amateurs like me.' He scowled across the room. '*And* her.'

Glass settled back with a sigh, visibly disappointed. Shaper had to look away – fingers wriggling behind his back – and switched on a protective scowl to bullshit his way clear.

'Go to the cops,' he said. 'They'll tell you. Nothing to worry about.' He slipped his hands into his pockets. 'I can't get involved.'

Glass considered for a moment with a faraway look, then seemed to reach a decision. His eyes were rich with sadness.

'Mr Shaper, my life is very complicated. At least, it *was*. I suppose it must seem rather simple to you, nowadays. I watch my fish, I look after my daughter and my grandson, and I try to remember the things I've forgotten. I think some of them might be useful. Mary helps me, you see?' He smiled at her, then dipped his brows and looked away. 'But with some things . . . some *recent* things . . . I'm a little more wary . . .'

'I don't follow.'

Glass sighed, glancing again at the girl. 'My dear, would you agree that I'm a . . . good person?'

Mary didn't miss a beat: dappy smile at full burn, eyes at maximum moist. 'You have the purest aura I've ever seen,' she blurted. 'You are sinless.'

Faker, faker, faker, thought Shaper, hornier than hell. And yet at the same time couldn't help inwardly conceding, inwardly *knowing*, that she was right, that Glass *was* good, that in this one batty old git he'd found a would-be client – for a change – actually worth helping.

(That lingering white glow, like a secret signal at the edges of his vision, merely aggravated the guilt.)

It's just the Sickness. It's just the fucking Sickness!

'I wouldn't go quite as far as "sinless",' Glass said, flashing Mary an indulgent smile. 'No . . . my sin is cowardice.' He turned back to Shaper. 'That's why I want your protection, you understand? And it's why I won't go to the police.'

'What's to be scared of?'

'The truth. The truths I've forgotten.'

Shaper shook his head, still not getting it. Even Mary was frowning now, tilting forwards in fascination.

'Some years ago,' said the old man, reaching towards his face, 'I found this.'

His slender fingers closed over his lower lip. They gripped the olive skin gently and peeled it forwards, exposing his lower jaw like some impromptu dental exam. For a moment Shaper was confused: the teeth seemed unusually clean and regular, but nothing extraordinary. Until his eye flitted a fraction downwards, and he realised the object of the presentation wasn't the white little tombstones above, but the slick fold of Glass's lip.

Its inside surface was marked with deep, blackened scars.

A burn-tattoo – a soldering-iron sigil – cut to form a word: CRIMINAL.

Glass let the lip close with a fleshy pop.

'I've no idea what I did,' he said, eyes not wavering, 'and I'd rather like to keep it that way.'

Chapter Seven

Shaper drove on autopilot.

It was a merciful mindset, as much a product of the impending narcotic crash as any special talent, which allowed him to set aside every hiss and clank of his overturned psyche, to dodge every strengthening distortion of his tainted brain, and to dislocate all thoughts of George Glass.

With his frightened, needy eyes . . .

Traffic-dodging through Canonbury, Shaper moved the wheel without conscious thought, driving along slippery rat runs without generating a single memory, and was as profoundly, numbly, abstractly content as he'd been in a long time.

The Sickness, naturally, couldn't allow that.

A slab of paranoia quaked up from nowhere and jolted him alert.

You're being followed.

A set of brighter-than-they-should've-been headlights splashed, for the fifth time, across his mirror. Someone, he judged, keeping their distance, ensuring two or more cars between them at all times.

(*Or*, said a more reasonable voice, *just some knackered office monkey, heading home after a late shift, avoiding the jams. This is not Bond. You do not pick up a tail in Highbury.*)

'It's nothing,' he whispered, as if saying it out loud could confirm it. 'Idiot.'

At any rate, the mental intrusion had disrupted his dissociative calm beyond recovery, and he thought back to Glass with a guilty buttock shuffle. All his own certainties and intentions – *fuck the job, fuck the money, fuck Tommy Boyle; get back to detox* – had faded before those old, amber eyes, and he'd ultimately fled the Samadhi Clinic before the man's childlike entreaties could undermine his decision.

Nobody could be so genuinely likeable.

It *hurt* to say 'no'.

Shaper jinked left along a narrow street, and briefly thought he'd lost the other car. But as he honked and heaved his way on to Camden Road, he spotted it again: the too-bright lights, butting back in from the outside filter.

Black Merc. Tinted windows.

Subtle.

It's nothing. Concentrate on the gig, dickwit.

At any rate, Glass's entreaties hadn't been entirely alone in threatening his fortitude. The money weighed on that front too, no denying it, and the sudden arrival of Mary 'big fucking liar' Devon into the picture – along with the magical resurrection of his libido – couldn't be ignored.

But mostly, he conceded, *yeah* . . . mostly it was Glass himself. The whole business with the lip tattoo had merely served to pique his interest further, as if he somehow *needed* to believe the old man was as decent and honest as he seemed, and the slightest hint of a contradictory truth generated an unignorable itch. Shaper yearned to scratch at it, perversely aware that by scraping off the scab to see what trickled beneath, he ran the risk of exposing Glass's 'purity' as a fraud. It was a maddening urge, hunting for flaws just to prove perfection, and it almost killed him to walk away from it. His dogged 'no' had thus spawned a sewer spout of guilt and regret which had chased him all the way out of the clinic, and now here he was, reaping what he sowed, approaching his home with a violent case of the jitters, fingers tracing back and forth across the pill file's zip.

And being followed.

(Except probably not.)

Finally tiring of the not knowing, he hard-turned into the side street behind his flat and leapt from the van before the engine had finished ticking. Straight inside and up to his landing, not pausing for breath or thought. Ziggy glared morosely as he stumbled in, and for once Shaper had the pleasure of being too preoccupied to care. He strode to the heap of matte-black gadgets and glassy little lenses by the wall – his expert arsenal for the pursuit of professional voyeurism – and grabbed a small blister pack from the top.

Then climbed out the back window. Along the crumbling dividing wall and into the piss-smelling pathway behind, dodging ragged plastic snagged in the wire fence.

'Just some bloke,' he mumbled, sweating too much. 'On his way home. Long gone. Idiot idiot idiot.'

Sometimes, he knew, it took a lot of really moronic effort to dislodge a paranoid conviction but it was always worth it. Letting the weeds of irrationality grow could only leave the rest of the garden smothered and dying. It didn't matter that the object of the paranoia would have seemed laughable in a more sober state of mind, it simply couldn't be permitted to gestate.

Pausing at the end of the alley, he peered round the blind corner – a long view of his own door, his own van – and permitted himself a gentle rush of relief.

The weeds: swept away.

'See?' he muttered, waggling a mental finger. 'There's nobody th—'

The Merc was parked ten feet away, angled slightly for a clearer view of his door.

Shit.

The shakes filtered into his hands like antifreeze in his veins. *Shit shit shit.*

He dropped back into cover and indulged in a full minute of concentrated swearing to chase away the jitters. Only when he felt fully cleansed did he finally scrabble across the pavement, staying low, dodging behind parked cars and dented mopeds. He reached the Merc without trouble, reasonably sure he'd evaded the wing-mirror views, and paused against its rear bumper to force a few breaths. He eased from his pocket the gadget he'd grabbed inside and delicately reached beneath the car's chassis, sliding its magnetic backplate on to the wheel trim. For an instant he zoned out in the adrenal high, imagining he could *see* the device bouncing its secret signal off the street: a spectral haze being guzzled high above by a fleet of frozen, glassy satellites.

He shook his head – bloody detox – and scuttled back to the alley.

Up the wall. Back through the window. Pausing to hurriedly chop a fresh apple for Ziggy – who continued to express his disinterest with a lazy tail flick – then back out through the door; dusting down his increasingly crumpled jacket.

Whistling as he went.

The only thing better than exorcising a paranoid delusion, he decided, is discovering you weren't being paranoid at all.

Outside he couldn't stop himself grinning, and as he reached for the van he turned his merry little smirk up the street towards the silent, sinister car.

And waved.

No movement.

Chuckling like a madman, he pulled the van away with a satisfying squeal and shot off, imagining the Merc's occupants scrabbling in pursuit, clammily aware they'd been made. He caught a blurred mirror impression of it lurching from its space – declaring a manic *Ha!* under his breath – and got on with losing it.

It wasn't hard. Not in London traffic. No Hollywood screech-turns or loud music required, simply a couple of false signals, a few random turnoffs, and an extra spin round every roundabout. The moment he was satisfied it was gone, he parked up and rummaged below the seat, withdrawing another part of his sneak's ensemble. It looked for all the world like a dashtop satnav but came complete with a few useful extra features, thanks to a specialist Internet retailer, who had helpfully included a freebie copy of the Regulations of Investigatory Powers Act with all the loopholes marked in red.

He flicked it on with a professional lip jut and, waiting for it to boot up, mused on the appropriate passage.

26(4). For the purposes of this part, surveillance is not intrusive to the extent that –
(a) it is carried out by means of a surveillance device designed or adapted principally for the purpose of providing information about the location of a vehicle . . .

Shaper always found it oddly disappointing if a particularly fine piece of skulduggery proved to be essentially legal.

On the screen a coloured map of North London flickered to life. Dead centre, a red blip threw itself around the side streets near his home, two miles east of where he was parked.

'Keep looking, gimp,' he mumbled.

After twenty minutes, when he came back from the petrol station over the street with a stagnant coffee and a nostalgic pack of jelly babies, the Merc had given up, shunting back on to the main road and cruising steadily away, evidently accepting that both stealth and skill had failed. *Here* was what Shaper had been waiting for, and as he craned over the little screen with eyes narrowed, waiting for his stalker to head home, he confidently predicted the red blip would swing south for Vauxhall, homing on the HQ of the Serious Organised Crime Agency.

Another of Canton's slick little minions, he wagered with himself, keeping tabs.

Instead the Merc turned east and kept going.

Shaper's face fell with every mile. By eleven thirty it had cleared the North Circular and was angling north for Essex. Inexorably returning, like a maggot to the corpse that had spawned it, to the gated communities, stone cladding, and satellite dish empires of Theydon Wood.

The home of the Coram family.

Shaper sat back in his seat, hands openly shaking now, crumpled shirt drenched, and let out a wordless moan.

Bastards.

Five years, staying out of their orbit. Five years repairing – or at least deadening – the damage he'd done while in their service. Five years just getting by, trying to ignore the fermenting grudge that had first set him against them, knowing that to act on it – to invite their ire – would kill him.

I needed you, you bastards. I needed you and you turned your fucking backs.

His finger began tracing at the pill file like some home-made instrument – *zzt, zzt, zzt* – and he had to stop himself before it synched with his heartbeat.

Bastards!

Why now?

'It's nothing to do with me!' he blurted, head craned back to address the sky. 'I already *said*, I'm off the fucking job! None of my business!' He bent down over the screen and shouted at the glowing red dot. 'Fuck off!'

A couple of boozy lads, meandering by en route from the

pub, jumped in alarm. Their startled faces made him feel fractionally better, though the clouds of guilt re-formed almost instantly, framing the serene, smiling face of George Glass.

As far as Shaper was concerned, the involvement of the Corams – in fact the merest hint of their attention – settled the whole matter. All the money in the world, all the perplexing brunettes and enigmatic tattoos and bizarre inducements wouldn't persuade him to risk a conjunction with his former employers.

Detox. Stick to the plan. Get straight.

Let it go.

Forget the old man.

It shouldn't have mattered. Shaper had more than a little experience telling would-be clients to go forth and multiply, and this one shouldn't have weighed on his psyche any heavier than the rest.

But it did. In the soup of his imagination, *it did.* Those liquid eyes dipping with disappointment; that frail smile drooping in anxiety. It mattered – *it stung* – and he almost sneered when a sudden idea struck him, assuaging the shame of his decision. He dived into his coat pocket, triumphant, and withdrew a white card.

Dr Mattheu I. Naryshkin, MB, BChir, GP

Glass's doctor.

He'd palmed it during the drama in Mary's flat, half suspecting it might be handy, half enslaved by the klepto instincts of his youth. He stared at it for a long time, trying not to listen to the quiet *bleep* of the bug on the screen.

And slowly – switching off the tracker with a lazy flick – he reached for his phone.

Chapter Eight

A phone rang in the dark.

Muffled with distance, its programmed ringtone an antique bell effect, dredged from some coppery corner of the mass mind – became flattened and plaintive, a broken, steely drum roll. In a bedroom two walls away a figure in black stiffened, listening to the night, then tilted its sapphire head like a quizzical dog.

And Dr Mattheu Naryshkin, endlessly capable, ever decisive, reliably calm under fire – cable-tied to his bed like a pin-skewered insect – peered up at the vile mask and screamed and screamed and screamed.

Uselessly.

Muted by the gloved hand crushing his mouth, slicing his lips against his own teeth, defeated by the detached grandeur of his own home, nobody heard. Nobody cared.

The knife was already an inch into his flesh. Prickling in its fleshy runnel – a fraction above his left nipple – like frozen fire. The blood was pouring freely now, soaking the sheets below him and puddling in his navel. The cut had been delivered thus far in slow, shallow fractions: a creeping line of meat unzipped, ten minutes since its first soft incision, which dug deeper millimetre by millimetre, second by second. A gentle torture, too slow, too surreal, to permit him the grace of passing out. Worse, he knew that to struggle – to jerk and flex as his body demanded – would be to impale himself fully.

And so he lay still, sweating and bleeding, and howled behind the glove until his voice gave out and he choked on his own spittle. And only then, as his faceless killer held the knife motionless in its slick ravine, as the doctor blinked fat tears of terror, did the phone at last fall silent.

The pause lasted forever.

And finally, off in the guts of the house, an answerphone clattered to life. The doctor listened to his own distorted, recorded self – *unavailable*, it said, *leave a message*, it said – with a deep, broken moan. A *bleep* drowned his misery.

'Uh . . . yeah, hi,' said a voice, tinny with lo-fi crackle. 'Dr Naryshkin? Are you there? It's . . . Actually, you're probably asleep, aren't you? Sorry.'

The voice coughed, awkward. The killer's head tilted the other way, moist eyes set sideways in glossy blue slits. The doctor tried again to shout, to cry out, to howl – as if he could somehow transmit his horror through the distant machine's electric heart.

But it was useless – pointless – and instead he sobbed and gurgled his misery in great, heaving gasps, snorting through flared nostrils.

'OK, look,' said the machine. 'My name's Dan Shaper. I wanted a word about a . . . well, I think he's a patient of yours – bloke called George Glass? See, I was supposed to do a job for him but now I can't, and . . . I just wanted to, I don't know, make sure someone was keeping an eye on him.' Another cough. 'I mean . . . I dunno if he's . . . all there, or . . . he's had a stroke or whatever . . . Point is, I think he could do with looking at, you know? He's being exploited by some real jokers, and . . . it's obvious he needs some h—'

The voice trailed away; deep, embarrassed chasms of concern weighting every word.

Looming above, blurred through tormented tears, the doctor watched the mask twist further towards the sound, as if the killer could somehow see the machine through the dividing walls or spy on the speaker himself.

'Look, sod it,' the voice grunted, firmer now. 'I ain't gonna relax till I've had a word. Someone's got to help him – Glass, I mean – and . . . it can't be me. I'm coming round, doc, I'm sorry. I'll see you in a bit, yeah?'

Click.

The doctor's eyes went wide.

A cruel pulse of hope broke across him; a stifled sob beneath the crushing hand. Above, nearly forgotten – eclipsed in the shaft of forlorn optimism – the killer clucked a wet tongue, theatrically thoughtful.

And nodded its grotesque face.

The mask loomed close, sparkling eyes in darkened, sapphire sockets, filling the doctor's world.

'*Yam*,' it whispered.

Then went on cutting – just a little faster than before.

Chapter Nine

The Naryshkin residence was only marginally less grand than Glass's fish-filled palace. Shaper treated it to a dour glance, suspecting it had been transplanted from some well-to-do suburb out in the commuter belt.

He'd spent the whole journey reassessing his decision to come here.

Am I really intending, he'd agonised, to disturb a medical professional at half past midnight, just to ask a few abstract questions?

Like: how come a mad old codger gets to believe he's three thousand years old? How come he can't remember what criminal scallywaggery he's committed? How does a socially fragile person like that, with more cash than links to reality, get to muddle himself with a bunch of New Age tryhards and their save-our-souls nonsense?

And above all: how the bollocks can I, Dan Shaper, an underworld fixer with a committed disregard for conventional morality and a pressing need for a decontamination holiday, stop feeling responsible for said old codger's well-fucking-being?

Staring at the Jag in the driveway, and the ornamental bronze cherub at the door – noting that this was the sort of house that had a name instead of a number – he suddenly didn't feel quite so bad about waking up the good doctor.

Class sadism. *Fun.*

He reached for the knocker with the first trace of an indecent smirk, which melted as swiftly as the door swung – unresisting – inwards.

'Um,' he said. 'Hello?'

He found the body quickly.

Halfway through his twentieth 'Anyone home?' rising up the stairs like a reluctant ghost, he glimpsed it in the midst of a sideways glance – an abstract impression of shape and colour – through an open door on the landing. With an instinct he neither expected nor understood he found himself ignoring the sight, arresting his own double-take, gripped by a cold, calm-surfaced desperation to deny and delay.

He moved past the door without so much as a gasp.

Pretending to be free from that grisly sight, he could peer into the other rooms with a measure of impunity, prying and poking at leisure, deaf to the promise that, eventually, he'd have to look again.

Glassy-eyed, he ogled medical encyclopaedias, sniffed appreciatively at Fine Organic Poshgrub™ in the fridge, and tried not to shit his pants whenever he spotted himself in distant, dim mirrors. This time he even made sure the front door was closed behind him.

The doctor lived alone. Here and there were odd traces of forgotten divorces and part-time families – a World's Best Dad mug, an unemployed shoe rack in an upstairs dressing room, a hallway cupboard whose left half was crammed with men's coats and the right side left barren. Old habits.

On sideboards, the doctor – white-haired, wiry specs, quiet smile – stared from off-the-cuff photos with his grown-up brood; an awkward patrician among dribbling grandkids. All oh-so-normal. Oh-so-still-alive.

By the time he started back upstairs, Shaper's denial was in trouble. The Sickness was poised to slink free – he could feel it – and in the growing clenches of his gut every shadow concealed a waiting killer, every shrouded nook held a blood-smeared knife, ready to strike. He forced himself to stand squarely wherever he walked, refuting the very notion of danger and refusing to acknowledge the gathering distortions of his vision, skipping lightly over any thought marked 'What This Death Means'.

And averting his eyes when he passed That Door.

A bedroom at the back was being used as an office, and there he lingered, eyeing medical certificates on one wall and, opposite them, like a Yin for their Yang, a photo of the doctor at some lavish dinner event, smiling beneath a bobbing balloon marked Happy Retirement Grampy. Oddities were lifelines for his attention, greedily seized distractions. An antique pipe sat beside a tatty tin with a hash-leaf sticker, and a thick wad of donation forms for a dozen charities lay arranged in one corner, from *Donkeys In Need* to *Cancer Research* and everything in between. To one side, a few bright paperbacks offered colourful relief from the fusty academia elsewhere, aberrantly titled *Heal the Spirit Heal the Flesh*, or *Subtle Bodies and Their Medical Practicalities*, or the ominous *Aurenema: A Guide To Chakric Irrigation*.

Shaper stared at them for a long time.

Hippy shit.

Here?

A half-used prescription pad gave the lie to the notion that Naryshkin's retirement had ended his doctoring days, and in a small filing drawer on one side, a compartment was marked Ongoing Pro-Bono. The files weren't alphabetised, and other than the one at the very front – marked 'Glass, George' – Shaper recognised none of the names. Long-term patients, he supposed, being favoured with post-retirement expertise and dosage. He took a deep breath and eased open Glass's record with a pen, a light shiver spidering up his neck.

Empty.

He was running out of distractions.

The doctor's desk phone caught his eye, briefly tempting him to do the right thing: to swamp the place with cops and medics, surrendering any chance of a first look for himself. But the body (*it's not there, it's not there*) wasn't getting any deader, the cops could wait, and in any case his attention was snagged by a leaf-green readout on the phone's cradle, which annihilated all other thoughts. 'No new messages.'

And oh, the hairs on the back of his neck.

He scowled at the 'Delete All' button as if personally wounded, squinting for the trace of a fingerprint, an explanation, an error . . .

Nothing.

He stood still for five full minutes, focused on breathing. Letting it sink in and trying not to think about it, all at once.

And finally, prepared now, he let his feet carry him along the landing like some disparate, dismissive eidolon, deliberately empty-minded, and cuffed open the bedroom door.

And stood.

And stared.

In those first moments of revulsion – staggering in his place, coming close to pressing treacherous fingerprints on to the wall – it was easy to read a record of frenzy in the scene before him. In that first adrenal rush, as the Sickness cackled and smashed at the cage of his skull, every detail spoke of a bestial savagery: the strip of shapeless meat ripped from the body's chest, left to hang like a deflated balloon across its abdomen; the ribs exposed below, shattered in three places like broken bars, looped across with intercostal gristle. The man's ghastly expression was somehow worse – flecked with arterial paste, lips peeled back like a braying horse, eyes stretched with incommunicable pain – and its silent stare cut deep into Shaper's rationality. On cue the scene came alive with all the nauseous art of his own imagination: hissing, rasping; vomiting fire and fear. The body became a hallucinogenic bogeyman, tainted by the same violence that had killed it, and Shaper dared not even turn his back, afraid it might pounce when he wasn't watching. He simply stared, dumb. Legs buckling.

And slowly, awfully, he saw the buried truth.

The shock dwindled to a morbid calm and the horrors gave way to a darker, stealthier distortion, senses filling hard-edged shadows like ghosts of movements that weren't there, and the recognition dawned in him that for every detail hinting carnage and rage, a second glance betrayed a process far more premeditated.

That wrinkled flap of chest flesh – still prickled along its skin surface with the doctor's wiry hair – wasn't ripped back in some bear-claw scrape as he'd first thought, but neatly sliced along three edges, peeled aside like a window folded on the pith of an orange. The ribs were the same. No frenzied splintering there, just a trio of stanchions strategically snapped like winter branches: an access point cleared inside. The sludge of blackening blood within was unable to fully disguise the variegated lung thus exposed, itself nudged aside to reveal—

And it was here, at last, that the realisation of what he was truly seeing swarmed into Shaper's mind with the buzzing of a billion locusts and an acid taste on his tongue, and he was tilted inexorably over the edge of rationality.

He got out while he still could. He stumbled downstairs before his senses overturned completely – before the rot began to appear on his skin and the worms of his past squirmed free – and even remembered to cuff the front door back to its almost-shut position on his way out. He curled himself on the driver's seat of the van until his stomach stopped pumping poison and the buzzing faded to an electric hum . . . and breathed until he thought he'd burst.

He'd swallowed two Xanax and a single fun-time Troparil before the world stopped pulsating around him, and when sensibility at last restored itself he couldn't even bring himself to regret the self-medication.

The detox was off.

Dr Mattheu Naryshkin's heart had been cut from his body.

By the time he was looping round Regent's Park – windows down, musty scents of the zoo creeping along the canal – the pills were kicking in hard. The horror slunk back to its cell with an impish giggle, sedated but not sated, and in its place came a tangled splat of trippy delights and uncomplicated pleasures. Shaper caught himself making *OoooOOooo* noises at the spooky tendrils of autumnal mist eddying off the park.

He decided to stop to get his brain straight, and pulled over in a bus stop just short of Camden. As he wobbled out of the car, an unhappy pigeon bumbled from the cover of the timetable sign – dank and dying from some daytime mishap – directly into the road. On cue, a rudeboy hummed past in a kitted-up Fiat Uno – a blur of go-faster stripes and pounding bass – and made absolutely no attempt to dodge the decrepit bird. A few sad feathers wafted in its wake, settling on a fresh smear.

'You heartless bastard!' Shaper shouted, waving a fist.

Then heard what he'd said and started laughing.

Heartless . . .

Then vomited down the side of the van and tried not to cry.

Don't think about it.

Don't think about it.

After ten minutes he felt calm enough – if still not entirely unmuddled – to reach for his phone. It rang for a long time before a voice croaked up through a shield of interrupted sleep.

'Mm? Yeah . . . yeah?'

'DI Canton?' Shaper said, affecting a Hilarious Birmingham Accent.

'Yeah. Who's . . . What fucking time is it, anyway?'

'It's an anonymous tip-off, loike. I know where there's a bodaaai . . .'

'Anonymous?'

'That's roight. A *bodaaaai.*'

A short pause. Canton cleared his throat. 'Dan, I know it's you. Your name comes up on my phone. Are you drunk?'

Shaper stared at the squished pigeon with an unexpected burst of empathy.

'Um . . .' he coughed. 'Wh-who's Dan, loike? Never 'eard of the bloke.'

'It's one a.m., mate. You're stoned, aren't you? You're stoned like a fucking infidel in a fucking quarry, as fucking usual, and I'm asleep.'

He almost squeaked, 'Bodaai?'

'Call 999.'

Click.

He found a payphone further up the road and called it in. By the time he got back to the van, a manky-furred fox was loping into the park with a fortuitous pigeon-meat dinner, and Shaper knew exactly where the universe required him to be.

It was 1.30 a.m. He was back on the chems, for better or worse.

Time to go to the pub.

Chapter Ten

The Dog and Ball on Highgate Road was the sort of place that diligently refused to change.

Like a venomous old veteran shouting abuse at German tourists, it strutted in its own intractability, a pivot around which the neighbourhood and the world revolved without itself ever shifting an inch. In recent years its patrons had seen the butcher's next door transform into a sushi restaurant, the little grocer's further along plunge into studio apartment hell, and the post office over the street collapse in the face of communal apathy, sprouting instead a thriving organic produce shop. The other pubs up and down the road flickered and redecorated with every blink-and-you'll-miss-him landlord, changing spots between dingy goth joints, well-to-do wine bars, real ale campaign-baiting gastropubs and a selection of generic chain outlets with chrome bar tops and 3-for-2 offers on flavourless curry-night pig swill.

The Mutt's Nut came through it all with grimy chin held high and corners packed with the same genus of scowling double-hard bastard that had raised its communal wrist there for decades. The only broken constants were the greyness of individuals' hair, their annual exaggerations of the same old stories, and the way they now smoked huddled in the doorway rather than inside, muttering mutinously at the ban.

Not that it was exclusively an old man's place. The clientele grew from the younger end as swiftly as it thinned at the elder: sallow-faced youths of a particular breed – recognising early in life that they had little time for the cattle-market crush and alcopops of the cool bars – would gravitate to the Mutt like maggots to a morgue, playing pool, sucking peanuts, enjoying the unfettered chance to be cheerfully surly without causing offence.

Shaper loved it.

By two o'clock, with thick maroon curtains keeping the nightly lock-in divided from drizzly reality, the comings and goings of the casual crowd had succumbed to the inertia of the regulars: clumping in ones and twos, nursing Guinness and unfizzed cider. Warhorses and legends every one, each unexpectedly outliving his or her reputation. Among these grizzled ghosts, Shaper knew, he was held in a sort of uncertain, amused regard, like a wolf who'd thoughtfully announced it had gone vegan. In the Mutt he always had the disconcerting feeling they were watching to check he was real.

Tonight, however, the old-timers were staring for an entirely different reason. Tonight Shaper sat at a glass-cluttered table with a young Indian man in a bubblegum-yellow T-shirt and faux crocskin waistcoat. In a bar where hair was something you traditionally shaved off – up until nature got the hint and did it for you – this kid had his jet-black mop spiked, draped and gelled in the most asymmetrically sculpted explosion imaginable.

His name was Talvir. He was twenty-two, awkward in his own skin, trying hard to be camp with little experience, and currently dividing his attention between Vince – at the bar, spending Shaper's money – and an expensive-looking white gadget more closely related to the Starship *Enterprise* than anything Shaper would have knowingly identified as a telephone.

'Hang on,' the youngster said, glancing up through camel-length lashes. 'It's coming.'

Shaper nodded and watched through the bottom of his pint, pleased to keep his fluctuating brain distracted.

By day Tal suffered a boring career in tech support at a Directory Enquiries exchange; by night he and his brothers – when they weren't hell-raising far from their parents' gaze – ran the finest forgery clinic inside the M25. From their cluster of bedsits in Bromley they churned out peerless driving licences and passports on a sliding scale of price versus demand. Tal had been a nice kid as long as Shaper had known him – the obvious go-to guy whenever a client needed dodgy ID – but he hadn't betrayed the bottled-up dynamo of his secret sexuality until a chance meeting with Vince three months before, and the battering-ram seduction that followed. Now, it seemed, he was making up for lost time, unleashing a barrage of tight jeans, eyeliner and ill-suited affectations. He'd settle down before too long, Shaper supposed – Vince wasn't the type for queens – but until then the regulars at the Mutt would just have to stare in silence. They'd seen what had happened to people who pissed off Vince.

Fortunately Tal was so overcome with gratitude at the initial introduction that he'd made it clear he owed Shaper some favours. Requesting that the lad abuse his daytime job skills – logging remotely into his company's database – was the first time Shaper had called one in. Watching him at work now, tapping efficiently at the gadget, he congratulated himself for having held off until something appropriately important came up.

'Mary Devon, right?' the kid double-checked.

Important. Ahaha.

Shaper nodded, trying not to blush. 'I called enquiries myself. She's ex-directory . . .'

Talvir gave him an *as if that matters* look and bent back to the task, leaving Shaper to quaff and fidget alone, afraid to relax. Every time he'd let his mind wander since arriving here the fucking thing had gone scurrying back to the doctor's home – the body, the cavity—

You're off the job!

Leave it to the cops!

Forget it!

And on instinct he'd decided to focus instead on the *other* thing he was having a hard time not thinking about.

'Here we go,' Tal muttered. 'D for Delta . . .'

Mary hippyshit Devon.

The faker.

The simple fact was that Shaper felt at his most comfortable around other liars, and there was a certain unselfish pleasure to be had in the acceptance of that. It provided him with a kind of fatalistic licence to surround himself with scallywags and criminals, to drink in places like the Mutt, and to move in circles of questionable morality that could never expose him as a purer, cleaner person. He didn't believe he deserved the chance.

He was just contemplating popping another Zoloft – wary of getting caught up in maudlin self-analysis – when Vince collapsed into the seat beside him with a tension-busting belch, massive hands clawing at three pints with a brightly coloured shooter balanced on top. He fished a pack of peanuts from a pocket and knocked back the shooter without a word.

'Any change?' grumbled Shaper, not optimistic.

Vince shovelled snacks and shook his head. 'Still owe me three, anyway.' He quaffed the first in a single soggy down. 'Shouldn't take long.'

'But they're well-earned, right?' Shaper leaned closer. 'What's the word on Boyle?'

The big man looked momentarily pained, then raised the second beer and pretended he hadn't heard. Shaper's heart sank.

'Vince? You said you'd—'

'I did, I did. Jesus.' He flapped a hand, conspiratorial. 'But it's like I said, you mention someone like that in a place like this, makes people uncomfortable.'

'So?'

'So . . . I sort of told 'em, didn't I . . . I was asking on your behalf.'

Shaper wobbled his jaw, silently reassessing the crowd. Suddenly seeing those curious stares in a whole different light. Coliseum spectators, waiting for lions.

'Thanks, mate,' he murmured.

Vince waved it away with another cheery chug. 'Anyway, nobody's heard nothing. No harm done.'

'Nothing?'

'Not a peep. Far as anyone knows, old Boyle's dead like a discoing dodo. End of.'

Vince still wouldn't meet his eyes. Shaper knew him too well. 'End of?'

'Well, yeah.'

'Vince.'

'End of. Really.'

'*Vince.*'

'Well, it's just that . . . I mean, it's nothing . . .'

'*What?*'

'I noticed a couple of 'em, is all . . . After I asked around, you know. I came back here, sat down. Had a drink. Bit of a snog – fair enough. Noticed 'em, sort of, nipping out.' He coughed delicately, then muttered into his beer, 'Probably just for a smoke, yeah?'

'Or?'

'Or . . . well.' He lowered the glass. 'Or . . . maybe making a call, sort of thing.'

Shaper slumped over the table with a groan. Suddenly the appearance of a lingering black Merc began to make sense.

'It's not *my* fault,' Vince whinged. 'You know how it goes. Stuff like this, it makes *ripples*. The Corams been looking for Boyle for *years*. What d'you expect?'

A barfly twitched and drowned in Shaper's pint. He knew how it felt.

Tal's phone abruptly pinged. The kid launched into a paroxysm of tapping and typing, giving Shaper an idea. He scrabbled in his jacket for the tracker handset and flicked it back on.

Vince, either flustered by his friend's annoyance or embarrassed at being uniquely gadget-free, drained his third pint in five resonant gulps and calmly got started on Shaper's. The barfly's day wasn't getting any better.

On the tracker, the red dot of terror sat firm, immobile – *safe* – over the heart of darkness that was chez Coram. Shaper's pulse returned to something approaching normality, and he even mustered the courage to shoot a defiant glare into the crowd.

'No fucking lions today,' he murmured.

'Got her!' Across the table Talvir waggled his phone. A number glowed enticingly on-screen.

'See?' Vince beamed, enveloping the kid in an avalanche-force bear hug. 'Isn't he great?'

The pair started kissing. Shaper waited until it was clear the sticky spectacle wasn't about to time out and reached gingerly through for Talvir's phone. He hammered the number into his own handset and stood up before the groping began.

'Dropping the kids off at the pool,' he explained, hooking a thumb towards the bogs. Neither of them looked up.

Mary's phone rang for too long.

Against all convention and expectation the toilets at the Mutt were clean, flower-scented and well lit, with a bare minimum of vomit in the urinal and a mere three pieces of marker-pen humour inside Shaper's stall. Two were variations on the classic cock and balls drawing, the third was a football joke Shaper didn't get.

He sat on the bowl with his trousers fastened and the lid down, checking the lock for the third time. His reputation for ice-cold bastardliness might not have held much water any more, but publicly stammering down the phone to a girl he barely knew, in the salubrious confines of a pub shitter, could easily present a knockout blow to what little respect he still commanded.

He had absolutely no idea what he was going to say. It was simply that he was already sporting an uninvited trouser tent at the mere thought of the girl, and after a week listening to orgasms without so much as a prick twitch he felt sure the universe was telling him something. He was high, he was traumatised, he was horny: he *owed* himself the right to pursue this woman.

'Hello?' the phone said, finally. Mary sounded entirely awake, with perhaps a touch of breathlessness. Shaper instantly decoded the hint in a welter of mental images including sex toys, jacuzzis and chocolate sauce.

Pig.

'Yeah, hi,' he said, stamping down on the desire to reach for the bog roll and knock out a glory shot. A pig, yes – but there were limits. 'It's Dan Shaper.'

'Hi!' Cheerful, bubbly, earth-goddess idiocy. Then, 'Wait – who?'

'We met earlier. With Mr Glass.'

'Oh.' The tiniest of pauses. 'You.'

'Yeah. I hope I'm not interrupting.'

'Actually you are a bit . . .' A sliver of displeasure had crept into the voice, bypassing the tie-dyed bullshit and emerging straight from the real her.

Phwoar.

'What were you doing?' Shaper asked, curious. This, he was confident, was the sort of thing normal people said when they rang each other. 'Up this late, I mean.'

'What's that got to do with you?'

'Just being friendly. Actually I . . . wanted to apologise for earlier on. I hope I didn't seem rude.'

He could almost hear her realising she'd slipped out of character, mentally reshuffling. 'Oh,' she said. 'Well. That's . . . Thank you. But don't worry about it. There was a lot of tension – bad energy, you know. And I was . . . I was yogic flying, if you must know. Just now.'

Shaper wobbled his jaw. 'Yogic flying.'

'Yogic flying.' *Almost* unembarrassed.

'What's that, then?'

'Well it's . . . You . . . you sort of sit and . . . *bounce* with your legs. It helps channel your energies. You go up and down for as long as y—'

'And you do this alone?'

'What?'

'Nothing.' *Idiot.* 'That's . . . You do that a lot, do you?'

'Well, I try, but . . .' The voice faltered. He imagined her blinking, remembering herself. 'Mr Shaper, I don't mean to sound rude but what do you want? It *is* very late.' An afterthought: 'And how did you get this number?'

'So do you bounce every night, then?' He couldn't resist.

'Look, I'd be happy to discuss the technique, but right now I'm just about to jump in the shower –' *oh god* – 'and unless I can help you with something, Mr Shaper, I'd—'

'Dan,' he said. 'Call me Dan.'

'*What do you want?*'

'Brunch. Let's have brunch.'

'What?'

'I'd like to take you out.'

'To . . . to discuss yogic flying?'

'No. *God*, no.'

Her voice went quiet. 'This is about Glass, isn't it? Look, is he in trouble?'

Shaper shook his head, not ready to be distracted by *that* just yet. He opened his mouth to reply, tingling with a strange pleasure at doing something as gloriously ordinary as chit-chat—

And scowled.

One of the cock-and-ball graffitos was so fat – so amorphous – that in his eyes it started to become a heart: bulging ventricles speckled with white, hairy bristles.

Pouring with blood.

Torn from a shattered chest.

'Uh,' he said.

Before he could stop it, he was seeing the body, the spatter, the horror . . . and all while sitting there with an erection like a harpoon. The gods of self-revulsion shat on his head.

Already? he panicked, reaching for the pill file to re-up.

'I want to help him,' Mary burbled, oblivious to the sounds of Shaper guzzling a tab. 'He's . . . he's so important to us. To the world. Please, what's the matter with him?'

'I . . . I can't really say.' The memory of the body warped behind his eyelids. The doctor's dead face became Glass's: frail form despoiled, quiet smile smeared in a silent shriek. A thick glut of nausea rose in Shaper's belly.

The Sickness, stronger all the time . . .

'Are *you* helping him?' Mary whispered.

'W-well, I . . .'

No.

'I don't know,' he said, lame. *Fucking coward.* 'I'm not sure yet.'

The dose was already tightening in his veins, and Mary's voice seemed to come from far away. 'Then we have nothing to talk about.'

The phone went dead.

Back in the pub, as if to compound his glumness, Shaper found the table empty. He followed the glares of a few muttering regulars to one side, half expecting to see his companions rutting on the bartop. Instead Talvir stood talking to a tall bald man in the corner, fiddling with the jukebox. Shaper had seen the elderly machine used just once in all the years of his patronage – by some beered-up lads on a pub crawl who thought a bit of Oasis was exactly what the place needed – and recalled the ambulance arriving admirably fast on the occasion.

He was on his way to warning off Tal from a similar fate when it occurred to him nobody was going to lay a finger on an official Vince squeeze, regardless of what they played, and the kid caught his eye first anyway, mouthing, 'He's out the back,' and miming a cigarette. The youth looked strangely tense, and Shaper guessed the lovers had had a tiff. He steered himself towards the back without slowing down – Vince could be trouble if both pissed and pissy – just as Celine fucking Dion started to warble.

The Mutt backed on to a dreary access lane, where late-night smokers were obliged to endure the smell of tramp juice and the yowling of tomcats to avoid drawing attention to the lock-in. Vince's slab-like frame was neither blocking the exit nor visible in the alley, but Shaper thought he could hear the big guy's voice from further along, and stepped out with his hands rammed in his pockets.

It had started to drizzle again – that special London omnidamp, like fog with extra gravity – and he decided after due consideration that yes, he would be thieving a warming cigarette from Vince.

His personal history with smoking was long and complicated, ultimately boiling down to the cunning self-deception that he found it so easy to quit he might as well do it every couple of weeks.

He followed the voice towards the corner, fumbling through his legion of pockets for a lighter, then slowed with a scowl.

'Look,' Vince was saying, 'just curious, wasn't he? Don't mean nothing.'

Shaper went still.

'Anyway, he ain't here tonight, is he? So you might as well sod off. No harm done.'

A second voice sneered, 'I'll be the judge of that, yeah? And keep your hands where I can fucking see 'em.'

The hairs prickled on Shaper's neck. People didn't talk that way to Vince unless stupid or unnaturally confident.

Armed, then.

He shuffled closer to the corner and moved sideways to see, finding Vince looming over a short man in a black tracksuit and red beanie. His podgy sausage fingers were closed tight round the hilt of a knife – a silly, chrome-effect toy – with the sloppy, half-raised tilt of an enthusiastic amateur. Vince, true to form, didn't look remotely threatened.

'I want you to know,' the brute said, casually lighting a fag, 'that if you don't stop waving that around I'll have to take it off you. And then what I'll do, yeah? I'll give it back. If you see what I mean.'

BeanieHat sneered, trying to front his way through it, but it was clear he was rattled. Shaper relaxed a notch, hand still dumbly ferreting for the lighter, and settled in to watch. Vince, he knew, had never bluffed in his life.

And then he froze.

A cold, toothless 'O' of metal had arrived against the base of his skull.

'If that is fucking shooter you getting for,' said a voice behind him, dripping Russian scorn in a curiously high pitch, 'I will make hole in you face.'

'Right then,' Shaper said.

The gun nudged him into the open.

Both men glanced up from their threat fest as he shuffled round the corner: Vince face-palming with an own-goal groan, BeanieHat's lips splitting in a smirk.

'Well now,' the little man said. 'We was just talking about you, Mr Shaper. Way I heard, you're not here tonight.'

'Coulda stayed in the fucking bogs, mate,' Vince spat. 'Made me look like a right plum.'

'Fancied a smoke.' Shaper shrugged, nonchalant. He knew this game. It went: *show no fear.*

'Thought you quit?'

'Been a tough day.'

'Bit tougher now, ain't it? Crap time to change your mind.'

'Story of my l—'

'Both quiet!' shrilled the voice over his shoulder. Shaper risked a glance, recognising the skinny bald guy he'd seen talking to Talvir, and an oily little pistol.

Glock 17, a forgotten corner of his brain chimed. *Beloved of reactivators everywhere.*

'Out from pocket, yes?'

Shaper withdrew his hand and wiggled his fingers. *Show no fear.*

'Here,' Vince grunted, a natural champion of the art. 'Did BollockHead there hurt Tal?'

'Don't think so. He was playing Celine Dion.'

'And that didn't fucking *warn* you?'

'How should I know what music the little princess likes?'

'Celine fucking Dion?'

'All right, all right, sorry.'

The two goons shifted uncomfortably. This wasn't how it was meant to go.

'I told already,' BollockHead barked, 'you be quiet now.'

Vince tilted towards Shaper, arching a businesslike brow. 'You want me to fuck 'em up?' he asked, as if they couldn't hear. 'No trouble.'

Shaper puffed his lips without conviction, as if pondering something incalculably unimportant. 'Best not, eh? I mean, you never know, they might be faster than they look.'

Vince just chuckled.

'Anyway, I already owe you three pints. Can't afford any more.'

'Point.'

'*Look*,' said BeanieHat, exasperated at his audience's unfair lack of bubbling terror, 'shut the fuck up, yeah?' He waggled the blade at Shaper. 'And *you're* coming with us.'

'Why's that, then?'

The man's fat little lips skewed in another smirk. He nodded sideways at the glossy black Mercedes steaming by the road, and in a flurry of abrupt indignation – *I checked the tracker! That car's in fucking Essex!* – Shaper discovered he suddenly wasn't enjoying himself any more at all.

''Cos Dave and Phyll want a word.'

Chapter Eleven

Max Vicar had glassy little eyes which never seemed to blink.

Max Vicar smiled like a viperfish. He smiled with the simple, lip-peeling desire to show off his teeth, and in the act brought to mind nothing so much as a cat – some soft-furred Siamese, long and liquid, which habitually yawns with its blue eyes held open.

Max Vicar wore a black shirt and a red tie. Always.

'Dannyboy.' He grinned from the marble steps, waiting like a bouncer at the stage door to hell. 'They been expecting you.'

BeanieHat and BollockHead prodded Shaper inwards, trying not to seem overawed themselves.

Chez Coram.

Welcome back, Dan.

Personally, he'd always felt the place shrieked unexpected wealth. It basked in its ostentatiousness like some suburban attempt to emulate a grand stately home, except without the bothersome fluff like bad plumbing and poachers. Theydon Wood was the playground of choice among lottery winners, lawsuit payees and dot-com luckouts, and there were five identical stone-clad compounds – each protesting its respectability – on every street. Here every baroque fountain was matched by a barn-door plasma TV, every concrete Doric column topped by a discreet A/C outlet, and every twiddly pediment detail surmounted by a satellite dish to shame NORAD.

The Corams had stag antlers on the wall of the lobby, next to a silver-framed photo of Princess Diana. That, Shaper had always felt, said it all.

He hadn't been here in five years. He would have appreciated five more.

Vicar closed the door behind the group and smiled his scary smile, waggling a teacherly finger at the goons' sweatily clutched weapons. 'None of that in here,' he trilled. 'Did you check him?'

BeanieHat, still pocketing his shooter, stepped smartly forwards: self-elected spokesman. 'Frisked him down, sir, same as you said.' Shaper half expected the little man to snap off a quivering salute.

'And?'

'Just this.' He passed over the tracker handset, helpfully switching it on as it went. Vicar greeted the extra effort with a frosty glare, deactivated the gadget without looking, and deposited it in his own pocket.

'We was all very impressed,' he whispered, tilting the tiger stare on to Shaper, smile wide enough to pedal-bin his head. 'Bug on the car. All very James Bond, innit?'

Shaper deadpanned and silently hated him.

'Lucky for us Phyll's got some kit to find that sort of shit. Never know who's keepin' tabs, these days. Dishonest types, y'know?'

He turned to lead them off with a sneer, then paused to glare at the goons. 'Nothing else? In his pockets?'

BeanieHat shrugged. 'L-lotsa pills, sir. But . . . no weapons.'

'You're sure?'

'We double-checked.'

'M-many pockets,' BollockHead cut in, 'you are see?' He had the look of a man who didn't want to get caught out later. 'Difficult to be finding all. M-maybe secretings . . .'

Shaper flapped his coat like Exhibit A, feeling unaccustomedly sorry for the men. BollockHead and BeanieHat hadn't said a word in the car the whole way here, and he'd liked to think it was because they were still mulling over Vince's parting words – *Hurt him and I'll eat your fucking kidneys*. Sadly it was more likely the wankers were just shit scared of entering the lion's den, and facing the toothy monster who'd hired them. If Shaper knew the Coram operation at all – and he did – there was every chance his chaperons had never even met, let alone come face to face with the bigwigs before tonight.

Bloody freelancers.

'Does his coat have any pockets,' Vicar sighed, 'big enough for a gun?'

'N-no, sir.'

'Then I expect you feel very stupid for wasting all this time, don't you?'

The goons bubbled like grilled cheese beneath the gaze. Shaper couldn't resist shooting them a sympathetic wink, which died like a pulverised roach as Vicar turned the laser beams his way.

'Unarmed. *Well.* How times change, eh, Dannyboy?'

'House rules, right?' *Show no fear . . . show no fear . . .* 'Respectable place, ain't it?'

Vicar preened. 'Quite so.'

Respectable my sweaty arse.

Shaper reflected, as the creep led them off with a foppish bow, on the secret that had miraculously evaded the notice of politicians and police, newspapers and novelists. It was an ugly secret, and he half suspected its untidiness was exactly what had prevented anyone from daring to believe it. The secret was this: organised crime, really, isn't that organised at all.

The truth was that the so-called 'criminal fraternity' was populated almost entirely by work-for-hire odd-jobbers like BeanieHat and BollockHead. There was no pseudo-military hierarchy, no rewards for loyalty, no doing time for the boss.

Freelancers were as interchangeable as bulbs or bog roll. They were paid cash in hand, they asked no questions and they told no lies. There was no sense of routine, no danger they'd consider their flirtation with villainy anything other than a part-time bid for some extra lucre. BeanieHat and BollockHead, for all their bluster, were probably more bowel-disruptingly terrified than he was.

These men were not In It for the career.

Max Vicar was a whole different matter.

Drifting through the blur of expensive tat with a permafrost grin, he slowed every few moments as this or that thought zapped past his electric attention. With one hand he might show off a designer vase, and with the other flick an irritable V at a snoozing corgi. He led the group through Bauhaus bullshit and mock-Tudor tedium like a schizophrenic tour guide, and Shaper shot psychic darts at his back the whole way, noting his strange, overly upright gait.

Icicle up the shitter, he guessed.

At one stage, passing a wide staircase, the man arrested the group with an arctic glare, a quietening finger pressed against bloodless lips. The goons cringed appropriately, and even Shaper – concentrating hard on maintaining his poise, sustained only by the lingering traces of that last dose from the pub bogs – couldn't resist a nascent tremor. He eyed the stairs like the steaming mouth of a dragon's lair and suppressed the urge to flee.

She's up there, isn't she? Trying to sleep, the old cow . . .

Oh so respectable.

Oh so not remotely criminal.

Vicar led them onwards, still smiling. They trailed in silence.

The truth was, Shaper knew, that if there *were* some idiot with a death wish – the IR, say, or a cop, or a shady fucker with a grudge – who attempted to trace upwards along the chain from street-level vomit like BeanieHat and BollockHead to the moneymen at the top, they'd find the links dissolving, the ghostly connections fading, the voices of dissuasion growing louder and stabbier. And if by some miracle of tenacity they trailed it to its utmost, it certainly wouldn't be the Corams they'd find waiting.

It'd be Max Vicar.

The Corams weren't in the business of getting their hands dirty. For such things – the tasks which couldn't be entrusted to pay-per-punch splatterers – they relied on a single professional shit.

This would be a man the Corams themselves rarely met, with no links – on paper, at least – to their lives. A man in a privileged position which combined the right to make decisions with the confident illegality to carry them out. He was the air gap between the commanders and the crime, and he had to be very, very good at his job. He had to have a profound lack of moral scruples, possess an inventive approach to creating and maintaining fear, and above all be completely and utterly temporary.

Shaper knew this because he had once been that bloke.

He'd expanded and extorted. He'd menaced and maimed with a bullish acumen that had swollen revenues as swiftly as it had spread terror. He'd done more awful, wretched things in those days than his brain could bear, until one bloody red winter five years before when his life had torn itself apart like a rabid fiend, and—

Don't think about it, idiot.

Remember the hate. Not the detail.

The very fact that his replacement was here tonight – that Max was in this house at all, threatening the Corams' respectability by association – spoke volumes about how important the family considered tonight's little chat. Shaper felt a secret shiver growing in his fingers, and for once was entirely confident it was a legitimate reponse.

'This way!'

The group descended white-carpeted steps into a wide, echoing expanse – glassed in like a watery greenhouse, thick with the stink of chlorine – and Shaper glanced up from his thoughts to meet the shuttered stares of the Coram siblings.

Lounging by the pool at three in the morning.

Arseholes.

Phyllis – she of the coffee-toned perma-tan and short hair – was pumping at a cross-trainer beside the water. Obsessively athletic, she'd spent years perfecting a boyish body and a permanently huffish expression, smothering all trace of physical femininity. Most people, Shaper knew, assumed her for an obstinately butch bull dyke, and she'd done little to confound the impression, all the better to segue with the chick-ogling, arse-slapping, wolf-whistling man's world she'd inherited. Privately, he recalled, she'd been married (and divorced) twice, and was once one of Kingsley the Cocker's most regular clients.

She smiled guardedly at his entrance, flicking sweat from her face.

'All right, Dan?' she said. 'How's it g—'

'Danny!' boomed Dave from the other direction. 'How the fuck are ya?' He sloshed whisky from his perch on a toxic-green lilo and didn't seem bothered when it slopped across his moobs. Dave wasn't fat per se, he simply radiated an air of such ineffable brick-in-the-face largeness – of character as much as form – that his tubby frame became obese in the eye of the beholder. He wore purple Speedos, had his hair dyed neon blue, and ostentatiously smoked his dad's old pipe.

Dave, Shaper recalled, always liked to be centre of attention.

The pair were thirty-one – the same age as Shaper – and he knew this for a fact because they'd been classmates at school.

He'd seen them grow from the pair of overly pampered pillocks who'd begged his protection from break-time weasels and vicious bitches alike, into stroppy adolescents whose mother despaired of them ever being useful, and finally into the enthusiastically manipulative business people the world knew and loathed today.

They were basically wankers. For a fairly major share of Shaper's life they'd also been his best friends.

Twins, though you wouldn't know it.

(Do. Not. Mention. The Krays.)

'Kids,' he said, civil through the hate. 'Long time.'

'You look like a piece of shit, mate!' blared Dave, toes splashing. 'Can't even afford a decent outfit!' He laughed at his own voice. Dave did that.

'Lots of pockets,' Shaper explained, flapping the coat. 'I like it.'

'Nah, mate! Not a patch on that . . . *whatsit.*' Dave wobbled an arm at Phyllis. 'That fancy shit he used to wear? With the funny collar?'

'Mandarin jacket.'

'Maaaan-darin jacket! That's it!' He slugged on the whisky. 'Like a fucking uniform, that. Give people the willies 'fore they could even see your face.'

Shaper kept his smiles to a polite minimum, seething inside. 'Not sure it compares to the new model.' He nodded across at Vicar.

Dave barked a laugh. ' 'Tween you and me, mate,' he boomed, 'I keep thinking he should lose the neck noose. Sort of an easy target, innit?'

Across the room Vicar raised his hands theatrically – making sure everyone was watching – and began to loosen the red tie. 'You're the boss, boss.'

Phyllis cut in on cue. 'Well, *I* like it. It's stark.'

Vicar barely registered the dilemma, grabbing BollockHead by the collar and sneering massively. 'Well, *you're* the boss too, boss.'

Arselick, Shaper didn't say.

Vicar wrapped the tie round the goon's bald forehead like a bandana, then stepped back with a ringmaster flourish. 'There, y'see? Still looks stark; less important target. Everyone wins.'

Both twins guffawed appreciatively. BollockHead stood frozen in place, reminding Shaper of nothing so much as that poor, doomed pigeon in the road.

One big, sinister circle jerk.

His impatience finally overtook his terror and he plopped down on to a deckchair without invitation, digging out the pill file and not caring who saw. Popping the tabs from their foils – a euphoric Zyban to kill the shakes and a low-dose benzo to blunt the edges – he became distantly aware of the twins' smirks trickling away.

Let them see, he thought. Let them know that scabby little rumour – didn't you hear, Dan Shaper's a junkie now – is bang on the money.

Let them see what they've done to me.

Not, he supposed, that it would help him much. And not that it was even particularly true, in the cold light of day. He knew only too well that he carried the balance of responsibility himself, for this chemical half-life he now lived. But it was all he had, in this place. The only protest he could present – the only accusation he could dare to silently make; the only way to stave off the guilty memories – and so he swallowed the pills and re-pocketed the file with a dramatic air.

'Problem, mate?' said Dave.

Shaper met his eyes. 'Is she joining us or not?'

The temperature plunged. Even Vicar shuffled, and Shaper dared to feel the first tenuous tendril of enjoyment.

'No,' said Phyll, designated serious one. 'Mother doesn't know. We haven't told her.'

'*Yet*,' spat Dave: a lame threat.

Shaper professionally slouched. *Show no fear.* 'Told her what?'

Phyllis started pumping again, rolling her eyes. 'Come off it.'

'Guys, I haven't a fucking clue what this is about.'

Unnoticed, cherishing the sudden lack of attention, BollockHead resumed his place next to BeanieHat and quietly reached to undo the tie.

'Look,' said Dave, presenting Shaper with what he probably thought was a chilling glare. 'Let's not piss ab—'

'Don't you fucking *dare*!'

All heads turned.

BollockHead, they saw, was on the floor, curled round his own belly. Vicar stood over him, face broken with rage, kicking him over and over in the ribs.

'Fucker! *Fucker! I'll* say when you take it off. Not you! Fucker!'

Shaper forced his mouth shut and kept slouching.

Show no fear.

Show no fear.

Vicar dropped to his knees, torso still ramrod straight, and began punching at BollockHead's face, protesting hands slapped aside. Beside them BeanieHat gingerly inched clear, abruptly fascinated by the ceiling.

Shaper just shook his head and kept quiet.

You don't interrupt Max Vicar.

Eventually, like a kid with a new toy, the man gave a bored huff and landed a final damp blow, splitting his victim's lip and slapping a gobbet of pink froth on the tiles. 'There,' he said. He grabbed for the tie and began wordlessly putting it back on, seeming to notice everyone staring for the first time.

'Oh,' he said, teeth flashing. 'Sorry.'

Shaper glanced back at Phyllis and Dave with a sigh, now returning their attention his way. 'You know, don't you,' he said, 'that your man's basically insane?'

Vicar gave a humourless *ha*. 'So says Captain Breakdown.'

'Boys, boys.' Dave's smirk was back in force. 'Put your dicks away, eh? You're both as mental as each other.'

'You were about to tell me,' Shaper said, refusing to rise, 'why I was dragged out here in the middle of the night.'

The twins exchanged an oblique look. Phyll gave a gentle flourish: *after you*.

'Our dad,' Dave began. 'He died when we was just kids.'

'Mine too,' Shaper snapped, reckless with nerve. 'Boo-fucking-hoo.'

The Zyban kicking in.

'Course he did, course he did. Poor little lost kiddies at boarding school—'

'Difference *is*,' said Phyll, cutting in, 'your daddy slipped in a paper-masher at work, ours got his throat slit and his tongue cut out.'

Shaper shrugged. 'Both occupational hazards.'

From across the pool: 'Stop being cute, you little fuck.' Vicar clearly felt left out.

'Shut it, Max.' Both twins together.

Shaper was too big a man to smirk. *Much*.

The truth was that the death of Sam Coram at the arse end of the eighties had entered the annals of underworld mythology. By the time he'd croaked, the era of the pie'n'chips gangster was long over – all the old scores rendered laughable by the ever-widening drugs trade – and gone were the days of rogues behind nightclub desks. Sam Coram had been a tubby little builder from Stepney who never wore a suit in his life, thought cigars were for poofs, cherished his ratty little Yorkshire terrier

Pok, and earned three million quid by importing high-quality heroin in specially quarried marble from the continent. Legend had it that the only time anyone ever saw him violent – directly – was when his shy little wife Maude gave birth to twins and some idiot at the christening compared them to the Krays.

'My kids,' he'd said, knuckles dripping, 'will not be fucking *thugs*.'

He'd died one summer morning when the twins were fifteen, before Shaper ever met them. The story went that the cops had found him locked in a stolen Audi, stark naked, covered in blood, with his tongue looped through the hole in his neck and the tip sliced off.

The tabloids loved it.

'The last time we saw Dad alive,' said Dave, flabby face tightening, 'he was heading down Camden to talk cannabis with the locals.'

'I know the story, Dave.'

'Then you know, don't you, that he was accompanied on this little territorial expansion by his good friend Tommy Boyle? Who, we later discovered, had been ripping him off.'

'Yes.'

'And who disappeared, Danny, the very next day. The same day Dad died.'

'*Yes*.'

Phyllis's voice slid in like an icicle to the guts. 'And who we've been searching for ever since, on account of wanting a word.'

'Yes, Phyll. I know.'

In fact – Shaper understood better than most – it was the twins' mother who'd nursed the vendetta. The cops, even the tame ones, had proved spectacularly useless, and so shy little Maude had packed the kids off to fancy school, 'accidentally' rolled over Pok in the Land Rover, and picked up the reins of the family trade. And to everyone's crashing astonishment had earned more in one year than her tubby husband had managed in his entire criminal career.

Maude was terror incarnate to the wrong people. And she'd been looking for Tommy Boyle a long, long time.

'Then maybe you can tell us, Dan,' said Dave, hooking his toes over the pool steps to stop himself drifting, 'since you know so fucking much, how it is that after all these years without a sign of the bloke, we hear this evening an old mate of ours – who if we're honest owes us a favour or two – is asking questions about that very same bloke . . . but didn't think to give us a call first?'

Shaper said nothing.

'Dan,' said Phyllis, stretching her muscles. 'What exactly have you heard?'

Shaper formed words with exaggerated care.

'I,' he said, 'do not owe you a fucking thing.'

The twins met each other's eyes.

And, eerily synchronised, twisted towards Vicar.

Who smiled. And pulled something slim from his pocket. And flicked it open with a *slt*.

'Let's see about that,' he smirked.

Shaper felt himself stand, lousy with chemical confidence. Heard himself say, 'Come on then.' Legs not trembling, adrenaline barely flowing. 'You crazy fucking fuck.'

He dug fingers into a rarely visited pocket below his right sleeve and retrieved the skinny treasure hidden there. The blade sounded like breaking ice.

Slt.

Vicar arrested his approach and cast a petulant look at the freelancers. 'Thought you said you searched him?'

BollockHead was still dripping on the floor. BeanieHat avoided his eyes.

Shaper slipped comfortably into a fighting stance, blade

angled, knuckles unimpeded – *no amateur fucking sword fights here* – and ignored the disgust at his own thrill.

Five years later, Dannyboy. Still a monster.

'That tie,' he heard himself say, 'is an easy fucking target.'

Which is when Vicar tossed away the flick knife with a merry shrug. Yanked open his shirt – buttons pinging like asteroids – and reached inside.

And withdrew the thing strapped below with the *schlop* of peeling duct tape.

He'd been carrying himself, Shaper recalled, far too upright.

Machete.

Fuck.

The man waggled the blade. His smile filled the world.

'Um,' said Shaper.

'Let's try again,' said Dave. 'No harm done.'

'No harm done,' said Phyllis, a watery echo.

Vicar kept smiling. 'What have you heard, Dan?'

Chapter Twelve

Shaper's first thought upon waking was, it's nice to have friends like the Corams.

The second was, it's nice to do them a favour.

Neither seemed entirely natural, so he scrabbled from unconsciousness with panicky haste, encountering as he went a headache, a desiccated mouth, and an unfeasibly clear vision of an enormous machete.

He was back at home. It was 10.30 a.m., Ziggy had shat on the floor and, naturally, there were birds on his windowsill. He was rummaging for the pill file before his eyes were fully unsealed, and staving off the *what happened* recall.

It didn't work.

He'd told the twins what they wanted to know, of course, and there was a guilty wound in his self-respect at that. Still, with his muscles untangling beneath a hot shower, it was easy to allow a gentle hint of pride at how much he'd also held back.

Tommy Boyle's fingerprint, he'd told them, had been found in the home of a recently deceased man named Jason K. Arbuthnot. The Corams had never heard of such a person, and Shaper had meticulously forgotten to mention the 'K for Kingsley' part.

Lying with too much truth. One of his favourites.

'Not much else to say,' he'd shrugged, dodging all reference to 3,000-year-old nutcases, scraggy-haired hippychicks and dissected doctors. 'I heard about it through a mate, that's all. A cop.'

They hadn't even bothered to ask which one. Possibly they didn't care – relegating all cops to a taxonomic platform somewhere beneath pond slime, undeserving of individual identity – but more probably they already knew about Shaper's little arrangement with DI Canton. There were old grudges there, too.

Ultimately he'd told the Corams that he had no intention of pursuing matters – or the unexpected emergence of Tommy Boyle's name – any further. 'None', as he'd put it, 'of my business. Right?'

And that was that.

Except on the way out, while Vicar showed him to the door and the two freelancers dragged their heels behind, Phyllis had dropped a skinny hand on his shoulder and murmured, 'Do us a favour, eh, Dan? *Make* it your business.'

'But—'

'And quick as you like, yeah?'

Then nothing but the silence of the drive home, punctuated only by BollockHead's moist pokings at his broken face, and the growling of his own guts.

And now, the proverbial morning after. The twittering of birds and the roaring in his ears. He sipped coffee and wondered where to start.

You know where, moron.

Glass answered the phone on the fourth ring.

'Hello?'

'I'm in.'

It took the old voice a moment to catch up. 'I beg your p—? But . . . M-Mr Shaper? Is that . . . ? Oh, thank goodness! Thank you. *Thank you!*' He sounded near hysterical.

'You've had another note, then?'

'Yes! How did you kn—'

'Dr Naryshkin?'

'A-another printout! They found him early this morning. Oh, that poor man . . . It says he'd been . . . he'd . . .'

Sliced up like a surgeon's dummy, mate? Cracked open and hollowed out?

'Any note with it?'

'No, just the article.'

'Right, listen.' Shaper took a deep breath. 'I think . . . maybe you *are* in a spot of bother after all. I'll do what I can to find out more. And I'll send someone round this evening to keep an eye, all right? But I want you to do something for me.'

'Anything.'

'Close your eyes. And no bullshit, all right? I'm sorry, Mr Glass, but this is serious. I need you to think. No past-life bollocks. Just try to remember. All right?'

'But . . . All right . . .'

'Mr Glass, do you know, or have you ever known, a man named Tommy Boyle?'

The silence stretched out. Shaper imagined he could almost hear Glass think. Could almost feel the slender fingers of memory questing into blackness, truffling through frightening histories. He remembered the old man with his lip peeled down, CRIMINAL scar picked out in black and red. The fear of the clouded past.

Shaper knew exactly how he felt.

'No,' the phone said. 'No. I can't say I know the name. But then . . . Th-that's not to say I've never known it. I'm sorry.'

Despite his frustration, Shaper couldn't help but mumble a reassuring 'Don't *worry,*' touched by the same weird sense of responsibility and concern.

Help him.

'Leave it with me,' he said, hanging up.

And then fidgeted. Drummed his fingers.

Get started. Make inquiries.
Help him!
Then growled in defeat and reached again for the phone.

'So,' said Mary, scowling over a defensive teacup. 'Why brunch?'

Shaper skewered a glossy sausage and guiltily enjoyed her awkwardness. Crammed with coughing vagrants, slacking builders and disconsolate jobseekers, Tony's Grill'n'Sizzler was Camden's antidote to cheerful, chatty, coffee-shop culture, and absolutely *not* where one went to be colourful. In her scrambled-rainbow dress and sequinned shoes, Mary had the look of a peacock among vultures or, more accurately, the look of a vulture in a peacock costume.

'Brunch?' he said, waggling the sausage. 'Best meal of the day. Only legitimate context for a fry-up if you get up late. Night worker's paradise.' He folded a slice of bread over a cremated bacon rasher and eyed Mary's own carbohydrate cataclysm. 'Do you, uh . . . ?'

She nudged the plate his way with more relief than generosity. Prickly, off-balance, disarmed; more desirable now even than the night before. Shaper guzzled a mouthful of her soggy chips and smiled through bulging cheeks.

For her – for just an hour of spoil-yourself company – the job could wait.

'So that's how you see yourself, is it?' she said. 'Nocturnal?'
'Depenf om fe work.'
'Which is what, exactly?'
He shrugged. 'I watch things. Closely.'
She fiddled with her hair and looked away.

To her credit, she hadn't even bothered with the whole sappy smile act this morning. Frankly, she was attracting quite enough attention as it was, without pretending to be something as unlikely as 'happy'. Customers at Tony's, Shaper knew, didn't *do* positive.

Besides, in the optimistic bowels of his brain he'd taken to decoding at least a small portion of her awkwardness as a sign of mutual attraction, and was therefore annoyed that the more sensible half of his mind kept butting in with a far neater explanation: Glass.

Glass, whom she'd asked about once a minute since arriving. Glass, whom she'd already phoned to confirm Shaper wasn't lying about accepting the job. And Glass, whose well-being had unexpectedly become just as important to Shaper as it so clearly was to Mary, to the extent that even in the midst of his disappointment at her preoccupation he couldn't bring himself to resent it.

The old man mattered. He wished he knew why.

'He has a sort of magic,' Mary murmured, and for an instant Shaper thought she truly had peered into his mind. But he looked up to find her simply staring into her teacup, a broody rumination along the same lines as his own. 'He just . . . he fascinates people. They want to be near him. And the thought of him being in trouble . . .' Their eyes met. 'Please. If there's anything I can do to help?'

Shaper puffed out his cheeks, a little irritated. Poised on the verge of a new job, facing narcotic collapse and evil, smiling machete-wielding cunts, he'd felt he *deserved* to give his attraction to this woman a brief blast of full attention. But no. Glass straddled the atmosphere like the hint of an inoffensive fart, impossible to ignore.

Fine.

'How do you know him, then?' he surrendered, glum.

Mary straightened in her chair, risking a smile. Straight into character.

'Actually, my mother found him. She had the Sight too.'

'Oh.' He treated her to his best heavy-lidded look. 'Gosh.'

'I was only little. Didn't meet him till much later. Mum always said he just . . . just showed up at the door one day while I was at school. He claimed he wanted to . . . reconnect with the world. Been on the sidelines too long – wanted to share himself.'

'This was before he lost his memory?'

'Oh yes, that was later. Anyway, she – my mother – she recognised instantly what he was. *Is*. It's the aura, you know.' Smile, enthuse, gesture. 'To her – and to me – he . . . he looks like a river of peace. Pouring this . . . endless energy into the world.' She waved her hands as she spoke, thoughtlessly raising her voice to lecture levels. Shaper noted several tramps eavesdropping at the next table, mugs frozen at lips.

'I mean, yes, there's the wisdom, the stories . . . He's lived three thousand years, how could he *not* be fascinating? But . . . it's the energy that really matters. This . . . rich vibration. It's like the pulse of the universe, you know, in his crown chakra . . . And if only others could tune in like I have, they could—'

'Mary.'

'They could feel the—'

'*Mary.*'

He waited until her eyes detached from whatever invisible audience she was addressing – halfway up the wall – and locked on to his.

'Would you please cut the shit?'

She stared. She shut her mouth with an audible click and slumped in her chair, and again Shaper found himself picking out expressions as they scrolled past: surprise, annoyance, shame; even a dark hint of red-handed guilt.

And perhaps something stranger too. Something Shaper put down to a random fluctuation of his chemicalised brain – a mid-morning hint that the drugs were already wearing off – which imbued her with a shiver of blossom confetti and a honking of horns. The strangest air, he thought, of relief.

Never one to play his cards close, he was preparing to blurt this observation when an apron-clad kitchen jockey appeared with fresh tea and an extra round of toast. The intrusion was so blunt, and so unexpected, that Shaper gaped like a fish.

Since when did Tightfisted Tony's do top-ups?

By the time he'd parcelled away his astonishment, Mary's expression had grounded in a surly, defensive scowl, and the moment had passed. He twiddled a drooping chip and blew mental raspberries. *Sod it.*

'Glass thinks there's a murderer after him,' he said. 'He wants me to find out who.'

He looked up, expecting shock and concern – and, yes, got them; saw the 'What? That's awful!' poised on her lips; the outrage and doubt lining up behind it.

But . . .

'And now Dr Naryshkin's been murdered,' he added, senses focused tight, watching so closely his eyes hurt. 'Did you know about that?'

But.

The shape of her brows. The corners of her mouth. The creeping, morphing chemical haze of pestilence and lies which crept and shimmered around her –

Not real, not real, not real –

And whatever the trigger, however his pickled waste of a brain chose to convey it, he knew.

She's not surprised.

'N-no,' she said. 'No, I didn't know.' Itchy nerves crowding in on her deep, hard scowl. 'He's dead? *Really?*'

Shaper sipped the fresh tea. 'You're bloody good,' he said.

'Pardon?'

'At lying.'

SIMON SPURRIER

The woman gave it all of two seconds' thought before pouncing out of her chair. Eyes flickering, chair scraping, body turning to stamp off; tramp heads twisting to see. But beneath it all, under the indignation and outrage, through the petulance and wounded pride, that same strange flicker of reluctant, painful joy. The perverse pleasure of being found out.

Not that it was quite enough to prevent the dramatic exit, and Shaper was forced to flap placating hands and blether panicky retractions, just to arrest her soap opera moment. 'Wait-wait-wait!' he cried. 'Just hang on! I'm not accusing you of . . .'

(Of what? Of murder?)

I'm not accusing you of *anything*. All right? Just . . . settle, petal.'

She hovered, uncertain.

'I'm just saying. I *suspect* you know more than you're letting on. But that's fine, no problem – par for the course. It's just . . . it's impressive, really. You make it look effortless.'

She made an icy decision – he could almost see it behind her eyes – ditching the cornered-fox look and sinking back to the chair. 'How dare you?'

'Sorry,' he said. 'OK? I'm sorry. Maybe I'm wrong ab—'

'You are.'

'Fine. And I'll find things out anyway, so it doesn't much matter. I'm just . . . interested. It comes naturally to you and I'm wondering why. What made you like this?'

'Like what?'

'A bullshitter.'

For a second he thought she might crumble then and there. She seemed poised on the brink of some vast precipice, tantalised at the prospect of a connection, frightened of stepping out.

But the hippy won. The smile flicked on like a bulb.

130

'Look, I don't know what you . . . you think you can tell about me. But I have a very complicated energy. Everyone says so.'

Shaper slumped in his seat.

'The last three limbs of the ashtanga can create a lot of . . . contradictory vibrations. It's like interference. It mixes up the messages. Makes people think they sense something that isn't there. Whatever you think y—'

'Mary, I'm not remotely interested.'

And oh, the silence.

'I get that some people buy this stuff,' he said. 'Or . . . or need a bit of mysterious bollocks in their lives. Or just like belonging to a gang – or whatever. I get that those people like the drama, yeah? But I'm not one of them, Mary. It's horsecock and I'm not interested.'

It was a vicious little spiel. And worse yet, a risky strategy, bargaining everything against his ghostly suspicion – more a hope, in truth – that she was as fascinated by him as he was by her. That she wanted – no, *needed* – to be exposed. That he could truffle out the reality with nothing but the threat of his own apathy.

'Not interested . . .' she echo-whispered, like scratching at a wound.

A white-clad arm appeared between them like a stray missile, offloading a plate of extra bacon and miraculously unburned sausages, before being borne away by its owner – another expressionless grease servitor.

'Hang on,' Shaper called, 'I didn't order th—'

The kitchen door *fwup-klunked* shut. For a second he spotted the frog-like face of Tightfisted Tony himself, watching through the mirrored slats of the peep window, before that too slinked away. Shaper eyed the bacon, suspicious, ignoring the envious glares of the vagrants at the next table.

'What makes you such a fucking authority anyway?' Mary

hissed, untroubled by the pig-product bounty, all floppy niceness now discarded. 'What's your fucking story?'

'I'm the world's first honest liar.' He shrugged, checking the sausages for booby traps. 'Ask me anything.'

She wobbled a jaw. Gave it some serious thought.

'You married?'

Shaper glanced up in surprise, noting the shadows of alarm round her eyes, as if she'd forgotten to switch off her mouth. She was suddenly fascinated by her teacup.

'I was . . . engaged once,' he said, recouping.

'What happened?'

Ah.

He stared at her and through her. Felt the landmines shift under the wheels of his psyche. Felt the Sickness purring its pleasure somewhere inside, itching to take over.

The shakes wormed along his wrists.

'She was shot by a one-bollocked Albanian,' he said Robot voice. Heart switched off. 'He was aiming for me.'

'P-pardon?'

'She died on an operating table an hour later. And I'll tell you this: I spent the whole time we were together, that's two years, lying to her.' He smiled, crueller than he'd meant. 'I was saturated – d'you understand? – *saturated* in deceit. Still am.'

The words came from a script etched on his spine, often rehearsed, rarely performed. 'I am an unpleasant shit, Mary Devon. But *I* don't pretend otherwise.'

She simply stared, aghast.

'Going for a piss,' he announced.

Let her fester.

A calming Zoloft, popped among screeching urinals. Watching the shakes rattlesnake away.

Hoping she'd still be there when he got back.

On the way, along the damp corridor from the bogs, he

sidestepped into a windowless office cubicle and fixed the pallid creature inside with a venomous glare.

'What the fuck's going on, Tony?'

Tony McCane's miniature eyes went wide in their fleshy sockets. Instantly his left hand groped for its opposite, like a father protecting a helpless child, and the bare scalp round his scraggy Mohawk prickled with sweat. 'Dan! I don't . . . What d'you mean, Dan?'

Shaper had known Tony for years. The man had started out in the protection rackets – everyone knew the story, these days – until the accident which had both derailed his criminal career and coined his nickname. Menacing a frightened shopkeeper one day, so the tale went, he'd jabbed his trademark hunting knife into the counter at a point of angry emphasis, and was astonished when, contrary to all the action movies which had inspired the gesture, his hand slid neatly down the blade and severed every tendon.

Thus, 'Tightfisted Tony'.

Nowadays – all skin and attitude, leather-clad and tattooed – Tony was overcompensation personified, trying to be, look and talk tough, when the world knew he was a crippled cafe magnate with halitosis. Not that he'd gone entirely legit, of course: the toilets at the Grill'n'Sizzler had seen more cloak-and-dagger deals than a CIA surveillance team, and Tony took a generous slice from each. He was a part of the loose confederacy of shifty types Vince would doubtless describe as 'mates' and Shaper would call 'people I know from the pub', and in all the years of their acquaintance Tony hadn't *once* offered him – or anyone – free bacon.

'Top-ups of tea?' Shaper scoffed. 'Extra toast? Do me a favour, Tone. What's it all about?'

'Just . . . being friendly.' The sweat ran like rivers.

'Tony, you're tighter than an oyster's arse. Everyone knows it. Stop shitting me around.'

'H-honestly, Dan, it's—'

'*Tony.*'

The punk deflated.

'It's just . . . W-we heard you're . . . back with the Corams. I was just showing some respect, sort of thing. Wouldn't want you getting a downer on my place.'

Shaper's shoulders drooped.

No bigger gossips in all the world than a bunch of crims.

'Tony, it's temporary. All right? And not by sodding choice.'

'I . . . I just thought. When you came in here, y'know? It might be . . . *business.* You know?'

Shaper knew all too well.

No bigger gossips. And no one with longer memories.

He turned for the door, guiltily aware of Mary left alone with things unsaid, then paused with a hand on the knob. 'Who told you, anyway?'

Tony shrugged. 'You know how it works, mate. You just . . . hear stuff.'

Information transfer. Invisible, silent, odourless. The essence of the underworld.

'Silly of me.'

She was still there. Waiting with an anxiety Shaper didn't feel he deserved. Cheeks flushed; no smile, no bullshit. Beautiful and ready to talk.

'My mother,' she said, not pausing for a prompt. 'She was very good at what she did.'

Shaper shoved the extra bacon towards the tramps, not looking. They descended like starved raptors.

'She . . . she could tell things about people the instant she saw them. I mean, that's spooky – if you're a kid. Growing up like that . . . So. I had a lot to live up to. You know?'

Shaper clumsily picked up the cue. 'That's why you went

into . . . uh . . .' He groped for the word, gesturing at her clothing, her hair.

'Yes. Well, no, it was more my brother's fault, really. Mum was perfect. Clever, loving. We had no dad – ran off when I was two – so it was all down to her. And Karl, that's my brother, he was kind of . . . troubled. Easily led. I mean, god, he was great with me, best big brother in the world, but . . . on the outside? Drugs, the wrong crowd, you know. Always a cop at the door. So Mum had to . . . give out to him a lot. In time, if nothing else. Took him everywhere, to all her clients, all her jobs.' Her eyebrows lifted, a flittered tangent. 'Matter of fact, Karl was there when Glass showed up at the door that first time – he'd been expelled from school the same day – so he got in on that action before me too.' She huffed and pulled a face, listening to herself. 'Look, I'm a grown woman, I know it's stupid. And I don't begrudge him – Karl, I mean. Not any more. It wasn't his fault. But when you're a kid and all you want is a cuddle . . . and your mum's too busy fretting over someone else, you just . . . you find ways to get attention.'

Shaper said nothing, feeling the beetle scuttle of synchronicity along his neck.

Amazing what people will do to fit in.

'So I started learning. Readings, regressions, therapies. Big books on occultism. Spells, dream definitions, tarot, all that. Mummy's little apprentice. "A natural talent," she told me, one day. I cried all that night, I was so happy. And eventually I got to meet Glass too, like . . . like I'd joined the club. Finally doing something to make her proud.' She sniffed, fighting tears. 'Oh, I stayed out of the hardcore stuff, you know. I was only young –' *Hardcore?* Shaper scowled but didn't interrupt – 'but I was in there. A connection. Something Karl didn't share. *Mine.*' Was this an admission? Shaper wondered. A read-between-the-lines confession that everything she was – all the floppy clairvoyant stuff, the fuzzy-minded jibber-jabber – was an affection-baiting fraud?

'Then one night Karl goes out. He's eighteen. Gets in a fight in Soho. Bloke's all set to kill him so Karl throws a punch. Self-defence, right?' Mary mimed a roundhouse, lost in the story. 'Turns out the guy's got a weak heart. Dead before he hits the ground.' She cleared her throat. 'Karl's packed off on a murder charge and Mum falls apart.'

'Understandable.'

'Yeah, now it is. But at the time?' She shook her head. 'It was like losing her all over again. Karl this, Karl that. She had a breakdown – I get that now. But all I could do then was step up a gear. Crystals and incense and . . . fucking beanbags! I took over the clinic, made a go of it. Quit college. Scrabbled about like a good little girl for the odd "Thank you, Mary" and made do.' She sat back with a whole-body sigh, looking away. 'Scratching for crumbs. Pathetic, really.'

Her eyes were moist, but she seemed so determined not to blink – not to let the moisture break its meniscus and invade her cheeks – that Shaper feared she'd be derailed or even insulted if he tried to comfort her. Instead he focused on repressing his lust for this calm, controlled, stunning woman exposing herself before him. He felt, for the first time in a long time, privileged.

She finished with a bullish shrug. 'Mum died in a motorway pile-up a few years ago. Distracted, they said. Using her mobile.'

Shaper saw the punchline coming. 'Talking to Karl?'

She nodded, jaw tight. 'His weekly call from inside. You've got to laugh.'

They didn't.

After several silent minutes, sipping tea and staring at nothing, Mary lifted her eyes and harpooned his gaze. 'Well?'

He drummed his fingers, building courage. Somehow, for

some reason – he felt it deep down, beyond even where the Sickness lurked – he *needed* her to say it.

'So it's . . . it's all bollocks, then? The clinic? The Sight? All that?'

And she seemed all set to reply – no longer angry, even giving the first sign of a nod – when he butted in with a last, thoughtless addition: 'And Glass.'

Idiot.

The last syllable killed the connection.

Her face clouded. The heart-to-heart shattered around them like—

Ha!

—like glass. As if it was OK for her to *hint* she was living a lie, to imply it was all phoney, to as much as concede the bullshit – up until it hinged around the old man. His name introduced the ring of accusation, and ejected them both quite suddenly from the heat of their shared moment back to the cafe; to the grease and stink and chatter. Two strangers eating brunch.

'*Not* bollocks,' she growled. 'That's *not* what I said.'

'But—'

But it was too late. She crossed her arms and powered up the shields in an electric instant. 'I was simply explaining how I wound up doing what I do. I thought you were interested. If you want to go around misinterpreting . . . or . . . or if you think I don't agree with the . . . the very compelling evidence that alternative therapies are a viable practice, then you can . . .'

Blah blah blah.

Back to square one.

Another waiter syruped by, spearing Shaper's attention and depositing a bizarre offering on the table: a glass of water, carefully and deliberately placed on a cardboard coaster.

From the kitchen window, Tony watched.

What?

And suddenly Shaper was knackered. All the thinking, all the fear, all the lust . . . He pinched the bridge of his nose and invited the drugs to soothe away the kinks in his muscles, letting Mary's prattle wash over him.

An honest liar, he'd told her. Fine.

'I'm very attracted to you,' he said, cutting her off. 'The fact that you're a fraud – whether you admit it or not – doesn't change that. It's quite exciting, matter of fact. I just thought you should know up front.'

She stared as if she'd been slapped.

He picked up the glass of water and stared at it, aware only abstractly that, across the table, the penny was dropping with a thud.

'This isn't about Glass, is it?'

'Hmm?'

'Inviting me here. It's nothing to do with your . . . the job.'

Ignoring her, still feeling Tony's sweaty gaze, he picked up the coaster and turned it over.

And stared.

2 men. Black Merc. Out front.

'Fuck,' he said.

Mary knuckled the tabletop for his attention. '*Answer me. Why did you invite me here?*'

'Shut up. This is . . . Fuck.' Clammy hands, aching guts. 'If they see you with me they'll think . . . Bollocks. Bugger, bugger, bugger.'

Fucking Corams and fucking leverage and—

'Don't you tell me to shut up.'

'Look, just . . . OK. OK . . .' He rose to his feet and flattened out his palms, calming her; brain rushing, muscles instantly re-kinking.

Of course they were going to keep tabs. Of course they'd be watching.

Don't get her involved.

'You need to go out the back way,' he said. 'I'm sorry. And . . . believe it or not, this *is* about Glass, sort of. Fuck knows how, but it is.'

'But—'

'Tell me this, how come he's forgotten everything?'

'What?'

'All his memories. Wiped away like that. How's that possible?'

She spluttered, caught up on the wave of urgency. 'Well, there . . . there are meditations. Ways of clearing the mind . . . I mean, memories are just echoes of a second plane, so there's no . . .'

He stared at her. In the heart of the whirlwind, he just stared.

Her voice faltered away. 'I don't know,' she said, lame.

And there was the breakthrough. In that simplest acceptance of her own ignorance, there was the admission.

It's all bollocks, Mr Shaper.

I'm a faker, Mr Shaper.

You're right, Mr Shaper.

None of it needing to be said.

And as he pushed her out through the kitchens – ignoring her complaints – and nodded gratefully at Tightfisted Tony on the way, he paused at the rusty fire door out back and kissed her, hard and urgent.

'I'll call you,' he said.

Chapter Thirteen

Shaper left through the front door, pausing on the kerb to dial his phone.

'Yeah?' gruffed a familiar voice.

'Vince? Job for you. Two grand.'

A dense silence trickled out. 'Uh.' It said. 'Look, don't take this the wrong way, but . . . This ain't got anything to do with the Corams, has it?'

'What?'

'Only everyone's saying you're back working for them again, and—'

'For fuck's sake! I'm not working for them!'

'You sure?'

'Yes!'

Sort of. Ish.

'Sorry, mate. Just checking.'

Shaper shook away the incipient annoyance, drinking in the street scene outside. By day Camden seethed with life. Tourist cameras snapping, theme-park punks waving Leather Shop signposts, prison-style smokers in emo black and a sense-battering medley of fast-food kiosk stinks. People weaved at leisure between kerbs, relying on the drivers of what little traffic dared run the gauntlet to be less drunk, less stoned, or less bloody stupid than themselves. Amongst the chaos of unconventionality, a solitary black Mercedes parked outside a pink tattoo temple stood out like a tyrannosaur among turkeys.

'Wankers,' Shaper muttered.

'Eh?'

'Nothing. Just some old pals. Look, about this job—'

'Two grand, yeah?'

'That's right.' He waved airily at the indistinct shadows behind the tints – imagining BeanieHat and BollockHead sinking lower in their seats – and hoped they hadn't spotted Mary. 'Bodyguarding. Nothing major. Bit of home security maybe. Call it five days, tops.'

'Yeah, *in*.'

A kid in a hoodie – so all-encompassing that Shaper couldn't make out his skin colour let alone his face – swaggered by with his trousers clinging valiantly to his thighs. 'Skunk . . . hash . . . pills . . .'

Shaper watched him dissolve into the crowd, dredging a random thought from the depths. 'Vince?'

'Yeah?'

'How's your Who's Who these days?'

He stared at the high-rise and cracked his knuckles.

Ten layers above ground, one lair below.

B-dum tsh.

The basement level was conspicuously segregated from the upper sections, as if shunned by the very bricks on its shoulders. The bulk was painted a skyline-confounding teal, which shifted to a patched and ruddy maroon where the kerb met a flotsam-clogged light well. Here the sunken windows – shafts tilted to eke a fraction more light – were packed behind metal grilles, like chutes emptying into a castle moat. This troglodytic level even had its own sleazy steps round the back – concrete and gum-pocked – where no one could see. The whole thing put Shaper in mind of some ballgowned baroness, peering discreetly over the trackside near the canal, hoping no one would realise she was tiptoeing on a toilet.

He took the stairs two at a time – *no buggering about, no nice guy: straight in and out* – and yanked open a fire door so graffiti clogged he could see a stratum of paint coats where the glass was cracked, like age rings in a tree.

Sixteen years since Tommy Boyle came here.

At least the walls will remember.

Inside, the hallway smelled of piss and breezeblocks. Somewhere a baby cried, a TV honked and applauded, and a prepubescent laugh – goblinoid and cruel – carried through the gloom. Motion-triggered lights followed him down the hall like a peristaltic ripple, a neon abyss sucking him in. The place brought the word *oubliette* to mind and, psyched-up, adrenalised, amphetamised, twitchy and snarly, he couldn't get it back out. It became a mantra in his brain, losing all coherence and meaning.

Oooo

Blee-et.

Oooo

Blee-et.

Shut up.

On reflection, the two extra Ampalex – nerve-tighteners knocked back with the dregs of a discarded beer can from the van – were perhaps too much. Every concrete edge looked blade-sharp; every static wall gripped by a heat-haze vibration.

Focus.

Show no fear.

'Number eight,' Vince had told him. 'Last on the left. Did some door work down there once – bloke pays pretty well.'

A bent school chair was set outside the door, occupied by a lump-with-eyes which resolved itself, with each step, into a monolithic teenager with biceps bigger than his feet.

Well-paid or not, the kid didn't seem especially attentive: reading a comic with his tongue jutting, oblivious to the world. Shaper came to an awkward halt beside him, desperately fostering his fearlessness.

He was still standing, feeling stupid, when the kid spat a magnificently uninterested 'What?' – not looking up – and turned a papery page. He had the word KIMOTA tattooed on his hand. Shaper didn't ask.

'Here to see Mouse.'

'Got an appointment?'

'No, but—'

'Just kidding. No one ever does. In you go, then.'

Shaper blinked, feeling oddly cheated. He found he almost had to stop himself blurting an objection, and instead shrugged, pushed open the door, and gazed into solid smoke. The sweet-and-sour of scorched marijuana roasted his palate.

Crossing the threshold, seized by an opportunistic thought, he turned back to the blob outside. 'There are these blokes following me,' he said. 'Two of 'em. Think I lost 'em, but . . . they might be cops.'

The kid finally looked up, sniffing, and gave Shaper an up-down appraisal of spectacularly rehearsed indifference. And then went back to his comic with a horse-like cluck.

Shaper entered the flat with reluctant admiration. This wasn't a system designed to prevent threats from getting in, he realised, but to convince people they weren't one.

He wiped it away. Today, here, now, he fucking *was* a fucking threat.

Had to be. Had to believe it.

It will be messy.

'Mouse' was hard at work. He barely glanced up as Shaper entered, lost in the acrid clouds. His name was well-deserved: small and hunched, coffee-black, with his yellow overbite masked by fag-stained fuzz. He fussed over a slab of skunk at a tabletop in the room's exact centre, puffing a liquorice roll-up with an asthmatic rattle. His fingers moved with a breathtaking dexterity which belied his age, chipping nuggets off the green block with a cup scale, then scooping each dose into a plastic baggie. Shaper struggled to avoid mesmerisation at the speed of the movement, his senses softening with the air's seductive payload. The block was gone before he'd even shuffled into the light.

The apartment was drab, grey, invisible. It didn't matter.

'Yes?' said the man, finally lifting his eyes. 'I can 'elp ya?'

Mouse's voice was thick with Jamaica, a honey-rum insouciance implied in every subsonic syllable.

Shaper ignored him.

Assess threats.

Three other occupants. A woman – for some reason wearing a sequinned cocktail dress – asleep and snoring on a thread-bare sofa, with a half-empty beer bottle slack in one hand. A white-skinned Rastalike, sprawled on an armchair by the door, spliff smoke roiling through ginger dreadlocks. And a twenty-something black kid, edgy, hairless, vest-topped and ball-shouldered, sitting on a school chair by the wall.

Eyeing Shaper sideways.

We have a winner.

The assessment was made on autopilot, a strategic eye flicker that dripped with the thoughtless, predatory joy of the bad old days. He almost cringed at the ease of it all.

Just go with the flow.

'I know you,' Mouse was saying, squinting. 'You that Shaper, uh? Good man, they say. You come t'buy fr'me, Mr Shaper?'

'No. No buying.'

'Mm. *Mmm.*' A grin in the dark. 'An' truly yes, I did eyah a story only today . . . They say you gone back work withem Corams.'

(For fuck's sake!)

The black kid rotated his face fully at that: confrontational, eyes preternaturally white.

'That true, Shaper?' Mouse drawled.

He shrugged – *show no fear* – and composed his actions playlist in silence, getting ready for when it all kicked off. He knew better than to hope it wouldn't.

''Cos I tell ya, Shaper,' the little man went on, presenting an untroubled smile, 'we don' like much the Corams down this place. Taken all the trade, they. Time was old Mouse in big money, free market. Workinna street, my man. Many dealin' too, no fella top. Now? Uh? You see?' He gestured round, hand cutting trails through smoke. 'Now Mouse in shit'ole. Scrapin' by, man. Corams ronnin' all the boys on the street – white shit in 'oods an' trainers.' He nearly spat. 'You wantin' close down what I got left, eh? That why you come, Shaper?'

'No.'

'Why then, uh?'

'To talk.'

'No talk, boy. Not this trade. You go now.'

'Here to talk about Tommy Boyle, Mouse.'

The little man blinked. Treacle-thick confidence liquefying; a heavy scowl dropping through grey brows. The change was so profound it somehow infected the smoky air, like a signal of uncertainty carried on the pall, and at the reaches of his vision Shaper felt rather than saw the kid's head twist away, uncertain at his boss's silence.

Don't think.

Settle it before it starts.

Shaper moved.

And, yeah, the kid was quick, head snapping back at the first hint of action, legs shifting from his seat, fists clenched—

But not quick enough.

Shaper threw himself into the sheared instant with such speed that his hands were closing behind the kid's skull before it was half turned, leg lifting, jerking his palms on to his knee with the kid's face in the way.

Blood geysered from a shattered nose. Eyes spastic, lips slack. Shaper didn't wait, spinning away as the limp form sagged and Mouse belatedly went foghorn loud.

Main threat down.

Don't think.

Back to the door. Flicking the latch before Fattie outside could react. Then back round, striding for the white Rasta, only now clambering up. Pausing to blast a savage, wordless shout into Mouse's face – forcing him down in a cringe – then onwards, room blurring, only smoke and energy around him.

His senses untangled. The Sickness borne on adrenaline now, bypassing its Ampalex restraints to gobble all his fear and doubt.

He leered the wolf-smirk of his old, caged self.

The Rasta went for a pocket, clumsy with the high, and Shaper laughed out loud, grabbing a fistful of dreads and back-handing the gurgling pillock across his face. Then followed him down – two punches to the gut, once with each fist – leaving him rasping and sucking through empty lungs.

Reassess.

The woman in the dress still comatose. Someone hammering at the door. The kid with the fucked nose blinking back to life. Mouse reaching for a desktop drawer.

Don't think.

He kicked the drawer shut on the little man's hand. Shouted over the startled squeal and grabbed a handful of Mouse's collar, dragging him back, twisting as he went. He dropped to his knees and straddled the dealer like a cowgirl whore – like a fantasy of Mary, arching and flexing with—

Focus, idiot!

Mouse was stronger than he looked. Pushing for clearance, bucking, he lashed out a lucky knuckle that cracked painfully at Shaper's cheek. He blotted the shock and hammered an elbow into the man's hairy little neck, ignoring his clogged choke and glancing back up.

FuckedNose was on his feet, pumped with anger, steaming forwards, snotting blood and hate.

Game over. Put it to bed.

Shaper dug into the pocket below his armpit and whisked out the slim little knife.

Positioned it with soft care.

And smiled sweetly.

FuckedNose rumbled to a halt.

The adrenal fug collapsed under its own weight. The pills reasserted their dominance and chased off the Crazy, repainting the background of his senses and restoring a crude botch job of time and space. The whole thing hadn't taken twenty seconds.

FuckedNose crossed his arms and scowled. The ginger Rasta got his breath and puked, muttering himself upright. The door kept thumping.

And Mouse, honey-voiced little Mouse, shivered at the blade against his throat and barely breathed.

Aaaand relax.

'Sixteen years ago,' said Shaper, blocking the wobble from his voice, 'Tommy Boyle came out here with Sam Coram. Right?'

Mouse nodded, then hissed as the knife broke his shifting skin.

'Best not move,' Shaper said, helpful.

'Yah. Tommy Boyle – yes.'

'I imagine he wanted to clear out all you hard-working independent types, right? Set up a proper system for the Corams?'

'Y-yes. Claimin' territ'ry.'

'Probably weren't too subtle about getting his way neither. Yeah?'

'Yah.'

'Good. Well done.' Shaper eased the pressure half a molecule: a reward for good behaviour. The door throbbed on its hinges. 'Only, before the night's out, old Sammy's dead in docklands and Boyle's done a runner. So what happened, Mouse?'

The little man fixed him with a confused scowl which melted, bit by bit, to a wry smile. 'Ya really tink they didn't ax at the time, man? Even the *po*-lis come wi'question. Everybody say same: nobody know *shit*. Why you wan'know *now*, eh?'

Shaper reapplied the pressure. 'I'll do the questions, thanks.'

Across the room FuckedNose spat blood and paced like a caged tiger. The Rastalike simply glowered. Shaper winked at them and returned his attention to Mouse. 'Did he come see you that day, mate? Tommy Boyle?'

'Man see *everyone* tha' day. Him an' he skinhead focks, visitin' al us supplier. Boss Coram watchin' from the back. Breakin' head, menacin'-op, ya know. "This owah turf now," them say. "You pay *os* if you wan' operate." Then away for th'next man.'

'So who was the last dealer to get a visit that day? Who saw Boyle and Coram last?'

'How th'*fock* ah know? Them see *everyone*, Shaper.'

That's a lot of pissed-off small-timers. A lot of grudges.

Thump, thump, thump. The door pulsing like a heart.

For fuck's sake.

'Just give me some names, Mouse. Who else did they rough up that day?'

The little man puffed his cheeks. '*Aye* donno . . . They's . . . Tamby Omoglu, Patrick Thyme . . . Big Rudy an' his brodder – can' remember him neam. Summa the whiteboys from down the crescent – jost kids, ya know. Crazy Foster was one. Ally

Smith. Odders too.' He scowled and smacked his lips, suddenly irritated. 'Fock, man, dey's too many. Nobody left *anyway*. Al chased away or get grey an' retire. Al *'oodie* kids these day. Only Mouse left now.'

The thumping at the door hit a fresh urgency. Shaper scowled angrily up from his victim, headache growing, and noticed with a gurgle of fear – *too late* – that both FuckedNose and the Rastalike were transfixed, poker-faced, by something behind him.

Which is when the woman in the cocktail dress, still pretending to snore, smashed her beer bottle across his head.

The knife left Shaper's hand. The carpet came up to meet him. His forehead smacked the ground, and even as reality went away, he could feel hands under his arms, strong fingers pulling wrists behind his back until his spine creaked and a hash-stinking breath warmed his neck.

'Little *fuck*,' said the Rastalike, bracing him hard.

His vision came and went. His hearing ghosted through an echo chamber of threats and spittle. The woman's laughter, Mouse's syrupy chuckle, the *fsk* of fresh fags. Somehow the thumping at the door was the only thing that seemed real: a static rhythm which glowed in his broken senses – now growing increasingly surreal – with a peculiar importance.

White light and swan feathers under the door frame.

What . . . ?

Something dripped down his neck. He imagined it was probably his brain.

'Fhnold him,' said FuckedNose, and Shaper couldn't help but laugh, drunk with abstraction, at the flu-voice from far away. 'Uhm gunna fhnucking *kill* im.'

The kid lined up for a first shot, face a mangled mask, arm reaching back—

Thump, thump, thump.

'Mouse?' the Rastalike grunted behind Shaper's back. 'Best let the fat prick in, eh? Causing a right racket out there.'

Mouse's voice impatient. 'Do it.'

FuckedNose aborted the strike with bad grace and stalked to the door.

'Woulf you fnut the fnuck *up*,' he snarled, yanking it open – just as DI Canton's boot lifted directly, with a damp *scrunch*, into his bollocks.

The kid hit the deck and stayed there.

'Hello everyone!' said the cop, smiling brightly. 'I have a gun!'

And, Shaper picked out through the blur, he bloody did.

Instants before the Rastalike released his neck, and the clouds of unconsciousness rolled in, Shaper caught a brief glimpse of the fat kid in the hall, sulking in cuffs, and beamed merrily at Canton.

'Have you got an appointment?' he murmured.

Chapter Fourteen

Canton's car smelled of pine cones and liquorice – chemical stink shields to smother too many secret cigarettes. Shaper sat alone with eyes closed and fingers gripping his seat, waiting for the universe to stop spinning. His head felt like a shattered egg, and he so far hadn't risked poking at it in case the yolk, as it were, had started to leak.

Eventually Canton clambered in and slammed the driver's door – *as loud as possible, the shit* – and gunned the engine to life.

'No arrests then?' Shaper noted, creaking open his eyes. 'They could've killed me.'

Canton shot him a Look. ' "That's right, yeronna," ' he panto-mimed, ' "there I was, minding me own business, when this nutter starts kicking the crap out of me mates. Then his pal shows up and bleedin' arrests me. Drugs? What drugs? Did I mention the unlicensed shooter, yeronna?" ' Canton shook his head and rummaged for the gun, passing it over. 'Glove box, please. And a little fucking gratitude, while you're about it.'

Shaper stowed the weapon with a grimace. It had been a long time.

'Is it real?'

'Twenty quid off the Internet? Course it's not bloody real.'

The high-rise dwindled behind them. Shaper noticed a fag

packet stashed behind the gun and thieved one without asking, hunting for his lighter.

The first puff felt like Communion. A whole-body event, shivering through his flesh, tickling at his bruised cheek and soothing the pounding headache. By the third drag it was easy to convince himself it didn't taste wretched and his lungs wouldn't hate him for it. He relaxed just a fraction.

Easy to quit. Done it loads of times.

Canton snaked the car down a back street and on to Camden Road.

Taking me home.

'So how'd you find me, then?'

The cop shrugged. 'Traffic camera with plate recognition. Black Merc in a no-stop zone pings an alert. Turns out it's registered to the Corams.' He waggled a pager on his belt. 'I like to pay attention.'

'Obsessive.'

'Committed.' The car dodged kamikaze goths. 'I stopped by to check it out, that's all. Thought I'd see who the twins've got playing goon-on-call these days.'

'You mean BeanieHat and BollockHead?'

'Do I? Anyway. Who should the meatheads be eyeballing but a certain fuck-ugly private eye? Figured it was probably worth hanging around.'

'So I didn't interrupt another stab at the lovely Natasha?'

'Sod off.'

'Getting the cold shoulder, are you?'

'That's none of your business.' Canton's face went devious. 'Or do I start asking about the chick in the cafe?'

Shit.

'No. You don't.' Then, 'I thought I lost the Merc anyway.'

'You did. Not me, though.' The cop preened, then seemed to catch up with himself. 'You want to tell me what's going on, Dan?'

Shaper let his eyes droop, gumming on smoke and wondering where to start. His head thumped like a second heart.

'It's this Boyle thing.' He shrugged, finally gathering the courage to probe at his scalp. 'Caused a right mess.' The wetness, he decided with relief, was beer not brain juice.

'How's that?'

He filled in Canton with a sigh, describing his late-night visit Chez Coram. The cop's face darkened throughout, goatee-clad jaw visibly tightening at each mention of the twins' names. Canton and the Corams had a special history of their own: an affair that had left both parties twisted with mutual hatred. Shaper knew the story all too well, because the episode had also seen his own introduction to Canton.

The pair had met at a turbulent, tumbling stage in Shaper's life, in the dying days of his stint as the Corams' Number Two, when the notion of getting out was a daily preoccupation. It seemed strange, nowadays, to think his eventual escape was catalysed by a fuck-up cop looking for cash, but in the event he and Canton, each in their own way, had saved one another. They'd been doing the same, on and off, ever since.

'So what you got for me?' Canton said, swerving past tourists. 'You been busy, right?'

Shaper contemplated the question at length. All his honourable obsessions with client confidentiality – what to share, what to withhold – swiftly eroded with the growing realisation that, well . . .

'I don't think I've discovered a single fucking thing, actually. Shit.'

'Well, *I*,' Canton smarmed, 'have.'

'The other deaths?'

'Yep. Up to and including Dr Unpronounceable from last night.'

'Linked?'

'Mm-hmm.'

'How?'

Canton pantomimed a scowl. 'I dunno, mate. You are a wretched criminal. And you did just thieve a fag without asking.'

'That's *my* lead, you horrible little Nazi. Cough up.'

Canton chuckled. 'All right. Start with the mugging victim. Bird found in Queen's Park. She's a—'

'What's her name?'

Canton blinked, derailed. 'Uh . . . Colquhoun. Alice Colquhoun. Why?'

Shaper just shrugged, staring into the cold. It had begun to drizzle again.

Alice Colquhoun. Victim number three.

'Anyway,' the cop pushed on. 'Seems she wasn't killed there at all.'

'Body moved?'

'That's the theory.'

'Like Kingsley.'

'Like you *think* with Kingsley, yeah. We can't confirm that one – too much of a mess. Anyway, this Colquhoun woman, they found bits of straw on her shoes.'

'Straw?'

'And sawdust, hay – shit like that. Just microscopic.'

'So?'

'So, she's rich. Business type. All about the image. She's got a thousand pairs of shoes, mate. These ones are for her evening run, same every night. Concrete pavement between her house and the park, then grass and mud. But here she is with half a farmyard stuck in the tread, and that's *underneath* a layer of wet dirt. So forensics figure the dry traces come from—'

'Wherever she was knocked off.' Shaper watched smoke coil,

brain racing. 'So – what? The killer takes the body back to the park, squelches her legs round like she's been jogging?'

'Could be.'

'So why sawdust? Where's it from?'

'Buggered if we know. Got helmets checking for links. Inner-city farms, stables, pet shops, all that. Long shot. Anyway, it gets better. Wait for this.' Shaper caught a depressing edge of enthusiasm in the voice. 'If she really was bumped off somewhere else, forensics think the killer deliberately brought a bunch of her blood with him, just to scatter around.'

'Fuck.'

The cop nodded excitedly. 'Nick the poor cow's iPod and Bob's your uncle – just a random mugging. This fucker's clever, mate.' A thrill in every syllable. 'This is gonna be big.'

Shaper watched him sideways and chewed a lip. Ambition had always been Canton's demon. Selling his soul to the Corams, all those years back, was just his first spastic attempt to frog-leap the hard route.

Oh, the family had plenty of other badges in their pockets, but none with Canton's prospects. And none who'd waltzed so willingly into the shadows. This tidy little tit had shown up one day from nowhere, proposing a two-way deal like an executive in presentation mode. The Corams, he suggested, would feed him their enemies, and in turn he'd engineer a blind eye for their operation. With his cheap suit and hilarious Organised Crime misconceptions, he was – so the twins had crowed – a prize haul.

Even now, years later, Shaper didn't fully understand why it was Canton who'd had such an effect on him. Over all his years of association with the Corams he'd inventively manipulated, controlled or just plain fucked over all manner of good people – cops and otherwise – and had barely paused to wash his hands. But with this one . . .

Maybe, he reflected, he'd felt some dim understanding, some hazy prescience, that this smug little tryhard could one day prove an irreplaceable ally. Perhaps Canton had simply been one decent soul too many, whose pending corruption had pushed Shaper beyond his own inertia. Or possibly – probably – it was simply that he'd been able to see the secret doubt, the tremor of self-disgust, lurking an inch below the cop's face . . .

Like looking in a mirror.

He'd taken the new recruit out for a drink, showing him a good time as the Corams commanded. And there, in a pub car park outside Chigwell, he'd kicked the living shit out of the snotty little tosser until he saw sense. Explaining a few things. Hammering in some home truths.

It had felt, he recalled, a lot like hitting himself.

Then he'd returned Canton's pay-off to the twins, told them the cop had changed his mind, and promised he'd deal with it. Then spent the few remaining months of his career – flaming and crumbling around him, by that point – secretly warning Canton every time someone was sent to break his legs.

Saving the cop – defeating his ambition – was the one good thing Shaper had achieved in those bitter, broken years.

Ancient history.

Back in the car, watching Canton smirk and preen at the prospect of a big case – the eyes of the world – Shaper felt an odd sense of gloom descend, which evolved his slow nod through the diagonal into a headshake.

'It doesn't make sense,' he said, deflating the excitement.

'What?'

'All this care. All the make-it-look-like-something-else bollocks.'

'Why?'

'Because of . . .' He coughed and looked away, abruptly chilled. 'Because of the doctor.'

Because of blood and skin and broken bone, and—

And don't think about it.

He lowered the window to flick away the dog-end, relishing the drizzle-flecked air. 'There was no attempt to disguise that. What's the link?'

Canton gave a dark, dangerous smile. 'Alice Colquhoun had her solar plexus missing.'

The world beyond the car hazed away. The wetness in Shaper's hair, beaded like pearls on his neck, froze in place.

'What?'

'It's like a . . . a nerve centre. Bit of gristle under the breast-bone.' The cop prodded himself, shadowed smile hanging wide. 'It was gone.'

'Gone?'

'Look, you asked about Natasha before. Well, she's the pathologist. Took her four hours to work it out, but she's sure. There's flesh missing.'

The Sickness shuffled its claws in the dark, as infected by Canton's excitement as the weakening, failing fences in Shaper's mind.

'And then matey stabbed her. We think forty to sixty times. Frenzied. Just *ragged*, you know – a mess. All to hide the incision.'

Shaper's eyes played tricks. Ugly flickers of liquid red crept at the corners of the windscreen, chittering plankton gusting through the blowers. Not drizzle out there, but a froth of blood, smeared and scabbing with every hiss of the wipers.

No no no no.

His fingers stroked the pill file. It had been barely half an hour since the last dose.

Fucking tolerance!

Beside him Canton took his eyes off the road long enough to stare directly, smile replaced by a hungry frown. 'Mate, we wouldn't have even looked if you hadn't dropped the hint it was linked to Kingsley. How the fuck did you know?'

Shaper shook his head. He realised he was smoking another cigarette but couldn't remember taking it, far less lighting up. 'Can't say,' he croaked.

'But I've got to put something in the report, and—'

'I can't fucking *say*!'

Loud. Shocking in the damp air. Dragging behind it a burning, uncomfortable silence.

Get a grip, wanker.

'Sorry,' he said. 'I just . . . You'll have to make something up. Say Natasha found it on her own. Anonymous tip – whatever.'

Canton wallowed in the silence for a while, but it was clear there was more. In Shaper's twisted senses it bubbled like molten gold: too much exhilaration bunched behind the man's face. Impossible to restrain.

'There's a very good chance,' Canton said, the outburst already forgotten, 'that your mate Kingsley had his bollocks cut off before he went under the train.'

Shaper shut his eyes and said nothing.

'Same trick, really. Do the fiddly stuff then mangle the body. They had to scrape up the poor bloke when they found him. Splayed, y'know? Legs akimbo.'

'I get it.'

'Literally minced.'

'I get it.'

'Yeah, but *I* saw the photos, mate. It stays with you, that shit. Killer could've taken the guy's whole bloody arse if he wanted, and we wouldn't've known at first gl—'

'I *get* it, Canton.'

Giggling hyenas in his ears now. The smell of diesel and damp. Hands useless with hypothermic shakes. The pill file already half out of his p—

Not here! Not with him watching!

Get it together! Get home!

158

Shaper concentrated on his breathing, invoking the last hard-edged glimmers of the Ampalex to restore order. Letting the car's hum soothe his senses.

'There's your link anyway,' Canton grunted. 'What we don't know is why the sicko picked these folks specifically.'

Finally, daring to creep open his eyes, Shaper saw with nerve-rocking relief that the distortions had faded to a spectral fog, and his own street was looming from the weather. 'So . . . so someone's . . . what?' he said, awash with relief. 'Stealing organs?'

'Maybe. The old dear – gardener who fell off her roof – she was buried yesterday. We've got an exhumation order in the pipe.' The cop slowed the car, eyes hunting a space. 'If we can prove there's something missing from her too—'

'There will be.' Straight from his brain to his mouth.

'Well then.' Canton pulled up and killed the engine. He turned to Shaper, ugly smile back in force, and played his ace. 'Then we've got a fucking serial killer, haven't we?

Shaper smoked and stared.

Stupid. Bullshit.

His guts bubbled.

'I'm serious,' the cop said. 'Even explains the way he did the doctor, all displayed like that. He starts with an organised MO, all calculating, covering his tracks, which breaks down over time.'

'Spare me the Wiki wisdom, Canton. This is London, not a fucking film set.'

'I mean it. It's *classic*. Before you know it, he's shitting down severed necks and leaving "from Hell" notes.'

The cop's excitement was a knife in Shaper's guts, a cancer long considered beaten, returning to pulverise a purified body.

Waving guns. Smoking in his car. Jonesing for success.

So much for 'saving' DI Canton from himself.

Even now – even on separate sides of the law and divided by

a gulf of fear and philosophy – Shaper couldn't help but feel responsible. Couldn't help but make it his mission to rescue the cop again, to protect him from his own ambition. He owed him that.

Five years before, when his breakdown was a fresh wound, when he'd escaped the Corams at the cost of his own sanity, in the midst of the horror of those early attempts to function, the news had reached Shaper that a hotshot young cop, recently rescued from a mire of self-inflicted corruption, had successfully captured a single-bollocked Albanian, wanted for the murder of one Anna Vlcek. Shaper's fiancée.

Ancient history.

'Please, mate,' he said. 'Just . . . tread carefully, yeah? Don't get too caught up in this. And don't bend the rules, all right? That's what I'm here for.'

For an instant Canton seemed set to riposte, snappy at the condescension. But he visibly hesitated, perhaps detecting in Shaper's eye a sliver of his concern, his obligation; his endless antique gratitude.

You got the fucker who killed her.

'Mate,' the cop said, kind. 'You don't get it. This isn't just about . . . catching a psycho. That's not even my department. I'm not even in *charge* of this shit.'

'What then?'

'We found more prints. One at the doctor's place, one at the roof garden. Wax, same as before.'

Shaper's cigarette forgotten. Ash coiling in his lap.

'Boyle's. Both of them.'

Dose, his brain screamed. *Dose! Dose!*

He reached for the car door, suddenly overwhelmed. 'I've got to go.'

'The Corams, Dan!' Canton hissed, a hand pawing at his arm. 'They need to fall!'

'It's—'

'I *need* them to fall, mate. So do you. Don't you pretend you don't.'

Like wiping the slate clean. Like exorcising a grudge . . .

'We can't do it on our own, mate. They've got too much shit on us. Both of us.' Shaper shook off the cop's hand and opened the door, blood steaming. *Get out get out get out.*

'But Boyle . . . He's got the dirt. He's the key, Dan. He can bring down Maude and those fucking *freaks* without the backsplash.'

Shaper slammed the door and hurried away, hearing the window hiss behind him.

'Get some ice on that head! I need you on top form!'

He didn't look back.

Chapter Fifteen

Shaper re-upped before he'd even reached the flat. Slouching in the stairwell, he let the womb-like rumblings of the world – sniping neighbours, shifting traffic; the stupefying background hum of London – cocoon his undignified hit. A coke substitute, Troparil, snorted off the edge of the pill file, and a single fat capsule marked 'CX-717'. Ampakine nuke.

Almost instantly the world tightened its screws. The corners seemed sharper, the horror spumed away, his hands went still. He *hmmmed* with pleasure through it all.

Until, that is, the pounding of his scalp phased back in and sent him scurrying upstairs to do as Canton had commanded. '*Get some ice on that head!*'

There was no ice.

Nor bags of frozen veg, coolbox gel packs or soft-packed TV dinners. Even a pizza would have worked, he decided, balanced like a comedy sombrero, but no, his freezer ultimately disgorged nothing but a single forgotten mackerel, eyes glaring accusingly through accumulated frost, which he duly strapped on with an old sweatband and tried not to feel stupid.

Determined to maintain his investigative momentum, and ignoring Ziggy's bemused glares, he scribbled down some of the names Mouse had blurted earlier. He found he could barely remember half of them, and those he could were just nicknames.

Idiot.

The paranoia came up from nowhere. The fruits of inaction, puffing out from spiny twigs to ruin the quiet moment, slinking into his consciousness with a graveyard whisper.

So what have you achieved, genius? Call yourself an investigator?

Useless!

He grabbed for the phone and called Glass. A perfunctory situation report, including reassurances of real actual progress (*liar!*) and vague references to a plan of action. 'I want you out of that house,' he said. 'That's the first step. Tova mentioned you had somewhere else.'

'That's right.' The old man sounded as genial as ever. 'Sandra and Freddie live there.'

'Good. Let's pack you off there this evening, and—'

'Oh. Oh dear. I'm afraid that's quite impossible. I've an important engagement tonight.'

Shaper pinched the bridge of his nose, starting to regret the yellow pill. His secret second stability – that high-wire plateau – was tilting perilously in the opposite direction.

'Mr Glass, *this* is what's important. You do understand that, don't you? You'll have to . . . disengage.'

'I'm sorry, it's out of the question. People are relying on me. I'm doing a lesson.'

'A lesson?'

'At the clinic.'

'Look, I'm sure people wouldn't mind if . . .' *Wait.* 'The clinic? You mean Mary's place?'

'Mm-hmm.'

Shaper mentally shifted gears. 'Rrrright. Right, well, I'll . . . Fine. Just this once. And I'll come along too.' *Creep.* 'Oh, one other thing: I've got you a bodyguard lined up. Big bloke called Vince. I'll send him over this evening. You ask him what goes

163

best with pasta; if he don't say "badger meat" it's someone else playing silly buggers. Got that?'

'Um. Pasta. Badgers. Right.'

'But first thing tomorrow you're out of there. Yes?'

'All right.'

'And you'd better give me Sandra's number too. I'll go see her, get things ready for you.'

(Snoop.)

He took Sandra's details, told the old boy he'd see him soon, and that was that.

Fish juice trickled along his spine. For a short while he dared to hope the paranoia was gone, as if the simple fact of activity, or perhaps something stranger in the old man's voice, had overthrown its hold. But the reprieve didn't last, and before he knew it the itching – the self-doubt, the crawling fear – was back in the nape of his neck, bringing with it the unsettling suspicion that someone was nearby. Thinking about him, watching him.

Hating him.

Push through it.

He called Sandra to arrange a visit. If she noticed the wobble in his voice she didn't show it, appearing positively friendly alongside her frosty, suspicious act from the other day.

'Dad told me about the letter,' she explained, almost apologetic. 'I'm very pleased you're helping him.'

He'd swing by at five-ish, he told her. He wanted to pick her brains about the old man's past, his dealings – all the things he couldn't remember himself. Abstractly, Shaper felt it was somehow unfair that he should have to invest as much time in investigating his client as the threat to the client's life, but then that was Glass all over: attention-gobbling, thought-thieving. Impossible to resent.

Sandra promised she'd be there but didn't expect she'd be much help.

'Dad and I were never exactly close,' she said.

Conversation over. Again, that brief sensation of progress – of positive, proactive momentum – warmed and protected Shaper from the chilly fingers of the Sickness, even as it matted his hair with melting fish paste.

But still the paranoia wouldn't shift. At its worst he became suddenly convinced there was someone in the hall outside the flat, certain he could hear a muffled snuffling like a great dark dog, thrusting its nose below the door, claws scratching . . . Yet when he summoned the courage to peer through the peephole, and then to creak open the door and double-check, the corridor was empty and silent.

Relax. Too wired.

Just relax. You shambling, chemical-veined fucking mess.

In the end, with a minor flash of inspiration, he rang Talvir and requested another favour: another behind-the-scenes glimpse at the Directory register.

'Karl Devon,' he said, feeling devious. 'I need an address. Or . . . actually, there's a chance he's on the inside. At Her Majesty's pleasure, y'know? Is that the sort of thing you can find out?'

'Well, *duh*,' Tal said.

Shaper showered while he waited, ditching the mackerel and gingerly washing off slime, then switched on the radio while chopping veg for Ziggy. Even that couldn't distract him for long: one teacherly voice apologised for the cancellation of an interview with 'celebrated urban artist' Merlin; another topped a news bulletin with the discovery of a savagely murdered doctor in the St John's Wood area. Shaper flicked it off with a growl.

The silence, like everything, seemed haunted.

Things undiscovered. Opportunities missed.

Dangers unknown.

And with them all, in waves, the unhappy certainty of his own stupidity.

He knew better than to believe any of it – did his best, even, to rationalise his way out: just the Sickness, just that hateful taint of the past. But eventually, inevitably, he reached for the pill file with a huff, resolving to tweak the chemical plateau with an anxiety-relieving diazepam.

The phone rang before he could pop the tablet from its foil.

'Tal!' he cried, expectant. 'Did you find him?'

Nobody answered.

'Hello?'

Something, somewhere, breathed.

Something snuffled and swallowed too loud, then began to emit an irregular, electric crackle. The hairs all across Shaper's body crawled upright. For no sensible reason his teeth began to hurt. The sound was lost in a fresh rasp of breath – a fresh snuffle – before returning faster and louder than before.

Shaper realised, slowly, exactly what he was hearing.

Someone licking the mouthpiece.

'Who is this?' he whispered.

And a voice without gender, without tone – without any apparent vibration of life – declared in a single moist breath, '*Hhhhham.*'

And Shaper's senses went wrong.

He staggered, knees weakening, and felt the room ripple around him. In an instant he became convinced he was trapped inside a great roaring ventricle – a house-sized heart, dizzyingly fast, mashing and pulping at the discs of blood around him. He cried out and scrabbled for the pill file, already knowing that whatever he took to chase this horror away, whatever tweak he made to the fine machinery of his medulla, it would work less well than it should; wouldn't last as long as normal; and would barely numb him from the writhing, self-hating taint of his own guilty brain.

Chemical resistance.

Fuck.

The snuffling at the door returned with a vengeance, sapping him of all oxygen. It rose to a monkey-like jibber, slapping palms against the outer surface and rattling the wood in its frame. Still fumbling the meds, Shaper caught sight of his own knuckles and gagged, eyes drinking in the festering flesh, the swarming worms and tiny flies; corrupted meat splitting along childlike bones.

Rotten.

Dead.

That same old delusion, no less wretched for its familiarity.

A dead man pretending to be alive. A cheating corpse, seething with the weight of its lies.

He dropped the phone and tore a downer from its foil, swallowing it without water, then gobbled a second on an impulse. He hunched himself down with his eyes slammed shut, teeth grinding like fault lines, hands knocking at the sides of his skull. And waited.

After five minutes the storm seemed to calm. The noise at the door went away and the bloody air faded like a bad special effect. His hands, his skin, his flesh: little by little it returned to life. And finally Shaper crawled, like a blind man among landmines, to the table where the phone's cradle waited. He notched it in place with a sigh.

It rang again almost instantly.

And again, a few minutes later.

And again.

Finally he summoned the courage to lift it, sweat barely dry, and croaked an uncertain, 'Yes?'

'Dan? It's Tal. Got that address.'

* * *

Later, medicated, caffeinated and fed, he paused on his way out of the flat.

There, on the outside surface of his front door, like a bullet wound for his psyche, sat a single fingertip smudge of white, odourless wax.

Chapter Sixteen

Karl Devon's home lurked in the shadow of a flyover like a feeder fish trailing a shark. Snagged at the heart of a grimy terrace, its scrubby patio was heaped with all the mouldering ejecta of a recent refurnish, and topped by a freshly lowered To Let sign. Its rudimentary rear 'garden' – judging by those visible at the ends of the row – withered in the shade of the overpass. The whole street seemed to cower below the roaring of passing lorries, and sulked among flows of gridlock litter.

The reaches of West London had always felt alien to Shaper, far from the bedrock of traditional scallywaggery out east. It was heartening nonetheless to note that the city had snotted out a few last-ditch nuggets of urban sleaze to mark its boundary. Here, beneath the M4 artery, among denuded trees and sooty parades of bleak anonymity, Shaper felt almost at home.

He stood at Karl's door and pondered. Three knuckle raps and still no answer.

Waste of time.

A little further down the street, he'd noticed, a small corner pub sat with peeling paint and a half-complete collection of shattered windows, with a knot of weathered humanity smoking in the doorway. It was the kind of pub Shaper loved at a distance: disdaining the seemingly intuitive need to attract new custom and favouring instead an air of thoughtless hostility towards all things unknown.

Inside, Shaper knew, would be Bastards With Stories.

He rummaged for the fags he'd picked up at a petrol station on the way – *in for a penny, in for a pound* – and contemplated the pub.

A smoke and a pint. *Nor-fucking-mality.*

He knocked dutifully one last time at Karl's door, wondering as he did so exactly why he'd bothered coming.

Officially – to the smartly dressed auditor in his psyche – it was because of a single disposable line Mary had uttered in the cafe this morning. '*Karl was there,*' she'd said, '*when Glass showed up at the door that first time – he'd been expelled from school that day . . .*'

If true, Karl was one of the few identifiable people who'd known Glass before the old man's memory meltdown. Since the others consisted of the man's daughter, a dead doctor, and a fraudulent deceitful apostle with whom Shaper was desperately in lust, he hoped Karl might provide a little objective opinion.

Besides, every mention Mary had made of Karl this morning had itched at something in Shaper's skull – the secret cop in him, perhaps – which had noted the man's delinquent youth, his history of violence, his jail time . . .

It was a feeble and patchy sort of lead, true, seasoned by nothing more than that troubling certainty that Mary knew more about Glass's case than she was letting on. Somehow she was at the centre of things, Shaper was certain, and so Karl was connected whether he liked it or not.

All of which was enough, just, to satisfy the inner auditor.

Deep down, he knew, the decision to come here owed as much to his terror of inactivity as anything else. He had a couple of hours before he was scheduled to visit Sandra and, still shaken by the last seizure, suspected that if he spent time twiddling his thumbs in the flat it might well just kill him.

This is proactivity.

And, since it didn't appear to be bearing any fruit (through no fault of his own), it seemed only fair that he reward himself for his uncharacteristic self-motivation. Right?

Right.

Duly convinced, he turned for the pub and fished out the cigarettes.

Twenty minutes later, all was well.

Wrapped in smoke, watching the rain – freshly dosed up – Shaper cheerfully eavesdropped on a yarn being spun from the next table, imaginatively titled 'When My Third Wife Tried To Cut Off My Todger'. It was an embarrassingly predictable affair involving garden shears, a pack of sausages and a Labrador, but in its familiar off-colour crudity it allowed Shaper the simple, happy opportunity to switch off his brain. To smoke a decent fag, to quaff a decent pint, and to huddle happily from the drizzle beneath a patched awning outside the front door.

Bollocks to everything else.

It was bliss.

And it didn't last.

'I knew you'd come,' said a voice, far too close to his ear.

Shit.

He was sure it was Karl the instant he turned. The pallid spectre had Mary's eyes and mouth – at least, the version of it that shone through when she was at her most surly – and Shaper blinked back from the todger story with the unsettling sensation of seeing something recognisable (and, worse, fanciable) in an otherwise repellent face.

Karl looked like shit. Too thin, old before his time, with a black shock of slicked-back hair and a wiry pair of glasses on an eagle's-beak nose. Set into too-deep sockets, his eyes were almost veiled, just a moist glimmer lifting them from the shadows. He inspected Shaper over a soggy dog-end, flicking at a lighter, then shook drizzle off his jacket and settled with a contemptuous spit on to the doorstep of the pub.

He'd come from inside.

He's been waiting, Shaper thought.

'I saw you come in,' the apparition declared, as if guessing his thoughts. Karl's voice was far softer than Mary's: a whisper with a shadow of tone. 'I knew you were after me. Knew you'd be coming.'

Shaper tried not to sound unnerved. 'Mary mentioned me?'

But I didn't even tell her I was c—

'Mary?' The man shook his head. 'I don't talk to her any more. Don't know where she lives. Haven't seen her in . . . ten, fifteen years? What's *she* got to do with it?'

'I just—'

'Doesn't matter. Don't care.'

'Then how did you know I'd—'

'Shut up, please.'

It was a snappy little command, almost cruel, but chased by a smile of such obscene earnestness that Shaper was forced to obey as if robbed of thought. In his senses the man fizzed and fumed with a thousand colours and shapes, a vibrating tumult of spastic glitter, and before he brought it back under control the Sickness almost seemed to recoil, as if the usual hallucinogenic bullshit was defeated by the man's sheer twitchy impermanence.

A fucking loon.

Great.

For a long time Karl just stared – incongruously long lashes dipped low across suspicious pupils – then quite suddenly reached for Shaper's pint and helped himself to a long, multi-swallow chug. Shaper didn't interrupt – he knew a performance when he saw one – and busied himself with an inspection of the marks in the crooks of Karl's arms: the train-track brands of a committed smackhead.

'You're a poker, aren't you?' Karl trilled, wiping foam from the pointed tip of his upper lip. 'A prodder. A digger in other people's business. I can tell.' He pointed at his own eyes and winked, as if that explained it. 'A parasite – that's you. What is it this time? Journo? Lawyer? Who *givesafuck*.' He spat again, a thick beery gobbit. 'You want to know what I did, don't you?'

Shaper shrugged. *Go with the flow.* 'All right then.'

'I punched him, is what. And he died.'

Shaper blinked. 'Um.'

'How was I meant to know? Prick starts acting up – *what you lookin' at, step the fuck up*, all that. Middle of Soho . . . Listen, what sort of a wanker picks a fight with a hole in his heart?'

'That's . . . that's not actually what I came t—'

'Down like a sack of spuds. Wasn't even that hard.'

'Listen, Karl, I don't w—'

'Then it's cops and cells and psychiatrists, an' all you fucking journos researching books. And your brain saying, you're a killer now, get used to it. You know what that's like? And all because of a flappy right hook.' The man waggled his fist, pouting. 'Don't even remember it well.' He sighed like a bellows and gazed into space.

Off at the mains.

Shaper coughed, wondering if he should set the lunatic straight – *that's not actually why I'm here* – then narrowed his eyes and ploughed on regardless, the first sickly strings of fascination stretching out.

'So . . . how long have you been out?'

'Out?'

'Of jail.'

'Ha.' No trace of humour. 'Wasn't jail, mate. They got me off, didn't they? "Accidental death." The system works!' He mimed a bitter applause and shuffled nearer, eyes bloodshot, mouth forming a sudden grin. 'You know what's funny?'

Shaper shook his head.

'Truth is, I probably would've done him anyway, given the chance. Dead, I mean.'

Something cold wormed in Shaper's spine.

'Deserved it, didn't he? Oh, I could tell he was coming for me. Could see what he had in mind.' The man tapped at his eyelids again and nodded into space. 'Yeah, he deserved it. Except . . . I wouldn't've done it so quick. I had a bottle. Fuck him up. Open his neck, maybe.' He moaned softly, lost in the image, then shrugged and met Shaper's eyes. 'Only he didn't let me, did he? One little tap, lights out.' He leaned back on his haunches, suddenly affable. 'Off my tits on acid, they said. I was giggling the whole time. Hard to say what I thought I was doing.'

Shaper just stared, nauseous with curiosity.

'So, no. Not jail. Nothing like that.'

'Right.'

'No, it was Thailand first, then India, then Brazil. White outfits and straps on the bed. "Purge the mind, purge the body!" All very private. *Rehab*, she called it – dear old Mum.' His face clouded. '*Bitch*.'

Shaper shuddered deep in his skin.

'Anyway, one month.'

'Sorry?'

'You wanted to know. How long I've been out, yeah? Only it's not "out", it's "back". I've still got tan lines, if you want to see.'

The lunatic leaned repulsively close, teeth showing. 'Soldiers came,' he whispered. 'Shut it all down. *Illegal*, they said. All foreign nationals repatriated. Guns and armoured cars and everything. Very exciting.'

'Your, uh . . . your sister.' Shaper flapped a feeble hand, clawing back to solid ground. 'She thinks you were in a normal . . . I mean. I don't think she knows about any of this.'

Karl's eyes smouldered, irises poisoned with amusement. 'Mary doesn't know about a lot of things.' He drained the last of Shaper's beer and burped through a smoky drag. And then . . . *shook*.

The shudder ran from his legs to his shoulders. A whole-body sneeze, flexing through his fingers like a player at an invisible piano.

And then he grinned.

Hundred per cent shitflinger crazy.

'Now please fuck off,' he said, affecting a haughty accent and nodding into the rain. 'For I grow weary of your company.'

Shaper coughed into a fist. 'Don't . . . uh. Don't take this badly,' he tried, 'but you've got me sort of wrong.'

'So you're *not* here to pick and poke? Eh? Not to delve?'

'Yeah, I . . . I suppose I am, but—'

'Well then.'

'Just . . . not about that.'

Karl tilted his head, lids sliding low, as if he could somehow inspect Shaper better from the corners of his eyes.

'Oh,' he said, oddly deflated. Then brightened up just as fast. 'Well, I got the concept, didn't I? Just not the detail. It's not a science, you know.' He tapped at his eyeballs for the third time, then nudged closer with a conspirator's whisper. 'And I know you do.'

'I see,' Shaper lied, buttock-shuffling for clearance. All his morbid fascination, he found, was mutating, helped along by a faint wash of white-noise distortion – into discomfort, dislike, even fear.

'So what *did* you want to ask about?' Karl breathed.

'Um. Bloke called George Glass. I'm trying to help him with something, but he doesn't remember anything ab-about . . . uh . . .'

He let the sentence sputter out. Karl's expression had changed.

'Glass?' he hissed.

From a man who'd shifted moods five times in as many minutes, Shaper shouldn't have been surprised at the transformation. But so deep and venomous was the loathing on this new façade – an ironclad emotion at last, unaffected by mercurial tangent – that it was almost unbearable in its intensity.

'You work for *him*?'

Shaper caught himself physically leaning away, wary of attack. 'Yeah. Afraid I do.'

Karl seemed to fold up like smouldering paper, peering over crossed arms. 'Well, I won't talk about him,' he said. 'I won't talk about *any* of them.'

'Them?'

'Fucking New Age gash. Fucking bollocks.'

'Wait, who do you m—'

'I'll tell you *this*.' The man dropped an intrusive hand on to Shaper's thigh, sneering. 'That lot, their type, all incense and juju, they're so twisted with the idea they're different, you know? Like . . . like persecution. Him and his little club. Burning bloody martyrs, the lot. "Us versus them" – that's the way they think! Locked away in that place in the woods, chucking bones and chanting . . .'

'Hang on. What pl—'

'I fucking hate them, d'you hear?' His eyes were blazing now, teeth clenched. 'They killed her. Did you know that, Mr Delver? *They* killed my mother.'

Shaper tried to shepherd the twitching maniac back to calm, lowering his own voice.

'I thought it was a car accident. She was on the phone . . .'

'She was. She was, yeah.' Karl seemed to take the cue, adopting a whisper voice with an air of childish enigma. 'Talking to me, wasn't she? Weekly call. Long delay – that's overseas connections for you. All family this, family that. Gave me Mary's number, even, *ha*, as if I'm going to use that. Then she starts going on about what they did . . . Her and the rest. All that naughty shit . . .'

Shaper tried to interject without success. Karl had sunk into a zombie-like shell, recounting in a dull monotone: a Dictaphone made of meat. 'Then it was as if her voice changed. Like a running commentary. Off the motorway, round the roundabout, back down the slip road, describing it all as she went. Wrong direction. She was still talking when she steered into the lorry. Phone didn't even give out in the crash.'

The man's eyes oozed back from nowhere, pinning Shaper in place.

'I listened to my dear old mum kill herself, mate. She was still cursing the name of your George cunting Glass when the steering wheel went through her lungs.'

The silence seeped like tar.

'S-suicide, then,' Shaper said, quietly. 'Mary doesn't know that either.'

'Probably best.' The man didn't even look up. 'Little Mary always worshipped the ground Mum walked on. No point spoiling it. I tell you, she's better out of it. Better off as far from me as she can get.'

'Karl, what did y—'

'I'd like you to go now, please. I have nothing else to say.'

'But . . . Look, you said "him and his little club". What's—'

'Mr Shaper, please.' Karl twisted his eyes oh so slowly upwards. 'I would like you, if you don't mind, to fuck . . .' He paused. Took a breath.

And screamed, '*OFF!*'

Top volume. Face distorted. Startling the old storyteller at the next table and making Shaper jolt in his place.

In the burning silence the man simply closed off again, hugging his knees.

Shaper tried a couple more times to get through – *What Club? What Naughty Shit? What Place In The Fucking Woods?* – but he might as well have been screaming from another galaxy. Eventually, with a glance at his watch and a muffled, '*Oops,*' Shaper stubbed out the remnants of his fag and turned to go, nodding apologetically at the other drinkers. Only when he'd emerged from the awning, when the drizzle seemed to simmer on his forehead, did he pause, a wave breaking behind his eyes.

'Karl?' he said, twisting back. 'You know what Mary's doing with her life?'

The fruit loop didn't move.

'She's got this clinic. New Age stuff. Regressions, séances, all that bollocks you're such a big fan of. She's faking it, mate. Bloody miserable, I'd say. And all down to . . . how did you put it? Worshipping the ground your mum walked on.'

Karl looked up, eyes red-rimmed.

'Still,' Shaper shrugged, 'it's like you said. No point spoiling it, eh?'

He left.

It wasn't until he was in the van and halfway back to Camden, preparing to pick up Vince, that he realised Karl had called him by name.

'*Mr Shaper, please . . .*'

He was almost certain he hadn't introduced himself.

Chapter Seventeen

Of all the questions Karl had declined to answer during his rant, one was resolved the moment Shaper turned his van off a winding lane and on to the driveway of Sandra's home.

What 'place in the woods', Karl?

This *place in the woods, Dan.*

'Fuck,' said Vince, slouching beside him. 'This is . . . *fuck.*'

It was huge.

Set like a winding gullet behind the poised jaws of an ornate gateway, the drive meandered through a bosky tangle of oak and elm, squirrels darting for pitted trunks. Here and there, where the brush was less dense, shimmering speckles of dying daylight hinted at a lake or pond, while odd flashes of masonry among the greens reported a full suite of statues, pergolas and artfully constructed ruins.

The drizzle died away as if it wasn't worthy.

Shaper smoked with an eyebrow arched and ignored Vince's towny gaspings – 'Is that a rabbit? Fuck!' – on the grounds that he'd had quite enough surprises for one day, and a few floppy-eared grass rats weren't going to quicken his pulse.

It had taken an hour to get here. Scudding round the North Circular from Vince's unexpectedly tidy little flat, then out into the bosky spaces of the Home Counties. If West London seemed an alien territory then the shires were a new cosmos, and these baronial grounds – pheasant-clogged, landscaped across centuries – were an entirely different dimension. Shaper half expected the laws of physics to change halfway down the drive.

After a few hundred metres the path hooked at a sharp dog-leg, crossing a too-quaint-to-be-true bridge and finally exposing – through a fringe of pampas grass and slouching willows – the house.

It loomed.

'This . . . client of yours,' Vince mumbled, a little strangled. 'He's . . . he's pretty minted, then?'

'Yeah.'

'So . . . this two grand I'm getting? Security arrangements and that? Keepin' out heart-thieving nutters.'

'Uh-huh.'

'How much're you getting paid? Out of interest.'

Shaper ignored him, wishing he'd never filled in the brute on last night's misadventures, and rolled to a gravelly halt, eyes fixed upwards.

The building had windows like a hedgehog has spines. It made no attempt at symmetry or grace, relying instead on a rambling brutality of scale to make its point. But in its mix of flinty greys and rosy browns, draped in great swathes of ivy, all its jagged eaves and square-set steeples hinted at an unexpected comfort, like an elderly hound that could be man's best friend or man's last sight. It conjured the strangest impression that it would provide a charming, safe home – just so long as it approved of its occupant.

Brrr.

The pair stepped from the van and stared at the colossal door, feeling stupid. No bell, no knocker. A great slate lintel above the frame, trimmed in black iron, bore the legend:

THORNHILL

(ST. GERMAIN)

Just as Shaper was accepting the frightening possibility that he'd have to knock, he caught a sound on the very fringes of his hearing: a promisingly human-sounding twitter.

'Round the back,' grunted Vince: living triangulator.

Shaper hesitantly scrunched across the gravel, wary of looking like an intruder but dimly aware – given the owner's recent death threats – that the distant sounds might very well be coming from one. He orbited the building's left wing with slow, creeping progress, Vince a disappointing four steps behind, and dodged rain-heavy flowers among wet foliage. He paused several times to nose through dusty windows, glimpsing empty chambers and dust-sheeted deserts. The voice grew louder and shriller, reassuringly suggesting neither stealth nor intruderliness, and – as Shaper rounded the final corner – resolved into the clipped, cold tones of the Valkyrie virgin.

'Tova?' he said.

She nodded from a perch on a low garden wall, as if the spectacle of a sleep-deprived man emerging from a rhododendron was nothing new, and wound up the phone conversation he'd been overhearing.

'Is right,' she said, 'as soon as possible, yes? No, fine, no need to come right in. I wait at main gate on the road. Ten minutes? Good.' She snapped the phone shut and presented a cool smile. 'Taxi,' she explained. Then threw a quizzical look at Vince as he blundered from the scrub. 'You know there is a path round other side?'

'Yeah, course.' Shaper brushed himself down. 'Just . . . having a recce, you know?'

'Recce,' nodded Vince. 'Checking the perimeter.' He had a leaf in his hair.

And, Shaper couldn't help noticing, was almost dribbling at Tova.

Officially gay, secretly bi. Way to keep your options open.

The back of the house was a far less intimidating prospect

than the front. A homely doorway, complete with bell and knocker, led via overgrown hanging baskets and a Thomas the Tank Engine welcome mat into what looked like a modern kitchen. Sure enough, on the far side beyond Tova, a neat path led from the driveway.

Recce.

'You, ah . . . you off already, then?' Shaper blurted, covering the directional blunder. 'I thought you stayed till late.'

Tova's smile went sour. 'Am off, yes. For good, in fact.' She lifted a sturdy suitcase and shot the house a bitter look. 'Got letter this morning from Mr Glass. Am fired.'

Shaper scowled, instantly awkward. He'd never been any good at sympathy.

'Aw . . .' he tried.

Sandra appeared in the doorway as if magically invoked. She'd clearly overheard.

'Please, Tova, you mustn't think like that. It's not . . . "fired".' She nodded to the men. 'That's not what he meant.'

' "Services no longer required",' Tova parroted, choosing Shaper as an unwilling judge. 'After three years – this!'

'Aw . . .' It seemed a safe bet.

'You want some help with that bag, love?' syruped Vince. Tova didn't let go.

Still in the door, Sandra mimed helplessness. 'You know what he's like when he gets an idea. I'll . . . I'll try and talk to him.'

'Is not the job,' Tova huffed, ventage still aimed at Shaper. 'He sent very big pay – all fine.' She plucked a cheque from a pocket and waggled it aggressively. 'Problem is Freddie! Letter say, the boy is getting better, not needing care full-time. Is bullshit! Is not getting better! Never get better!' She sniffed and looked away, repocketing the payoff. 'Who will treat him, eh?'

Shaper considered another *aw*, but the woman pre-empted it

with a disgusted *Pah!* and tramped off along the path. Vince scuttled after, still groping for her bag.

'At least wait a while!' Shaper called. 'We'll be going back to town after this. Give you a lift?'

She smiled back, not slowing. 'Is fine. Taxi get me. Want to get out quick.' Her eyes flicked to Sandra. 'Please give Freddie cuddle from me? Will miss him very much. And also . . . look after yourself.'

Shaper watched Sandra nod, biting her lip, and wondered at what strange understanding was passing between the women. Tova interrupted with a cluck of her tongue, aiming a narrow stare directly at him.

'I will be in touch, Mr Shaper. Will call soon. We should talk.' *Er.*

'OK . . .'

She turned the corner with a last mournful nod and vanished. Vince sloped back, baggageless and surly, then gave Sandra an appraising look and brightened. All not lost. Shaper rolled his eyes.

'Right then,' Sandra muttered, and led them in.

The inspection seemed to last for ever.

Hectic and huffish, Sandra led them through a dizzying array of empty, dust-sheeted rooms, Vince dragging his heels and staring at her arse, Shaper far more interested in her demeanour. His delusions were becoming more intrusive all the time now – the drugs relegated to keeping the Sickness on a fraying leash rather than imprisoning it altogether – and he swiftly reconfirmed his first impressions of Glass's awkward, uncomfortable daughter. He came to imagine her at the heart of an interpersonal cloud of mirror glass and metal, an orbital flock of radar-proof chaff, camouflaging and concealing something frailer, but warmer, beneath.

When he'd first asked her if he and his 'security consultant' – *ha!* – might have a look around (to best prepare for Glass's stay), it was entirely the woman's impenetrable 'outer' self which had responded, marching them about with all the brusqueness of a tour guide on unpaid overtime. But among the slammed doors and disinterested trivia ('That fireplace is original . . .' or 'The Prime Minister slept here in eighteen sixty-five') the softer Sandra emerged in hints and secret sighs. Ultimately, as if battered down by the sheer unrelenting redundancy of the mansion – ninety per cent of its gorgeous rooms an inch deep in dust – the force fields faltered and the woman simply sagged, arms hooked over the parapet of a second-floor landing.

'The truth is,' she said, 'I sort of hate it here.'

She gazed at the walls with such abrupt melancholia that Shaper even caught a sympathetic glance from Vince, a man famously oblivious to emotional states.

'Hate it?' he said. 'How come?'

'Oh, it's . . . it's too big. Lonely. And it's not as though Freddie can even enjoy it. Sixty acres of woods – that's every kid's dream, isn't it?'

'I . . . suppose so, yeah.'

'He can't even stand up for more than a minute.'

For a second Shaper thought she might cry. It was as if she had only the two emotional settings, one formidable, one helpless, and no gradient in between.

'It's cold at night,' she blurted. 'The heating takes hours to warm up. There are mice. And things creak. I *hate* it.'

Just when it seemed the first tearful globs couldn't help but hop her lashes – and Shaper noted Vince visibly engaging Comfort Mode – she blinked it back and got a grip. 'I shouldn't complain,' she said, dramatically brave. 'We get to stay for free – Father's been very generous. I just . . . I wish we were a bit closer to things, you know?' She nodded through a vast window.

'It takes a bloody hour to get anywhere. All my jobs are in London these days.'

'What d'you do?' Vince blurted, keen to engage.

'It's . . . Well.' She shrugged, half-smiling. 'Sex, actually. I get people to have sex.'

Vince blinked, disarmed, and Sandra almost giggled. She gestured them onwards with a smile. 'This way.'

Trailing in horror, Shaper dared to think the unthinkable.

Is she fucking flirting with him?

The woman elaborated as the tour inched onwards. She worked, she explained, as a specialist counsellor, visiting couples in crisis and encouraging them to re-engage in a loving, meaningful partnership.

'By making them fuck?'

'You'd be amazed,' she said, now conspicuously preferring to direct herself at Vince, 'how often the wider issues boil down to the bedroom. I know, I know, it all sounds so bloody *male* when you say it like that, but it's true. And mostly it's just the taboo getting in the way.' She waggled a finger. 'People's libidos change – fact of life. So do their tastes, their desires. But they won't bloody talk about it! They hide it away and pretend all's well, then can't understand why everything's going up the creek. All I do is get them to talk. You know, open up a bit.'

She opened another door, revealing – for once – a prominent lack of dust sheets.

'My bedroom.'

Shaper desperately hoped he'd imagined the significant look she shot at Vince.

Sandra's room was so perfectly bland that he was put in mind again of Kingsley's place back in Clapham: an antiseptic lie smothering the flourishes of life. The difference was that here the woman's most revealing effects were neither disguised nor hidden, she simply had too few to dispel the room's wider anonymity.

Her lone bookshelf groaned with a mix of grim textbooks –
psychiatry, counselling and sexual politics – and a few medical
guides on the subject of Gaucher's disease. But clustered at one
end, within easiest reach of a bedtime arm, lurked an incongruous
collection of glittery, girly kids' books, all fairies, princesses and
huge-eyed unicorns. Nearby, on the bedside table, a packet of
Serax sleeping pills sat brazenly on view, and above them a pair
of fluffy black handcuffs dangled from the headboard. Shaper
caught Vince eyeing them speculatively.

A flash of colour snagged his attention, peeking from a skirting
board nook where the wallpaper had started to peel. Sandra saw
him staring.

'Damp,' she explained. 'That's another thing. It's all falling
apart.'

'Mm.' Below the curling paper, a layer of bright paint sat
exposed. 'Someone certainly liked their pink.'

'Guilty.' The woman shrugged. 'I was a very girly girl.'

'You grew up here? Same room?'

'All my life. Why bother moving?'

'So . . .' Something itched in Shaper's brain. 'So your parents
would have been around too, back then?'

'Just Dad. Mum died having me.'

'Sorry.' He coughed, ignoring Vince's stop-killing-the-mood
glare. Sandra's breezy tone, he noted, was softly seeping away,
the shards of metal gathering like clouds. 'But . . . OK, your dad.
When did he stop living here?'

'Not until his memory started to go. He got bored
of the place. Wanted to be more central. Twelve, thirteen
years?'

'And, uh,' *go for it,* 'what was he like before then?'

'What do you mean?'

'Well, all this . . . New Age stuff. Unascended Master, auras,
you know? Was he into all that before . . .'

Vince chimed in with a helpful smile. 'He means, before he lost his marbles.'

The last echoes of Sandra's easy-going self withered away. Her mouth went straight-line stiff.

'Yes,' she said, holding Shaper's stare. 'Very much so.'

'Like how?'

'It's no good asking me, I didn't get involved. There's a reason I picked a bedroom all the way up here.' Her voice was bordering on frosty now. 'I don't believe in that rubbish.'

Shaper couldn't help himself. 'Do you happen to know a woman called Mary Devon?'

The temperature dropped another degree.

'No,' Sandra said. 'I don't know her.'

But—

'I don't know the little cow who's been trying to suck cash out of Dad for years. "To renovate the clinic," he says.'

Ah.

'I don't know the devious little witch who replies to my letters – telling her to leave him alone, Mr Shaper – with god-awful essays called "New Age Revelation" and "The Proof Of The Prophet". I don't know her at all.'

Vince, warming to the explanatory role, leaned in again. 'She's being sarcastic, mate.'

'Ah.'

'And most of all,' Sandra hissed, 'I don't know the sick little bitch who's made him stop taking his pills, *twice*, because, and I quote, "it interferes with his aura".'

Shaper fancied he could see steam curling from her eyes.

'No, I don't know her. I know *of* her. And if you're interested, Mr Shaper – honestly? I think she's a cunt.'

Shaper almost staggered. The woman held the look a second too long then strode for the door.

'*Anyway,*' Vince boomed, lamely attempting to resurrect the cheer, 'about this job of yours. What sort of sex does th—'

'I expect I'll have to give it up,' she snapped, fixed in arctic mode now, ushering them out. 'I can't possibly get to appointments. Not without Tova tending Freddie.' She shut the door behind her. 'What was he *thinking*?'

Shaper caught himself jumping to Glass's defence without knowing why. 'Maybe he figures, y'know, since he'll be staying here too . . .'

She shot it down with a sneer. '*Him?* I wouldn't trust him to look after a pot plant, Mr Shaper.'

And she stormed off to conclude the tour, as if her sad, lonely, flirty doppelgänger had never existed at all.

Chapter Eighteen

The tour ended near where it began, at Freddie's room.

Set beside the stairs on the ground floor – by necessity, Sandra said, gesturing at wheelchairs, oxy bottles and trolley beds – it contained more warmth and life than the rest of Thornhill's creaking mass combined. Freddie, propped up in bed, paused in his spasms just long enough to notice – and smile enormously at – his guests. Shaper grinned back without thinking, noticing even Vince's slab-like face cheerfully crinkle. Stranger still was the transformation that swept over Sandra – an even deeper expression of her inner self – upon seeing her son. Shaper had never encountered such tangible love, and found himself feeling weirdly embarrassed.

All the way down the stairs he'd been worrying at something Sandra had said, flagged by that antique flash of pink from her wall; gathering a layer of callous implications like an oyster wrapping mucus round a pearl.

'*Why bother moving?*' she'd said.

Because, love, your terminally unwell son is two floors down on his bloody own . . .

So insidious was the notion, tangling itself in all kinds of unwelcome detritus concerning his own so-called-mother, about families and affections and Mrs Coram and, and –

And all that stuff—

– that by the time they'd arrived at Freddie's bedside, Shaper's subconscious had efficiently assassinated Sandra's character, poured scorn on her loathing for Mary, and was formulating a theory on Why This Heartless Bitch Murdered Four People.

Watching her now with her son, he instantly regretted it. Freddie's delight at seeing her was almost religious, and she – all trace of cold efficiency gone; all hints of simmering anger forgotten – was no less demonstrative, nibbling at his neck until he gurgled in delight, then hugging him with eyes scrunched shut.

Shaper packed away his cynicism and quietly hated himself.

'Freddie,' Sandra said, meeting the boy's eyes. 'This is Mr Shaper, and Mr . . .'

'Vince,' said Vince.

'You'll probably be seeing more of them. OK? They're nice.'

Freddie did something that might've been a nod.

'Actually, mate,' said Vince, perching gently on the edge of the bed and beaming at Freddie, 'I'll probably be staying here a few nights – if that's OK by you? I'm helping look after your grandpa for a little while.'

Another rolling half-nod, another smile.

Still lurking at the door, Shaper felt more a fraud than ever. Even Vince had fitted himself into the soft-focus tableau without effort, and though he tried to imagine himself doing the same, all smiles and tender tones, the vision wouldn't coalesce, resisting his intrusion like a sealed socket.

You don't deserve it.

Across the room Sandra fitted an oxygen mask on to Freddie's face and peered at Vince. 'You're staying?' she murmured. Not displeased.

The brute shrugged, all square-jawed modesty. 'Bodyguard. From tomorrow, I think.'

'Well . . . I hope we're not dragging you away from your own family.' An unmistakable twinkle in her eye. 'Kids, wife, whatever?'

For god's sake.

Shaper could already feel the words corkscrewing up – *Yeah, Vince, how does your boyfriend feel about that?* – when Sandra abruptly squinted at the oxygen bottle and tapped at its gauge.

'Damn. Tova always brought up the new ones – she's stronger than me.' She chewed a lip and glanced at Vince. 'I don't suppose you'd . . .'

The man lit up like a gunpowder puppy dog. 'No pr—'

'I'll go!' Shaper cried. 'Where are they kept?'

Get me out of here!

'Who,' he muttered, 'has a fucking wine cellar?'

Glass does, genius.

The stairs crept down from a dusty pantry behind the kitchen, and in a disappointing break with convention were neither gloomy and dank nor creaky. The distant aural fluff of Vince and Sandra's prattle dwindled as he clumped downwards, and the silence – as thick and suffocating as it was – was a distinct improvement.

At the foot of the stairs he found a squat chamber, unexpectedly warm, crammed with household tools, old mops, geriatric vacuum cleaners and a thriving colony of wellington boots. The only dust-free fixture was the phalanx of gas cylinders beside the lowest step, and Shaper gripped the nearest one with a preemptive surge of effort.

And stopped.

Something, somewhere, rustled.

Mice.

She said there were mice. It's just mice.

He peered around with an undignified tremor nonetheless, flicking a glance over his shoulder, and froze. A quiet *oop* escaped his lips.

There was blackness behind him.

Hidden beyond the eyeline from the pantry above, an archway beneath the stairs yawned on to inky nothing. With a crazy flash of mammalian panic he shuffled to face it, pivoting round the canister, instinctively unable to bare his back to the dead space. It radiated a thick, earthy heat.

On the fringes of what little light slunk through, a weird mass of hexacomb cells dwindled into the gloom. With another unmanly shiver he caught himself imagining he'd strayed upon some vast prehistoric beehive – fossilised mega larvae entombed in honey.

Wine racks. Just wine racks, idiot.

He relaxed just a fraction.

And then, as if watching someone else from far away – some Hollywood-scripted moron – he felt himself release the oxygen and shuffle, inch by inch, towards the brick-lined threshold.

Just a quick look.

This is how horror films start, pillock.

Something primal raised goosebumps along his arms, and he realised with a moment's thought he could feel a gentle movement in the warm air. He dared himself to creep closer, sensing rather than seeing the stony lintel pass above.

Here was the darkness and dankery he'd been expecting. Here were the secret hints of mildew and damp, the imagined susurration of a million worms burrowing through packed earth . . .

From further in he could see that the empty racks extended along one wall as far as his eyes could penetrate, lost to distance and dark. The opposite side was even less substantial, a few vault arches hinting at recessed spaces and secondary rooms. Without daring to venture deeper, he could only see into the nearest one: a low-roofed cavern with a few hints of odd furniture. Sharp corners jutted among beady, glossy reflections.

Like spider's eyes . . .

Bees, earthworms, spiders . . . His rotten brain was curiously bug-fixated today. He almost smirked at his own foolishness, preparing to turn back and retrieve the oxyg—

Fsk.

The sound again. Filtering from the distant nothingness, far along the wine-rack wall.

In a flash he found it abruptly difficult *not* to imagine how he must look, framed against the light, to anyone lurking along that inky, febrile gullet. He shuffled away on his heels, the notion of turning his back still inconceivable, and slowly retreated, heading for the cooler air of the storeroom while watching his own shadow stretch out bef—

Two shadows.

Fuck.

He shouted out loud, spinning in place with hands clutching. And then again – a honk of wordless alarm – as an explosion of light boiled his vision.

Blind, he awaited the fatal strike.

Amazingly, no murderous blow descended. No blade slunk between his ribs, and nobody, in the shell shock of the sudden bedazzlement, prised open his chest and thieved his heart. His hands closed instead on something soft and warm, and he finally eased open his eyes, squinting in the electric glow.

It was Sandra.

Standing in the archway, hand resting on the light switch he'd entirely failed to notice.

'Ah,' he said.

'You're touching my breasts, Mr Shaper.'

'Yes. Sorry.'

He rammed his hands into his pockets and stepped away. And then, as a sudden memory hacked through the shame, twirled in his place to inspect the cellars with the benefit of light.

No mice. No murderers. No giant spiders.

The ghosts of his paranoia giggled in silence.

'We wondered where you'd got to,' the woman said, icy. 'The oxygen's right there.'

'Yes. Sorry.'

'Your friend's gone upstairs. Security checks, he said. He seems like a decent enough chap.'

I bet he does. 'Right then.'

He wandered vaguely along the corridor, doing his best to seem nonchalant, secretly checking Sandra wasn't about to flick the lights back off.

'They go on for ever,' she grunted, unimpressed. 'More vaults, an ice house, a coal store, a few larders. We keep it locked up.' She hooked a thumb at the stony ceiling. 'It'll suck the heat out of the house if you let it.'

No shit.

Sure enough, where the racks finally gave out, an iron door barred the way. It seemed to smirk at him, smug in the knowledge of his fear, and he couldn't stop himself pulling a face at it when Sandra wasn't watching.

Just as he'd imagined, the arches to the side held secondary cavities: most empty, others rather boringly heaped with unwanted toss. Unused wallpaper, spattered paint pots, rusting stepladders. One niche contained a bric-a-brac of plumbing equipment round an antediluvian bathtub, another contained only a single mahogany chair – cobwebbed and scratched – like a throne awaiting its king.

Creepy.

Only the vault nearest the entrance warranted a closer look – that beady-eyed spider's lair – and Shaper inspected it with a frown. It looked for all the world like a chemistry lab.

'LSD,' said Sandra, as if that explained everything.

'I'm sorry?'

'You didn't know?'

'Know what?'

She fired him a look which contrived, with no more than an arched brow and a reflective tilt of the mouth, to seriously question his skills as an investigator. 'I did say no police,' she grunted. 'You must have wondered why.'

Shaper stared. 'He . . . made drugs?'

She shrugged. '*He* never called it that but, yes. Him and his pals. Down here like Bunsen and bloody Beaker.' She shook her head. 'You asked why he lost his memory, Mr Shaper? You can bet all this didn't help.' She blew dust off a grubby flask. 'For all I know the police are still looking for the black-hearted mastermind behind the Camden acid revival of ninety-four. "Like a slice of the sixties," he used to say. "Groovy."'

'Used to?'

'Doesn't bloody remember it now, does he?'

Shaper just shook his head, bewildered. He kept flashing back to Glass's fleshy CRIMINAL tag.

All that, just for making a few tabs of the cosmic crazy?

'Was he . . . was he a pretty major supplier?' he probed. 'Like . . . enough to piss off the big boys?'

Like maybe the Corams?

Like maybe Tommy supposed-to-be-dead Boyle? That would explain the link betw—

'No, not really.'

Balls.

Sandra scowled into space. 'Not that I know of, anyway. Like I said, I stayed out of it. But as far as I know there was never much . . . demand, you know? Select clientele. Mostly they just made it for themselves.'

'They?'

'Him and his friends. Getting high, chanting. "Opening the Third Eye" – all that. And then the . . . You know.' She flapped a hand. 'The orgies.'

The . . . ?

Fuck.

'Anyway, sometimes they made too much and sold it to a dealer. Strictly small-time. Just a way to spread the bull-shit, really. They used to wrap each tab in one of their pamphlets.'

For someone who'd stayed out of it, Shaper reflected, Sandra was amazingly well-informed.

'So you can't think of anyone who might have it in for your dad?' he said, a prickly little link forming behind his eyes.

Mary said Karl was on acid, that night in Soho . . . A murderer with one punch.

'Not one.'

Did Glass feel responsible? Is that why he didn't want to remember?

'And I don't suppose you'd recall the name of this dealer? The one your dad sold to?'

'No.'

Lying.

'Oh well.' He shrugged, hamming it up. 'Doesn't matter. I mean, now I know what I'm looking for, shouldn't be too hard to find out. Bit of a rarity these days, acid. Folks tend to remember that sort of thing. I'll just ask around.'

Unless you want to change your story, love?

He pretended to inspect a sooty test tube and watched her fidget from the corner of his eye.

'Actually . . .' She coughed. 'Maybe—'

'Dan! Oi, Dan!'

Vince. *Sod, shit and piss it.*

The brute's shadow wobbled massively down the stairs. 'You better see this, mate!'

Sandra didn't miss a beat, setting off towards it with her face hidden. Shaper flicked off the lights and trailed after her, stooping to grab the oxygen, and almost resisted the urge to throw a final, cautious glance into the dark.

The air kept moving.

'Recognise him?' said Vince, smug, when they joined him in the kitchen. He passed over a dusty oblong with an I'm-so-fucking-smart smirk. Shaper cast a sneaky glance at Sandra as he took it, deciding she seemed as interested as him.

'On the left,' Vince pointed. 'At the back.'

It was a photo – buried in a frame of beads and shells – of a group in a restaurant. A passing waiter had doubtless been commandeered for camera duty, obliging half the subjects to lean and contort uncomfortably in their seats.

'Where'd you find this?' Sandra said.

Vince nodded through the door and across the cavernous hall. 'Big room at the front. Chest of drawers. All sorts of odd bollocks in there.'

Security checks, Shaper thought, one eyebrow arched. He reminded himself to turn out Vince's pockets before they left.

'That's the sunroom,' Sandra mumbled. 'No one goes in there now. That's where they used to . . .' She caught Shaper's eye. 'You know.'

The orgies.

Sexually liberated or not, the diners made an unlikely group. Each sported the incongruous combination of a cardboard party hat and a bindi, but otherwise couldn't have been more varied if they tried. Shaper could tell immediately what had caught Vince's eye, and the sensation of importance – of links forming and progress being made – blossomed from the photo like spores from a fungus.

On the left at the back, barely out of his teens, was an angel-faced youth with a lascivious smile and twinkling eyes, instantly recognisable as one Jason K. Arbuthnot.

'That's Kingsley, innit?' Vince grinned, tapping the glass. 'Kingsley the bloody Cocker as a lad.'

Shaper nodded, mute. Next to the youth was a frumpy woman in late middle-age, sweater-clad, whose no-nonsense expression sent his mind reeling to another photo, cut from inky paper.

Heidi Meyer, a keen gardener and frequent exhibitor at the Chelsea Plower Show . . . neighbour spotted the body at the foot of a communal light well . . .

'Um,' Shaper said. He felt bizarrely as though he were sinking into water.

They were all there. Next to Heidi, a prim-faced woman flicked a thin-lipped smile at the lens, ('*She's rich,*' Canton had said. '*Business type. All about the image . . .*'), and Shaper whispered her name: *Alice Colquhoun.* He felt a tremble growing in his fingers – the Sickness uncoiling as if sensing his excitement – and swapped the photo to his other hand. His toes tingled.

'All right, mate?' Vince asked, uncharacteristically perceptive.

He lied with a nod.

Two seats from Alice Colquhoun, twisting in his chair, Dr Naryshkin beamed an alcohol-fuzzed grin. His heart still beating. Ribs still intact. Chest flesh unpeeled, eyes not bugging with terror and torment, arms not pinioned out like—

Stop it.

Stop it stop it stop it.

Shaper pulled out a chair and sat with a throat-clearing grunt. Breathed.

Vince and Sandra – he could *feel* it – were both watching him. He ignored them.

In the photo, at the head of the table, smart in a black suit and violet tie – smiling with such serenity that it became almost impossible to drag the eye away – was George Glass.

A line of text dropped over Shaper's eyes, unravelling in a single, gasping flurry.

YOU'RE ON a LIST

'*What we don't know,*' he heard, '*is why the sicko picked these people specifically.*' Canton's voice, like a ghost in his skull.

Shaper took a moment to arrange his thoughts. 'Sandra? Do you know who they are?'

'I told you, they're Dad's friends. Chanting, candles. All that stuff.'

'Orgies, et cetera?'

'Yes.'

Vince glanced up. '*What?*'

'I don't know their names,' Sandra said, ignoring him. 'They never used them.'

'Hang on, you did say orgies? I'm j—'

'Shut up.' Shaper kept his eyes on Sandra, ignoring Vince's pout. 'What do you mean, never used them?'

'They had these, like, code names. I never really got it. I told you, I—'

'Stayed out the way, yeah.' He looked back at the photo, chewing his cheek.

Four dead. One old man. And a pair of faces he didn't know.

'These two,' he said, tapping them. 'Anything you can remember. Anything at all.'

Sandra fixed her eyes on the first. A thirty-something black man with a neatly clipped beard and a baggy, buttonless shirt, waving a glass of wine.

'This guy was crazy,' she mumbled. 'I remember thinking that. Very well-spoken, but . . . never made eye contact. Spaced-out most of the time. He talked to the walls.'

Shaper dropped his eyes back to the image, confused by the sudden suspicion that he recognised the mystery man after all, but try as he might he couldn't place the face.

Sandra was scowling. 'They called him . . . Vish, Vish something. Sounded sort of Indian. That was his code name.'

Vince, still sulking, spat, 'Vishnu.'

'Eh?'

'Hindu god. One of the top blokes. You got Brahm the creator, Vishnu the maintainer, Shiva the destroyer. Trimurti, all together.' He spotted the others' bemused expressions. 'What? I read stuff! I'm informed.'

'You're weird.'

Sandra shook her head. 'It's not that anyway. Sorry.'

Shaper *hmmed* and tapped at the final member of the group. 'And this?'

She met his eye as if checking for tricks. 'You don't know?'

He inspected it again. It was a woman's face, and a more clichéd hippy he'd never seen. Long red hair hooked in a green band, with a loose-woven dress haemorrhaging colour. She wore a strangely familiar expression, one of almost supernatural openness, and it took Shaper a moment to realise he recognised it only through emulation, through an attempt by someone he *did* know to reconstruct it.

To fake it.

Sandra said it an instant before he did. 'That's Mary's mother.'

Shaper went one better, still mulling over the afternoon's creepy encounter.

Karl's mother too.

'*Him and his little club,*' the twitchy, eerie man had said. '*Burning bloody martyrs, the lot. "Us versus them" – that's the way they think! Locked away in that place in the woods, waving candles and chanting . . . I fucking hate them, d'you hear me?*'

200

Shaper put down the photograph slowly, shakes building in his other hand, and nodded at Vince.

'I think we ought to have a little look through these drawers of yours, mate.'

Chapter Nineteen

'Sod all,' said Vince, an hour later.

The drawers had contained precisely nothing of use. Emptied across the sunroom floor, they'd disgorged a dusty smattering of coloured ribbons, some long-crumbled incense, a few badly carved ethnic musical instruments and a wad of hyperbolic pamphlets with titles like *Blavatsky Knew!* (featuring a woodcut of a chubby woman and a crystal ball), *Occult Technology: What We Forgot!!* (fronted by a dramatic magician with a hand-shaped lantern), and *Embrace The Seventh Ray!!!* whose badly painted cover model bore an uncanny resemblance to Glass. To Shaper it all hinted at a rather joyless culture – over-earnest, over-serious – and he hadn't been able to shake the unhelpful image ever since of a roomful of psychedelic trainspotters nervously getting naked. He had to keep reminding himself that to Glass and his cronies – like those hungry-for-mystery customers at Mary's clinic – this kaleidoscope of chakras and chanting was a serious business, a faith, no less, and therefore beyond the jurisdiction of his own heavy-lidded contempt. These people *believed* in this stuff – or at least wanted to enough for it to amount to the same thing. Given that someone had now taken it upon themselves to start killing them, Shaper's own views on the topic didn't seem remotely relevant. It had therefore dawned on him that if he was to have the slightest handle on the sorts of irrational motives involved, he was going to have to do some homework.

So he'd crammed the pamphlets into a pocket, paused to thank Sandra for being so accommodating and, with a hint of impatience, studiously ignored the hazy delusions enveloping her.

That, of course, was the other problem.

Spooky bollocks.

Shaper had spent years chemically dodging his own illness. But despite understanding that his symptoms arose from the chaos of his damaged psyche, still he had to concede that the hallucinations themselves were not fundamentally chaotic. If each fuzzy brainfart truly was, as he suspected, little more than a reflection of his own subconscious – jumbled through his imagination, yes; exaggerated and confused, fine – then he also had to accept that they were, broadly speaking, honest. If it weren't for the miseries that came with them – the headaches, the fits, the incapacitating rush towards that final awful vision of decomposition and death – then he might even have grudgingly considered them useful.

They showed him, after all, what his conventional senses could only hint at.

But then how was that any different from the clairvoyant, aura-spotting nonsense Mary had been shilling for years?

You hypocritical bastard.

So he'd rammed Vince into the van, shot one last glance at the ivy-drenched bulk of Thornhill, and left its dreary shadow behind.

'Sod all,' Vince said again, smoking on the passenger side.

'What?'

'Honestly, mate. I have sod all interest in that woman.'

Shaper had forgotten he'd even asked. Now, scudding through the western approaches to Holland Park, he flicked his friend a sideways glare. 'Pull the other one.'

'I'm gay.'

'Bollocks. You biffed that traffic warden's missus last year.'

'*Pft*. That was just revenge, doesn't count. Sandra's nothing, all right? Zero interest.'

'If you say so.'

'I do.'

Whatever the truth of Vince's schizophrenic libido, Sandra was certainly of interest to Shaper – and not just for her patchy access to Glass's bizarre past. Moments before leaving Thornhill he'd felt her hand on his shoulder – one final, hesitant emergence of the inner shy.

'About that dealer . . .' she'd mumbled, unable to meet his eye.

'The one who bought the acid?'

'Mm.'

'You've remembered his name.'

'Yes. It's Fossey. They called him Fossey.'

She'd ejected the word with a hesitancy born of far more than just guilt. It wasn't the fear of being found out Shaper saw in her eyes – he'd learned to recognise that all too well – but a more painful, personal association. She'd been reluctant to speak the name, he guessed, simply because to do so would require her to remember something she'd rather forget.

He recognised that too.

'You and him . . . you were an item?'

She'd looked away. 'It didn't last long.'

'Oh?'

'He wasn't a nice person.'

'And where is he now?'

'I haven't the foggiest.' The force fields slammed back up. 'Dead, for all I know. He was going the right way about it.'

And that had been that.

The drizzle picked up as they approached Glass's home, as if a guilty cloud had been hanging above London, waiting for Shaper to return. Stuck in traffic, he caught himself peering along the needle shafts as they fell, slicing at the tombstones of slick roofs. Without warning the dreary sight triggered an abstract link to the black man in the photo – *Vish something* – and left Shaper scrolling through mental mugshots of his old acquaintances, cautiously unearthed from the buried past. None fitted the bill, and he was left with the added bewilderment of why a few moisture-clogged buildings should have brought the stranger's face so swiftly to mind.

Three days of detox. Amazing how much clearer things would have seemed.

Too late to go back now, idiot.

'What if he asks about the case?' Vince grunted, derailing Shaper's thoughts for a second time. 'This old git of yours. What do I say?'

'Tell him I'm making swift and serious progress.'

'Are you?'

'Yes.'

'Liar.'

He turned into Glass's street and pulled up at the kerb, refusing to fork out for the privilege of parking. The building lurked like a deserted temple.

'Just keep an eye on him, all right?' Shaper instructed. 'All these deaths have been at night, so don't you bloody nod off. And don't scare him, either.'

Vince looked hurt. 'Me?'

'You. He's old, all right? And a bit . . . eccentric. No frights. No blue stories. And no fucking flirting! Oh, and he'll ask you the pasta question, for security. Unless he's forgotten.'

'Badger meat. That really happened, you know. Funny story.'

'I've heard it.'

'But—'

'A thousand times, Vince. Go earn your keep.'

The big lug grinned and clambered out. Shaper called him back with a sudden rustle along his spine.

'One thing, mate. Someone might post a letter, come dawn.'
'That'll be a postman, Dan. There are quite a few ab—'
'Someone else, smartarse.'
'Who?'
'Precisely what I'd like to know. Feel free to employ physical unhappiness in the course of your inquiries.'
'Roger-roger.' Vince snapped off an ironic salute, blew a kiss, and headed up the steps.

She was waiting on his doorstep.

Arms round her knees, clothes sodden, hair bedraggled. She wore black make-up, panda dense, which had smeared down her cheeks in radial curves like the spines of a bat's wings. Gone were the tie-dyed skirts and baggy jumpers, her lithe body packed instead into dark, vac-form jeans and a red/black top, all buckles and straps.

She shivered in the street light and dripped.

A butterfly dipped in oil.

'Mary?' he said, just checking.

He could tell instantly she was either drunk or high. She lurched upright with an uncertain focus which skyburst in recognition and relief, then collapsed – wobbling on unfamiliar boots – into his arms.

'I didn't know where else to go,' she drawled, smearing a Rorschach blot on his shirt. 'Y-you were in the phone book.'

He *ahhed* politely, feeling abstractly as though the universe expected him to hold her tight, to mutter reassurances and sniff her hair. Frankly he could smell her perfectly as it was (vodka and damp fags), and in the rush of surprise and uncertainty at her appearance he fell back on the familiar need to have a little space. He pushed her gently upright, checked she was steady on her feet, and gingerly backed away.

'Right,' he said. 'Let's get you inside.'

* * *

A shower didn't do much to improve her sobriety, but at least cured the shivers. Shaper occupied himself with a carefully calculated dose and a few cigarettes, then brought her coffee when she reappeared. She flapped on to the futon amidst a shapeless bundle of towels, and he was perplexed to find that she'd somehow managed, in spite of obscuring all hints of a body shape, to imply nakedness.

She's rat-arsed and susceptible to persuasion, scumbag. Don't even think about it.

He didn't have to, as it happened.

'C'mere,' she gurgled, lunging for his face. 'Kiss me.'

He held her back and mumbled *let's-just-wait-a-minute* sounds, clocking up a few self-conscious brownie points on his decency slate. Oblivious, she broke into a soft schoolgirl blub, thoughtlessly wiping at errant nose trickles with a towel. Impossibly, she made even *that* look lascivious.

'Listen,' Shaper croaked, way out of his depth. 'You're OK now. What's this about, eh?'

She sniffed away the misery and breathed deep, an exaggerated regaining-one's-composure routine that put him in mind of a pulled-over drunk.

'I was scared,' she said. 'I . . . I got a phone call.'

Hhhhham, Shaper remembered, shivering.

'I-it was Karl. Karl called me. He was so *strange* . . .' Another brief burst of tears, subsiding in a spasm of breath: *h-h-h-h-h-hhh*. 'I haven't heard from him in years. And then right out of the blue, you know? All long pauses. Strange noises. He sounded *mad*, Mr Shaper.'

'Dan, please – for god's sake.'

'He frightened me. He was *spooky*!'

So says the clairvoyant, Shaper carefully didn't say.

'Look, I'm . . . I'm sorry,' he mumbled. 'I think this might be my fault. I went to see him earlier today.'

Mary threw him an inebriated scowl. 'Why?'

'Just . . . wanted to check him out. Thought he might be involved in the Glass thing.'

'No. No no no,' she shook her head, eyes lagging on each sideways jolt. 'He's not bad. Just . . . messed up. Just . . . He's not a *criminal*, Mr Shaper.'

'Just Dan, yeah? What else did he say?'

'He wasn't happy, that's all. About what I do. My job. "Waste of your life," he said. As if it's any of his bloody business!' She started crying again, the brief zephyr of anger slumping with her shoulders.

'If only he'd said,' she whispered. 'If only he'd . . . s-sooner, you know? Told me what he thought of it. Told me everything. Th-then . . . then . . .'

Shaper finished the sentence for her.

Then maybe you wouldn't have wasted your life on crystals and crap.

It was swiftly occurring to him that Mary Devon lived and breathed for what other people thought of her.

It was also dawning, worryingly fast, that whatever *he* thought of her was growing stronger all the time.

He was still tangled in this sweaty little revelation when she tried to kiss him again. This time the lunge connected, and for a moment he let himself relax into the breathless attachment: tongue creeping out, hands gripping her arms—

She's pissed and you're a shit. Stop it.

He broke off and eased her away, terrified of causing offence. She slurped more coffee and slouched back on her haunches, apparently uninsulted – *more honour points* – then blinked with uncertainty.

'There's a lizard,' she said.

'Yeah.'

'Just there.'

'That's Ziggy.'

'He just shat.'

'That means he likes you.'

'Karl told me about Mum.'

A sultry little silence chased the non-sequitur. Shaper mouthed a wordless, '*Ah.*'

'She sent him away,' Mary said, voice low. 'Like . . . like she was fucking *ashamed*. That's her own son! All that time! And she told me he was in prison! *Liar!*'

The tears were gone now, trampled by growing bitterness, and before Shaper could respond she coughed out a hot, acidic laugh. 'That's not even the worst though, is it? 'Cos . . . 'cos even when he was gone, she . . . she was still being eaten up by it. I thought I finally had her to myself, but oh no. No! Poor cow hops in her car and . . . and . . .'

'Yeah,' said Shaper. He wondered if he should try and touch her – to comfort her like a normal person – but was so panicked with inexperience he missed the chance.

She looked away and whispered, 'My whole life. My whole life I thought she was . . . you know?'

Perfect.

'But she only saw him, didn't she? It's always been about him.'

An electric idea suddenly seemed to grip her, and she met Shaper's eyes with a mad, manic grimace. 'Do you have any idea how much I fucking hate incense? All for her, Dan. All for her! The . . . the clothes! And the *people*, Dan! They're a *joke*.'

'Yogic flying,' he thoughtlessly added.

Mary stared as if he'd shat himself.

And then she began to laugh. Ragged and unconvincing, a desperate hyena vent – 'Yogic! Fucking! Flying!' – which writhed like a dying snake back down, by degrees, into tears.

He watched her, silent. Ziggy ate an apple on the sideboard, enjoying the drama.

SIMON SPURRIER

After a minute or two she sniffed and dragged hands across her eyes, chin-jutting determination spiking through the misery. A glimmer of sobriety, even; a toxic yellow aura with a power-chord whine.

'*Anyway.* It's not your problem. I just wanted to be, you know, around people. Away from the clinic. I went to some bars, but . . . well.'

'You got pissed.'

'And I couldn't go home – it didn't feel safe. Karl was a bit . . . a bit creepy.'

'Well, you're . . . you're safe here,' he lied.

'Thank you.' She looked up, misery and drunkenness parting like clouds. 'Really. Thank you.'

And this time when she came in for the kiss Shaper's defences snapped like brittle bones, his good behaviour was erased from the karmic scoreboard in a hot instant, and his inner decency had just enough time to giggle before the pair's weight carried them down on to the futon.

Ziggy got bored and wandered off.

Chapter Twenty

It was 10.30 p.m. before the cosy little spell began to break.

Side by side – touching but not embracing, smoking but not talking – they sat in bed and listened to the rain on the window, each alone with their thoughts. Shaper's had been souring for a while already, infected by the growing need to get out, to get *on* – and at first he clothed himself in the same prickly paranoia he'd felt the day before: the doubt at his own progress, the need for momentum. But even after a discreet, calming Amytal – popped while flushing the latest jellyfish johnnie – the urge to get back to the case didn't diminish.

Help the old man.

Now!

Besides, there was a second, grimier itch, gathering strength in his soul, borne on the realisation that Mary was sobering up. Her expression gradually solidified from inebriated carelessness to actual emotional investment, and the bouts of fucking duly became less chaotic, more considered.

Better, if anything – but that was hardly the point.

She began to take an active interest in her surroundings – scratching at Ziggy's head, standing nakedly to poke through books and CDs, at one point even getting up to make herself coffee. And as much as half of Shaper's brain dared to cherish the effortless familiarity, even angrily snarling that *this is what you wanted, idiot!* – still the other half pulsed with sudden, unforeseen panic.

You don't deserve this, fucko. You do know that, don't you?

And so he cleared his throat and stubbed out his fag, shooting her a nervous smile – just as she turned an inquisitive eye on the closed bedroom door.

'What's through there?'

'Let's . . . Let's get you home, eh?' he mumbled.

She looked as if she'd been slapped.

'Bollocks,' she spat. 'It's all bollocks.'

Shaper slowed the van, hunting kerb space near the clinic, and cast a nervous glance at his passenger.

'Well, bollocks or not,' he mumbled, 'I could use the help.'

Mary just glowered.

Things had iced over fast.

He supposed he couldn't blame her, being angry. In the unkind version of this evening's events he'd essentially fucked her then booted her out, all under the grubby umbrella of intoxicated vulnerability, and he didn't have the first clue how to explain himself in a more gallant light. In the wake of a tough day and tougher evening, Mary's newly exposed 'real self' had almost certainly needed to be handled with more care, and Shaper belatedly wished he'd had the tact or experience to know it sooner. She now had about her the manner of a woman scorned or, worse, a woman *disappointed*, and in the crawling silence of the journey – desperate to demonstrate that this wasn't a rejection, this wasn't some sleazy liaison – Shaper had instinctively tried to keep her talking.

It wasn't going well.

'Just an introduction to what it's all about. Please? The job you do, what people get out of it . . . Like an overview?'

'There's no such thing,' she snapped. 'I already told you, New

Age, alternative medicine, fucking magic, whatever you call it, there's a million different variations. No two people practise the same thing – that's the point. That's how the fish get hooked. It's all about discovering meaning for yourself.'

Shaper pulled into a space as slowly as he dared, drawing things out. 'But . . . there's got to be some common ground.'

'Barely. And when there is, it's just people building structures. Rituals, rules . . . That's human nature. Stupid.' Arms folded, emanating frost, she spoke with deep and lasting bitterness. She'd gone from high priestess to angry sceptic within the space of a day, and the soppy enthusiasm of the first didn't seem to be mitigating the venom of the second.

'Tarot,' she suddenly spat, like pulling a trigger. 'Gypsy wisdom from the fucking Pharaohs or a fifteenth-century card game crawling up its own arse? Doesn't even matter if you know what you're talking about, 'cos there's a list of interpretations as long as your arm. It's like paint-by-numbers for credulous dickheads.'

'Uh.'

'Or crystals, right? Lumps of fucking mineral. Different stones match different parts of the body, fine, but you think anyone agrees on which ones? Or how best to use them? Or how they fucking work in the first place?'

Shaper just stared, gingerly killing the engine. Mary had suddenly developed the manic look of a spree killer, gleefully knocking down targets, preparing to turn the gun on herself, and he realised her eyes were fixed, unmoving, on the clinic across the street. Roving the posters inside the window.

'Spells, regressions, auras, astral fucking journeys. I've spent the last decade talking bollocks to gullible wankers and now *you* want an overview? Fine. It's this: *bollocks*. Waste of time. Bollocks, bollocks, bollocks, *bollocks*.'

And then she was gone, van door slamming behind her, and

Shaper bundled out with a gurgle. He chased her across the street, desperately mumble-citing how afraid she'd been earlier that evening – 'Maybe I should check inside, eh?' – then fighting the urge to duck when she rounded on him with keys brandished.

'I'll be fine! Karl's harmless – doesn't know where I live anyway. I let my imagination get the better of me.' She slotted the keys into the lock and shot Shaper a dark glare. 'I'm stupid like that.'

'I should . . . probably have a look anyway,' he persisted – oh so manly – gently nudging past her and unlocking the door. He paused at the threshold to make a speedy, secret inspection of the keyhole – hunting a telltale smudge of wax – then slipped through.

Nothing.

Inside he stamped about like a SWAT commander, flicking on lights, peering into corners and throwing open cupboards, and only realised Mary wasn't even following him, let alone watching, when he declared the all-clear to an empty space behind him. He tracked her down, finally, to a small table in the bedsit, nursing a fresh coffee, and shot her a hopeful grin.

'Off you go, then,' she said.

He shuffled in place. 'L-look . . . about before. I didn't mean to suggest that . . . that I don't want to see you ag—'

'Just fuck off, Dan? It's a bit late for chocolate and roses.'

'But . . .' He flapped about for an olive branch. 'But you hadn't finished telling me about – y'know.' He gestured at the incense on the sideboard, the dreamcatcher in the window. 'All this.'

Homework. Researching the context of the investigation.

(Keep her talking!)

'Doesn't exactly matter now, does it?' She fell suddenly morose; mood still mercurial with the tail end of the booze. 'Not after all this. After . . . Karl. And Mum.'

Shaper sat slowly, half expecting her to kick his chair away. There was a small heap of coins stacked on the seat – emptied from her pockets, he supposed – and he gingerly shifted them aside, afraid to make any sound. She seemed too wrapped up in the sulk to notice.

'Supposed to be a session tonight,' she muttered. ' "Midnight Meditation".' Her voice assumed a dramatic, self-mocking tone, like an actor rehearsing bad lines. 'The Apogee of Darkness, when the walls 'twixt worlds are thin!'

'Glass mentioned something, yeah . . .'

'Poor old sod.'

'So will you tell him, d'you think? About . . . y'know . . .'

About being an enormous fake.

She absorbed the question slowly, anger and sadness muddling together, mollifying whatever frosty ire she felt towards Shaper and his romantic FUBAR – and nodded. 'Funny thing is, it really does feel like he's . . .' She waggled a hand, hunting the word.

'Special.'

'Yeah.'

They sat in silence for five minutes.

Finally Mary stirred, surfacing from the introspective sludge, and seemed to notice Shaper all over again. Irritation clouded her face. He could almost see the command to piss off forming on her tongue, and cast about with growing desperation, eyes finding a poster on the wall.

'There!' he demanded, pointing. It showed a human silhouette, in negative, with a string of bright discs along its spine. 'Chakras, right? Everyone's heard of chakras. Glass was on about 'em during his trance the other day.'

'So?'

'So . . .' He raised a hand, affecting a schoolboy squeak. 'Please, Miss, what the fuck is a chakra?'

Even in the grip of a strop, Mary couldn't hide a slender smirk.

Progress.

Slowly, thoughtfully, she clambered to her feet and approached the poster, voice seeming to change, all annoyances forgotten. A sermon, delivered from far away.

'Chakras are . . . Well. They mean different things too. It's an Indian idea originally – most of this stuff is. Plus a couple of centuries of Western meddling, all jumbled up.' She touched a finger to the paper, tracing along the coloured discs. 'Lot of different interpretations.'

'Like?'

'Like . . . oh . . .' She sighed, pantomime-reluctant. 'In Qigong they're seen as a circuit, pumping spirit energy around. Same in Reiki. In Bönpo they're more like . . . filters, or lenses, kind of – changing the way you perceive things. Like whichever one you focus through, you experience reality differently.'

Shaper felt a prickle in his neck. 'Why would you want that?'

She shrugged. 'The aim's the same in all the versions. Achieving divine bliss.'

'Is that all?'

She ignored him, still stroking softly at the coloured orbs.

'In tantric yoga, chakras are like . . . manifestations. Places where all the different layers of . . . of spirit and self . . . they come together. Everyone gets this portion of primal energy – kundalini, it's called. Lives at the base of your spine, coiled up like a snake.'

Thoughtless, unaware she was doing it, her hand dropped to knead slowly at the top of her jeans, pressing at the meat of her buttock. 'The idea of yoga is to arouse it.'

Shaper watched with his breath in his throat. Entranced.

'To let it . . . rise up the chakras one by one. Each more subtle than the last. And if you can do it all the way up, out through the crown? That's called samadhi.'

She seemed to remember herself, removing her hand and glancing back at him. 'That's a union with God, basically. You don't get to do that unless you're pretty much perfect. You know?'

Shaper shook his head.

'Like Glass,' she prompted. And turned back to the poster.

Ah.

'So . . . so that's what he follows, is it?' said Shaper. 'Tantric yoga?'

'No, he's . . . He doesn't really belong to any particular school of thought.' Shaper could see her smiling gently, a faint ray of hope for his inner defeatist. 'Or he belongs to them all, maybe. He helps people feel calm, that's all. Achieve happiness. It's just hints, mostly, bits and bobs of different techniques. He says he's forgotten the rest. It's enough to keep people coming back, anyway. You've seen the effect he has on them.' She sighed. 'The closest you'd get – trying to categorise him, I mean . . . That's probably theosophy, which sort of mixes everything together. But even that's mostly . . . well . . .' She wobbled a hand, palm down. Settled on, 'Bollocks.'

And then ripped the poster to shreds.

Before Shaper could react, paper was fluttering around him and she was storming through the doorway to the clinic, annihilating any other hangings she found with a long, unbroken moan, until the walls were bare and she was left, cheek against the paint, energies wasted.

A ray of hope. Right.

'You OK?' he mumbled.

She straightened without a word, swept her hair to one side, and sat back down as if nothing had happened.

'Most Western views share common ground,' she said, voice

back to sermonic neutrality. 'Seven energy points along your core – that's shakta theory. Linking between the physical body and the spiritual self. Each chakra's associated with different actions, different emotions. The more energised a particular one, the more influence it has on your personality.'

'Like drugs?' Shaper blurted, neck still prickling.

She just stared, blank-faced. 'No. Nothing like that.'

'Oh.' He fiddled uncomfortably beneath the steely gaze, turning over a shredded piece of the poster. He ran his finger downwards from a blue symbol at the figure's throat – where the page was slashed apart – through a green disc on its chest, a yellow mark below its ribs, then orange and re—

Wait.

'You're going the wrong way,' Mary grunted.

'What?' Something ugly unclenched in Shaper's guts.

'The energy flows up, not down,' she said. Then snapped a scornful, 'Supposedly.'

'What d'you mean?'

She huffed, clearly irritated to be dwelling on something she'd so spectacularly renounced. 'Rule of thumb: the higher the chakra, the more "spiritual" the qualities. Lower down, that's more about . . . corporeality, material stuff, you know.' She tapped at the lowest disc on the diagram, a circle of baleful red enclosed in four pointed petals. 'Let's say you're ruled by your base chakra. It's called Muladhara. You've got a predominantly red aura, and—'

'You're a filthy materialistic shitbag?'

'No. Not that simple. There's no value judgement on these things. No "better" or "worse". I mean, the ideal is to energise all your chakras equally, but that's – well. The crown chakra's basically impossible.'

'Unless you're Glass.'

'Unless you're Glass.'

Another odd little pause.

'Anyway,' she picked up, 'no, the base point's all about . . . growth. The earth. Nature. Red auras tend to be animal lovers, collectors, hoarders, that sor—'

'Gardeners?' Shaper blurted, surprising himself. The idea had slithered into his mouth without pausing to fill him in, and only now poured its poison, goosebumps riffling along his arm.

An old woman, tripping among rooftop flowers . . .

Mary shrugged. 'I suppose. Why?'

Shaper tapped at the next disc up: an orange flower with six petals, positioned over—

Shit.

Over the silhouette's crotch.

Canton's voice scurried along his veins: '. . . *very good chance,*' it hissed, '*that your mate Kingsley had his bollocks hacked off before he went under the train.*'

'This one?' he croaked.

'Svadhisthana. That's . . . unconscious desires. Relating the physical to the personal, like . . . relationships. Conversations.' She met his eye; a hint of bitterness rediscovered. 'Sexual desires.'

Kingsley the Cocker . . . best of the best . . . a grand a night . . .

'And this one?' His finger dragged upwards as if caught in a vacuum, now jabbing at a yellow disc – '*solar plexus . . . like a . . . a nerve centre . . .*' centred beneath the ribs.

'Manipura. Dynamism, energy. Willpower. Decision-making on a material level. Business . . . acquisitions. Someone decisive.'

Alice Colquhoun. Dead in a park.

Fuck, fuck, fuck.

'And this?'

Mary's patience started to break. 'Look, I don't know what th—'

'*This one!*' He rapped at a green circle over the figure's heart, voice quaking. 'It's . . . healing, right? Charity, compassion, all that?'

'Well, it's more to do w—'

'A doctor? A bloody doctor, Mary!'

'I . . . y-yes. Maybe. But—'

'They're all defined by one each! Don't you get it?'

'Get *what*?'

'He's fucking *stealing* them!' Shaper was on his feet now, digging in a pocket for the photo of Glass's little gang, hammering it on to the table. 'He's working his fucking way up!'

Mary almost cowered, all her bitterness turning to confusion. 'What . . . what d . . . Is that *Mum*?'

'Do this one!' Shaper cried, stabbing at the blue disc on the diagram's throat. 'This one's next! Who *is* he?'

Mary just shook her head, transfixed by the photo.

'*Mary!* Please!'

'It's . . . The throat chakra. Expressive, creative. Communicative. It's called Vishuddha, it's—'

'Wait.'

And the crackle in his ears died. The panic withered away.

Stop everything.

In the froth of his memory he heard Sandra's voice, curdled with the effort of remembering.

'*Vish?*' she'd said. '*Vish something. That was his code name.*'

He snatched the photo from Mary's hand and gawped.

The smiling black man. The one Shaper was sure he knew. Number five.

'What is it?' Mary whispered.

'Creative, you said, expressive.'

And then he had it.

'I have to go,' he blurted, hand already groping for his phone. 'I'll . . . I'll be back later.'

'Why?'

He stopped in his tracks.

Mary had spat the syllable with such barely disguised venom that it punctured the storm in his head. He could see it scrawled on her face as if etched with acid.

Go on then, you shit. Fuck and run.

'It's . . . Mary, it's not like that. It's complicated. But I'll be back. All right? I'll be . . .'

She just stared.

He went.

Talvir received his request with a barrage of huffs, evidently starting to begrudge the favours, and Shaper was obliged to inventively promise a romantic-weekend-for-two bonus on top of Vince's current fee. Then screamed, '*Just fucking hurry!*' and hung up.

He shuffled the van into traffic on the usual mental autopilot, awaiting the callback with no notion of destination. He wanted to be ready – already moving – as if physical momentum could substitute for genuine progress. His brain was groaning from the evening's revelations, and with the first dull hints of the Amytal crash (*too soon, too soon!*) and the accompanying shakes, he swiftly dosed himself straight; as mindless as breathing.

Calm down. Think.

He ferreted again for the phone and called Canton.

'Yeah?' the voice spat, impatient. Somewhere in the background a TV roared the baritone mess of a football game.

'Heidi Meyer,' Shaper hissed, fingers still trembling. 'The gardener. You dug her up yet?'

'What? Yeah.'

'And?'

'I can't discuss that with y—'

'She had something missing from the bottom of her spine. Didn't she? Or her . . . I don't know, her arsehole. Her bloody tailbone! Something around there!'

Muladhara.
The base chakra.
The football sounds died away. Canton's voice went tight.
'How did you know that?'
'Did she or didn't she?'
'Yes! Bloody yes, all right? A piece of her coccyx.'

Shaper punched the air, hooting in triumph, then thought about what he was doing and shook the pleasure away. The drugs were already creeping warm little tendrils through his fibres, but the Sickness wasn't going without a fight; his fingers were still determinedly quivering. Somewhere up ahead, he saw, a bar brawl had spilled on to the street – two human knuckles in beer jackets pushing and spitting – and drivers were judiciously nudging round the fringes. For some reason the ghosts of distortion in Shaper's eyes favoured the scene, gathering round the bar like a faint plume of white noise.

Canton's voice broke through from far away. 'Fall like that,' it said, 'bones are as good as powder anyway. We wouldn't have known there was something missing if we hadn't been looking.'
'How was it done?'
'That's not something you want t—'
'Canton!'

The voice sighed. 'He cut up inside her. Through the rectum, we think. Hacked out the last bone then dropped her off a fucking roof. No external signs.'

Shaper tried not to think about it. The revulsion only galvanised the Sickness, scabbing at his vision and jumbling the sounds of the fight, the bright jackets of sprinting cops, the cheering kerbside crowd. His heart bellowed beneath his ribs – a physical pain – and he fished out the pill file for the second time (*more! more!*), disturbed at the mess he'd become.

'No sign of a struggle in the flat?' he managed. 'N-no blood in the garden?'

'Never was. He took her away, same as numbers two and three. Sliced her up, brought her back, chucked her off.'

'And no sign of restraints? Bruises and that?'

'None. And no drugs in her blood.'

'Right.'

'Dan. Forensics think . . . they say she was conscious, when she fell. They think she was still alive, mate, even after he cut her. What sort of freak would *do* that?'

Shaper's skin spiked him like ice. The distortions strengthened, focusing above the brawl, and he gulped a stim at random, feeling sick. *Don't think about it.*

'How did you know, anyway?' Canton growled. 'You've got t—'

'Doesn't matter. Look, I've got to go. I'm waiting for a . . . a . . .'

He let his voice trail away, suddenly dumb.

The hazy crackle had *winked*. Looping like a worm, it coiled his attention up and away from the ruck of shouting helmets and flying fists outside the bar, as if possessed of some secret design, as if the brawl had never been its true target and it could now tweak his gaze – as it always intended – towards . . .

What?

A glowing sign, jutting from the corner of the bar like an out-thrust tongue. Utterly normal, utterly unremarkable, it nonetheless seethed with all the nauseous chaos of his imagination, and shunted his brain sideways for just a second.

Fosters, it said. *Served ice-cold.*

Links snapped together. Mouse's deep Jamaican purr filled his skull – running through the names of dealers menaced by Tommy Boyle – then hazed neatly into Sandra's faltering voice from just that afternoon.

'Summa the whiteboys from down the crescent – jost kids, ya know. Crazy Foster was one . . .'

'*Fossey . . . We called him Fossey . . .*'

'Shaper?' Canton crackled in his ear. 'You still there?'

And as if its job was done, as if all the heart-hammering effort was worth it, his brain succumbed to the deadening fog of the combined dosage and let the Sickness fade back to its standard, sleazy hum.

'I need you to check someone out,' Shaper gasped, still reeling. 'It's possible he's . . . he's important.'

'Who?'

'Foster. Bloke called Foster. Petty dealer, Camden area. Mornington Crescent. Anything you've got.'

'Why? Who is he?'

'I don't know.' A cheery chime pinged at his ear. *Call waiting.* 'I've got to go.'

He ignored Canton's outraged '*Wait!*' and stabbed the kill key, opening the second line.

It was Tal. With an address.

An address for the smiling black man from the photo. A man ruled by his blue chakra – if you believed that sort of thing – whose associated propensity for expression and creativity was all it had taken to remind Shaper of where he'd seen the face before.

Buildings. Architectural art. Modern masterpieces.

He hurled the van along side roads, heading east. Racing to save an 'urban artist' – self-styled – called Merlin.

Chapter Twenty-one

Walter Clarke stared at the knife tip before his face and realised, with an inappropriate stab of self-awareness, he was crossing his eyes.

Ever conscious of appearances, he slipped back to normal focus and allowed the bright point to become a blurred streak on his vision, almost – but not quite – touching his face. He found himself seized by a sudden need to know how it would feel against his skin, and had to fight the urge to prick the ridge of his nose against it. He leaned away instead, as if to remove the sick temptation, and bumped it against the bare brick of the studio wall.

The knife didn't follow. The figure holding it didn't move, and couldn't have changed its expression even if it had wanted. Its face, nonetheless, remained lovely, and Walter found it hard to think of anything else.

He'd always had issues with his concentration. Always hunting gratification of his senses; always distracted by beauty or wonder far above dreary context. Like some surreal companion piece to this awful, self-containing tableau ('Man Prepares To Die'), he remembered standing among friends long ago, as a news bulletin replayed the death of the Twin Towers over and over: jetliners slamming like apocalypse angels into fiery flanks. Oblivious to the others' groans, he'd calmly praised the gorgeous fluctuations of the smoky pall, then been mystified at their disgusted glares.

Another time, not long before that, he'd stood for hours admiring the movement of maggots on a road-splattered fox cub. Once he'd fished used condoms from a canal then carried them, in bare hands and fabric pockets, back to his workshop – only to forget them for weeks. Once he'd raced home upon witnessing a robbery, not to call the cops but to grab his camera, entranced by the sticky beads of the victim's blood he'd seen strike the pavement. Like binary stars, he'd thought, connected by an umbilicus of solar fire.

He was, he readily conceded, a bit weird.

Nonetheless, it usually came as a surprise when people took umbrage at his quirks, so dissociated was he from the supposedly 'proper' responses. But even he, right now, could gather the necessary rationality required to understand that, no, it probably wasn't normal to be entranced by the inherent beauty of his own impending death.

Nonetheless.

'You're perfect,' he whispered.

The killer's face tilted quizzically, all sapphire-blue creases and golden whorls, snarling mouth glossy above a blood-bright tongue. The knife didn't move. The arm stayed outstretched. The eyes behind the mask blinked – too slow – and in spite of the bunched hatred of the façade somehow conveyed such deep disinterest that they perturbed Walter far more than the blade itself. 'Right now,' he breathed, as if to reinvigorate the killer's passion, '*we're* beautiful.'

The eyes just stared. Empty, dutiful. Dull.

In the gloom of his workshop, surrounded by pieces he'd long since wearied of, Walter scowled and worried at the intruder's apathy.

He'd been expecting all this, of course – or something like it – for a long time. Oh, he'd lost touch with the others from that mad little group years ago, partly sharing the communal guilt at what they'd done, more pertinently growing abruptly bored of the beliefs he'd once advocated so strongly. They'd lost the flame of originality, and he'd spiralled off towards new passions, new excitements. Still, the disappointment of their failure stayed with him – a worthy expressionism that had gone hideously wrong – and in some abstract way he supposed he'd always expected it to catch up. He'd changed his name during a brief obsession with Arthurian myth and, as the 'urban artist' Merlin, gradually allowed his contemporary work to eclipse the guilty exuberance of his youth. Aural cityscapes, transient architecture; acts of aesthetic terrorism.

Fame and acclaim.

But he'd recognised the faces all the same. Picked out from the white noise of local news broadcasts, even fifteen years later – even though he'd never known their names – he'd deciphered the pattern.

The gardener. The rent boy. The businesswoman. And the doctor.

The doctor, whose death scene they'd described live on air this morning – splayed, ruined, *beautiful* – with the carefully worded suggestion of a slow, orchestrated ordeal.

'Abhorrent,' they'd said. 'Torture,' they'd said.

Idiots.

Walter had felt his own turn drawing near. He'd suffered – at first – a shameful twinge of horror. He'd contemplated contacting the cops, falling on the mercy of his would-be destroyers, then shuddered at the notion of revisiting that past. He'd considered, even, contacting the ones left over – insightful Ajna and inscrutable Sahasrara – to warn them of what was coming.

He'd been, in short, afraid.

Until today. Until this afternoon, when the cops had given their breathless, fusty little press conference – all their dour-faced understatement failing to defuse the tabloid resonance of the 'serial killer' tag – and at last Walter had let the murders trickle into his soul for what they truly were.

A masterpiece.

And he'd been invited to participate.

He swallowed and tried to stay calm, the knife never leaving his view. Now the time had come, his body was reacting on its own, full of treacherous shakes and cold sweats. It felt a lot like a betrayal, filling his brain with flimsy fears and miseries at a time when it should have been *exulting*; awaiting whatever fabulous display his killer planned to create.

He'd been waiting all afternoon. He'd cancelled a radio interview and draped sheets over his old works, gloomy that he'd never made anything exceptional but excited to contribute to just such a thing.

It would happen at midnight, he'd supposed – remembering all too many hokey sessions with the old group, kick-started with the drama of a chiming clock and as the hour approached he'd stripped naked to prepare, imagining the care taken to display the doctor's body.

'Make me like that,' he'd whispered, touching himself.

But when the killer came at last, his nerve – that great traitor – had collapsed. Holding its eerie instrument, tiny flames flicking at wet eyes, the figure had slunk inside like a mist and shattered his resolve. He'd fled, screaming and crashing among his own works, loathing himself, until at last he was backed against the wall, sweating and shivering as the shadow slinked nearer, and there he froze.

Adrenaline trickling away. Courage finally returning.

Transfixed.

The killer had extinguished its terrible lantern and stowed it in a backpack, then simply stood, knife poised, the threat indefinitely prolonged. Every few moments it glanced off to one side, as if so thoroughly unabsorbed it could barely maintain its attention. The sheer flimsiness of the drama and ceremony which, Walter felt deeply, should underscore the scene – *his* scene – sent the first crustacean scuttles of panic up his spine.

'*Hhham*,' he prompted. 'Yes? *Hhham* . . .'

The killer met his eyes. Sweat glittered in the dark cavities behind the mask, deepening his fear, hinting at an act far grubbier, far less orchestrated, than he'd imagined. As if reaching a decision, the knife was abruptly lifted away, tensed in its latex grip, and there held aloft, ready to fall.

Preparing for a single, savage, *artless* chop.

'No!' Walter shrieked. 'Please! Do it ri—'

And the knife hilt smashed him across the face.

Walter howled. Fluid spumed from his nose, and the pain arrived in a thick wave, shattering from cheek to cheek. Before he could blink through it, he was on his hands and knees, foamy blood gurgling across lips and into eyes, spattering on the floor. Even thus cowed – supplicant at the feet of his tormentor – what shuddered through him worst of all wasn't the agony or the shock, but the blazing *wrongness* of it all. The horror of an imperfect, common little death.

'Not like this!' he gurgled, vomit scalding his throat. 'P-please . . .'

A foot smashed at his ribs, flipping him like a grounded turtle, and as he wheezed and thrashed, he sighted on the looming figure, even now still distracted. Still staring at the studio's side door.

And then sheathing the knife with a single, economical move.

And oh, the *relief*. The gratitude that washed through Walter, then; thick with promise that there was more to come, that there was *design* at work; there was *art*. He wept through bloody eyes and murmured, 'Thank you, oh, thank you . . .'

Which is when the front door smashed off its hinges and everything went wrong.

Chapter Twenty-two

Shaper didn't think.

The crazed impression he'd snatched through the letter box – a confusion of liquid reds and swift-moving bodies – hot-wired his muscles and lashed at the door without the distracting influence of thought.

The lock shattered at his second shoulder barge, and in the flush of power that followed, what greeted him was no less fleeting: a flash frieze, a lightning-strike instant frozen in time, shrieking for action before any analysis could occur.

There was a room – warehouse-wide, bare-brick walled – haunted by sheet-covered pedestals.

There was a body on the floor, and blood, and movement.

And there was a figure in black.

He charged it. He screamed as he ran – a broken, unintelligible howl that rose straight from his balls without bothering his lungs or heart – and groped in his armpit for the flick knife. The figure spun to meet him, head twisting, and—

Oh god.

And the howl died in his throat. His feet faltered.

The figure *festered*. In Shaper's eyes it drowned in a halo of pestilent energy, an optical overlay simmering with every sweaty, palpitating pain his fucked little brain could invoke. It dragged him back to the seizure in his flat, the snuffling at the door, the snake-like voice on the phone – *Hham* – and for a second he thought he'd lose it again; nausea rising to overwhelm him.

His knife – flimsy, useless, *laughable* – clattered to the floor, as if to even brandish it were an insult to the devil he faced.

Black-clad, hoodie raised over the back of its head, wide shoulders and barrel chest unmistakably male, its face atomised his soul.

No time to rationalise it as a mask. No space to pause and dismiss the horror, not with his collapsing legs dragging him nearer. Not with the simple, ghastly certainty, fed by the drama-loving excess of his Sickness, that it was Evil.

Like a varnished corpse, every brutal crease of its surface glittered in the studio's light, glossy blue and grooved by a distorted sneer. Etched across it all, a maze of white and gold webs stood in stark relief: war paint slashed across cheeks and jaws. The mouth, open and ruby-bright, gaped with a shriek of such animal rage that its tongue protruded, pointed like a bloody red eel, at a sinuous, organic tilt.

And then the eyes.

Sunken from the glossy plate, they stared like secret beasts, prowling in their lairs: white, moving, moist. Blazing with hate.

Shaper stumbled to a halt, crippled with the horror. Tremors guttered from his ankles, multiplying along his spine and prying at his mouth – loose, wordless, *worthless* – then raising hairs across every scrap of his skin. The black fire of his Sickness rippled across the figure's limbs, blurring its form and adding its own sly, secret energies: making it dance.

Hellish.

Somewhere – on another planet, far beyond the searing gaze – a curled form choked in a corner of the room and gurgled moronic nonsense.

The victim, a rational voice whispered. *The man in the photo. Still alive.*

The monster twitched. Its every movement felt like a violation of the air, as if Shaper's brain, already disarmed by insincere senses, refused to accept that this vile thing was part of the reality it was obscuring. The figure hunkered slowly on to its haunches – a spring wound with care, ready to explode – and then clucked wetly behind its unreadable, unbearable face.

And then –

Oh god no shit please—

– bolted in the opposite direction.

Shaper blinked. *What the fuck?*

It blurred like a smoky smudge towards a loading-bay door, where the night sat open and damp. Shaper merely gurgled, brain lagging behind.

'But . . .'

Across the room the victim moaned. Wiping blood from his nose, he dragged himself upright to sit and drip against the wall. He looked, against all logic, utterly grief-stricken.

'Go . . .' he mumbled.

'What?'

'I'm fine. Fine.' The man raised a trembling finger after the killer. 'He's getting away.'

Shaper fought a weird pulse of irritation. 'Don't you want me to . . . to stay? You need an ambulance . . .'

You ungrateful bastard!

'I'll call one. Fine. I'm fine. You've got to go after him.'

Shaper fidgeted, surplus adrenaline jabbing at his ribs.

'Please!' the artist snarled, gaze locked on the doorway, a crazy glint in his eye. 'Leave me alone. Get him. Leave me!'

Fine. Shaper stabbed a vicious finger towards the man – 'Wait here! Call the fuzz!' – and chased.

In the wake of the adrenal storm, swaddled in the candyfloss of delusion, the pursuit assumed the sureality of a dream, a jarring montage which somehow built to a smooth momentum, despite its fractured rhythm.

Run. Go. Take him!

The loading bay behind the workshop merged like an urban gullet with a tangled alley, shattering across his senses in a spume of drizzle. Footsteps scampered far away, distracting him from a spurious shiver of danger at the doorway, and he spied a frenzied shape slinking round a side-street corner. A flash of black, a trailing hand . . .

Go!

The passage jackknifed at an intersection, puddle-spattered and litter-clogged, and opened among startled pigeons on a desert of quays, forklifts and cranes, underscored by the fecund stink of old Mother Thames, oozing and sucking in the distance.

Dockyard. Right.

The sound of his own footsteps changed at each fresh junction, each new surface, and as the mustard dome of the night-lit clouds wobbled overhead, he became abruptly convinced he'd strayed on to the river itself, prancing lightly across its viscous foam. In his state – in his dream – it didn't seem implausible.

The Sickness made him cackle like an idiot even as it inflated his heart like a straining balloon and sent stabbing waves through his guts, and he speeded up on instinct, eyes fixed on the distant, sprinting speck. *This* was detective work at its purest – *chase man, catch man* – and despite the stimulant thunderhead raging inside him, he couldn't help feeling a clammy kind of joy.

At one stage his distant prey paused to glance back, its shadow scuttling like a great roach across corrugated sheds, sapphire sneer catching the light, and for a second Shaper's rush collapsed, momentum tripping on a knuckle of dread. But the beast instantly fled again, and he rushed ever onwards, shouting without words. Crumbling and dying – a toxic man in a toxic race – he wound through channels of stacked steel and leapt crippled oil drums, spastic larvae twitching in rimmed puddles, until – finally – his spidery quarry stopped in its tracks.

It flexed in the distant dark, all insect agitation, then syruped sideways between rotting sheds. Shaper accelerated again, ignoring the pain, sensing an end, and took the corner wide to dodge the imagined ambush.

And then stumbled, smirking, to a halt.

Dead end.

Sheds loomed at the mouth of a shadowed cul-de-sac like mouldering sentinels, boathouses with sealed gates and the stink of fish guts, and for an instant his spirit soared. *No escape now, fucker!*

But the killer wasn't there.

Just darkness and, as his eyes accustomed, the chilly presence of nooks and crannies. Broken windows, splintered planks:

Places to lurk.

Second by slow second all the savage joy evaporated, leaving behind it only aching muscles, pounding blood and the spinning sensory spoor of the Sickness. The shadows seemed to creep and cringe, screwing with his balance, and as the rush death-rattled away, it whispered the question he should have asked at the start: *what do you do when you catch him, genius?*

He reached for his knife.

You dropped it, remember?

Wanker.

He tried to ignore the exhaustion, the doubt, the slithering fears, clinging to the last ragged traces of his resolve, and stared into each patchwork shadow in turn, each shivery recess, hunting a flicker of movement that wasn't generated by his own psyche.

Nothing.

And so he inched deeper. Knuckles rapping at the soft wood

of the nearest shed, as if to exorcise a threat lingering in the silence itself.

'Come on,' he said, out loud. 'No way out of it now. Might as well show yourself.'

A name trickled into his mouth, alight with the ghost of a hunch made real, and he found himself gently shocked at how readily – how effortlessly – his secret suspicions had coalesced.

The phone calls . . . the history . . . the twitchy, freaky little fucker . . .

It was out of his mouth and hanging on the drizzle before he could stop himself.

'Karl. Please, mate . . .'

Airborne, the name tasted right.

But still, silence thicker than stone.

He reached the first gap and shuffled to a halt: a dingy abyss partly shielded by a flap of tarp. He tightened his nerves and yanked it aside with a shout, hands raised for the strike.

Empty.

His second candidate was a non-starter – a shallow recess on the front of a squat shack, too small to fear. And the third, when he kicked viciously at the decaying MDF propped against its hollow, disgorged nothing but a clan of woodlice and a single earthworm.

And then he saw it. A shadow within the shadows, a patch of matte black no darker than its surroundings yet somehow discrete, hunched in a half-covered channel by a grit bin. *Moving.*

His heart hurt. His eyeballs throbbed with his pulse, and he clenched his jaw so tight his gums ached. He stepped slowly forwards, watching the shape shift and tremble, ignoring the buzzing of flies, the stink of sulphur . . .

Not real! (Probably.)

'Hey,' he said.

The shadow bobbed, rustled, *clicked*.

'Hey.'

He took a breath. Stretched out a hand, fingers flexing claw-stiff, and reached into the dark.

It exploded.

Screaming like a devil.

Detonating in a burst of shock so pure that Shaper collapsed on to his back, hands covering his face, as black feathers frenzied and a demonic something cackled into the night.

He lay there for a long, long time.

'Crow,' he said. 'Shit.'

Fucking birds.

It wasn't until he'd swiftly checked the last few hiding places – all empty – and was walking away with a guilty tang of relief, that he thought to check what the bird had been pecking at. By the time he returned, it was fluttering off a second time, clenching something long and pale in its beak. On the wet tarmac behind the grit bin, knees damp on the ground, he found nothing but a faint trace of crumbled wax – just like the smudge on his door. And as he walked back towards Merlin's place, mind a pall of exhaustion, he glanced once over his shoulder and thought he saw – far in the distance beyond the river – a flash of gold and blue, coiling from a seething shadow.

But he couldn't be sure and so didn't dwell, clamping down all thoughts of sensible or rational observation. His brain, he knew, couldn't be trusted.

The shakes were back with a vengeance, and he doubted now that any fresh dose of soothing barbiturate could chase them clear, any more than a re-up of Adderall or Troparil could sharpen the dullness at the base of his skull. Nothing seemed real any more, and he supposed with a sigh he was simply going to have to get used to it.

Which is why he was barely surprised at all – stepping back

into the airy studio with his hair dripping sweat and drizzle – to find the urban artist Merlin hunched where he'd left him, slick in an ocean of blood.

His throat had been cut.

No. Not just cut, not just neatly sliced from jaw point to jaw point, but opened up, cross-sectioned like a diagram in a kid's comic. Its cavities and tubes lay exposed, carotid artery long since slackened, jugular in a slippery slouch, and at the centre the creamy trachea sat slick with gore – an inky hole in its centre. A fold of cartilage cut out and gone.

Vishuddha.

The throat chakra.

The horror slunk back up. This time Shaper was waiting for it, too crazed to care, and simply decanted it into the morass of his already bubbling mind, like shitting straight into a sewer. For a brief second of rationality – unable to conceive of the killer returning here so quickly, of such fiddly work being conducted in the time it took him to walk back from the docks – he wondered if the artist might have done this to himself. After all, Merlin's lips were twisted in a wretched smile as if relieved, a blood-dribbling perversity which only added to the scene's revulsion.

But then he saw that his own knife was missing from the floor, that the front door had been carefully pulled shut, and when he lifted his hand to wipe his brow, the skin of his palms was abruptly blackened and peeling, and *oh god I'm dead I'm crumbling I'm rotten and sick and—*

And something a little like a brain sneeze shivered through him, and mercifully, joyously, he tuned out of the real.

Chapter Twenty-three

He awoke – such as it was – driving. His mind clocked in with a blink of restored self-awareness and a disbelieving smirk at its own trauma-dodging brilliance.

He'd been on autopilot again. A comforting fugue, permitting him the time and space to shuck off the shock, to calm down, to reboot; brainlessly twisting the wheel along silent, night-lit streets. He discovered his skin was mercifully unblemished, no longer appearing mouldering or vile, and before he'd even finished shaking himself down from the mental backflip, noticed he was cruising past a familiar pub, long since closed for the night.

The broken windows, the table where the todger story was told, the doorstep where he'd enjoyed a much-deserved smoke. He pulled up a little further along the street and festered in silence, gently unnerved that his standby navigator had crossed the entire city, east to west, in the service of a secret hunch.

Karl's home looked dead. Lights out, curtains drawn, the same as all of its neighbours. For a moment Shaper imagined the man asleep, swaddled in lunatic dreams, then discarded the image with a scowl.

Not sleeping. Probably not even home yet, the little shit. Racing back with bloody gloves, sweaty face . . .

And my fucking knife in his pocket.

He half expected a black-clad bogeyman to prowl past the

van on its way inside, and caught himself peering along the street just in case.

He took drugs to cover the usual bases. Not enough to retrieve normality, to kill the shadows and purge the pains – too late for that – but at least to maintain, to keep on going. *Just get the job done, mate. Then sleep for a year*.

His phone rang. He yelped and fumbled through pockets, the shrill tone somehow an affront to the notion of a stakeout. 'Hello?'

'Shaper? Canton.'

'Yeah?'

'Dispatch sent some guys round. They've found the body, like you said.'

'What? What are you t—'

He stopped.

Across the street, shadow-drenched, a curtain *pulsed*.

'That's number five,' Canton burbled, oblivious. 'CID's never been happier. They're calling him the Tourist, if you believe that, on account of he likes to take souvenirs. *Wankers*. They've got profilers, Yank experts, the works. Not releasing it to the media till everyone's had a look. On which note, how'd you find this one?'

Shaper struggled to concentrate, eyes fixed on the window. 'Wait, Canton, how's . . . What d'you mean, "same as you said"?'

There . . .

Between the curtains, continent-slow, a coal-black gap sneered open. Somehow, in the pits of his misfiring senses, the certainty of attention – of the eye behind it, the hot breath beneath – sat like a ragged weight on Shaper's spine.

He beat me here. He fucking beat me back . . .

Again.

'You all right?' the phone said.

'Y-yeah. Yeah, why?'

I seeeeeee you . . .

'Not pissed?'

'No.' He drew himself deeper into the van, a snail recoiling into its shell, and forced himself to look away. 'No, I'm not bloody pissed. What're you *talking* about?'

'You called me twenty minutes ago, mate. Directions to the fifth victim.'

'No I fucking didn't.'

'I'm afraid you fucking did. You sure you're OK?'

Autopilot. Shit.

The cop abruptly sounded embarrassed. 'Listen, Dan, I had to report my source this time. The case officer's a right shitbag – asking questions, you know? So I need you to come down the station tomorrow. Make a statement.'

'But—'

'No buts. Four o'clock.'

'Canton! No! It'll lead to my client. Or worse yet, it'll lead to bloody *me*. That's—'

'That's what happens when you play Poirot, mate. You're expected to be vaguely fucking accountable.'

'But—'

'Sorry. Four o'clock.' The phone went dead.

Shaper shouted. A lot.

And by the time he'd got a grip, daring at last to squint back up at the watching window, the chink had closed like a meaty scar, and the world was as still and silent as a tomb.

Fuck stakeouts.

The Samadhi Alternative Therapy Clinic wasn't much livelier.

Shaper hammered on the door in short bursts of increasing volume, trying not to get swept up in paranoia.

She's asleep. She's exhausted after confessing to a room of dedicated hippy types that she's a vile black-hearted liar, and has justifiably nodded off.

Or:

She's still pissed off with you for treating her like a disposable inebriated fuckmonkey, and would sooner open the door to an enraged stegosaur.

Yes.

Definitely one of those two.

Or something's happened to her.

Shut up.

After the fifth round of knocking – aware curtains were starting to twitch in the flats above – he backed away and sulked on the kerb, a valiant cigarette defying the damp. A few late-night pedestrians staggered by, one even shuffling up – clutching at a foam tray containing either the world's least appetising kebab or an aborted elephant foetus – to conspiratorially request an eighth of skunk.

'Sorry, mate,' Shaper grunted, not sure if he was pleased or annoyed at the misidentification. 'I'm all out.'

Just when his patience was going the same way as his imaginary dope stash – as he was glumly contemplating heading home, and worse still was starting to fearfully analyse why he'd come rushing back to Mary's place at all – he caught a strange movement from the corner of his eye and twisted to stare. Someone, he realised, had stepped round a corner up the street then darted out of sight. He frowned and approached the turning, fists clenching. He wouldn't be the first person to let his curiosity goose-step him into a late-night mugging, but he'd be fucked if he was going to stand on the pavement like an idiot while someone played silly buggers with his paranoia.

And, he conceded to himself, in the grubby little pocket of his soul, *I want a fucking fight*.

The anticipated ambush never came. The side street was

241

deserted, except for a battered old jalopy parked in the light bleed from a 24-hour Internet cafe. Which was now, Shaper couldn't help noticing, abruptly pulling away. He glimpsed two drivers, one unmistakably bald, one wearing a skull-hugging beanie, and with a momentary clenching in his gut – *they've got her!* – spotted a single passenger in the back. But before he could react, the third figure twisted through dappled reflections and flashed a predatory smirk directly at him.

Vicar. Shit.

The creep touched two fingers to his eyes, widened the sneer, then twisted the gesture into a finger-point directly at the net cafe.

Watching.

Watching what?

His confusion was short-lived. No sooner had the car dwindled away than a scrawny shape stepped from the dingy establishment and lit a fag with gloved hands – then glanced up and noticed him.

'Shaper?' said Mary. 'Shit!'

He tried to read her expression, but the usual synaesthetic clutter was unhelpfully jumbled – *Anger? Guilt? Relief?* – before something solid clicked behind her eyes. She ditched the cigarette as if it disgusted her and strode, almost running, towards him. He was still grappling with the crazy urge to cover his bollocks when she swallowed him in an embrace and kissed him hard.

'You came back,' she kept saying. 'You came back.'

In the bedsit there was a moment's awkwardness. Mary flung off her coat – a little violently to Shaper's eye – and poured two glasses of wine. She kept staring at him, as if to check he was real.

'I didn't think you'd come back,' she muttered.

For his part, Shaper fidgeted and wondered what would

happen next; bobbing in unfamiliar waters. It was clear he'd somehow salved all her former anger without much effort, and though he had no idea how, he dimly supposed he should move on to instigating some sort of Affirmative Emotional Intimacy. But in all the panic, the best his flailing brain could do was buy time, scatter-firing professional concerns.

'The, uh . . . the Internet place . . .' he coughed. 'What's that all about? Bit late to be surfing, isn't it?'

'I couldn't sleep.' She shrugged.

'It's just – there were these blokes. Waiting outside, like.'

She recorked the bottle. 'Who?'

'They didn't talk to you?'

'What blokes?'

'Never mind.'

She shrugged, as if minding had never been on the cards, and passed him a glass. He sipped gingerly, trying to identify where all this unmanly terror was coming from.

It wasn't as if Shaper had lived some testicle-witheringly monkish existence for the past five years; merely that his dalliances had tended to come at the end of a beery night, when "getting the ball rolling" was as natural as staggering into one's giggling conquest. He hadn't tried his hand at anything more . . . *complex* since the catastrophe that had changed his life, and he was loath to dig back into *those* memories for inspiration. That, after all, hadn't ended well.

Mary just kept staring with a lopsided little grin. 'You came back.'

Her phone rang. The smile went brittle and something shifted in the air – a pulse of darkness and fear, wiring itself through Shaper's brain as a leathery shriek and a flicker of tawny light. She lifted the receiver with an oddly frozen expression, then dumped it down unanswered. 'No interruptions,' she said.

Something, Shaper grasped, *is fucking going on.*

He cleared his throat. 'So, uh . . . how did it go?'

'What?'

'The meeting with Glass. Coming clean.'

She wrinkled her nose. 'Let's not talk about that.'

A sooty little bell rang at the back of his brain, but as she theatrically set down her glass and stepped forwards, unhooking a shoulder strap and firing a lascivious smile straight through his pupils and into his balls, there wasn't time to give it a thought. Unclouded by tears and tequila, writhing sinuously out of her clothes, her intentions came screaming out with such force that Shaper was almost staggered: a snack in the lair of a dragon.

He could hardly be surprised, he supposed. She'd spent her whole life playing the cheery little earth mother without sleaze or seduction; no wonder the inner vamp was making up for lost time.

'D-did you meet Vince, then?' he gurgled, watching her pour from her skirt like liquid. 'He was with Glass, right?'

She nodded and kept coming, lifting her top over her head.

'Yeah. I . . . I think you'd like him. He's a mate. And, listen, I wanted to talk to you some more about chakras, because—'

'Shut up, Dan.'

She kissed him. Down to just her underwear, body warmth palpable through his clothes, a hand snaking tenderly across his crotch. He stumbled back another step, legs weakening, idiot brain still whispering *something wrong, something wrong*, and felt his arse nudge at the table. A few coins spilled to the floor, clattering in crazy constellations, and he seized the distraction with undignified haste, dropping to his knees to gather the mess.

'How much was there?' he croaked, scrabbling at the linoleum.

She sounded annoyed. 'I don't know . . . about a fiver. Just leave it.'

'I've got . . . four twenty. The rest must have rolled under stuff. I'll just—'

'Dan.'

He looked up. 'Mm?'

'Get naked.'

They fucked, or had sex, or made love – whatever – just once.

Quality, he thought, slinking unresisting into gorgeous nothing, *over quantity*.

He slept without dreaming for eight hours, an experience of such religious wonder that he could almost feel it filling his black soul with milky calm, brain unscrambling like a decaying protein – and then woke among the first glimmers of prickly withdrawal to find Mary tucked in a ball beside him, nose nudging at his chest.

And instantly he knew.

Instantly the shards of a broken image clicked together like a paranoid jigsaw, needing only the pause for breath to be seen for what they were. That creepy sense of *wrongness* he'd felt before, the distracting overkill of her sledgehammer seduction, even the damn money on the table, all of it amounting – without resentment or judgement – to a simple conclusion.

Lying.

Lying, lying, liar.

He slipped out of bed and fished in his coat for the morning dose, remembering as he did so the unusual force with which she'd ditched her own jacket as they came in. He tracked it to a crumpled corner and, with a shiver of Modafanil courage, rummaged in the pockets.

And sighed.

It was shit, being right.

* * *

He woke her gently, chewing his cheek.

She smiled warmly as she came round and he kept his expression at a carefully controlled room temperature, deciding on impulse to give her the chance to confess for herself.

'How much,' he said, 'can you remember about your mum's friends?'

She was still rubbing her eyes, *nyup-nyupping* with a distracting stretch – perfect little nipples poking from the edge of the sheet – and grunted a frazzled, '*Whuh?*' before nuzzling back into his side.

He moved away with a soft spasm of anger – *or fear, Dannyboy, at the effortless intimacy?* – and dug for the photo from the sunroom drawer.

'The group,' he said. 'Your mum, Glass, all the rest. What d'you remember? You must have met them?'

She sat up with a scowl, perplexed by his change of tone. 'I told you, I was kept out of it. Don't remember much. What's this about?'

He just nodded at the picture, blank-faced and silent.

'Is this . . . is this them, then?' She wouldn't meet his eye. 'I don't recognise them.'

Dosed up or not, even with the delusions at a bearable remove, it wasn't hard for Shaper to see: *liar.*

He wondered if she could tell already the jig was up, but it was clear she wouldn't be taking the easy way out. He drew breath to begin the accusation, awkward in the heart of the red-handed moment, then couldn't resist a pulse of relief equal to her own – a sensory gobbet of yellow and cream – when the phone rang. She tumbled from bed to snatch at the distraction, barking a bullish, 'Yeah?'

And her face changed. Brows falling, then gathering abruptly in a spike of anger. She slammed down the receiver even harder

A Serpent Uncoiled

than before, and stepped away as if the phone could infect her, hugging herself. She'd turned unmistakably paler, and Shaper found himself uncharitably suspecting another act.

'Karl,' she whispered. 'Again.'

'Like yesterday?'

'N-no. Like last night. He must've called ten, twelve times . . .' She sat forlorn on the bed, still naked. 'Th-that's why I went round to the web cafe. I was a bit . . . you know? Public place, I thought. And I didn't think you were coming back.'

It took every last dribble of Shaper's resolve not to hold her. To cling to the scraps of rage still percolating inside.

'What did he say?'

'He sounded so . . . so *angry*. Just shouted and screamed.' Tears were gathering in her eyes. 'Didn't make any sense. Kept talking about . . . about bodies and fire. He said, "They deserve it, don't they?" Then just swearing, calling me a bitch, a whore. Then just the breathing.' Her lip trembled. 'He *frightens* me, Dan . . .'

Tears trickling now. He couldn't hold out any longer, flouncing down to embrace her, hoping against hope that on *this* stuff at least she was telling the truth. The delusions – too faint and confused, a riot of suspicion and attraction – couldn't help him.

Too involved. Too fucking muddled.

When the worst of the sobbing was over, and the silence needed plugging, he lifted his arms off her shoulders with a sigh.

'I know you sent Glass those letters,' he said.

There.

And yes, she tried to front it out, feigning confusion, and for a second he hated her. But it was an impossible thing to maintain, not with her sitting naked and miserable, so as she shook her head through drying tears, he calmly raised a hand to cut off the case for the defence.

247

'Don't,' he said.

'But—'

'Mary, nobody visits an Internet cafe at two in the morning except backpackers and perverts.'

'I *told* you, I was scared of Karl and—'

'Karl, who lives on the other side of London. Who doesn't even *know* where you live. Not exactly knocking on the door, was he?' He shook his head. 'You could have just taken the phone off the bloody hook. *Or* called the cops.'

'Look, I don't know what you think y—'

'You were waiting for the story, weren't you? News updates, BBC website, all that. Shit, you can even scan police dispatch online these days. Victim number five, right? You knew it was going to happen. You were waiting for confirmation.'

She just stared, cheeks burning.

'This . . . this is bollocks, Dan.'

'Yeah? There's four pounds twenty on your kitchen table.'

'So?'

'Very precise, that. No coppers, no five pees. Laid out specially. Funny thing is, I needed exactly the same amount myself the other day. Remember thinking what a rip-off it was. Coincidence.'

She crossed her arms and jutted her jaw, silent.

'Parking, see? Street where Glass lives. Whack an envelope through the door, same as yesterday. Same as the day before.'

Lucky for you you didn't, he silently added, imagining Vince poised behind the letter box.

'That's all you've got?' she hissed. 'A late-night stroll and fucking pocket change? You're paranoid. You're mental.'

'Almost certainly.'

'Well then.'

'Enough for a hunch, mind.'

'So?'

He sighed again. 'So there's an empty envelope marked for

Glass in your coat pocket, Mary. Kiddie handwriting and all. So cut the bollocks, yeah?'

She sank back on her haunches, affront punctured like bubblegum. Her face said: *busted*.

He might have felt smug if it weren't so fucking depressing.

'So,' he grunted, headache gathering. 'Did you get it?'

'Get what?' Little more than a whisper.

'Confirmation. News of the death.'

'N-no. No, there was nothing being r—' She stopped, brows tangling. 'You mean there *was* one?'

She seemed genuinely surprised.

But that means—

'Ohhhh!' He tilted back his head with a humourless smile, palm to his forehead. 'I get it! I fucking *wondered* why you were so pleased to see me.' He aimed a finger. 'You thought it was all over, didn't you? Danny Shaper comes back from his emergency all horny and happy, equals no fifth murder.'

She covered her eyes, nodding.

'Well, there was one.' He sniffed. 'The cops are withholding from the media. And I came back anyway.'

They sat in silence for a while. She pulled the sheet round herself, crashingly awkward, while Shaper ranted and screamed in the silence of his skull.

Fucking liars! Fucking liars everywhere!

He realised, guilty, that he had an erection again.

'So why, Mary? You've seen these poor sods dying one by one. You recognised their faces, right?'

She nodded.

'So you know what it means. You know how it ends.'

'With Glass.'

'So why not call the cops? Why not tell the old man himself? You see him often enough. He'd listen to you.'

She sniffed, surly now. 'Why do you think?'

'Well, that's it, isn't it? Way I see it, there's only two options. Either it's like Sandra thinks, and you're trying to get cash out of the old boy somehow –' her face shot up, aghast – 'or . . .' He took a deep breath, almost afraid to say it. 'Or you're protecting the killer.'

She looked away.

And oh, the silence.

He helped himself to a shower and shrugged on his clothes while still damp, rushing to get out. Isolated among the choppy seas of his anger and hurt, a whiny little voice promised: *it wouldn't've worked anyway, mate. Better now than later, eh?*

He silently hated it and got on with feeling terrible, stamping for the exit. To his surprise, she was waiting for him, half dressed, crumpled on a beanbag by the door, eyes red.

'Don't hate me.'

'I don't,' he grunted, not slowing down, and meant it.

'Don't be disappointed with me, then.'

Perceptive.

He stopped with his hand on the door and turned, not knowing what to say but feeling, instinctively, it had to be said. He roved the room for inspiration, and it dawned on him slowly that the clinic was too tidy: chairs and beanbags in their neat circle, equipment stowed away, incense stink clinging like a ghost. He figured it out.

'Lying's just what you do.' He shrugged. 'Can't blame you for it. You can't help it.'

'That's not true. That's not—'

'Course it is. Look.' He slapped a hand against a poster on the wall, one among dozens. 'You put 'em back up.'

'So?'

'So you never told Glass, did you? Last night, your big confession? Your brand-new start.'

She hid her face.

'You went through the bloody paces. Regressions, writing notes . . . Unascended fucking Master, all that. Same as every week.'

'I couldn't tell him!' It was almost a howl. 'His face! He would've been so . . .' She ran out of words, then rallied with a choke. 'It's the only thing I'm *good* at,' she whispered.

'Like I said. Can't help yourself.'

He turned back for the door.

'The letters!' she shouted, urgent. 'I couldn't tell the cops! I *had* to send them!'

Another doorway pause, another desperate burst of attention-gravity sucking at his back. 'Why?'

'It's . . . it's Karl.'

Yes.

He felt himself turn again, arms crossing. 'Listening.'

'He . . . *oh god* . . .' She fought herself, eyes sidling for an escape, until at last her shoulders slumped, her neck craned, and defeat settled on to her. 'I *told* you he hated Glass. Didn't I?'

'Yeah.'

'Well, there's more. At the . . . at the trial. Mum took me, the first day.'

'This was after the thing in Soho? When Karl killed that bloke?'

'*Accidentally*. Yes.'

Shaper shrugged, tasting the man's sickly little voice like psychic reflux. '*Truth is,*' he'd said, '*I probably would've done him anyway, given the chance . . .*'

'It was during the opening statements,' Mary murmured. 'Glass was a character witness. Mum's idea.'

'Karl wasn't happy?'

'No, but . . . I mean, so what? Glass said all the right things.

SIMON SPURRIER

"He's a nice boy, wouldn't hurt a fly," all that. Then he got kind of . . . eccentric. You know how he can be. He started saying Karl had "the Sight". Saying he had . . . abilities. "Too important to lock away," he said.' Mary sighed. 'His idea of an alibi, I suppose. He meant well . . .'

'But it didn't go down too well in court?'

'No.'

Shaper imagined some ruddy-faced judge, wobbling his jowls in outrage at Glass's airy-fairy nonsense.

'Anyway, in all the commotion Karl stands up and starts screaming. Says he hates Glass. Blames him for everything. Doesn't want his help. Hates Mum, hates them all. Keeps shouting, "It's all bullshit!" And right when the judge's got everything back under control and there's quiet again, Karl points up at Glass –' Mary acted the part, aiming a sinister finger at Shaper – 'and he says, "I'll kill you."'

Mary blinked as if returning to herself. She broke the eye contact and released Shaper to whistle under his breath, a long, descending tone, like a bomb from a blue sky.

The acid, he remembered, fuzzy with uncertainty. *Karl was high when he got in the fight.*

Glass and co. were making the fucking stuff.

Grounds enough for a lunatic's grudge?

'So the case gets adjourned for the day.' Mary shrugged. 'Karl gets fined a couple hundred quid for contempt – I think Glass paid it, actually – and Mum wouldn't let me go back to watch the next day. Actually that was . . . that was the last time I ever saw Karl.'

'And your mum never told you he got off, at the end?'

She shook her head, still pained by the secret, then made a show of waving it away. 'Anyway, that's not the point.'

'What is?' Shaper's eye was drawn back to the posters on the wall, finding with a dull inevitability yet another chakra diagram

252

in the centre, and counting up the coloured blobs like an abstract death toll.

'Come on, Dan, think about it. Suddenly all Glass's mates are getting bumped off and here's me knowing the connection, calling the cops like a good girl. What's the first thing they do when they link it to Glass?'

Aha.

'They look back at his history,' Shaper mumbled, pennies dropping like mortars. 'And they pay Karl a visit.'

'So I . . . I sent the letters instead. To warn him, y'know?'

'Why not just tell him?'

A bitter sneer. 'You think Sandra would've let him spend all that money, hiring help, on my say? No, I had to frighten him. And I couldn't contact any of the others – I've no idea who they are. Just the faces . . . But the idea of someone going round and . . . hurting him. Hurting Glass . . .' She covered her face.

Intolerable.

'So I warned him. And he hired you.'

She made it sound like fate. Like, so that's OK, then.

Shaper sighed. 'And Karl gets left to do what he wants?'

'He's my brother.'

'So?'

'So . . . Look, I was so sure, OK? There was no way he was involved.'

Shaper fidgeted, awkward at the certainty. He reminded himself he'd had siblings once, of a kind. Phyllis and Dave Coram, the family he'd lied for and cheated for and done a thousand and one hideous, bloody, soul-scarring things for. Not because they'd deserved his help, but because the notion of *not* helping them – *family!* – was more wretched than the acts he'd committed in their name.

Then they turned their fucking backs anyway.

Mary knew none of it. Didn't even seem aware of Shaper any

more, mumbling to herself in some insular little world of unconvincing self-justification.

'Karl was always so gentle. Soppy idiot. Oh, he . . . he got cross now and then, shouted and stamped. But he never *did* anything. Never hurt anyone. He wouldn't! So I had to protect him.' She seemed to notice Shaper again, shaking her head. 'But the cops wouldn't see it like that, not after one look at his record. So I . . . I thought I was doing the right thing.'

'What about now?'

She wiped at more tears and dropped her eyes on to the phone, face scrunched with fear. Like a stink rising off her.

Not an act.

(Probably.)

'Now? I don't know,' she sobbed. 'He sounded so *angry.* So *sick!*'

'So he really did call last night?'

'Yes! I'm not lying about that!'

She was crying out of control now. Shaper held himself back, refusing to go to her, knowing in the sweaty pits of his soul that for him to stand in judgement was the height of hypocrisy. But unable to overcome his pride all the same.

'I need to think,' he said, toneless. 'You should consider going somewhere safer.'

'What?' She frowned through the tears. 'No . . . No, Karl wouldn't do anything to hurt m—'

'No?' He pointed at the chakra chart, thin-lipped. 'I'll be honest, Mary, I haven't a fucking clue why matey's working his way up this thing. Not known for their logical motives, your basic nutcase. I don't know if it's Karl, or Tommy bloody Boyle—'

'Who?'

'Or whoever. But it's someone. And people are dying, Mary. And this fucker's collecting bits along the way.' He tapped dispassionately at the sixth symbol on the chart, an indigo triangle winged by a two-petalled flower.

Ajna, the label read. The Third Eye.

'This one's your mother's, right?'

'But. But she's—'

'Yeah. She is. So who'd be a decent replacement, eh? Who's been playing at clair-fucking-voyancy for years?' He narrowed his eyes, feeling cruel. 'Who's always been second best?'

Mary just gaped.

Chapter Twenty-four

His brain whooped like a howler monkey all the way across London. Gyrating on an uncertain axis, it worried at the details of the case like a nail at a fresh wound, chewing throughout on the unfamiliar gristle of emotional entanglement.

In the end Mary had categorically refused to leave the clinic, flatly denying she was in any danger, and he'd left her to sniff and eye-wipe without further affection.

He'd regretted it almost instantly.

Where, he wondered – wishing he'd stayed longer, said something else, done things differently – did this leave them?

Was there a 'them'? Would she contact him? Should he contact her? Why did . . .

And so on.

And all along, buried like a code in the confusion, a deeper anxiety.

What else are you lying about, Mary Devon?

Still, the drizzle had stopped at least, and by the time he arrived at Glass's house to ferry the old man, along with his new shadow Vince (baggy-eyed from a night 'on patrol') out to the countryside, Shaper found he'd achieved a sort of muddled Zen, accepting it would be pointless to keep agonising over unsolvable uncertainties.

i.e: *Women.*

i.e: *Liars.*

i.e: *Women liars, Dannyboy, you're falling for like a pilotless plane.*

And then Glass was beside him anyway, warm and distracting and reassuringly eccentric, and suddenly all the dangers of romantic turbulence seemed rinsed away. They spent the journey discussing tropical fish (left, he was assured, with electric feed timers), *The Archers*, the laxative effects of coconut milk and the paradoxical nature of sublime truth. Or rather, the old man 'discussed' them, Shaper simply made interested *oom* noises and tried not to let Vince's snoring ruin the soothing prattle. Glass seemed positively buoyant, citing an especially productive regression meeting under Mary's direction ('I was an advisory envoy at the palace of Siddhartha Gautama!') and cheerfully noting the lack of a letter in his postbox that morning. Shaper didn't have the heart to puncture either mood bubble, and gently steered things away from the case.

Even dosed up, even more rested – physically, at least – than he'd felt in days, still the Sickness was teasing him with stealthy peripheral flickers of that same, strange aura: streaming white and violet from the passenger seat. Smoothing away every sharp edge, every fear. By the time they arrived at Thornhill – greeting Sandra, saying hello to Freddie, carrying Glass's luggage to his room and finally sitting down for a nice cuppa – Shaper was feeling thoroughly at ease with the world, noticing that even his shakes were almost gone. It seemed peculiar that Glass could effect such a change in him, if indeed Glass's influence it was, yet couldn't cure his own quivering, quaking frailty, which seemed to worsen the more genial he became. It was as if whatever beneficial effect he exerted on Shaper was a finite resource, some deep, healing radiation, and the more he poured into the world, the less he retained for hims—

Hold it.

Shaper scowled at the gloomy reflection in his teacup, batting away the soppy thoughts with a mental chorus of *New Age bollocks! New Age bollocks!* He shunted back into 'job mode' on cue, deciding his dignity would be imperilled by any further idle pondering, and shot Glass a thoughtful smile.

'Let's go for a stroll, eh?'

'Echo!' the old man shouted, grinning like a schoolboy.

His voice boomeranged back with a sepulchral resonance, making him giggle, and he waddled excitedly into the gloom, stick clicking.

The cellars. *Again.*

It was something Shaper had been planning since his own creepy moment in the dark: plunging Glass back among the relics of a past he claimed to have forgotten. Shaper hoped it might dust a few cobwebs off the entombed history of the man's mind, triggering a useful memory or two, but as he shuffled after his employer with a nervous lip lick, hurrying to keep the wrinkled face in sight, he conceded to himself his second, grubbier goal. If he could only watch Glass's ploughed little expression close enough, perhaps he might discern some telltale sign that the man's clean and abrupt memory loss was exactly what, logic demanded, it had to be: a convenient fraud.

You suspicious shit, Dannyboy.

But no. Glass betrayed not a glimmer of familiarity, and even when he poked among the glossy detritus of the lab, his simple, guileless eyes underlined his confusion with unmistakable honesty.

'What's all this, then?' he said.

You're an acid merchant, mate. A kid off his tits on your product killed a bloke in Soho.

Again, he didn't have the heart to tell him, and again bridled at the weird risk of digging up too much truth by mistake.

Maybe you're not as perfect as all that, eh?

He loathed the thought on instinct, even as he felt inwardly urged on to hunt answers, to settle the matter. For better or worse.

At any rate, the old man seemed positively enervated by the gloom of the tunnels, tapping into each newly opened abyss with walking stick brandished like a depth gauge – impatient for Shaper to reach the appropriate light switch – and his enthusiasm was infectious. He shuffled, chortling, through corridors without end and junk-cluttered side rooms without number. Once or twice Shaper tried, almost experimentally, to listen out for the horrid rustlings he'd caught the last time, or detect the faint movement of warm air. But in the face of Glass's cheery explorations – currently contained beneath a WWII Observer Corps helmet he'd found in a storeroom – any atmosphere of spookiness was swiftly annihilated.

Not that there weren't mysteries to be pondered, still. Even the huge bunch of keys Sandra had provided couldn't crack open several of the heavy doors, and at each inaccessible barrier Shaper was obliged to derail Glass's petulance by discovering other diversions nearby: a mouldering puppet theatre; a frog's skeleton; an eighties ghetto blaster with a selection of decaying tapes. At either extreme – delighted or distracted – it was clear the old man recognised none of it, frequently muttering, 'It all belongs to me?' as if he couldn't quite believe it. Before long Shaper got fed up with the whole thing and commanded an abort to the so-called 'stroll'.

'Probably just as well,' Glass said, brave amidst disappointment. 'I could use a nap.'

But as they turned for the stairs, Shaper saw the man pause in place, head turning, legs seeming to falter. For a second he feared Glass might fall, and as he lurched forward to help, he glanced sideways, following the ageless gaze.

It was the chair. The gnarled mahogany throne Shaper had

SIMON SPURRIER

noted before, still awaiting its royal occupant: alone and eerie in its recess.

Glass wasn't unsteady. He was transfixed.

'What?' Shaper said.

'I'm not . . . *mm.*' The old man's shaggy brows knotted. He looked suddenly exhausted, as if crippled by the effort of remembering, and Shaper felt wretched for silently willing him to *think, think, think . . .*

'What is it?'

Glass took an unsteady step towards it, as if caught in its gravity, and scowled deeper than Shaper had imagined him capable. He leaned slowly towards it, shoulders rising, head tilting to one side, mouth creaking open . . .

Then straightened with a dismissive huff. 'Ugly thing, that,' he said, shuffling for the stairs.

'Hang on – wait. You recognised it.'

'What? No.' Glass shook his head. 'No, I . . . I just thought it felt . . . *sad*. Why should a chair be sad?' He seemed thoughtful for a moment, as if infected by the same melancholy he'd detected, then shrugged out a careless, 'Silly old man, eh?' and hobbled off.

Alone now, Shaper slunk towards the chair almost furtively, listening to the cane tap away up the stairs. It was a dark and unlovable thing, but clearly sturdy. Thick, bevelled struts, carved with rolling foliage and varnished petals, took the strain above a wickerwork seat and latticed back. The dust was unbroken across it, and spiders had made homes in the gibbet crossbeams of its legs. Shaper ran his eyes up from their desiccated victims to the strange landscape of the armrests, scowling at an odd blemish behind the pommels on either tip. He shuffled closer still, feeling insanely like a trespasser in the item's nook, and bent to squint. They were screwplates, he saw; simple metal rings untidily affixed to the wood, rusting clasps clinging to each surface.

A chill treacled along his veins.

Strap buckles, he realised. Restraints.

Fascinated, he eased on to his knees and examined the pommels themselves: orb-like rests; smooth planets of swirling wood grain, whose undersides hid a starker topography. There the continental crusts were broken by short, violent scratches, as if torn apart by seismic convulsions, which sent a shudder through Shaper's body and flared up the spectral lunacy in his eyes. He fancied he could almost see into the static of time, like a magic-eye picture resolving from a meaningless hiss.

Just the Sickness, mate. Just the drugs, getting weaker by the hour. But still . . .

He imagined Glass and the group, tripping and chanting, clustered like courtiers around the hateful seat . . .

What did they do down here?

In the vision, a figure screamed and shook on the chair, arms pinioned, fingers bleeding as they splintered at the only surface they could reach, straining its neck with every fresh shriek of—

What? Terror? Anger? Pain?

Ecstasy?

What the fuck do a bunch of hippies need with a torture chair?

Something caught his eye, visible even through the ghost show: a jagged flake of creamy yellow, slicked in age-old dust, poking like a shard of shrapnel from the mahogany.

Fingernail.

He eased it out with care and stowed it in a pocket of the pill file, standing with a final shudder. With Glass gone, it was increasingly difficult to ignore how profoundly creepy the cellars had once more become. He coughed into a fist and made for the exit.

He found the others on the main stairs.

Sandra and Vince fretted around Glass as if he were made of his own namesake, the woman steadying him on one side, the brute lurking a step behind with a goalkeeper's stance, ostensibly to catch the old sod if he fell, more plausibly to ogle Sandra's arse as she went. It had been Vince's professional judgement that the mansion's most secure bedroom was a squat chamber on the first floor, so it seemed only fair he should be involved in the rigmarole of installing Glass therein. Shaper stood in the main hallway, unnoticed, and couldn't help grinning up at the whole clumsy, creaking arrangement.

And reading between the lines.

Like, for instance, when Vince 'accidentally' strayed too close and bumped against Sandra. Like the back and forth smirking, the soft blush on Sandra's cheeks, and a whole suite of unspoken gaze-fucking between the two.

Shaper rolled his eyes and hoped Glass wouldn't notice.

Glass noticed.

'You,' the old man grunted, pausing to point a trembling finger at Vince. 'Stop that.'

'Sir?'

'You know.'

Shaper frowned from below, softly surprised at the genuine annoyance in the frail voice.

'Anyway,' it went on, 'you're meant to be protecting me, not playing nursemaid.' Glass swept the whole debate away with a disapproving wave and, having reached the top, snatched back his stick. 'Tova's perfectly capable of all this, and *she*'s not a pervert.'

Sandra, looking away, happened to catch Shaper's eye: a shared moment of confusion and concern.

'Tova!' the old man yelled. 'Where's she got to? Tova! Get up here!'

'Dad?' Sandra took his hand. 'Tova's gone, Dad. You . . . you fired her.'

'What?'

'Don't you remember? The letter you sent her. It came yesterday.'

'Well . . . I . . .' He leaned against the banister as if over-exhausted by his own confusion. His creased face took on an aspect of such unbearable uncertainty that Shaper found himself climbing the stairs two at a time, already forming unfamiliar words of comfort.

It's all right, mate. I'm just the same. Forget me own head if it weren't screwed on.

'Fired her?' Glass muttered, pre-empting the sympathy. And then quite suddenly brightened, smile spreading. 'Yes, that's it. I remember. And quite right too – never did like her.'

And with that he pottered towards his room, swinging the door behind him.

Sandra hovered for a moment, worry infused with indecision, then strode in behind him with a lingering glance at Shaper. 'I'll just . . . He needs a hand sometimes.'

The two men lurked awkwardly outside, listening to Sandra's muffled voice – the same sweet tone she used with Freddie – through the door.

It didn't take Vince long to rage against the quiet.

'That bloke's fucking mental!' he hissed – too loud – stabbing a finger at the bedroom.

'Shh!'

'I mean it!'

'Fine, but keep it down!'

The brute waved a dismissive hand. 'Sod it, he's half deaf. I spent all evening saying everything three times.'

'Well, Sandra's bloody not.'

'Nobody can hear – you're paranoid. Anyway, it's nothing she don't think herself. He's mental.'

Shaper simmered down. 'There was no trouble, then?'

'You mean no ninja assassins in the night?' He scratched his balls distractedly. 'More's the pity. Would've been a lot more fucking interesting than tropical fish and Radio Four. And that notebook of his – *Je*-sus!'

'Yeah.'

'Three thousand years old! For fuck's sake!'

'I did tell you.'

' "Eccentric," you said. Not touched by the bleedin' moon.'

'All right . . .'

'And we went to this . . . this group thing. All these wankers fawnin' over him like he's bloody royalty, and all he does is talk bollocks for an hour. It's stupid.'

Shaper was on the verge of dumbly agreeing when an oblique little enquiry scampered up, intrigued at Vince's scathing tone.

'So you don't like him, then?'

'Aw, no, it's . . . it's not that.' The big man looked uncomfortable. 'I mean, he's definitely mad but . . . nah, he's all right. You sort of can't help wanting to . . . y'know . . .'

Help him.

'Yeah,' Shaper said. 'I know.'

Vince sniffed, clearly as uncomfortable at Glass's magnetic effect as Shaper, and quickly changed the subject. 'Anyway. I can see why you like her.'

'Who?'

'That Mary chick at the hippy fest. Blimey.'

'You're supposed to be gay.'

Vince's eyes bulged, an alarmed glance flicking at the bedroom door. A beefy hand dragged Shaper further down the hall. 'Keep it fucking down!'

Shaper hid his smirk. 'Thought you said no one could hear?'

'Look, gay or not, I'm allowed to . . . admire.'

'Long as that's all it is.'

'Meaning?'

'Meaning, mate, that half-deaf old git's had three thousand

years – ho ho ho – to collect cash, and right now a fat wad of it's earmarked for me. I won't have your bloody libido buggering things up.'

Vince went sly. 'Funny you should mention money, mate, 'cos the old boy did happen to say – just in passing, like – how much he's paying you.'

'Oh, here we go.'

'And it seems to me, given my central role in the ongoin' operation, that my own fee don't accurately represent the very real risks involved. If you catch my drift.'

'Loud and clear.'

'Well then.'

'Well then,' Shaper kept his voice honey-smooth, 'there's also the small matter of Talvir.'

Vince opened and closed his mouth. 'You . . . you stay out of that.'

'Very fond of you, that lad.'

'Just . . . you . . .'

'I mean, I wouldn't want him to find out about any funny business.' Shaper feigned indifference, inspecting his nails. 'Not for the sake of a few extra quid anyway. Wouldn't want to see him getting hurt, you know?' He silently added: *not so long as the little queen's doing me favours*.

'Bastard!' Vince croaked. 'You wouldn't!'

Shaper fixed him with a look, judging the banter over and the advantage unquestionably his. 'Just do your job, mate. And keep your cock in your keks.'

'Everything all right?' said Sandra, appearing beside them as if summoned from the abyss.

Shaper watched the titanic clash between anger and embarrassment on Vince's face, which peaked in a thoroughly entertaining sort of overwhelmed panic. The big bastard actually *blushed*.

'All fine,' he grunted. 'I'm . . . I'm off for a nap meself. Knackered.'

He stalked off, muttering every step.

Sandra watched him go. 'Is he all right?'

'Fine. How's your pa?'

'Oh, tired.' She lowered her head and assumed a businesslike expression. 'If you don't mind me asking, Mr Shaper, have you made any progress? All this worry is wearing him out.'

Shaper privately supposed all the running about in cellars probably hadn't helped either. The mental memory of those cloying corridors toppled a series of dominoes in his mind – the dark, the chair, the restraints, the fingernail – and before he knew it dumped him back into the crackling white noise of the last delusion: that writhing, seated figure, thrashing to escape.

'Progress?' he mumbled, finger thoughtlessly probing the pill file. 'Oh, yeah.'

The heaving body formed a face: sharp cheeks and sunken eyes appearing from the storm, as if trying them on for size.

'Listen, Sandra,' he said, shaking it away. 'Did Karl Devon ever come round here? In the old days, I mean.'

'Karl?'

Her reaction would have spoken volumes even if Shaper's senses hadn't been reeling: a crumple-faced discomfort masking deep, crawling revulsion. She couldn't have been more disgusted if he'd shat in his hand and thrown it at her, and he could almost see her brain diverting away into cold, impersonal disengagement.

'Sometimes, I suppose,' she monotoned. 'Once or twice.'

The armour briefly slipped, admitting a secret shudder, before slamming back. 'Why would you ask about him?'

'Oh, just wondered. You two must be about the same age . . .'

'He's a year older.' Flat, unemotional, cold.

'Right. And you're, uh . . . If you don't mind me asking . . .'

'Thirty.' She almost smiled, softening at his awkwardness, and he coughed into a fist with the decision to push it.

'Did you two ever fuck?' he blurted.

Instant ice.

He hastily backpedalled, hands flapping. 'I mean, your folks are down in the sunroom getting high, having orgies and all that . . . You two never . . . passed the time together? Sort of thing.'

'I hated him,' she hissed.

'And vice versa?'

'Does this really matter?'

'Might do.'

He watched her work her jaw then sigh – a deep reluctance valiantly overcome.

'Karl hated everyone. But, yes – since you ask. He was especially unhappy with me.'

'Why?'

'Jealousy. I told you before, I was seeing Fossey at the time. Karl hated that.'

Ah yes, the mysterious Mr Foster.

'So, OK, you're with Fossey. Karl's pissed off. I bet your dad wasn't too wild either, eh?' He remembered the old man's curious outburst on the stairs. 'His little princess, mucking about with a dealer? Especially since, hey, here's Karl instead. Nice boy, right? Your dad even said so in court. Much better suited . . .'

He left it hanging, a hook baited with a dozen random worms, an optimist's trap.

Sandra simply scoffed. 'For one, I was never *anyone*'s little princess, let alone Dad's. And two, he didn't disapprove of my relationships, whoever they were with, because I wasn't in the habit of telling him. All right?' She glared at Shaper as if she'd found him in the tread of her shoe. 'Is this an example of your investigative technique?' she tutted. 'Because I have to say, my father's paying you a lot more than you're worth if the best you can do is throw about silly scenarios until something sticks.'

Busted.

'No, I just—'

'You think Karl's involved in all this? Is that it?'

Balls deep, love.

'I don't know.' He tried to regroup, unbalanced by the sledgehammer of derision. 'What do you think?'

Sandra contemplated for a long time, that secret spark of revulsion still alive in her eye. 'Maybe. But I doubt it. He was a sick little worm, that's all.'

'He killed a bloke.'

'Oh, *please*. He slapped an idiot whose heart popped. I wouldn't credit him with the wit for anything more ... orchestrated.' She rubbed her hands as if rinsing them clean. 'Karl Devon was a sneak. A watcher. The sort of twitchy creature who reacts without thinking. He doesn't destroy things, Mr Shaper, he *takes* them.'

'So ... what? Did he ... watch you with Fossey? Is that it? Tell tales, maybe?'

She shook her head as if impatient, and it stole over Shaper that in her bristly, barricaded way, Sandra was trying to tell him something – or at least to steer him towards a revelation she daren't express herself.

'No.'

'Did he see you sleeping together, maybe?'

'*No.*' Irritation spiking now, every moment visibly weakening her faith in his flailing intuition.

'How can you be so sure?'

'Because I wasn't sleeping with *anyone*, Mr Shaper. I was fifteen, do you understand? Not a slut.'

'But . . .' *Try again.* 'Is that why you split up, then? You and Fossey? You weren't putting out?'

The indignation almost steamed out of her at that, fully eclipsing whatever ugly truth she was fidgeting to expose. 'That's none of your business!'

'It's just . . . You did say it didn't last long – you and him. And he wouldn't be the first bloke who dumped a schoolgirl because she wouldn't spread her legs . . .'

He thought she might storm off at that, or even punch him. But she clamped down on the frosty flames in her eyes and merely waggled a teacherly finger, lips bloodless. 'That's not what happened.'

'What, then?'

'Father intervened.'

'But you said you never discussed it w—'

'I know what I said! He just . . . he found out.'

Shaper held his tongue, recognising all too well that he'd wound her up to a manic tension, and needed only to let her unravel.

'There was . . . Something happened. Fossey got angry about it and we argued. He got . . . violent.' She looked away. 'I told you, he wasn't a nice person either.' She prowled from side to side, a steam-powered tiger, then suddenly stopped and forced a measure of calm, like mist falling across her face. Shaper almost gaped at the transformation, synaesthetic flickers frozen in place above her head.

'Dad rescued me,' she said, perversely serene. 'Heard the commotion and came bursting in. Threw Fossey out.'

She hugged herself and leaned against the wall, just waiting.

She's given you everything you need, idiot. Think!

His brain raced. Somehow he'd missed it, whatever kernel of truth this broken, repaired, strange woman was unable to say.

'You . . . you said something happened. Something that made Fossey angry. Was that to do with Karl?'

She trembled, eyes equine wide, lip curling, as if the language didn't exist to express how thick he must be to not get it, and how thoroughly she therefore despised him.

And at last – always late to the party – his brain shat a nagging chain of thought with an ugly *Aha!*

She's thirty now.

She was fifteen then . . .

'How . . . um . . . How old's Freddie, Sandra?'

She whispered it – fourteen and a bit, of course – but no voice came. Instead the words were carried on a bow wave of tears, all the anger and hate caving in on a chasm of misery. The delusional mesh of her defences, ever orbiting, dissolved like smoke, and the frightened rodent within drove her along the corridor with a moan.

She was pregnant. She was pregnant and Fossey found out.

He replayed her voice over and over, shivering deep in his bones.

'*The sort of twitchy little shit,*' she'd said, '*who reacts without thinking. He doesn't destroy things. He takes them.*'

Karl.

Karl, you bastard. What did you do?

And as he jumbled the ragged spew of epiphanies away, stowing it in a ball at the back of his skull to percolate in silence, he passed Glass's room and flicked a glance inside.

The old man was sitting upright in bed, facing the door, an image of confusion and sadness.

Half deaf my arse.

Chapter Twenty-five

He stopped at his flat on the way through town. His present shirt had reached its three-day limit and he scrabbled together something vaguely fresh to eat: a few lumps of fruit and nuts thieved from a stash earmarked for Ziggy. He did a quick stride around the place – neck prickling at the notion of intruders in the night, waxy fingerprints, breathy voices on the phone – but could find nothing out of place. He paused only to ram a small baggie into one pocket – a mischievous idea forming – and then . . .

Time to face the music, Dannyboy.

He bundled into the van and clanked into traffic.

DI Canton's unit was nominally based in Vauxhall, and for Shaper it held little to fear. The Serious Organised Crime Agency enjoyed a relationship of, if not quite cooperation with, then at least grudging tolerance towards his own murky, quasi-criminal world. It, after all, was the ocean in which the SOCA's prey swam, and the Mob-busters had sensibly realised they wouldn't catch sharks if they scared off all the sprats along the way. They'd reluctantly arrived at the heretical notion that a person could be a good guy, a useful resource and technically a criminal all at the same time, which is why it was so disastrously unfair that both the SOCA and Canton had precisely fuck all to do with Shaper's current errand.

Vile, blood-spattered lunatic killers were, apparently, the sole preserve of the CID, and in the present case Shaper's friend and protector hovered abstractly behind the sanctimonious pomp merchants at the helm. Canton's involvement began and ended with the appearance of the name Tommy Boyle in the case notes, and until it could be demonstrated convincingly that the deaths were irreparably linked to the missing enforcer – and thus to the Organised Crime scene – that was as far as the prim detective could poke his nose.

Today's replacement hard-arse was based in Brixton, a Lambeth Borough DI into whose territorial jurisdiction the first part of the investigation – the 'accidental' death of poor, bollock-splattered Kingsley the Cocker – had plunged. Shaper cruised the cop shop a couple of times just to get a feel for the place, and very nearly went straight back home.

Here be dragons.

Worse still was his lack of preparation. He should have spent the journey getting his story straight, fixing in mind a satisfactory explanation – in a way that utterly occluded all mention of George Glass, Mary Devon, or his own scabrous past – for how it was that he came to discover the violently murdered body of a semi-famous artist in a workshop in Limehouse, and then didn't call it in for twenty minutes.

Typically, his brain was refusing to cooperate.

Karl raped Sandra, it kept hissing. *Right? That* is *what she was saying?*

Karl raped Sandra, then Fossey got chatty with his fists when he found out she was pregnant.

Right?

He pulled up two streets away, eschewing the official car park with its forest of cameras and attendants, and walked the remainder slowly, every footstep another revolution of the grinding wheel.

So who was in the chair? And where the fuck does Tommy

*Boyle fit in? And what's with all the chakra bollocks? And . . .
and . . . and . . .*

He almost beat his hands against his temples: too many
variables, too many headaches. And worst of all the cruel
suspicion that there was already a solution packed inside,
obfuscated by too much irrelevance and too many layers of his
own contrary, curmudgeonly Sickness.

*The figure with coloured circles along its spine. The chink in the
curtains.*

The blue face.

The—

A slab-like hand slammed him, hard, against a wall.

He blinked up from the thought swamp far too slowly, and
before he'd even begun to react, an elbow was against his throat
and a purple-patched face filled his vision. For a second he
thought he was being mugged, and a shard of the old indignation,
thick with predatory arrogance, bolted up from the shuttered
doors of his memory. *Rob me? The Corams'll eat your eyes, you
little shit! Don't you know who I am!?*

But the voice was five years out of date, and it wasn't a
mugging.

'Hellos, Mister Daniel,' said BollockHead, face a blue/black
paint spill, arm crushing Shaper's larynx. 'Is good to be seeing
again.'

Shaper attempted to respond, gulping furiously, but could
manage only a strangled *uurhg*. He tried lifting his arms just in
case, but the pressure soared the instant he twitched.

'Not to move, yes?'

Right you are, boss.

For the first time since leaving the van he checked his
surroundings, eyes darting along a silent backstreet, slate-grey
sides of the cop shop compound tantalisingly near. He wondered
if his bruise-faced assailant even realised what the building was,

then decided it didn't much matter either way. Unless some bored helmet peered from the top floor during a tea break from crime, there'd be no help from that department.

As if sensing the prisoner's resignation, a second shape seeped from a nearby car – another jalopy, Shaper noted, annoyed that he hadn't watched for a tail – and began patting down his coat, leering.

Hi, BeanieHat.

'Well, well well,' the little man smirked, breath toxic. 'Fancy runnin' into *you* . . .'

'*Unnh.*'

'Mr Vicar asked us to come 'ave a word. Wants to know what's what. You've 'ad long enough, he says.'

'*Nnk.*'

'Loosen it up a bit, eh, Mik?'

The elbow stab withdrew a fraction. BollockHead's technicolour visage dipped across Shaper's frame, inspecting the point of contact. 'Is plenty loose! He can to talk.'

He can to gurgle, mate.

'Yh bys bhn *fllwing* muh?' he wheezed.

'We can to find you *wherever*!' BollockHead snarled, warming to the intimidator role. 'Can to follow like ghosts. You never know we there!'

Shaper missed the opportunity to look impressed, too busy choking. BeanieHat just scowled at his partner – muttering, 'I'll do the talkin', yeah?' – before jabbing the captive in the chest.

'So what's new, Dannyboy? Where's Boyle, eh? You promised results.'

'*Actlly* I nvr . . . nv . . .' He fluttered his eyes, unconsciousness imminent.

And the Oscar goes to . . .

'Loose it more, Mik. He sounds like bleedin' Gollum.'

'But is already not tight on h—'

'Just do it! He's no fuckin' good passed-out, is he?'

The elbow crept another millimetre, and Shaper turned up the 'woe is me' another notch, Adam's apple bobbing like a baseball.

'Don't know anything yet . . . No new inf—'

'Not fuckin' good enough!' BeanieHat tried his hand at a little explosive anger, finger still prodding. 'You tell me everythin' you fucking know!'

'Cn't . . . cn't *brthe* . . .'

He strained the muscles of his neck, feeling the blood ruddying his face

'Is bullshit!' BollockHead snarled. 'Am barely touchi—'

'Just let him breathe, fuck's sake! He's not going nowhere, is he?'

Another slight slackening, set to a chorus of Russian complaints. Shaper began to prepare himself, letting the latest dose of attention-tightening stims flow to the fore. Despite their sharpening shield, the Sickness flexed in agitation, sensing the coming storm. Harpoons of pain worked – almost gently – into his guts, and through the haze of bloody, bruise-toned distortion he barely cared that BeanieHat was talking again. For a second he became fascinated by the man's repugnant little face, by the single thread of spittle connecting his lips, by his squinting porcine eyes . . . then sideways, entranced now by the purple sprawl of BollockHead's nose, so close to his own that they became a blurred nebulae, galactic bonds of—

Concentrate, wanker.

Be ready.

Briefly, BeanieHat's words coalesced from the murk, '. . . that sweet bit of cunt up in Dalston, she's on the menu 'n' all . . .' before it happened.

Siren.

A distant howl of primal fear – a banshee's *fuck you* to the world – which rose from two streets' distance and pummelled directly on the criminal psyche, hurtling off to some who-gives-a-crap disturbance out in the shitty city.

Shaper had been waiting for it. The freelancers hadn't.

Their heads snapped round as if electrocuted. Already tensing to run – or at least to scream an instinctive protestation of innocence – it took them less than half a second to realise the danger was imagined, the cop car too distant; the sanctity of their ambush intact. But by then it was too late.

Shaper nutted BollockHead in the remnants of his nose, and laughed through the *squelch*. The man roared as if his brain was pulp – body collapsing, pink mist chasing him down – and Shaper shoved past him without pause, snatching at BeanieHat's outstretched fingers, still dumbly chest-prodding at empty air.

He snapped them like pencils. Didn't let go. Rammed the heel of his spare hand into the man's face before the first shriek was even released, knocking him backwards too and dislocating the crippled fingers with a nasty little *pop*.

Somewhere, BollockHead sobbed through slime.

Shaper ignored it and squatted beside BeanieHat: lip gashed, mouth filling with blood. In shock.

I'll do the talking.

'Stay away from Mary,' he said, calmer than he'd felt in days, 'or I will push maggots up your cock hole.'

They were still screaming, moaning, gurling as he walked away. The Sickness stroked his soul like a lover – tender for once; *approving* for once – and he shut it out with a grimace, shouting in the silence of his skull.

I didn't enjoy that.

I didn't enjoy that.

He paused outside the station to puke in a public bin, then ferreted for his pills like a drowning man, avoiding the I-don't-want-to-know stare of a cop going off duty.

I didn't enjoy that.
I didn't enjoy that!
(You fucking liar.)

The fat man scowled from a corner. The cute woman read the statement back.

'. . . *had been jogging for about ten minutes,*' she said, eyes tracing her own biro scrawl, '*when I stopped for a breather. I like to drive out to the docks to run, see, because the air is cleaner. Also, there are less people to laugh at the Lycra, you know what I mean? Anyway, I noticed a nearby door was open and, being a good citizen—*'

'Can you capitalise that, please?' Shaper cut in, slouching in his chair. 'G for Good, C for Citizen. Added gravity, y'know?'

Interview room seats were always fucking uncomfortable.

The WPC reached for the biro and amended the page, sighing. The fat guy in the corner – Jabba the Hutt's uglier, greasier cousin – just kept glaring.

'. . . *being a Good Citizen,*' the woman resumed, '*I decided to investigate. I stood at the doorway and shouted, "Hello." Nobody answered. I tried this several times. After a while I stepped inside to check everything was OK. It looked like an art gallery.*'

She had nice eyes, Shaper thought, but man's hands. And she blinked too much.

'*It was then that I saw the body. It was a black man I did not recognise. He looked like he was dead, and there was blood everywhere. I did not go nearer to check because I have this phobia of blood, you see. I completely wigged out, Jesus, and ran for it. It's totally an instinct. No thought involved. It's creepy. Oh fuck yes.*'

The WPC sighed again. He'd made sure she was thorough in transcribing. '*It wasn't until some time later – maybe twenty minutes – that I got my shit together. I didn't want to call 999 because I thought I might get in trouble for not ringing sooner, so I called this bloke I know from the pub who is a good guy but also a cop. His name is DI Canton. He said he would call it in to dispatch straight away, so that's all OK.'*

The fat man muttered under his breath.

'I hereby acknowledge that this statement is true and correct, and I make it in the belief that a person making a false statement in the circumstances is liable to the penalties of perjury.' The WPC gave him a questioning look.

'Perfect,' Shaper said.

'Sign here.' She passed the paper and watched him sign, wordlessly folded it away, and headed for the door. It shut like thunder.

'What,' said the Jabbalike, not moving, 'a load of festering shit.'

Shaper put his feet up on the table and grinned. It was, he couldn't help feeling, an inspired account. He'd even demonstrated jogging round the room at one point, just to prove he could. Wheezing notwithstanding, the WPC had looked totally impressed.

'Who're you, then?' he asked.

'Vehrman,' the Jabbalike growled, disconnecting from the wall and planting himself opposite Shaper.

'Got some ID? They say you should never trust a str—'

'Keep it up, Danny.' He had a voice like ice in a blender.

'Thank you, I shall. There's s'posed to be a number I can call, isn't there? So if I can just get your warrant ID, I'll—'

'Shut up.'

'But you said—'

'*Shut up.*'

Shaper feigned indignation, enjoying himself. 'Well, I can't be held responsible if you tell me to do one thing then when I do it you—'

'*Shut up!*' His face went red. Shaper cheerfully supposed this hadn't been on his script.

'Phobia of blood . . .' the Jabbalike spat, visibly simmering himself down. 'Is that right?'

'Can't stand the stuff.'

'Really.'

'Really.'

'You've got some on your face.'

(BollockHead. Whoops.)

'Ketchup. Late lunch.'

The cop craned forward, smiling like a cannon. 'You're a disgusting little fuck, Shaper, you know that?'

'If you say so.'

'I do. We know all about you here. Don't you worry about that.'

'I wasn't.'

'Lot of nasty shit swirlin' round you, Dan. Lot of water under the bridge.'

Shaper nodded, polite. The Jabbalike waved an airy hand.

'Reckon we could get a testimony or two, if we went digging. Old victims. Old enemies.'

'Could be.'

'Nothing major, of course.'

'Of course.'

'You're too clever for that.'

'Thanks.'

'Leave no stone unturned, right? Cover your tracks.'

'Very wise advice.'

'But maybe a testimony or two, yeah. Enough to make things difficult, I should say. Year or two inside, even.'

Shaper shrugged again.

'Course, multiple murders might stain your record a bit. Not sure if even your mates in SOCA could help you with *that*, eh?'

'I beg your pardon?'

'This "Tourist" thing.'

'What about it?'

'You're in it up to your cunt, sweetheart.'

Shaper feigned innocence, abruptly bored. 'Afraid you've confused me with someone. I just spent the last half-hour explaining all that, didn't I? Surprised you didn't catch it, stood right there.' He glanced round the room, theatrical. 'Speaking of which, I note that my lawyer isn't present, and now that I've done my civic duty and helped police with their inquiries, I believe I'll be fucking off.'

He started to stand. The Jabbalike reached into his jacket with a growl – '*Sit!*' – and produced a boxy little MP3 player with a jowl-wobbling sneer. Shaper sank back on to his seat just as the cop hit 'play', a sinking feeling bubbling his bowels.

'. . . *just callin' to say,*' a tinny tone declared, lousy with a comedy accent, '*oi've fahnd a bodaaaii . . .*'

It was unmistakably Shaper's voice.

Shit.

The doctor's corpse. The first fucked-up night. The phone in the park, the smeared pigeon, the too many fucking pills.

Shit.

'Who's that then?' said the Jabbalike, orgasmic.

'S-sounds like someone from Birmingham,' Shaper croaked. 'And now I should be off.'

He walked for the door just a little quicker than he'd intended.

'See you soon, sweetheart,' the blob called after.

He was scurrying along the hall – already planning his next chemical barrage – when Canton stepped from a side room and deftly steered him along an intersecting corridor.

'All right, Dan?'

'You saw all that, I suppose?'

Canton nodded, swiping an ID card at an electric door and

failing to notice Shaper's hesitation. Heading deeper into the dragon's lair was not a survival strategy he felt comfortable with.

'This is *balls*, mate,' he hissed, faceless blue figures wafting by. 'If fattie back there gets a voice expert to confirm that's me—'

'Then it's still not enough for an arrest. Relax.'

'But—'

'Look, Vehrman knows as well as I do you're more involved than you say. Difference is, the idea of basing his investigation on your "intelligence" – *ha*, sorry – makes him want to puke blood.'

'But not you?'

'Well. Not blood.'

'Funny.'

'Point is, he'll do anything to squeeze it out of you. Wants it all looking nice and neat on paper, doesn't he?' The pair descended a set of stairs, footsteps deadened by bland, wall-to-wall whiteness. 'Anyway, it's nobody's fault but your own. You can't go running about doing cop work and not tell the cops.'

'I told you.'

Canton shot him an as-if-that-counts look. 'You just better hope there's nothing else to link you to the crime scenes, or Vehrman goes from a pain in the arse to a menace.'

The knife. Shit.

'Or,' the cop smirked, 'you could save yourself a lot of bother by giving him – or, say, me – everything you know up front.'

'Bollocks.' *Nobody gets Glass.* 'Sorry.'

Canton shrugged, helpless but unsurprised, and Shaper mentally tightened the screws on his already-creaking psyche, silently adding a second option to get him the fuck out of trouble:

Find the killer, quick. Make it all go away before your brain dribbles out your nostrils.

'Fossey,' he blurted, the thought spewing up like a reflex. 'You were going to check him out.'

'Mm-hmm.' Canton turned along another corridor, not even bothering to check Shaper was following. 'Matthew Foster. Record as long as your arm.' Canton framed a significant look. 'Dangerous.'

An excited little light flashed on in Shaper's mind.

'Bloke starts out slow. Minor dealing, public disorder, six months in Holloway in ninety-three. Then mid-nineties he starts getting wacky. Bites off a tourist's ear in Leicester Square. Still on bail for that, he shows up in Green Park stark bollock naked. Rangers' report said he was catching pigeons and – get this – pulling off their heads. Then throwing the bodies at cyclists.'

'Nice.'

'Yeah. So he gets picked up. Screaming, shouting, the whole circus. Doesn't even make it to court.'

'Sectioned?'

'Quick as you like. Shuffled around a bit, various places. All of them rubber-stamp him a fucking loon – he's getting in fights, terrorising other patients, collecting hair and nails, all very weird. That is, up until—'

Don't tell me. 'This year?'

Canton had the grace to look apologetic. 'Actually, no. He's been out just over three.'

'Oh.' Shaper couldn't quite hide his disappointment. 'So why'd they let him go?'

'Very good question. See, at some point the doctors figure the problem isn't mental illness per se, but a bona-fide personality disorder. Psychopathy, most likely. But that's not a "medical" condition. Far as the shrinks are concerned, it's incurable.'

'So?'

'So this bloke's in a hospital, not a prison. You can't hold him captive if you can't fix him. Mental Health Act. So . . .' He waved a prompting hand.

Shaper gaped. 'They let him go?'

'Yup. Incredible, eh? Happens all the time, apparently.'

'That's . . .'

'Ridiculous, yeah.'

'No . . . no, it's *brilliant.*'

Canton stopped in his tracks. 'What?'

'Sorry, but come on! Fossey's perfect! Violent, nuttier than squirrel shit, plus the collecting thing . . . OK, the timing's a bit off – he's been knocking about for three years off the radar – but still . . .'

'Plus there's the link to Tommy Boyle,' Canton slyly muttered.

'You know about that?'

'Give me *some* credit, mate. I've spent the last five years poking through the Corams' rubbish. Foster was one of the dealers Tommy Boyle visited, day before he vanished.'

'Yeah, well . . .' Shaper rubbed his hands together. 'Like I said, perfect. Prime suspect material – gotta be. Did you pick him up?'

'Nope.'

'Why not?'

Canton paused at the head of a long corridor, lined by steel doors. It stank of bleach and fear, and two of the strip lights were blinking torturously: an instant headache. Canton looked thoughtful.

'Fossey's dead,' he said.

'*What?*'

'Vehrman sent some helmets round his flat.'

'You told Vehrman about this?'

'Couldn't very well not, could I?'

Shaper sighed, rubbing his temples. The lights seemed to be

flickering at some secret evil frequency, resonating with his own inner interference. 'Anyway . . .' he prompted.

'Yeah, so, Fossey's flat. Resettlement programme, place up in Harlesden. You know what they found?'

Shaper shook his head.

'Three fire crews and a smoking shell. Place went up sometime in the night. Arson, they think.'

Shaper sagged against a wall. He felt as if someone had given him a million quid then taken it away before the yacht brochure even arrived.

'He was inside?'

Canton nodded, setting off again at a funereal pace. 'Crispy-fried nugget. ID in his wallet.'

'Fuck.'

'It's not all bad.' Canton grinned, as if delivering a punchline he'd been prick-teasing all along. 'The helmets caught a lurker.'

'What?'

'Standard procedure for a dodgy fire: keep an eye on the crowd. Lot of arsonists like to watch.'

'So?'

Canton paused beside one of the doors and tapped a nail against the metal. 'So this numpty's standing there bold as brass, up to his elbows in soot. Sobbing.' He eased open the peephole. 'I'm dying to know who he is.'

Chapter Twenty-six

'Karl John Devon,' said DI Vehrman, leafing through a folder of notes. 'Age: thirty-one. History of violence. Dodged a murder charge, aged nineteen. Said some stupid things in court. Out of the country till recently, whereabouts unknown. No further record.' He placed the sheaf down and steepled podgy fingers, unnecessarily slow. 'Where'd you go, Karl?'

From the viewing room next door, Shaper pressed close to the mirror-glass window and watched the Jabbalike with a scowl. *Thinks he's being intimidating. Knobhead.*

Karl, across the table, conspicuously failed to look intimidated. He and the fat fuck glared at one another inside a carbon copy of the interview room where Shaper himself had sat just an hour before, albeit this time in a deeper bowel of the station. Huddled with Canton in a side room – cloying with the stink of concrete and mould – he was not enjoying his peek behind the scenes. He kept expecting to bump into some petty criminal acquaintance, recently arrested, and having to explain what he was doing drinking cheap coffee in the enemy HQ.

Canton, blissfully ignorant of his discomfort, slurped annoyingly and eyed Karl with wolfish interest. 'You know him?'

Ahahahah.

'No,' Shaper lied.

Through the mirror the sickly-faced freak simply stared and

said nothing. He looked, if anything, even more twisted and grotesque than when back at the pub: hair lank across his forehead, shoulders hunched and vulture-like, buried in a filthy dark hoodie. His eyes were so puffed and bloodshot that his irises seemed mere specks in a sea of ruddy red, and Shaper wondered if the effect was down to the sobbing Canton had reported, or – remembering the smackhead threads on the man's arms – a crash from a heavy score. Today the train tracks were hidden, thick sleeves covered in soot and filth, and Karl kept running slender fingers through the grime, staining pallid digits a smoky grey.

'Nothing to say for yourself, eh?' Vehrman sneered. In Shaper's voyeur chamber the Jabbalike's voice emerged – disorientatingly – from a speaker high above, creating the odd sensation that the fat arsehole was simultaneously in plain sight and poised to drop from above.

'Nothing to say for myself,' Karl echoed, voice oddly girlish. Shaper subconsciously shuffled away from the speaker, neck prickling.

'Funny-looking fucker,' Canton said beside him, flashing an odd grin. Shaper squinted at him, wary of the out-of-place smarm. 'Funny looking. Yeah . . .'

'Suppose his sister got the looks, eh?'

Shit.

'You bastard.' He aimed a finger of betrayal. 'You checked her out, didn't you? After the cafe!'

Canton smirked. 'Got one of the lads to tail her home. Checked her records.'

'That's *low*, man. That's—'

'Oh, spare me. If you're gonna play pic'n'mix with the info, you better believe I'll take what I can get.'

Shaper simmered for a moment, watching Karl blink and moisten his lips.

The query worked its way up from his feet, making him fidget, and when at last he sighed and turned back to Canton, the cop was already smiling, waiting.

'What's it say, then?' he grumbled. 'Her record?'

'Relax. Clean sheet. You're tupping a saint.'

A lying, deceptive, corrupted . . .

. . . saint.

'Right then.'

The speaker suddenly blared, making Shaper jump. 'What interests *me*,' Verhrman boomed, tilting forward in his chair, 'is why the sudden change in MO?'

Karl pouted. 'Don't understand.'

'Murder, mate. Thrill kills. Interesting topic.'

'Don't know anything about that.'

'Maybe you don't, maybe you don't. But I'll tell you this, we've got a certified loon down in the morgue, black like fuckin' charcoal. Mr Matthew Foster, Karl. Bloke's linked to some bad shit.' He gestured expansively at the mirror, though Karl's eyes didn't follow. 'See, when my colleague – he's just through there – told me a little shit like Fossey might be muddled up in this, I got kind of excited. Always nice, getting a new suspect. Got a little justice hard-on, I did.'

'Bullshit,' Canton whispered in the dark, like adding a secret footnote. 'He wanted to know where I'd got the name. Almost spat when I told him. "Inadmissible," he said. Fucking hypocrite.'

Shaper didn't return his friend's grin, silently appalled at how much Her Majesty's finest were hinging their efforts around the few crumbs he'd flicked their way.

In too deep.

On cue, the Sickness sprouted a crop of cobweb itches in the small of his back, making him fidget.

'Man like Fossey,' the Jabbalike was saying, 'history like

his . . . Well. It fits, don't it? Definite arrest material, that.' He curled a flabby lip. 'Then *you* went and killed him before I could even say hello.'

Karl shook his head. 'No.'

'Why would you do that, Karl?'

'I didn't. I wouldn't hurt him.'

'So you *did* know him?'

'Yes!'

'Good.' Vehrman settled back, leering. 'That's *progress*.'

Canton tutted. 'Smug prick.'

'So. Since you and the human barbecue downstairs were such good pals, Karl, maybe you can tell me about him. Like I said, I'm interested. Why the change in method?'

'I . . . don't know what you mean . . .'

'It's simple enough, mate. These murders, they start out pretty clever, yeah? Disguised as accidents, ain't they?'

'I don't—'

'Then see for yourself.'

The Jabbalike produced a set of photos like a hustler playing his ace, spreading them on the table. As the freak bent to see, the cop shot a triumphant smirk at the mirror, face declaring *behold my genius*.

'Does he know I'm in here?' Shaper mumbled, discreetly shaking a mischievous shiver from his left foot.

'Nope.' Canton sounded weary. 'That one was for me.'

'Departmental rivalry?'

'Nah, he's just a cunt. Thinks he's bloody Cracker. "Keep the suspect off balance." '

Through the window, Karl's eyes wormed across the photos, sweat beading his pallid skin. Cunt or not, Vehrman's technique appeared to be working.

Karl seemed to have stopped breathing. Slowly, his fingers traced with a disgusting sensuality across the gloss.

The gardener, Shaper imagined. *Crumpled in a light well, bones powdered below bunched skin . . .*

The gigolo: a mere red chaos, bisected by a steely track . . .

The businesswoman: sprawled among nettles, clothes shredded in a storm of blades . . .

Slowly, thoughtlessly, Karl jutted the tip of his tongue and hooked a pearl of sweat from the base of his nose. Shaper could feel the delusions flexing to life, hungry to swirl and sluice around the gargoyle next door.

Vehrman just kept leering. 'See?' he grunted. 'All nice and innocent. Accidents, muggings . . . But *then*, oh ho ho!'

He slapped down two more prints, repellently pleased with himself.

The doctor.

The artist.

Cut, opened, unzipped. Displayed.

Karl's body was shaking now, and Shaper blinked through the gathering distortions, trying to distinguish what sultry emotions were crumpling the sallow face. Horror? Revulsion? *Delight?*

'So what changed?' Vehrman grunted. 'Eh? Your mate Fossey, Karl, why'd he go all exhibitionist?'

'F-Fossey's not a killer,' Karl groaned, effort in every syllable. 'He wouldn't.'

'Is that so?'

'Yes.'

'Is that *right*, Karl?'

'Yes. I said.'

'Then maybe it's someone else, eh? Maybe you.'

'No.'

'Maybe – let's pretend – maybe you and Fossey done it all together.'

'No.'

'That why you had to get rid of him, Karl?'

'No!'

'Or maybe you just done it all yourself? Did he find out? Had to keep him quiet? Whoosh! Bonfire!'

'*No!*'

Canton whispered in the gloom, 'Man's gonna pop . . .'

'Or maybe, maybe it was *you* who found out? Decided to punish him all by yourself?'

'No!' Karl screamed, slamming hard on the table. 'It wasn't like that!'

Abrupt silence prowled the air. Shaper's blood buzzed. Next door Karl was on his feet, fists forming frustrated claws, cheeks pouring with sweat.

'Then maybe you can tell me what it was like, Karl,' Vehrman leered, waving him back down. 'Since you know so much, 'n' all.'

Karl slunk on to the seat slowly, eyes closed, mouth clenched.

And then transformed.

To Shaper's eyes it was like a flower ratcheting open. Like dead leaves peeling free, exposing iridescent petals of sabre sharpness to the world.

Karl stopped shaking and opened his eyes. The muscles of his face seemed to slacken and smooth, and only the thick rings under his eyes remained, like speckles on a pale orchid. It was as if he'd simply stepped out of himself, as if a switch had been thrown in some rust-clogged war room in his mind, and – now that the missiles were airborne – there was nothing to do but relax and wait.

He put Shaper in mind of a junkie taking an invisible hit.

'It's a simple matter of excitement,' he said, voice utterly changed.

Opposite him, Vehrman sat back with a scowl. Even Canton muttered a breathless, '*Whaaaat . . . ?*'

Shaper barely listened. In his senses the man effervesced with noxious colours and discordant screams: the Sickness reaching deep into his spine and twisting a tortured helix.

Vehrman was scrabbling to regroup. 'What d'you mean, excitement?'

'The compulsion becomes unbearable. One feels one has a . . . a mission . . . a righteous task . . . and to begin with that's enough. You do the job, you cover your tracks—'

'You're talking about murder?'

'But as time goes by you come to resent it. This . . . this perfect thing, this just cause . . . It's not right – is it? – that you can't share it with the world? It's not right they can't be *shown*.'

Watching, flesh writhing, Shaper was put in mind of Mary the first time they'd met: the clairvoyant skit, *channelling another energy* . . .

Karl, he decided, was a lot better at it than she was.

'Isn't it fair,' the man whispered, eyes rolling, 'to seek a little recognition? Hmm? To be celebrated! To display one's craft.' His shadowed eyes dipped once more to the photos, touching unctuously at the last two victims. 'To advertise in blood and bone. To be *proud*.'

He settled back into his seat, giving a limp little smile, and appeared to simply switch off. Shaper's senses responded in kind: settling to a slower, headachey dance, and beside him Canton breathed out in a rush, turning a bewildered face his way.

'Was that . . . was that a confession, just then?'

Shaper could only shrug.

Vehrman seemed just as confused, shifting in his seat. 'You admit it, then?'

'Admit what?' Karl scowled, voice back to its girlish lilt.

'The deaths, Karl. The fucking murders!'

The man mimed an astonished *oh*. 'I'm so sorry . . . I thought we were being hypothetical. *Obviously* I'm just guessing.

I mean . . . why else would someone change from . . . from *this*,'
he tapped at the first three pictures, then stroked the final two,
'to *this?*'

'He's fucking mental,' Shaper gurgled.

Vehrman re-pocketed the photographs with the air of a parent
dragging a child away from a stranger. 'Why did you kill Matthew
Foster?' he said, obviously unnerved.

'I didn't.'

'There's a smoking hole in Harlesden says you did.'

'I wouldn't hurt him.'

'Why?'

Karl shrugged. 'Fossey and I were in love.'

In the side room, Shaper traded an uncertain glance with his
friend.

Jealousy, he remembered Sandra saying. *I told you, I was seeing
Fossey at the time. Karl hated that.*

Shaper whispered an '*Ah*' under his breath. *Wrong end of the
stick, there.*

'What was the extent of your relationship?' Vehrman ploughed
on.

'We knew each other briefly. This would be . . . ninety-four,
ninety-five.'

Right before Sandra fell pregnant, Shaper quietly calculated.
Right before Fossey went crazy, and Glass lost his marbles, and
Boyle vanished, and . . . and . . .

And what the fuck happened back then?

'He was straight, more's the pity,' Karl shrugged. 'At least, he
was then.'

'What do you m—'

'I had to go away for a little while. It wouldn't've worked out
anyway, not at that stage in our lives.'

Vehrman rummaged through the file on the desk. ' "Go
away",' he echoed. 'That'd be "got locked up", would it? Some

shithole overseas, that's my bet. No records, right? What was it? Smuggling? Kiddy-fiddling?'

'Only dangerous people get locked up, officer. My mother . . . she was *helping* me.'

The bitterness and hate rang out in every clipped syllable, and Karl abruptly covered his face with a sigh. For a second Shaper felt a deep tug of sympathy for this mercurial, confused creature, then noticed with a start that those needle-blue eyes were peering through the gaps in his fingers – *like the chink in the curtains* – directly at the viewing mirror.

No. Worse:

Directly at him.

The freak's mouth stretched, a toxic sideways smirk, and in Shaper's eyes the clouds were back, the tumbling snow globe of distortion and filth spiralled up again, and coalesced little by little above the man's face . . .

And then Karl was relaxed again, smiling at Vehrman without a trace of malice, and Shaper couldn't tell if he'd imagined that awful gaze or not.

'We wrote, anyway,' Karl declared. 'Fossey and me. Back and forth. Such letters! That's how I know he loved me all along.'

'Then why start the fire?'

'What fire?'

'You know what fire.'

'Do I?'

'*Fine.* Those letters, we'd like to see them. Where are they?'

'Oh, I'm very sorry, I'm afraid that's not possible.'

'We're en route to a warrant already, pal. We'll be checking your home.'

'Please do.'

'So the letters aren't there, then?'

Karl's face split in a frog-like smile. 'I believe they may have recently gone up in smoke.'

Vehrman almost growled, and in the side room Canton made a dry little spitting sound: revolted. Shaper itched to be away, to sleep, to clean himself with wire wool: to vomit and vomit until all the drugs and Sickness and stress was gone.

Some hope.

'Karl Devon,' the Jabbalike suddenly said, face set. 'At this time I'm going to halt the interview, with a view to resuming in the company of a member of the Crown Prosecution Service. I shall be recommending, based on the evidence available to us, that . . .'

Shaper allowed the drone to fade away, bending all his attention on Karl's face. The man seemed to be barely listening either and as he sat back in his seat with a secret smile, the distortions boiled all the stronger: deep purples and blues emerging, engorging like blood-filled mosquitoes round the centre of his face.

Oh god . . .

'. . . nsidered opinion should be charged forthwith with the crime of murder, and . . .'

The colours iridesced, and no matter how much Shaper blinked and shook his head, no matter how deep he dug for the soothing chemical reservoir in his skull, the vision wouldn't dissolve, forming instead an awful, solid shape.

'. . . ulting in the death of one Matthew Foster of 23 Tubbs Mews, Harlesden . . .'

And there it was. Set like a crater into Karl's forehead, a bruise-coloured eye suppurated bloody tears and rolled, inexorably, to stare at Shaper.

His skin turned to ice. His legs locked in place and the gentle sound of Canton's voice – 'Let's go before Vehrman sees you, eh, or it'll be my bollocks' – faded to a cobwebbed nothing.

'Anyone you want to call?' the Jabbalike boomed through the speaker. 'A lawyer? Family member?'

The third eye burned through Shaper like fire.

'No,' Karl whispered. 'I have no family.'

Shaper fled.

Canton was decent enough to wait outside the toilets.

Just as well, Shaper thought, fingers shaking, washing down tablets – indeterminate, now; innumerable – with handfuls of tap water.

Re-upping in a cop shop: a new low.

He dared a second's glance at the mirror, noting that a muscle below his left eye had started to spasm. He hadn't even felt it.

He looked crazier than Karl.

Canton escorted him out.

Every footstep brought the promise of fresh air and freedom closer. In the sagging aftermath of the brain fuck – waiting for the meds to take effect (*any effect!*) – Shaper stalked through a world of faceless shades and cop-shadow shapes, glowering and suspicious. He stayed close to Canton.

Approaching the final door – soul crying for the daylight beyond – he spotted his companion's slight sideways glance: bespectacled eyes darting to an upward staircase and a sign marked Forensics Dept. He remembered the half-baked idea that had grabbed him back in the flat, and though it tortured him to delay his escape, he forced a mischievous smile.

'Just a minute,' he said.

'What?'

'She's up there, ain't she?'

Canton poker-faced in a flash. 'Who?'

'Your bit of fluff. What's-her-name . . . Nadia . . . Natalie . . . ?'

'Natasha.'

He smirked. 'That's the one.'

Canton crossed his arms, a cherry-red glow infecting his cheeks. 'So?'

'So how's it going, you and her? Still no good, eh?'

'That is none of your b—'

'I can help.'

The cop glowered, jaw working, then grabbed his lapels and yanked him into a quiet recess; human traffic flowed by beyond earshot. Out of sight, Canton's anger caved like cardboard. 'How?' he squeaked.

'It'll cost you. Just a little favour. Could help both of us in the long run. Ooh, *and* it'll give you a conversation-starter with the lovely lady into the bargain . . .'

Canton gave him a hateful glare. 'Expand.'

Shaper dug in his coat, chuckling. After a couple of pocket errors he clucked his tongue and produced a pair of strange objects.

In one hand, a tiny sliver of broken fingernail. 'Forensic analysis required,' he said. 'Very important.'

And in the other, a small baggie of brown powder. 'Instant irresistibility. Your wages of sin, sir.'

Three cheers for tiger cock.

Chapter Twenty-seven

The last remaining Tafil finished him off. He sank gratefully on to his futon in a candyfloss fog of false calm, pretending not to notice the blur-edged distortions obtusely refusing to dissipate, and even remembered to set an alarm on his mobile. An hour? he wondered. Hour and a half?

Fuck it. One hundred and twenty minutes – be a devil.

Karl, he reassured himself, festered in a cell. Game over.

He dreamed, of course. A hypnogogic clusterfuck of tortured fantasies: short-term memories bubbling with whimsical horrors and the ghastly ghosts of his past, all shot through with sick psychedelia.

Anna was there, he remembered that much afterwards. So too was Mary, and among the nonsense narratives and twisted traumas – a thousand beatings, a million menaces, a torrent of blood spilled and tortures presided over – he kept catching them giggling together, comparing notes.

At some point they were joined by George Glass and the Coram twins, all spiralling round to poke and prod, and he realised with sluggish logic they weren't interested in him at all, but in a chair of polished wood with leather straps behind his back. They gathered and honked, multiplying and changing, faces hidden, clothes lost beneath orange robes, and Shaper searched among them with rising panic, trying to find the people he knew and loved. None was interested, shoving him aside in their haste, grasping for the spiny seat and the figure in its chilly clasp.

A faceless man. A broken devil, fingers scrabbling themselves raw on the mess of the chair's pommels, writhing in pain and terror. The noises of it filled Shaper's world, lingering even as the dream faded and the figures accreted like oil on water.

Scritch . . . scritch . . . scritch.

Nails breaking, wood rasping. Voices chanting all at once, dying to silence.

And in a slick of sweat and toxicity, Shaper awoke – probably . . . *maybe* – back in his home, and realised with dawning horror that the scratching sound hadn't ended.

He drifted to the entrance as if disembodied. Around him the flat seemed colourless with fag smoke, a barcode of dying daylight puncturing the blinds. In the molten haze he was barely aware of having moved, until his hands were pressed to the inside of the door. The scratching continued, joined now by a deep nasal snuffling: damp, breathless, excited. Shaper's neck crawled.

The peephole glittered with distortion. Like some miniature kaleidoscope its inner surfaces tumbled with fire and blood, and he had to stop and breathe – to scowl and calm and blink and *think* – before the chaos faltered and he could gaze through unimpeded.

There was a demon in the hallway.

(Ohgodnopleasefuck . . .)

His breath died, body frozen.

It was a figure, he saw – more or less. Seething with noxious gases and abstract angles, its face shifted and burned, now a blue mask, now a balaclava, pale skin clammy in ragged slits, now a shield of televisual crackle.

(Keep it together! Breathe!)

The figure raked at the door, and Shaper almost recoiled from the eyehole, overcome at its closeness. But no, he couldn't move, couldn't look away, could barely even think. His last sliver of rationality grumbled its confusion in his skull – *Karl's in a cell! What the fuck?* – but the question which condensed in his mouth – 'Who *are* you?' – refused to be uttered. Frozen, in stasis, like the rest of him.

The figure slinked and dipped across its enclosed circle, and only when it briefly straightened did Shaper momentarily glimpse what it was carrying.

It was a withered light. A ghastly lantern of bony steeples and congealed crags, which made no sense to his eye – except to revolt it. One of its stodgy juttings was capped by a sickly flame, tracing exposure contrails across Shaper's slow vision.

A candle.

It was gone as soon as he'd seen it, dropping from the tunnel of his view, nudging with a soft scrape at the wood beside the handle.

And something *clicked* in the lock.

Shaper's body pulsed like a bomb blast. A thunderclap of fury shattered the ice in his arteries – the Sickness shrieking its outrage – and at last he could raise his arms, could hammer his fists hard against the door.

'I can *see* you, cunt!' he screamed, knuckles smashing, hinges drumming in sockets. 'Get away from here! Get the fuck away!'

The room raged around him. Colour swarmed back like a depth charge beneath his brain, quaking red and purple through the walls. Somewhere Ziggy raced in a blind panic across the floor – a flutter of bird hops and tail spines – and still Shaper pounded at the wood, hands aching, tumbling to his death through the cruel nonsense of hallucination.

Finally, exhausted, he dared a final glance through the peephole.

A black coil, like soot on the wind, was creeping down the stairs and round the corner.

And then only silence. The sound of his own breathing returning by degrees, and the rushing of blood in his ears. And . . .

A phone?

And Shaper awoke, lurching from the futon with a gasp, to the scream of his mobile ringing. It took him a long, long time to get his bearings.

It was dark outside, he saw. The alarm hadn't gone off when it was meant to and his head howled in indignation at its chemical vacuum. Ziggy, he saw, was still hiding under a chair. He shut his eyes and pretended to be calm, bundling it all back into place, and jabbed a key on the handset.

It was Canton.

'Thought you might want to know,' the cop said. 'We had to let Karl go.'

Shaper stared at the inside of the door and felt the ache in his fists.

No shit, he thought.

'I'll call you back,' he said, reaching for his coat.

He drove too fast, horns dopplering around him, dosed so violently on introspection-murdering uppers that the comforts of the usual autopilot seemed a galaxy away. He snuck through traffic lights and thumped over speed bumps, a pounding in his chest and forehead like a great cathartic drum.

'Tell me everything,' he snapped at his mobile.

'Post-charge bail,' said Canton. 'Home curfew pending further inquiries.'

'How the fuck did he pull *that*?'

'Crown-appointed lawyer. Got the little creep saying he was first on the scene of the fire – trying to help survivors. Thus the soot.'

'Bollocks.'

'Obviously. But we've nothing else to hold him on.'

Shaper ignored his wing mirror *cluck-clucking* at parked cars, and wondered at the hint of breathless excitement in Canton's tone.

'Nothing to hold him on?' he spat. 'It's a fucking murder charge! You can't just turf him out and—'

'That's just it. It's not murder.'

'What?'

'Look, we've done some prelim tests on the body in Harlesden. It's been dead years, mate. All mangled, fucked-up. Barely had any meat on it *before* the blaze. "Recently exhumed." That's, uh . . . that's what Natasha thinks.' The cop gave a weird little sigh of satisfaction.

'Natasha,' Shaper deadpanned, getting it.

'Dan, what the fuck's in that stuff you gave me?' The cop's voice went high. 'She can't keep her hands off me! Just cornered me in the evidence locker and—'

'Canton.' Shaper dodged a couple of kids on a zebra crossing, sighing. *Hooray for simple, reciprocal sexual shenanigans.* 'Canton, listen.'

'This thing she does with her tongue, *Jesus*, and—'

'Canton! The fucking body!'

'Oh. Yeah . . . Well, it's not murder, is it, if you just set fire to someone already dead? And like I said, there's no guarantee Karl even did that.'

'So who's the stiff?'

'We're still assuming it's Foster, for now. Explains how he's stayed out of trouble the last few years, anyway. Natasha's doing DNA checks to confirm.' The voice went quiet. 'She'll have a go at your fingernail too, by the way. But don't get your hopes up, the database ain't exactly exhaustive.'

'Right.' Shaper groped for the kill key, ready to sever contact. 'Thanks.'

'Uh, mate? There was something a bit weird . . .'

His finger paused.

'The body . . . There's, ah . . . Well. It's lacking a few bits.'

'Bits?'

'Yeah. I mean, if it's been buried all along, like Natasha thinks, you'd expect some . . . some loss of mass. But this?'

'What's missing?'

'Soft parts mostly. Eyes, tongue – things like that.' Canton coughed. 'And half an arm, mate. It's missing half an arm.'

Cogs meshed in Shaper's brain, booming with contact.

A candle, fluttering in the night. A waxy smudge . . .

A crow, pecking at tallow.

Shit.

'Did Karl say anything when he left?' he croaked, hands tight on the wheel.

'No. He asked a squad car to drop him at his sister's place, and—'

'You what?' Shaper's blood dropped another degree. 'But she's ex-directory! Her address isn't on the—'

'Hello-o? *Cop* here.'

'Tell me you didn't take him there.' He gunned the car faster, heart on fire. 'Canton! Tell me!'

'Nah. We looked it up, gave her a ring. No answer. Anyway, Vehrman wasn't about to spaff any more resources on the bloke. Waste of time, far as he's concerned, and all thanks to you. Sent him home in a taxi.'

'But Karl knows Mary's address now?'

'So? She's his sister.'

Next on the list, he thought. Ajna, the clairvoyant.

'Is someone watching him?'

'Home curfew, eight till eight. Electronic tag. He's not going anywhere.'

'But is someone *actually watching him*?'

302

'Shaper, we can't waste resources like that.' The detective was starting to sound stroppy. 'We've got nothing on the bloke except a maybe-connection to a fire, which is maybe connected to Fossey, and all of it based solely on *your* bloody say-so.'

'But—'

'Vehrman's already talking about bringing you in for obstruction, mate. We're not bloody monkeys, here – and you're not the organ grinder.'

'Canton, please—'

'Karl's just a creepy sod on the dole, all right? Let it go. And leave it to us.'

But it's him!

He's opened doors! He's carried bodies in and out of murder scenes like a fucking ghost, Canton, and you think an electric tag's going to stop him?

'It's him,' Shaper whispered. 'It just *is*, all right?'

It doesn't need to be more complicated than that. There don't need to be twists and fucking turns. It doesn't need to be Hollywood!

He killed the line before Canton could reply and let the night blur past him. Somewhere near Canonbury, when the tension was too much to bear and the Sickness was threatening to cripple even his ability to see where he was going, he groped for the phone again and speed-dialled Mary.

It rang far, far too long. He mumbled and sweated, and squinted through the lights and urban murk to make out the coloured façade of the clinic far ahead.

Don't let him have beaten me again.

Don't let him have beaten me again.

Don't let—

The phone answered. 'Yeah?'

Mary's voice. *Ohthankfuck.*

'It's me. You OK?'

'Dan?' She sounded surprised. 'I didn't think you'd call.'

'Are you at home?'

'What? Yes.'

'Alone?'

'Yeah.'

A horn blared past. He ignored it. 'Mary, listen—'

'No, please,' she said. 'I need to . . . Look, I wanted to say . . . I'm sorry I lied. I'm sorry for everything. I want us to be honest with each other from n—'

'Mary, shut up.'

'What?'

'I need you to pack a bag.'

'What?'

'I need you to get out of there, Mary. It turns out I'm sort of into you, and I'd quite like you not to die.'

'But—'

'Now, Mary.'

He sped past the clinic and didn't slow down, heading east and north, to beg help from the devil.

Chapter Twenty-eight

Maude Coram had put on weight.

Like some vast dollop of raspberry ice cream, scooped on to a white sofa then neglected to soften and slump, she bulged with a fruity corpulence. Draped in a pink bathrobe like a fluffy hillock, she passed the time – waiting for Phyllis and Dave – by clutching at her cherished corgi and indelicately munching pork scratchings. Every bite, every crackling retort of her jaw, was like a shotgun to Shaper's concentration. Sitting opposite her, fidgeting, he breathed as calmly as he could and fought to soothe the Sickness.

Here, in this place – in her company – it *yearned* to explode through his psyche.

'So . . .' he managed, adrenaline still shrieking from the warp-speed journey. 'How've you been?'

The woman blinked slowly, never looking away, and bit down on another rind.

(Wickerwork in a grinder.)

From a corner behind Shaper's back, like a goblin haunting a shadow, Max Vicar giggled in the silence.

'I see,' Shaper mumbled, neck prickling. 'Well, OK then.'

When the grinning monster had first led him in, five minutes before, the she-witch who haunted his heart was engrossed in a recorded episode of *EastEnders* on a plasma TV the size of Wales. At his arrival she'd switched it off without a word, turned solemnly to face him, and had been simply staring – with that special unreadability reserved for the faces of the morbidly obese – ever since.

And chewing.

(Roaches underfoot.)

'It's, ah . . . It's been a while, eh?' he tried, diverting his bottomless gulfs of anger and hate towards an unlikely nervous friendliness. Something, he was sure, was transposing the moisture from his mouth on to his forehead.

Maude said nothing. Didn't move at all, except to shudder the first of her several chins up and down.

(Trees splintering in deserted forests.)

(Bubble wrap in a mangle.)

(Sheet-ice shifting in a thaw.)

Vicar giggled again. Shaper gave up on chit-chat and wormed shaking fingers inside his pocket, thumb eagerly tracing along the pill-file zip. He found himself abstractly annoyed that Maude was doing the sulking and *he* was making the effort.

I'm the one who got hurt, bitch!

Ma Coram, he remembered, simply had that effect on people.

—scronch—

(Jackal jaws on baby bones.)

In a certain light this blobby matriarch was sure to put the beholder in mind of nothing so much as a flamboyant cream pastry: all indulgence and sugar with no hard edges. Where Phyllis had found her place in the underworld by emulating the machismo around her, her mother had pushed so far in the opposite direction she'd become almost a caricature of herself: a frilly-edged nuke of pinkness and pearls. Shaper knew only too well it, too, was an illusion, an archetype she'd spent years cultivating. She presented herself as a woman quick to give affection, easily wounded, impossible to resent, and all of it packaged in a disarming air of silky helplessness and enough scent to confuse a *musth*ing elephant.

—*scronch*—

A big, fat lie.

Over the years, lest he forget, Shaper had seen, planned and committed atrocities without number, all at the order of this blush-faced blancmange. He'd observed her enemies so fooled by the act that when the sword fell – when the veil was whipped away and the knife slipped between trusting ribs – they refused to believe the truth with their dying breaths.

'Isn't she lovely . . .'

No, she's fucking not.

Another pork scratching vanished into the maw with a planet-shattering crunch, timed to a lazy-cat blink.

At least today she wasn't bothering with the act, sweeping aside the doughy dearie and letting the bulldog out to snarl. A small mercy, that; a simpler sort of menace. Not that it changed Shaper's bubbling perceptions of her, shuddering now with arterial reds and pestilent purples, set to the strains of discordant fiddles. It was all he could do to share her oxygen without vomiting, and his thumbnail gathered fresh urgency on the zip of the pill file.

Bitch. Traitor.

(I miss you.)

Fidgeting under the laser inspection, he desperately sought distractions, twisting to peer out of the window and avoiding Vicar's stare. BeanieHat and BollockHead were sulkily sharing a cigarette in the drizzle, one with a fist laced in plaster, the other's face swaddled in a bandage like a whole-head condom. They'd studiously avoided eye contact when he'd arrived and, watching them now – doing their best to keep their backs to the window – it was hard not to smirk.

'Fuck you grinning at?' a voice snarled.

The Coram twins blundered in with typically bad timing, crossing the path of Shaper's smarm. He let his face drop, guilty.

Dave splashed robustly on to an armchair like a rugby prop hitting a tackle pad, nodding at Maude and ditching a landslide of scatter pillows on the floor. Shaper eyed his purple-and-maroon suit and determinedly didn't mention Batman villains. Phyll settled rather more quietly beside her mother, wiry knees and elbows held in, mantis-like. The corgi glared balefully and farted.

With the room at last achieving a *Jackanory* air of ripeness – *if you're sitting comfortably, let the threatening begin* – Dave finally met Shaper's eyes.

'On the phone,' he said, 'you mentioned you had a name.'

Shaper, ever the good boy, had called ahead.

Eight eyes bored into his brain. Three mouths set and unsmiling, one smirking like a barracuda at the back of his head. *Happy fucking families.*

In the domes of his skull the pestilent pall of memories – seething, repressed, unvisited – flapped in the murk like a deep-sea beast. The Corams simply stared, filling his world with serpents of contamination and echoes of spilled blood, radiating impatience.

Let them wait.

It had all started, Shaper supposed, with his own mother. Whatever nicotine-stained affection existed between them had turned to ire and ice long before his father died – mashed in a defective paper mill, of all things – and merely mutated thereafter via resentment and rage. She hadn't even pretended to mourn, revelling in the ability to at last entertain her lovers without artifice. When the compensation money came through, it was more than enough to pack Shaper off to boarding school – inject a little discipline, the logic went, into a troubled child – and the old cow had even squeezed out a make-up-clouded tear at the school gates, all for the benefit of whatever hard-eyed boyfriend had been on the scene at the time. Appropriately embarrassed in front of the floppy-haired snobs he'd be spending the next four years among, Shaper had turned his energies towards inventive delinquency, feeling somehow more real than his hawhawing classmates. They did their best to torment the pikey, the scally, but they could see the knuckles behind his eyes and, after a few enjoyable run-ins, left him alone. Entirely, completely, awfully.

And there, just when he'd needed them – every bit as out of place except defenceless with it, crying out for a defender – were the Corams. Scions to a dark crown, sobbing for their mummy at breaktime.

And now here they were, years later, all grown-up and glutted with power, trying to intimidate *him* for the second time in one long, freaky, frightful week. He almost sneered.

'You told her, then?' he said, eyes flitting between them. 'About the Boyle thing. Only I'm sure you said you weren't going to . . .'

Telltale tit, telltale tit . . .

The twins shifted in their seats. 'Obviously,' Phyll spat.

'A name,' Dave repeated.

Podgy little Maude just kept smiling, too clever to rise to it, mouth crunching away like shin bones under hammers.

Shaper sighed.

'Does the phrase "Hand of Glory" mean anything to you?' he said. He half expected Dave to waggle his jowls and launch into some blue belly laugh about 'this Korean chick I once knew', but the glares didn't falter.

'No.'

'Right. Well. It's a bit mad. I'm just saying, in advance. It won't make sense. Just bear in mind the world's full of crackpots who'll believe any old shit, and it'll all be fine.'

Scowl, scowl, scowl. He took a deep breath.

'It's a dead man's hand,' he said. 'A wicked man, specifically. It's coated in tallow – that's like wax made of animal fat – and turned into a candle.' He winced, listening to himself. 'It's magic.'

The leaflet had explained everything. The one he'd taken from the sunroom drawer, with the dramatic wizard on the front and enough daffy bullshit to drive a dynamo. 'Occult Technology.'

'Magic,' echoed Phyll, appropriately heavy-lidded.

'It freezes you where you stand, all right? Opens any door.' Shaper caught Phyllis's lips creaking open and pre-empted the dismissal, hoarding the initiative. 'That's just what these loonies believe, all right? I'm not saying it works.'

The waxy shape in the hallway . . . The wan light flickering . . .

His own blood, turning to ice.

'J-just bollocks, yeah?' He almost sounded convinced. 'Point is, right now a creepy little fucker's running around out there killing people, and . . . and he's got one of these things with him. I've seen it.'

(The crow at the docks, pecking at a snapped-off finger. And the prints. The smudged marks on victims' doors; a match in the cops' file . . .)

'It's made from the stolen fist of your mate Tommy Boyle.'

Thick, clotted-cream silence drowned the room. It took Shaper a moment – heart hammering in his mouth – to realise that even the crunching had stopped.

Slowly, in perfect union, the twins twisted their heads towards their mother.

Maude kept staring at Shaper, hand poised above the snack-pack; tongue clearing pig fat off gold-filled molars.

'I think I'll have a cuppa,' she said.

Her voice alone was enough to set off the Sickness, and

Shaper lurched half out of his seat to pre-empt its spasm, old habits honking in his muscles. *Two sugars, one shot of brandy.* 'I'll get it!' – before pausing, knees still bent, feeling like an idiot.

'*I'll* get it,' Phyllis corrected, voice low.

Vicar giggled in the gloom. Phyll unfolded and stalked out, pausing at the door with an oily, 'Don't go on without me, yeah?'

And then the silence again, and Shaper's fingers kneading at his pills.

And again the chewing.

This time Dave broke the tension, clearly as uncomfortable in the fetid atmosphere as Shaper. '*Harry Potter*,' he grunted, flashing a guarded smile.

'Pardon?'

'Your Hand of Glory whatsit. There's one in *Harry Potter*. I've read them all.'

Shaper felt oddly disarmed. 'Oh.'

Maude flicked eyes at her son. 'Shut up, you.'

The man grinned, childishly disobedient. 'We miss you, Dan.' And then settled back into the sofa, humming gently beneath his breath. Maude's eyes swiftly reaffixed to Shaper's.

And I miss you, he thought, suddenly overwhelmed. All of you.

He'd grown up a second time with the twins, thick as thieves among dusty libraries and frosty mornings at school. Persuading them to smoke, smuggling in porn, scribbling one-liners in soggy exercise books so they could defend themselves if he wasn't nearby. A second adolescence, built on the platform of a second family.

It was just odd weekends, at first, a guest chez Coram, in the lap of luxury. Then half-terms; holidays; even trips away with the whole clan. Christmas around the Coram tree. It wasn't as if his real mum gave a shit.

Perhaps, he conceded, there'd been a sliver of consciousness in the way he'd wheedled into their cell: a broken boy, lacking structure, borrowing one already formed, like a benign little cuckoo. But nothing sinister, no weird courtship of Maude's maternal instincts, no playing up his vulnerability. Probably, knowing her as he now did, she'd loved him so readily precisely because he wasn't vulnerable; because he was smarter than her own kids, more ruthless, more cynical, more capable. Better equipped to handle the world.

At least, to handle *her* world.

The odd jobs began the same week they sat their A levels. Little stuff, at first: driving things around, picking up, dropping off. Sometimes he worked alone, more often with the twins in the back, squabbling over music. Always a fifty note waiting when he got back to the ranch, an indulgent wink from Maude when the kids weren't watching, the secret thrill of favouritism. And the long, slow slide towards the thing he became.

And with every trusted request, every 'For your eyes only', every 'Show those idiots how it's done, eh, Dan?' he'd slipped another inch into the heart of the family.

The memories were abruptly blown clear, shattered by Phyllis's crockery-rattling return, a multicoloured tray gripped in tanned knuckles.

'So,' she said, presenting Maude with a steaming mug and firing Shaper a look. 'That's the best you've got, is it? Magic?'

'Listen, a little earlier today this bloke, this creepy little cunt, was caught burning a body.'

'I don't give a—'

'Boyle's body, Phyll. One hand missing. Tommy Boyle's fucking body, all right? You with me?'

The twins traded a slow look. Maude, silent as a grave, stirred sugar into her tea.

'Who is he, then?' Dave grunted. 'This bloke of yours.'

Shaper hesitated, instinctively withholding the ace.

'A name, mate. That's all we n—'

'Hang on, hang on.' Phyllis threw her brother a glare. 'This is bollocks. Why should this guy have Boyle's body?'

Shaper shrugged. 'I don't know. Not exactly. He's mental, for a start – that helps. He's got ties to one of the dealers Boyle went and saw in Camden on that last day. Maybe he knocked off Boyle in revenge for roughing up his mate? Fuck knows. It's sort of irrelevant, isn't it? Right now he's the only sod out there who knows any more than you do about what happened to Tommy Boyle.'

Phyll still wasn't biting.

'Tenuous,' she spat. 'And all this "magic" crap . . .' She glanced at Dave. 'You buy this?'

The big man just shrugged, and Shaper scratched at his forehead with a surge of impatience. *He's out there, you idiots!*

He's out there, and I don't know for sure that he did the things I'm saying, but he's as crazy as an otter's arse and the last thing he did was ask for his sister's address, and . . .

And I'm worried he might . . .

'It's bullshit,' Vicar trilled from behind him, uninvited. 'A fob-off.'

Shaper snapped. 'Yeah, it's bullshit. Right up till you actually *pay fucking attention*. There is a mentalist out there *right now*, OK, with the disembodied hand of the last man who saw your dad alive, leaving splodgy fucking fingerprints all over the place. Does anything else actually *matter*?'

Get him! Go fucking get him!

Get him before he gets her!

'Thing is . . .' Even big, gullible Dave sounded softly unconvinced. 'That don't necessarily connect this bloke to Dad, does it?'

Shaper reached for the nuke. 'You've been watching the news, right?'

Phyllis nodded. 'So?'

'String of nasty deaths, yeah? Bits being taken out. Stolen away.'

Across the room – just a flicker in the corner of Shaper's vision – Maude Coram closed her eyes and didn't reopen them.

She gets it.

'Now I seem to recall,' Shaper went on, 'someone cutting off your dad's tongue. Someone chopping it off, right out of his mouth, *snip*, just like that, and ramming it up th—'

'That'll do,' hissed Maude, white like an iceberg.

He took a sadistic pleasure in finishing the sentence.

'And ramming it up the exhaust of his car.'

Maude looked away.

Shaper, 1: Evil trog fiend, 0.

'And now,' he said, twisting the knife, 'there's a man chopping bits out of people just the same, and he's got a bit of your dad's Number Two goon right there in his pocket. I have no fucking idea how that's all come about, but I think if anyone's going to persuade the cunt to spill his guts – metaphorically speaking – that'd be you lot, no?'

It was a spurious link, he knew. The six dead, the paying gig, this insane chakric scheme centred round George Glass, it all had about it the ring of something carefully orchestrated, not the sleazy horror of Sam Coram's end. It didn't feel right to connect them so closely – but what else could he do?

Ajna, the clairvoyant. The Third Eye chakra; next on the list.

Mary.

No. No other option. He would eliminate Karl before allowing the slightest chance the nutter could reach her, and he'd do so with whatever tools he could muster. Up to and including the evil empire.

'What's his name?' Dave whispered.

And Shaper breathed, enjoying the tension despite the clock pounding inside him, the Sickness draping its froth-red visions across the room. It uncoiled around the three Corams – razor-tipped nuggets of a lost past, pox-ridden and broken-boned – and painted them in shades of sickly, strawberry gore.

Oh, my family . . .

It had all gone wrong, of course. With hindsight it was obvious that it was him who'd been seduced by Maude, not vice versa. She'd recognised in this bony little youth a companion, a teacher, a useful influence on her spawn, and had drawn him into the nest with all the art of a born manipulator.

The odd jobs had grown in complexity, as the footwork slowly metamorphosed into knuckle-work. 'Show the twins the ropes' became 'Cover for their fuck-ups'; then 'Keep an eye to make sure they do it right'; then 'Watch their backs but leave them to it', and finally 'Just do what they tell you, Dan, like a good little soldier'. Even when it at last became clear that he'd built his comfort on a lie, still he'd clung to it. Good at his job, quick with his wits, he'd been the perfect Number Two for years and years, jonesing for the winks and favouritisms of his younger days.

He'd split his fists every night. He'd snapped fingers and cut skin, broken faces and shattered lives. He'd watched junkies die on shit he'd sold, sent sobbing girls out to earn their keep, ruined businesses guilty of nothing more than inconvenience, and spread fear like an infection through his world. And all of it in the name of the empire he'd once called brother, sister, mother.

And little by little the doubts had trickled in: the regrets, the guilt. He'd started calling up his real mum, after years out of touch. Started getting nightmares, headaches, puking in secrecy and silence after every job.

And then he'd met Anna.

Beautiful Anna. Anna who thought before speaking. Anna who scratched his neck like a dog and whispered Romany nonsense – sexier than the clearest English smut – into his ears.

He'd met her and extended his family on instinct. He'd grasped like a maggot for the human warmth she represented, sinking hungry fingers into the promise of company, affection, structure.

And, like everything, he ruined it.

And when it all came crashing down, when the horrors overflowed and dumped him deep into madness, when all he needed was family – the Corams washed their hands of him.

And now, you evil old cow?

Now he felt like a god. Now he held all the cards, gripped as firm as their attention on him, and as the distortions swarmed up to chitter like a tsunami of bats, and his fingers dripped sweat down the covers of his pill file, he felt a mad scalding urge to laugh.

He would use these twisted fucks as his weapon. He would manipulate them to eliminate a frightening little bastard, just to protect the woman he l—

Really liked.

'Karl Devon,' he said. 'His name's Karl Devon. You should definitely go ask him some questions.'

And the Coram twins looked slowly at their mother.

And Maude nodded, just once.

Vicar showed him out.

For a man of such creeping feline affectations, his pushes and shoves seemed strangely uncouth. Shaper tolerated them with good grace, eager to get out, to hold the past at bay once more; to clamber into his van and batter the rising memories with as many bright little bombs from the pill file as he dared.

Not until he was safely ensconced in the cab – wheezing with relief, daring to believe it was over at last – did he dig for the meds and come back empty-handed.

Back inside the house, visible through the front window, Vicar was drawing curtains. He paused for a second before killing the final chink of light, squinting out towards the driveway.

Waggling a familiar black shape.

He smiled. And vanished into angular dark.

Pushes and shoves, Shaper thought. Hands in pockets.

He sat, sweating like rain.

'Fuck,' he said.

Chapter Twenty-nine

The girls fussed round him like an explosion of chickens. They squabbled to hang off his arm as he shuffled inside, a battering ram of lascivious gratitude, and the punters were no different: old men in shaggy towels creaking up to slap him on the back and point at their crotches. 'Back to full speed, lad!' 'Full mast!' 'All down to you!'

It was nice to be appreciated, and Shaper almost dared believe that the brothel's grateful welcome – sealed by a slice of cake and mug of cocoa from little Mrs Swanson – could eclipse the sunbursting dread at the loss of his meds.

The missing next dose. The Sickness uncoiling . . .

Keep it in. Squash it down . . .

But then, a secret voice whispered, as accidental hands brushed his groin and botox lips whispered two-for-one offers, why bother? Why should he give that bastard Vicar the satisfaction of all this clammy, crashing fear? The job, after all, was done; the hounds of hell were off the leash, George Glass's proverbial bacon was saved, and the suspect's proverbial card was proverbially punched.

The danger, it hissed, was gone.

Yes?

The Corams would handle it.

So why mourn the drugs at all, Dannyboy? Why should he resist the Sickness and all its pulsing venom a second longer, when the detox his body and brain so desperately needed was already – accidentally – under way? When the only impediment to its progress – the unhappy need to be functional – was . . .

Was soon to be . . .

(Karl, you poor sod. I hope you're high, mate. I hope you don't see it coming.)

Was soon to be dealt with.

(And I hope your sister never finds out it's all down to me.)

With his flailing mind thus briefly refocused on Mary, he tamped down the roaring delusions one last time – a nuclear chorus of sex sounds and glossy-wet walls – and reminded himself why he'd come here, gently extricating himself from the gaggle of girls.

'Actually,' he said, smiling at Mrs Swanson, 'I just popped by to check Miss Devon was OK.'

Somewhere safe, he'd told her. Somewhere safe where nobody can find you.

It had seemed like a good idea at the time.

The Madam gave him a blank look. 'Miss Devon?'

'Yeah. I mentioned her on the phone? She was going to stay for a bit?'

'Y-yes, of course – it's just . . . I rather assumed she'd be coming with you, dear. She's not here.'

What?

'Have some more cake, eh?'

He tried to call her, over and over, but each time the phone rang for sweaty minutes before chiming into the hopeless gulf of voicemail. The twittering girls drifted off to get on with the night's work, stroppy at his disinterest, and he crumpled on to a bed in one purple-toned room to think. He rummaged abstractly for the van keys, tensing himself to tear off across town, to reach the clinic, to *save* her . . .

But he could already tell it was useless.

The Sickness had him now.

Fed by his fear, the shakes occupied his whole body like some truculent, trembling ghost, palpitating his heart with every second beat. The hallucinations ripped free of his meagre resistance and inked his reality with a patchwork resonance between present and past.

You couldn't save her. You couldn't save either of them!

He saw Anna, then; bleeding out in a hospital bed five years before. Her muscles softening, hands going limp. And he saw Mary, as if somehow part of the same experience, whimpering alone as the monster drew near. Lantern-lit, eyes wet beneath their sapphire shell . . .

Too late.

All the momentum of the day came crashing down around him, gripping his every muscle, and he found that in the face of the maelstrom where imagination met memory, he was frozen in place, baulking at his own uselessness.

Oh, Karl. Karl, you shit . . .

You beat me again, didn't you?

In the haze of his senses he watched the fiend slip in through the clinic door, Mary too busy packing a bag to notice. Perhaps the killer would pick the lock, secret-sly, or ooze in through an open window. Or – *fuck* – maybe he'd just knock, convincing himself in the spasms of his crazy brain that it was all magic, the power of the Hand of Glory, and giggling as he drew his knife.

Shaper saw surgery. He saw scalpels rise from the crackling vision, green robes and linen masks invading Mary's death scene, lifting a veil on a different dream. He saw electric lines on white machines, and heard the synthetic bleeps of lingering life phase into a solid tone. Anna, dying with his lies in her ears. Mary, cursing him for being too slow.

One loss running into another. One death breeding a second.

He felt something hot in his mouth and realised he'd bitten into the wall of his cheek – then couldn't bring himself to stop gnawing it. The pain felt clean, somehow.

Will you display her, Karl, he wondered, *when she's dead?*

(He'd missed Anna's funeral. Comatose, jibbering, sick with his failure and the lies that had spawned it.)

What will I find, Karl? What slick artwork will you leave me, when you're done killing your own sister?

(He'd thrown away all the photos he had of Anna – even the grainy ultrasound prints. Too much to bear, even later when the drugs were working well.)

How long will it take you, Karl, to let her die?

(The ECG – video-game noisy – hiccupping to its last, unbroken note.)

Mary's heart . . . Pounding with terror, slowing to silence with each cut of the knife . . . Throbbing. Crashing. Hammering at—

'Mr Shaper?'

He awoke with a cry, legs kicking out – unaware he'd even dropped off – and felt brothel noises fade back from a distant world. The bedroom door was sealed – *how long have I been asleep?* – and someone was knocking hard.

'Mr Shaper?'

'Y-yeah?' he gurgled, panic undiminished.

Mrs Swanson cringed through a cautious doorway gap. 'I'm sorry to disturb you, dear, but . . .' She looked worried.

'What is it?'

'Well, there's . . . there's a woman outside. She's stamping up and down in the rain.'

'S-stamping?'

'Well, swearing mostly. And . . . and mentioning you quite a lot.'

He felt his face split open. A bubble of evil and tension bursting deep inside him, its toxic pus evaporating in the light. The Sickness sulked, briefly brought to rein, and diminished beneath the wave of his relief. 'Is she . . . is she OK?'

'Oh yes, seems to be. It's just that she's . . . she's scaring off the clients, you see?'

He laughed for far too long.

For the second time since he'd met her, the rain had made a thicket of Mary's hair and left her shivering in her boots. This time, however, it was clear the furnaces within were far from doused.

'It's a fucking *brothel*, you dick!' she kept snarling, when finally installed in the purple room. 'One of the . . . one of those men *smirked* at me.'

Shaper couldn't stop doing the same. 'They're nice people. It's safe here. Why didn't you come sooner?'

'It's a fucking brothel! It's . . . I can't *believe* you'd . . . And . . . and I'm not going to come running every time you make a . . . a fucking booty call, you . . . I should've stayed at home and . . . Look at me! I'm in a fucking nunnery!'

He chuckled and let her vent herself clear. It was obvious, even without the steely little ball bearings of secrecy he alone could see spiralling around her, that there were far deeper annoyances at the true heart of her mood.

Something's changed.

Eventually he grew bored with the rant and shushed her with a kiss. She dropped silent and stared as if he'd gone insane.

'I was worried,' he said, 'that's all. That's why you need to stay here, all right? It's safe and your place isn't. Don't ask why.'

'I . . .' She looked away, mouth opening and closing, then seemed to slump, defeated. 'I would've come sooner. I was on my way and everything.'

'But?'

'Well, I . . . got a call. A delivery at the clinic. I needed to sign for it.'

'And you went back? Mary! That's . . . that's exactly how you set someone up!' *(Been there, done that.)* 'You've got to be more careful!'

'Spare me the James Bond bollocks, it was just a package.' She dug in her handbag and produced a small jiffy bag, plastered in the courier firm's stickers, already opened.

And then she folded, as if all the head-wobbling indignation, all the chin-jutting capability, was so much gas in a limp balloon, wheezing out of her in one long gust. She waggled the package weakly, passing it over.

Inside was a notebook. Old, battered, with a black leather cover and a decaying spine, like wrinkles on a withered lip.

'You should probably read it,' she whispered.

And there at last were answers, in red and black and blue, and every other loopy gel pen the author had been able to find.

Scrawled one across another, the scribbled patches criss-crossed pages like the stumblings of stoned spiders. Mostly the text – arranged in nuggets of one or two lines, disjointed without syntax or grammar – was lightly scrawled, whimsical lists of words Shaper didn't know: *shakta, relaxatia, prana*. But inter-spersed among them lay patches of angrier annotation, letters pressed deep into the paper, infecting everything with a spiky urgency. On odd leaves the flow was interrupted by alien objects: sketches in black biro, out-of-proportion diagrams, muddled quotes from this or that parent text.

Is this Karl's? he wondered, recognising a hint of mania that felt somehow familiar, and left him almost recoiling from the artefact at the thought. But no, that didn't seem right. Here was an object heavy with inquiry – an investigation, a communal plan – not the mercurial solitude he'd come to associate with Mary's brother. He noted that the messy scribblings grew neater the further one flicked into the book, and the cursive less frantic, hinting at a mind approaching a happy state of ordered formality.

Definitely not Karl's.

The notebook was only a third full. After its final entry, the pages lay untouched, and Shaper returned to the front leaf with an uncertain scowl at Mary.

She said nothing.

'*Been at it months,*' read an entry on the first page. '*Good dedication, integration etc. Think #s 1–5 suspect more going on than they thought. No sense nervousness: just excitement. (Plan reveal soon?)*'

Patterns trickled down the sheet from that opening bait like unconscious telephone doodles, leading into the maze of intertwined text below. He allowed himself to tune out and leaf onwards, eyes and brain relaxed, grudgingly trusting his spastic senses to find the buried truths, the lines of greatest value.

> . . . *inner state of all practitioners = point of reliability & consistency. Each mastered indi. role. 2nd stage? (Have persuaded SG we're ready.) Meeting called 2nite.*

Another page, another storm of scribbles, another passage leaping from the dross.

> . . . *group shocked, 1ˢᵗ, at plan. SG persuaded them (typ!). Now all = ready. Hadn't seen potential. Chance to **externalise**: turn personal efforts outwards. Treating reluctant (**disbelieving!**) world. 'Heroic idea' (how SG put it). How could they refuse? Each has homework.*

Shaper glanced at Mary, pursing his lips. 'SG?'

'St Germain.' She didn't even look up.

'Eh?'

'As in, the Count of.'

'Who the fuck's . . .'

A memory bubbled up. A name, inscribed above an unused door at Thornhill. And a fragile old voice, explaining the impossible to a cynical listener.

'*My name is the Count of St Germain*,' it had said. '*I'm an Unascended Master of Theosophical Doctrine. I once held the knowledge of the Universal Medicine . . . am an occultist, a thaumaturge, and a necromancer . . .*'

'Glass,' Shaper muttered. Mary said nothing.

He turned a page and roved onwards.

Caught M rooting in the clinic files. Told her off, tho feels wrong 2 exclude her. K's court case affecting her a lot. Will understand, 1 day. All for her anyway – her generation. Changing the future!

(Meds for the soul: what a world to grow up in!)

'M and K . . .' he mumbled, thoughtful. 'This is your mother's, isn't it?'

She nodded.

'So what's it all ab—'

'Just read it, Dan.'

He huffed and speeded up, already annoyed by the esoteric bollocks. Each page introduced more and more fiddly little drawings, scrupulously coloured symbols and mad snatches of foreign text. Buried in the mire, even the readable passages were rendered barely legible.

. . . discovered unexpected confluence/blockage of Ida and

Pingala, preventing prana circulation, but sure that . . .

. . . must strive: greater mastery of Ajna locus. Am finding tabs help – small dose only!!! Too much = no focus. Impossible to control stimulating energies if . . .

. . . last shreds sex/excitement dying. Suspect #2 & #5 only inv. for that at first. Now all on-message. (SG persuasive!) All in room at once: feel we can do anything, change everything!

. . . planning simple mantra each. Prep. host for arousal/ stim. Req. thought/testing/love. Must be perfect, accurate; precise. No fuckups.

*Simple trial stage. Theorising process may cause discomfort? SG bankrolled appropriate equipment. (Sahasrara or not, couldn't do this w/o his resources. A **gift** from the universe!!)*

On the next page a particularly intricate diagram had been drawn, traced in red and black. It showed a human form, seated and sedate – a sleeping king on a scribbled throne. Along the figure's torso and head, Mary's mother had drawn neat little whirlpools, each with its own colour, each attended by a hovering symbol and a name in Western text: svadisthana, vishuddha, sahasrara . . .

Yawn.

Except at each of the chakric points a toxic-red arrow swept in from the side, so fussily packed with crazed patterns, it was impossible to tell which were foreign characters and which simple doodles. Each halberd tip speared into its target spiral, blinking out little commas of activity like shock beams round a comic hero's head. Stranger still, beneath the seat of the chair, patterned with a childish set of stripes and diamonds, a ruby-eyed snake coiled between the figure's legs.

And a final detail, almost unbearably crude beside the carefully composed detail elsewhere: thick metal bands, drawn in blobby silver, over the figure's wrists and ankles.

Restraints.

It took everything Shaper had, then, sitting in the brothel with muffled moans from the next room, with Mary tutting under her breath, with sick and mysterious *some-things* planned on the page like a warped experiment, to avoid tumbling back into that ghastly vision from the cellars at Thornhill.

The seething white noise. The victim: screaming, scrabbling at armrests.

The cloaked figures reaching out—

He bit into the mess of his cheek – still tangy with the taste of iron – and ground his eyes back on to the page, noticing a minuscule thread of text wavering beneath the diagram.

> *Awaken the serpent.*
> *Cleanse the unclean.*
> *Disinfect the infected.*
> *(Uncoil the beauty.)*

He sniffed and lowered the book, probing thoughtfully at the sore in his mouth.

'This,' he said, 'is creepy.'

'Just fucking read it, OK?' Mary glowered and dripped rain.

The next page bore a heading with elaborate serifs, underlined three times, like a new chapter: 'The Treatment'. Beneath it the text was tighter, less notational, a new sobriety in the tone.

*Confident now: efficacy of the **Process** above doubt. Stimulation of specialist areas can be demonstrated (in isolation) on each other. We've hesitated to go beyond two or three opened*

*loci in one sitting – (pain is intense) – but methodology =
sound.*

No one expects it to be easy. No one will back out now.

*. . . at last have our candidate. Host for the first miracle.
Closer to home than we could ever have imagined. I pray it
works for his sake. It **will**. It **must**.*

*. . . treatment ultimately far simpler than we expected.
Will be the merest matter of chanting mantras, laying on
hands, **forcing wills**. Each = master of one node. Together?
What glorious circuitry! We must stiffen our resolve against
cries/pleas.*

*Discoveries thick and fast. Secret nature of chakras,
our revelation! Each like a fortress door: **opens only from
within. But,** same analogue: **may be battered down
from without**.*

*#1 expressing doubts today – qualms, weakening. SG
settled it: 'No pain, no gain.' How true. (Subject's pain = the
world's gain.)*

*Process will begin at the root. Let the Kundalini awake.
Each stage joins the chorus 1 by 1. Each door pushed open
by its own master. No pause, no respite. Estimating treatment
will take several hours – none of us knows for sure.*

. . . Coaxing the Little God upwards.
***Cosmic Ejaculation**.*

Shaper stared at the last line with an eyebrow arched. 'Great
band name, there.'

'What?'

'Nothing.'

He found himself almost at the end of the annotated sections.

On the penultimate page, before the gulf of untouched paper, a seven-pointed star had been drawn, each of whose tips was a clumsy circle of black ink coloured in orange. At the centre a square enclosed yet another blob, this time effervescing with a crazed confusion of colours and shapes. And, as before, a set of silver bands.

Shaper realised he was seeing the same diagram as before, albeit now from an aerial view: the seated figure enclosed in a ring of others, pinioned to that hateful chair, each tormentor stretching out hands to grope and stroke. Again the static fell like a curtain before his eyes – Karl's face gagging in pain, the Sickness keening in sympathy – and he flicked over the final page with a shiver, racing to cut off the eruption before it began.

It bore a single word, neatly written without underline or flourish.

Tonight.

Shaper stared at it for a long time. In its simple solitude it drew perverse pieces towards vacant gaps in his mind, hunting for close fits and watertight joints.

How had Mary put it, he floundered, sitting at her kitchen table among the ruins of shredded paper?

'*The idea of yoga is to arouse it . . .*'

Kundalini, she'd called it – he remembered that. The primeval energy snake; the airy-fairy fucking god eel, coiled up like a mystic turd in the cosmic arsehole.

Mary had said, '*To let it . . . rise up all the chakras, one by one.*'

She'd said, '*If you can do it all the way up, out through the crown? That's called samadhi . . . That's a union with god basically. You don't get to do that unless you're pretty much perfect.*'

Shaper sighed and stared at the notebook, at that last damning word, *Tonight*, and began to understand what the group had tried to do.

Across the room Mary noticed his wandering gaze. She touched his arm and nodded at the book, voice tight. 'Check the back.'

He frowned at her tone, flicking to the inside of the back cover. A sheet of paper had been taped there, folded into quarters, and he opened it out at her urging nod.

It was a letter.

Dear Ajna,

As per your request, I've established a trust (technically based in the Cayman Islands, though accessible through various UK providers), to autonomously apportion funds for medical treatment and associated care of the Subject. As you'd expect, this has been conducted in the utmost secrecy and anonymity, with access regulated by code number alone. I'm confident that no linking evidence (this letter notwithstanding, which I would urge you to destroy) remains.

I estimate the monies raised should, depending on variations in cost, procedure and response, last six to eight years. After this period it falls to Master G's discretion to provide additional monies, until such time as he deems the dangers sufficiently mitigated.

The professionals involved have accepted sweeteners, as discussed, and we can be confident of the utmost discretion in executing this plan – at least until the funds are exhausted.

I trust this brings the matter to a close, and – as we have communally agreed – the dispersion and silence of the group are the final, and lasting, stages.

Yours,
MANIPURA

'I see,' Shaper said. And for once, with something a little like surprise, realised he meant it.

Manipura, he remembered. The solar plexus hub. The third chakra on the list.

Alice Colquhoun. The businesswoman. Who better to arrange something like this?

'So?' Mary said, hugging herself. 'What do you think?'

He stared into space and felt the universe knot around him. Insanely, unexpectedly, everything was beginning to fit.

They took someone wicked, didn't they?

They took someone tainted – in their eyes at least. Someone who wouldn't or couldn't fix themselves. Someone who wouldn't sit and meditate and chant with all these earnest, happy-clapping idiots. Someone who couldn't be arsed – or more likely didn't believe a word of it – to . . . what? To master their chakras alone? To energise and open each in turn? To uncoil the fucking spine snake?

So the bastards took him and did it to him anyway.

He could feel Mary still staring. He kept his eyes on the letter, scored with neurotic precision along its four quarters, then folded it away with a grunt.

'It went wrong,' he said, thinking out loud. 'This thing your mum tried. It all went to tits, and they packaged off the poor sod like he was crazy. "Treatment and associated care for the subject." Jesus.'

Even amidst the pleasure of progress, questions still nagged. Shaper scratched at his chin and mentally gnawed on numbers. If Karl had been locked up for just 'six to eight years', he realised, the freak would have come slithering back almost a decade ago, yet he'd claimed at the pub to have only recently arrived home.

So who was lying? The accountant with the dodgy deals, or the twitchy little freak with his foreign asylums and military manoeuvres? Or did something happen? Did Glass top up the account before his memory crumbled and he forgot the whole thing?

Even the uncertain details couldn't derail Shaper's blossoming triumph – the bigger picture, with its clear culprit, primly unchanged – and he packaged it away with a mental asterisk.

Mary, he saw, had softly started to cry.

'Who sent you this?' he asked, too exhausted to comfort her. She wiped manically at her eyes, digging in the jiffy bag for one last clumsily folded sheet of paper.

It was signed 'Karl'.

M.

Thought you should see this notebook before everything ends. It got to me in Brazil just after mum topped herself i spose she sent it knowing what shed do. Sort of a confesson??

Ive kept it ever since hope it helps you understand.

1 other thing. That man your fucking – hes like me.

He sees, Mary. Hes dirty on the inside and he sees. Dont forget that.

Shaper stared and stared and stared. He felt strangely as though he'd been punched by an inanimate sheet of paper, as though with a simple reference he'd become as inseparable from the very thing he was trying to investigate as the victims and suspects themselves.

He had absolutely no idea how this should make him feel, except that it took him in his spine and his skull and his stomach, and all of them hurt like hell.

'I didn't think he knew my address,' said Mary, leaden.

Making it easy on me. Ignoring that last paragraph. Not talking about it.

'He . . . yeah, he got it,' Shaper croaked. 'The cops, they . . . He found it out.'

An uneasy something buzzed behind his eye. *But*, it whispered, *Karl got her address so he could come after her, didn't he? Surely not just for . . . Not just to send her a package?*

The doubt came creeping back for just a moment. The it's-too-simple, the there-must-be-more-to-it infecting his certainties like mould across damp walls. Had he missed something? Had he miscalculated?

Karl, sent abroad for rehab, kept out of trouble: Thailand, India, Brazil . . . 'Treatment and associated care of the subject', just like in the letter.

'Yeah,' Shaper blurted out loud, as if convincing himself. 'It does fit. It *does*.'

Karl had got out from whatever malarial shithole they'd sent him to – long ago, recently, it didn't matter when – and came zipping home like a toxic boomerang, hungry for payback on the incense-burning, bindi-faced fucks who'd . . .

Name it.

Who'd experimented on him. The ones who'd seen the accidental death of a drunken idiot in a Soho brawl as a blot on his soul, a blockage on the path to nirvana, to be cured whether he liked it or not.

'You knew, didn't you?' Mary breathed, eyes wet. 'You knew he's the . . . the one who . . .'

The killer.

'That's why you made me come here. You knew he'd found out where I . . . Y-you thought he might be coming f . . . fuh . . .'

Shaper just nodded. It didn't matter that Mary had no part in this 'treatment', that Karl had no rational reason to come for her. Rationality was a virtue the frothing little freak had shown himself utterly beyond.

'It's OK,' Shaper heard himself say, determined not to fight it, not to worry that it was all too cosy, packed with holes like his own spongy cerebrum. 'It's OK now. I've handled it . . . It's under control.'

He could almost see it happening. BollockHead and BeanieHat piling into a car. Creepy Max Vicar and his fucking machete. The Corams, hungry for blood, jonesing for revenge on a man who . . .

Ha. Who probably had fuck all to do with the death of their dad, in truth, but that's hardly the cocking point.

'It's being dealt with,' he murmured.

All my weapons.

And then his phone rang. And everything went wrong.

Chapter Thirty

Somewhere halfway across town, with Canton's voice replaying on a loop in his ears and the van's newly developed choke – like an old man hacking through a plug of phlegm – providing a maddening counterpoint to the Sickness already pounding at his brain, Shaper realised he was losing it.

The world beyond the windscreen became a thing of jagged corners and apocalyptic sights, and every wave form of noise and light seemed to chant a secret, divine condemnation.

Yoooou—

Fucked up.

Yoooou—

Fucked up!

'We've got DNA results back,' Canton had said, a hyena howl cackling in Shaper's soul. 'You'll never believe it. That body in the fire? It's—'

'Tommy Boyle. Yeah.'

'But . . . How could you possibly know th—'

'Fuck the body, Canton! The nail! You got a match on the fingernail?'

'Yeah. Yeah, we know whose that is too. Where'd you find it, anyw—'

'It's Karl's, right?'

There was a solidity, he'd felt, in that. Clinging to the solution, gripping tight to the one calculation which absolved him of all further effort and justified his every move.

Karl. Strapped to the seat; restrained by a traitor mother, fingers tearing and bleeding at the wood, mind pushed past the brink of reason into—

'No, actually,' said Canton. 'It's Matthew Foster's.'

And oh, the plunge. All Shaper's certainties Atlantised into the mire, and the ragged remnants of his logic frog-leaped the new truth – and the thought-storm it conjured – to spit a far more urgent priority.

The Corams, Dannyboy! You already pulled the trigger, remember?

He could barely tell how he was managing to drive, now. Closing on the M4 approaches like a demon, the old autopilot fugue had transformed into something far uglier, a haunted, mechanical nightmare, and the memory of his brusque dismissal of Mary still rang in his ears.

'Stay here! Don't move!'

He cursed himself with every mile. He'd been so *certain*! He'd been so busy building the centre of the jigsaw, delighted at the perfect fit, that he'd forgotten the edges, those misty peripheries of uncertainty and doubt.

The elusive Mr Foster.

He'd forgotten his brief excitement at the police station at the news of the drug dealer's past: the violence, the lunacy; the perfect suspect! The whole brainthread had been washed away with the knowledge (no, the supposition) that Fossey was dead, burned to a crisp in his own home.

Washed away – but never restored when the evidence changed.

It wasn't Fossey's body, was it? And you knew that, you moron, from the second you heard about the missing arm. You knew it, but you didn't think it through, oh no, because Karl fitted the bill too well. Karl and the threat to Mary. Karl and the whole twitchy, creepy act.

He remembered the pestilent aura he'd imagined around the man. The scintilla of evil; the filth and sadism, all of it implied by a . . .

A fucking delusion! A fucking hunch, Dannyboy! Nothing more!

Clattering through Acton, it came to him like a grenade blast, like a stroke made of laughter and screams, that he'd been fooled, utterly and inexcusably, by his own venomous brain.

The truth, in the final analysis, was that Fossey fitted the bill just as well as Karl.

Mouse had called him 'crazy Foster': a letch, a pusher, a dealer. A man certainly 'tainted' enough for the meditation group's purposes, to abduct, to purify: '. . . *At last have our candidate. Host for the first miracle. Closer to home than we could ever have imagined . . .*'

Shaper berated himself for even thinking they could have used one of their own children – how could they risk *that* for a trial run? But a man like Fossey, some unmissable speck of criminality . . . He was a far more bearable proposition, should the treatment go wrong.

Which it did. And in so doing cued a chain of damage limitation and sculduggery which left Fossey institutionalised despite having no discernible 'mental illness'. DI Canton's file had made it clear that the ill-defined diagnosis of a 'personality disorder' should have seen the man released straight away – 'untreatable', the law said – so what had kept him inside all that time?

I estimate the monies raised should, depending on variations in cost, procedure and response, last six to eight years. After this period it falls to Master G's discretion to provide additional monies, until such time as he deems the dangers sufficiently mitigated.

The professionals involved have accepted sweeteners, as discussed . . .

'Fuck, fuck, *fuck*!' Shaper shouted, slapping trembling hands against the wheel.

'Master G's discretion' didn't hold much water if the senile old git couldn't remember a single thing about it. Sooner or later, Shaper supposed, the money in the trust fund simply gave out, the whitecoats stashed their bribes, and crazy Foster slithered from his hole.

Fuck.

Karl and Fossey. Two nutjobs, two tainted men, both packed off in secret. And Shaper had backed the wrong horse.

Why? Because, he admitted to himself, he simply hadn't met the right one. He'd built a case around a fucking *impression*, a fucking *feeling*, a Hollywood fucking *hunch*, and a tenuous fear for the life of the woman he was tupping.

Idiot.

'Who and where,' he snarled out loud, addressing his misery to the mucal, maggoty drizzle on the window, 'is Matthew . . . bloody . . . Foster?'

He sensed now that there were still too many loose ends flapping, and in a jolt of self-revulsion understood – *knew* – that this dismal human mess he'd become was useless in the face of the lingering mystery. But with the keenness of that conviction arrived an equal and opposite certainty, a blade of urgency which sliced through his hopeless hopes of stitching it all together – of figuring Glass and Thornhill and Tommy Boyle into the equation, of finishing this insane toxic jigsaw – and concentrated what little focus he could muster on the now.

Now belonged to the Corams.

Shaper had set the hounds of hell after the wrong man, and they weren't in the habit of being brought to heel.

* * *

It was already kicking off when he arrived in Karl's street: a kaleidoscope of flashing lights, blue helmets and silver buttons. He eased the van past it all at an inconspicuous twenty, skull quaking – *too late?* – and parked at the pub further along, grabbing an unattended pint on a whim and joining the clutch of beery punters stood on tables, keeping watch like the world's ugliest meerkats.

Even at this distance – even through the glitterball of hallucination tainting the whirligig blue – he could make out two knots of activity: separate scrums of Her Majesty's finest, struggling to restrain hollering bodies.

You're fucking kidding . . .

It was BeanieHat and BollockHead. Each screaming for all he was worth, kicking and thrashing in a nucleus of swearing bodies and click-a-clacking cuffs.

Karl's door, Shaper noticed, wasn't even open, curtains resolutely drawn, silent as the grave.

Hm.

At the roadside the congregated cop-fleet was already thinning – lights killed, engines fired, officers drifting into the night – and Shaper could tell, even at this distance, what had happened.

'Canton,' he muttered, trying to clear the buzzing in his ears. 'You lying little shit . . .'

Electronic tag, the cop had told him, dismissive. *He's not going anywhere.*

The prim man had raved about Vehrman throwing out the whole line of inquiry, accusing Shaper of obstruction, refusing to waste resources on twitchy little Karl Devon . . .

Then a pair of bungling wankers show up to bust down the guy's door and the whole fucking Met swoops like a nuclear eagle.

'Not being watched, my arse,' Shaper mumbled.

Outside the freak's house, wheezing almost audible across the street, the blobby silhouette of the Jabbalike waved fingers and snarled instructions, dispersing all non-essential troops and chivvying along those still grappling with the freelancers. BeanieHat and BollockHead, Shaper could see, weren't going quietly.

He watched the brawls and permitted himself a molecule of relief – administered to his raging senses like a natural medication. The Corams had sent a pair of morons to do a fiend's work. The cops had done what cops do, and poor sick little Karl wouldn't be wrongfully knocked off on Shaper's say-so tonight. He polished off the pint like an 'up yours' to the Sickness, lighting a fag and hopping off the bench, and managed to get almost all the way back to the van before common sense caught up.

The Corams aren't dense.

He stopped walking. Behind him the two goons continued to make a fuss, louder, crazier with every jolt and jerk, the entire spectacle rendered in a suspicious, piss-yellow hue in his eyes. More cops came piling in on cue: Vehrman shouting, curtains along the street twitching.

And nobody . . .

Oh fuck.

. . . nobody watching the back.

Shaper broke into a run, silently begging his brain for just a moment's more function, an extra second of peace. He clambered a fence at the terrace end down the street, utterly ignored by all, and skipped over shrubs, walls, hedges on his way back. He fixed himself at every step with a simple, predatory mindset – an echo of the old him, appeasing and *using* the Sickness, compressing it down to a brittle point of intention. He counted the houses as he passed and listened for the goons out front, still in full diversion mode.

He clambered a shed – stifling a reflexive impression of the drizzle-damp roof as bloody mahogany, scratched and marked like some gargantuan version of the chair in Thornhill's bowels – and paused to rummage in his coat for the last pair of foil key picks, left over from his invasion of Kingsley's home.

Not enough . . . Not enough . . .

And then he was dropping down among the weeds of Karl's garden, eyeing the back door – too late to go back, too late to change his mind – and felt his balls gently recess into his body.

The door was already ajar.

It was shit, being right.

It was Vicar, of course. Vicar with Karl.

Shaper spotted them from below, sprawled at the top of the staircase like ghastly waxworks, sealed in a bubble of low voices and strange sounds. Far from any doorway or window, Karl lay cuffed to a radiator beside a hissing airing cupboard, while his tormentor – teeth glittering, hands moving – commanded an uninterrupted view of every approach.

Vicar knew his stuff.

Shaper tried his best to creep up all the same. He went slowly, at first. Barely glancing at the horrors above, except to check Vicar's gaze was elsewhere, bent on his squirming, crooning prize. Nor did he pause to get a sense for the house as he ghosted on to the lowest step – beyond a dim impression of unpacked boxes and too much dust – nor the awful sounds of torture: each sticky slice and gentle moan feeding the cyclone of his brain.

The drugs were barely a memory, now.

He got further than he expected. Taking each slow step at a time – hilariously close to the fiend, hilariously unnoticed – he paused only when it seemed ludicrous to continue, five steps short of the landing, when any further movement would betray him as surely as to stamp his feet and shout. It dawned on him with a rising cringe that his only hope of stopping this, of ending the gory business, would be to rush in and stamp Vicar like a cockroach. Falling on the man's mercy, after all – trying to explain his own mistake, to appeal to reason – was a laughable proposition.

Thus fixed in place, electrified by surreal fantasies of his own invisibility, Shaper let slip his focus at the critical instant and stole his first full look at the tableau. At the gag in Karl's mouth and the bruises on his cheeks and chin. At his trousers and underwear, pulled down to bunch round the electric tag on his ankle, and the narrow blade threads sprouting on his thighs and groin. At the man's dick, shrivelled and buried in a stain of black hair, with its own fresh wound – like a pen line along its shaft – already dripping. Each cut shallow: skin unzipped, alive with the promise that the next would be deeper.

Torture 101, thought Shaper, heart fit to explode. Been there, done that.

He tried to stop himself looking. Tried to break his eyes away, tensing for the attack just as he'd planned – but it was too late for that. Too late to release the breath in his throat, to coax his body into anything more than its junkie-like quivering, to sweep aside the palls of pure and opaque delusion as they scaled his eyes.

He wallowed in it. He spiralled through lunacy, and every detail his senses drank was fermented, corrupted; transformed. Vicar's hands, latex gloves, silver scalpels; then chrome and diesel insects, the sound of refracted light, the smell of time . . .

(You're going mad.)

The earth, spinning so hard he felt sure it must throw him off.

(Get a grip!)

He glimpsed through it all for a second, like a break in the clouds, to note the rubber cord round the meat of Karl's leg, Vicar's hand dipping into a sports bag, and the grimy-bladed thing it removed.

Hacksaw. Oh god.

'Now then.' The bastard grinned, teeth flashing. 'Either you'll oblige me with some fucking answers, Karl m'lad, or I'll be forced to cut your foot off.' He tapped the tool playfully against Karl's knee, drawing a soft moan. 'It's this tag bollocks, innit? Bleedin' gadgets, mate. Not your fault – but what's a feller to do? Can't have a proper chat here, can we? Not when you're keeping secrets, Karly-Karl. Not with the fuzz out front. So either you gimme some details – that's your choice – or we go see a specialist. Can't be helped.'

He smiled wider than his head seemed to allow, tilting his eyes to drink in Karl's face – and the shadows behind it.

Shaper stopped breathing. *He can see me, he can see me, he can s—*

'Well?' said Vicar, too absorbed in his prey, idiotic with domination. 'What's it to be?'

Karl nodded and said something ragged in his throat.

'Good man,' Vicar congratulated, gently loosening the gag. Even Shaper, a ghost on the edge of a half-lit stage, tilted inwards a fraction to hear.

Karl took a moment to moisten his mouth, thin little lips moving.

And then smirked.

'Hello back there, Mr Shaper,' he said.

But he's not even looking at m—

Fuck fuck fuck!

Shaper tried to move. All initiative gone, all surprise stolen, he pulsed forward with his fists swinging, an indignant whinge rising uninvited.

I'm here to save you, you little shit! Why'd you go and d—

Vicar was too fast.

The hacksaw bit into Shaper's forearm. It tore at his coat, aborting his first punch and snapping the blade with a musical twang. The sound magnified itself in his senses – distorting, assuming a weird synaesthetic glow – and he focused on the hot pain under his sleeve to exorcise the abstraction, snatching out with his other fist to clutch at Vicar's face and shove it away, hard.

The arsehole snarled as he went down. Shaper caught a crazy impression of bunched skin round baby-like eyes, before the man's head bounced on the airing cupboard door and shat out a gobbet of pink slime. He almost cheered, driving onwards to finish the job, trippy with the Sickness.

Quicker than Vicar! That rhymes! Ha ha h—

Except not.

The fucker's foot caught him full in the gut and exploded the air out of him. His skull filled with fireworks and frenzy, and before he knew it, he was stumbling back, tripping on Karl's form and tumbling downwards, skidding off the top step then–

Oh no.

His knees crumpled. His coccyx hit a hard corner with a jolt and everything turned over. The world flip-flopped – a bottomless shaft gulping him down – and something cracked him in the back of his skull, unleashing a supernova before his eyes.

Falling down the stairs. How embarrassing.

He flailed out an arm and felt the banister slap at his knuckles. Shoulder screaming, body flopping like a fish, he gripped the wood and hung on for his life, blood like bubble wrap in his ears.

The silence trickled back like dawn on the heels of a storm, but the echoes in his brain wouldn't fade – *couldn't*, now – roaring and raging even as his bearings returned.

He puked down the steps.

'Hello, mate,' said Vicar, bruise-nosed and bloody-toothed. 'Nice of you to join us.'

Grinning.

Shaper rose to his feet, groggy. Too wired to test himself for damage – just a confused jumble of pain signals and aches; too many to tell which were serious and which just spectres of his condition – and fixed Vicar with a glare.

'I got it wrong,' he tried, gasping. 'Wrong name, wrong bloke.' He pointed at Karl. 'It's not him.'

Vicar just smiled.

'Let him go, eh? It's not him, Max. He doesn't know a thing. I'm serious.'

Vicar's eyebrows pantomimed shock. 'Serious? *Gosh.*' He wiped blood and spittle off his lip and, not even looking down, nudged Karl with a foot. 'Karly-Karl? Mr Shaper here says I've got the wrong bloke.'

Karl moaned.

'*He* says you don't know nothing about it.'

Even from a few steps below head height, with a broken view of the spreadeagled victim, Shaper could see the wetness of Karl's eyes, tears streaking the cuts on his cheeks, a pestilent halo again condensing around him . . .

Why the fuck is he still smiling?

'So why don't you tell him, Karl, what you said to me when I first got here? Why don't you do that?'

Despite himself, body all but beyond control, gripped by a curiosity far stronger than fear, Shaper climbed back to the lip of the landing.

At his feet, Karl's voice was a sand-clogged hiss.

'I killed Tommy Boyle,' he said. 'And Sam Coram. It's all me.'

Shaper's brain gave in. All his inner certainties collapsed, all his convictions tumbled, shattered, dissolved.

But that's not possible.

Why the fuck are you doing th—

A lobster's claw snapped round his arm, and beyond the fog

of shock – *Vicar!* – he tried to struggle, throwing an exhausted slap. It did little more than scrape at the snake-like smile, and before he could summon the dregs of his energy, his old friend the machete had appeared in Vicar's hand. The fight seeped out of him, the Sickness settled a fraction, and all the world seemed dimmer, softer: less real.

There was a sick joy, he knew, in resignation.

'Good man,' Vicar said. And giggled.

And swung the machete at his face.

Shaper had a starburst instant of terror at the curious notion of his head being split in two, but as swift as it came, the shadows rolled in like a bloody tide, and swallowed the fear away.

He dropped, bodily, into tar.

Chapter Thirty-one

Shaper woke up and wished he hadn't. Again.

Somewhere a phone was ringing.

It took him some time to realise he was in the airing cupboard. Sweltering, with just the hiss of the boiler for company, his prison was invaded only by a laser beam of light from between the doors, and the distant moans of Karl Devon.

It took him even longer to realise his head was all in one piece.

The handle. The bastard hit me with the machete handle.

The phone, he realised, was his own: not a ringtone but an alarm, mercilessly cheerful in its pinging, bouncing cadence. It didn't help his headache.

He hurt *everywhere*. His wrists seemed to be bound, constricted behind his back, dull with a pins-and-needles fuzz, and when he opened his mouth to shout about it, his jaw protested: a dry clog between his lips.

Gagged.

His forearm twinged with every movement – skin tight with the sticky-yet-powdered feel of drying blood – and besides the bruises through his back and shoulders, a single flourish of agony marked his left cheek where the blade hilt had hit him. But around it all, worse by far than any of the thudding pains, was the storm in his skull.

It was all falling down. The weight of his crumbling energies held him like a claw to his scalp, psyche bubbling through molten lead. The soft membrane of his rationality, a thin gauze at the best of times, had stretched too far: raggedy holes tearing open.

The pain, the bleating phone, the terror, the heat – all just triggers. All just sticks to prod at the Sickness in its cage, enraging it, coaxing it to hurl itself again and again at the splintering bars of its jail. He found spiders tormenting the edges of his vision, racing beneath his skin to nudge upwards wherever a dainty hair follicle itched and stood erect. The buzz of a billion fruit flies hung in his ears, and he realised with discomfort that the blur of movement all around was caused by his own shaking body – even his eyeballs were infected by the spasm. He fought not to vomit.

The alarm wouldn't shut up. It had failed to go off earlier when he'd stolen a brief nap, he remembered, and he now decided – with a stroke of bizarre mental clarity in the heart of the chaos – that when he'd asked the gadget for 120 minutes' sleep, he'd somehow fucked up and instructed it to chime at twelve o'clock instead.

Midnight, then.

The apogee of darkness, Mary had called it.

As if on cue, the cupboard doors quaked: a hand hammering at the outside. 'Shut up that fucking racket, you!' Vicar snarled. 'We're trying to talk, here!'

Mercifully, magically, the alarm fell to silence.

Thank fuck, Shaper thought, for snooze mode.

With an effort so supreme it left him rasping for breath, he heaved himself forwards and pressed an eye to the gap. The scene was just as he'd left it, except that Vicar, pausing in his sickly administrations, was holding his own mobile to his ear, apologising for the distraction.

Shaper caught, 'Not a problem, boss,' then, 'Tell your ma it won't be long,' before the creep's scarecrow arm set aside the handset and reclaimed the hacksaw. A new blade fixed in place. 'C'mon then,' he trilled, 'Karl, me old shitter. No more distractions, eh?'

And got back to it.

And *oh*, the rasping, the barcode view of the bastard's arm, sliding back and forth; the wet then dry sounds.

But there were no screams, and that somehow made it worse. Only Karl's gentle moans, the odd *clank* of his cuffs against the radiator, and the sounds of Vicar hard-breathing with effort.

Shaper fielded another pulse of nausea and a new pain in his chest. He could feel the old horror rising up without needing to see it: his skin peeling and rotting, his eyeballs loose in their sockets, muscles squirming with the weight of worms packed along their fibres . . .

Something hissed abruptly behind him, and in the armpit of his panic it was so much easier to let the delusion absorb it – to whisper the name of the kundalini serpent, that bright wyrm slithering in his spine – than to listen to the voice of reason.

(Just the boiler, idiot.)

In a panic he hammered his foot against the cupboard doors, screaming through the gag, but they wouldn't budge. Something steely rattled between the hoops of the handles outside, penning him in, and he found he could almost see it – as though detached from himself.

The machete. He's locked me in with the fucking machete.

And somewhere, like a ghost's voice, Vicar giggled and kept on sawing.

Panic electrocuted Shaper, then. A black storm, sparks hopping from the tips of every sharp edge. He pushed his head back near the light, like a snorkel to a drowning man, and prepared to scream and scream until the world caved in and the Sickness went away and the cutting stopped and . . . and . . .

And someone gives me some fucking DRUGS.

But he couldn't move.

And the world went weird.

A silence settled, a void so complete that Shaper could no longer even detect his own breathing, and the insane idea gripped him that what he was hearing was *anti-noise*, a secret volume so dense that it drowned out its equal and opposite vibrations.

(You junkie. You crazy, crashing, junkie fuck.)

And then a candle flickered through the gap.

A stair creaked under someone's foot, and – like oil – something black shifted into the silver of Shaper's view.

And a voice – Vicar's, he thought, choked as much by the unfamiliarity of fear as by the fear itself – hissed, 'Wh . . . who the fuck're *you?*'

And something blue-gold-white, with a flash of liquid red where its mouth should be, leaned down, smoke-slow and steam-serene, and said, '*Shush* now.'

Fossey.

The thought stole over Shaper like mould, corrupting and bloating every cell of his psyche. *He's come . . . Why here? Why now?*

Something flashed silver. A latex hand danced from his fogged perspective to scrabble at the cupboard doors, tugging feebly at the machete, before slinking away by weak degrees, grip failing, in a chorus of wet noises and startled gurgles.

'You came . . .' Karl's voice, impossibly strong, flooded with joy and, *yes*, Shaper could almost feel it, with *lust*. 'Oh! You came for me!'

'Yes,' the beast whispered.

'I knew you would. I waited. I've . . . I've tried to *help*. The body . . . the body in y-your . . . I burnt it, Foss! I made them think it was you! I helped!'

'Yes.'

The voice crawled in Shaper's bones, a thing of gasps and

cobwebs, of tombstones ground together and slick knives on steel. A snake voice. *Fosssss.*

Somewhere Vicar groaned, sly tone modulated through liquid, and Shaper forced himself forwards one last time, balance tilting like a tormented ocean, to press his eyes to the slit.

Vicar was on his knees, a red fountain pouring beneath his chin and a copper gloss staining his teeth. His eyes rolled, mouth gaping, body refusing to accept it was dead. Beyond him – beyond that one gasping, collapsing form which made a modicum of sense – Shaper's vision was met with only chaos: with blood and pain and sweat, with a limp victim and a bloody leg, with a merry flame on a waxy fist, and a tender glove tracing lovely lines on a sweaty brow.

And a black thing. A devil sneering in blue and gold and red.

'I love you,' Karl panted. 'I love you, and you've come for me.'

The killer hunched lower. Shaper grimaced at the storm poised behind his pupils – the full weight of the breakdown humming in storage; his body electrified with the rotting, mangling delusions – and twisted his wrists violently in their noose, cleansing his senses with pain.

'Not for you, Karl . . .' the voice breathed. 'I'm sorry. Not for you.' A black finger uncurled, pointing straight down. 'Just for your eyes. Your special eyes.'

The storm burbled closer, and like a swimmer before a tsunami, Shaper's brain raced along cruel chasms.

His eyes? But . . .

And he remembered. He saw Karl waiting for him in the pub, recognising his intentions before they'd even met, already knowing his name. *'You're a poker, aren't you?'* the man had said. *'A prodder . . .'* He remembered the inky attention through the curtain chink and Karl's venomous glare in the interview room: a baleful wink through an opaque mirror. And he remembered Mary describing a courtroom panic, fifteen years before. '*He started saying Karl had "the Sight". Saying he had . . . abilities . . .*'

And Shaper rolled his eyes in his black little prison and cursed himself for an idiot. He'd thought Mary was the target. Mary with her pretend gift and her make-believe clairvoyance. Ajna, the Third Eye chakra. Sixth on a list of seven.

Wrong sibling.

Outside in the awful Real, everything coiled and bulged at once. Vicar was beginning to fall sideways, Karl burbling in fear and betrayal.

'I'm sorry . . .' the monster whispered. 'I'm sorry, but . . .' It looked up. Twisting towards the stairs. 'But it's not up to me.'

And just as Karl began to moan, Vicar collapsed against the cupboard doors with a final rattle, and the slit of light blinked out.

And Shaper's Sickness – finally, like some cataclysmic eruption – unleashed itself across the domes of his perspective and drowned him. Utterly.

His flesh crumbled. His soul mouldered. His past came up to meet him in the gloss of a woman's eye – recognising his treachery but saying nothing – and as he slunk into unconsciousness, uncertain whether this time he'd emerge at all, what chased him down like a cruel punchline from beyond his cage was a single word, delivered by a voice made of water and wind.

'*Aum . . .*'

There was darkness, and a moment of discovery. There was excitement and noise – a bramble of disengaged sense impressions; an abstract semaphore of places and people. There was something red on the floor, and people wearing white plastic, and yellow fluttering tape. There were questions.

Shaper whistled to himself through it all, a long descending note, like a nuke falling with a smirk. He supposed, swaddled in a billion layers of disconnection and apathy, that the bomb was his mind, endlessly plunging down a comforting well shaft. If he wanted, he could even imagine the 'o' of light at its head receding away to nothing, but even that seemed like too much effort.

There were bad things up there.

Later, there was a too-bright place. It smelled of bleach, and beneath the aeroplane hum of air vents, people's voices were distant and low, nightmare mutterings, sickly coughs behind membrane curtains. Someone bandaged his arm. Someone in a blue jumper and a bright yellow jacket watched.

More questions. Always, always, always.

He kept falling.

After that came a slate-grey place: the same smells but a different hum. Here there was a table and two chairs, and a mirror which (he somehow understood) was *not* a mirror. There was brown liquid in plastic cups and a fat man who asked more questions.

After a few minutes, or possibly hours – or grinding epochs of mass extinction and flourishing civilised life – a thin man came in and shooed off the fattie. There was talk of *jurisdiction*. There was mention of a death – something about a vicar? – which somehow put the younger man in charge. He had a familiar face which, at the bottom of the well shaft, triggered hazy links to Chinese food and desiccated tigers.

Shaper shrugged – *weird* – and stopped thinking about it.

He found himself mummified in bloodless candyfloss, which occluded the truth but cruelly permitted the pains and aches and Sicknesses to come and go as they pleased. He hurt. A lot.

He fell some more.

The thin man was trying to talk to him now. It sounded

friendly, but still thorned with questions. Shaper ignored them.

He dumbly remembered another time – *another episode*, a quiet voice whispered – like this one. A time of recuperation and convalescence, scatter cushions in his mother's flat and an endless taste of hate and helplessness and debt. He remembered a sluggard's inertia gripping his every muscle, and wondered if it had all happened again. Sitting there in the grey place, guts moving as if he was looping on some invisible roller coaster, he considered probing harder into his own mind, trying to get to the bottom of this claggy, no-living malaise . . .

What caused it the first time? Some . . . some deep and dark betrayal, he was sure. Some heartbreaking thing, almost remembered, which had changed him—

Don't go there, mate, the voice whispered, a primal safety valve. *Don't think about it. Seriously.*

The thin man was talking about a bloke with no eyes now, and Shaper pretended to pay attention. But his hands on the tabletop were still, calm, unshaking, and that seemed somehow far more important than anything else.

'Won't last the day,' the man was saying. 'Deep shock, you know? Had to lose that foot too. Fucking mess.'

Even through the clouds Shaper thought he detected an unspoken question there, an appeal for explanation. He recoiled on instinct, waving his hands and asking if he was allowed to leave.

The voice just sighed and told him to calm down.

'Unless you can use a machete to bar yourself in a cupboard,' it said, 'and not trek any blood in with you, you're not a suspect. We're just talking here.'

He nodded, nodded, nodded, with no idea or interest in what was going on. He fell and fell some more.

The thin man asked what had happened, wheedling and huffing and chiding. There was something about an electric tag going stationary, about a dawn decision to go in. About *that's when we found you.*

Shaper asked if he was under arrest.

The thin man mentioned alibis. 'Some old dear in Hackney got in touch,' he grumbled. 'Claims you were working for her on the nights the first three got done. Crown Prossy says I couldn't hold you even if I wanted.'

The word 'brothel' came up. A head shake, a long sigh. 'Only you could use a knocking shop to get out of trouble, Dan.'

Bored now, Shaper decided to stand, and noticed only distantly something gripping his arm.

'You said there'd be one more,' the man said, insistent. 'When we found you. A right state, you were in. You said, "One more. Just one more."' The grip tightened. 'We can help you with this, Dan. But you've got to tell us who.'

A shining man, he remembered. *A Jesusalike. An odd scowl on an old face, and 'No cops', and* CRIMINAL, *and, and, and—*

And just thinking about him made the falling slow down.

Abruptly decisive, Shaper stared at the hand holding his arm until it let go, and headed for the door. *Brothel*, he thought.

It was a place, and it wasn't here. He went there.

Later, he sat in a van.

There was daylight, there was rain, there was a city; there were no questions.

Progress.

But still falling.

He supposed – noting the wheel and the seat belt – that he must have driven here. He supposed he might recall something about the journey if he tried, but it seemed barely worth the effort, and he satisfied himself instead with sitting and whistling, aching all over.

There was a brothel across the street. It didn't look like one, and he didn't concern himself with how he knew it was. The place meant something to him, he was sure; as if there were something vitally important inside. He wondered if he was supposed to go in – he even put his hand on the van door to exit – but after a century or two of thinking, of wading in cerebral syrup, decided not to bother. This, after all, this sitting here, this inertia, seemed reassuringly familiar.

Except . . .

Wasn't he supposed to be listening to someone? Grunts and screams and sticky slurps?

There didn't seem to be anyone around, so he occupied himself by listening to the rain – until that too became an effort and his mind wandered away. The slow certainty was stealing over him that there *was* something missing, something he'd grown so accustomed to hosting inside himself that in its absence, despite suspecting it was a terrible thing he'd always secretly hated, he felt somehow diminished.

Chemicals?

Another abstract idea, chased by an eye-rolling rebuke.

'Everything's made of chemicals,' he mumbled. 'Idiot.'

In any case, he found himself unwilling to probe the mystery, piqued by an awkward sense of urgency – *something you've got to do!* – which was bundled away in shaggy silk as fast as it arose. He fell away from it, not caring.

Somewhere, something began to bleep, shrill and uncomfortable. It made him think, '*Midnight*' – which was a strange thought for the middle of the day – and he dug from one pocket a glossy black box of plastic and glass, turning it over and over without aim. Unbidden, his thumb jabbed a certain key with precocious muscle memory, making the bleeping stop, and a voice squawked out from nowhere.

It said it was called Vince. Shaper stared at the little device with a doubtful eyebrow arched and said, 'Hi, Vince.'

It jabbered away. It said something about watching the news, and something about uncertain glass. It yawned loudly.

Uncertain glass? The words tasted important and, stranger yet, did something to Shaper's brain, shucking off a layer or two of apathy. He rapped his knuckles against the van's windscreen, experimental, but it felt certain enough to him.

The voice just kept on twittering. It asked questions, and when Shaper didn't answer – wishing it would be quiet and go away – it blurted, 'I'm passing you over. He wants a word, mate, OK?'

And then silence.

And Shaper fell some more.

And then a voice said, 'Hello.'

And—

Chapter Thirty-two

Dan Shaper achieved consciousness approximately three hours after technically waking up.

'Hello?' said a voice, weak and worried in his ear. 'Mr Shaper?'

It kneaded something in his skull.

Like some epic jolt of clarity, puncturing the clouds of dissociation that had wreathed him, his brain shat a scalding volley of flashbacks and analyses. The horror, as it poured free, came close to overwhelming him a second time, presenting a memory mosaic of the long night in the cupboard: the wet sounds, the narcotic barriers seeping away, and above all the *thing* outside, that crackling black beast, hunched over Karl . . .

He felt himself beginning to sink under again, but the voice, the voice in his ear . . .

'Mr Shaper? Are you all right? This is George Glass. Are you there, Mr Shaper?'

That voice was a white knife. An aural scalpel, swiftly and effortlessly excising the corrupted thoughts. Not destroying them, nor simply blocking them away in some cluttered corner (as his own mind had crudely attempted), but disarming them, rendering them harmless.

The voice lifted him from the swamp of memory with the merest tonal hint of care, concern; *love*.

'Yes,' Shaper said into the phone, eyes suddenly wet. 'I'm here.'

'I still need your help, Mr Shaper . . .'

And reality slammed into place, physically rocking him. He became aware without lingering to agonise or fret that in the storm of this week's events, nudged on by the final chemical void, he'd fallen into an abyss every bit as deep and dark as the breakdown that had ruined him five years before, except that this time . . .

This time he'd been salved by no more than a voice. This time the escape – the means of retrieving function – wasn't some sleazy junkie regime but . . .

But what?

Magic, Dannyboy? Is that what you think?

Whatever the cause, the muscles of his shoulders and neck unknotted like earthworms writhing apart, and he could almost hear his own heart slowing, sighing in oxygenated relief.

Undrugged.

Well, fuck.

'Mr Glass?' he said, wiping his eyes, praying it would last. 'Just . . . don't worry about a thing, OK? It's all under control.'

'But . . . W-we saw the news this morning. They're saying there's been another incident. This Tourist fellow . . .'

'Have you been talking to Vince, Mr Glass?'

'Well, he did mention there might be a link . . .'

That unbelievable wanker.

'Mr Glass, please, it'll all be over tonight, OK? I promise.'

He didn't add, '*One way or another.*' Didn't mention – nor even dare think about – the final death, the last victim on an insane list. He rubbed it from his mind, too busy enjoying his unfogged state to risk it all in a test of his fears, and comforted himself even as he comforted his client.

'No more fretting, all right? I know who's behind it now. I know what's happening.' *(Ish. Sort of.)* 'I'll be over there soon myself. I'm not going to let anything happen to you.'

And he meant it. *Oh god*, he meant it. Whatever Glass's involvement in the mad "treatment" Mary's mother had overseen, the old man's empty memory had re-cast him as an innocent, whose simple forgetful grace transcended any past mistakes. With the man's frail tone scraping the shit off Shaper's soul, leaving him more focused, more alive, more *him* than he'd felt in years, he made a silent vow that he would die before letting Matthew fucking Foster get close enough to hurt George Glass.

'I'll be there soon, OK?' he said. 'Could you . . . could you put Vince back on, please?'

The phone crackled and bumped. Shaper rubbed his eyes and stared idly at the brothel across the street, confused by a strange something nagging at his attention. He mentally berated his overactive senses, a manifesto for the new era.

No more paranoia. No more neurosis. No more fucking nagging, you hear?

Vince reappeared on the line.

'Yeah?'

'What the fuck are you doing,' Shaper said, too relaxed to put much ire into it, 'telling him about this Tourist shit?'

'Huh?'

'He's got enough to worry about without knowing what his own personal nutcase is up to.'

'Well . . . yeah. S-sorry.'

'What's wrong with you, anyway? You're slurring.'

'No I'm . . . I'm fine. Just a bit tired. Not much sleep.'

Shaper worked his jaw, eyes still scanning the brothel. 'That'll be because you were on guard all night, yes?'

'Well . . . Yeah. That.'

'Good. Listen, I need you to get a couple of extra heads. Trustworthy types – I'll pay.'

'Like who?'

360

'Oh, I dunno . . . Tightfist? He's still got that sawn-off, hasn't he? And Tal too, tell him to bring those radios he was showing off down the Mutt last month.'

Vince's voice seemed to come from far away. 'M-maybe . . . maybe not Tal, eh?'

'What?'

The big lug coughed. 'Sleeping arrangements are a bit . . . *uh.*'

Shaper closed his eyes. 'Vince.'

'Look, it's—'

'Vince.'

'No, listen—'

'You've been fucking the old man's daughter, haven't you?'

'Sh! Shhh!'

'Hence the lack of sleep.'

'Look, for fuck's sake, it's n—'

'Hence you sounding like a retarded caveman.'

'I'm *sorry*, all right! It's just . . . She's . . .' The voice went urgent, contrition drowned in a bubble of blokeish excitement. 'She's a fucking *goer*, mate! I can barely *move*, I'm that knackered!'

Shaper tried not to imagine. 'I haven't got time for this,' he said, astonished by his own calmness. 'Just get Tal and Tony, OK? I want them there this afternoon.'

He gazed out at the brothel, eyes narrowed, and the mental itch finally gathered the self-respect to formally introduce itself.

Oh, crap . . .

'Fine,' Vince was still muttering, oblivious. 'But look, about this thing with Sandra, it's—'

Shaper wasn't listening. Already spilling from the van, phone stranded on the seat.

The brothel door was hanging off its hinges.

Kicked in.

361

And so he ran, and had just enough time to reflect – sour – that clear-headed or not, cleansed and purified or not, preternaturally relaxed or not, it still felt a lot like he was falling.

Inside, certain things were immediately apparent.

That the door had been so violently opened told Shaper a lot and, perversely, mitigated a little of his dread. There was none of the invasive creepiness he'd seen elsewhere: no waxy prints, no subtle penetration. This entry had been crude and brutish, a shock-and-fear job rather than some slinking assassination, and the interior had been methodically savaged. The walls stood dented and scraped where furniture had been publicly executed. Thin doors yawned like crippled jawbones, leering on twisted frames. Every flourish of Mrs Swanson's homely charm – the prints, the doilies, the discreet sex toys among china knick-knacks – lay shattered and scattered, as if a bomb had detonated without heat or fire or epicentre. Nothing stolen. Nobody hurt.

Just for show. A message.

It didn't take a genius to work out who'd sent it.

The twins have heard what happened to Vicar. They knew I'd come here. Which means—

Damn.

They knew Mary was here too.

The inner panic lifted a notch, even as the physical unwind continued. The place seemed deserted: no girls, no punters, no smiley old ladies, and no sign whatsoever of the damaged, suspicious, lovely liar he wanted. Just an odd scratching sound, from off among the detritus.

It turned out to be Mrs Swanson. On her hands and knees, she rasped at a patch of something flamingo-pink on the carpet with a silver butter knife. She saw Shaper approach and shot him a look of such concentrated accusation that he almost staggered. It felt a lot like being savaged by a kitten.

'Bubblegum,' she muttered, indicating the carpet. 'The fat one with the stupid hair.'

Dave. They came in person.

Fuck.

He started forwards to help – lips forming words he barely dared think: *did they take her?* – but the old lady froze him with a silent, venomous waggle of the knife. He showed off his palms and slunk back to the door, gnawing at the hurt in her eyes. Another life, fucked up by the bow wave of his own.

But then, even that shame was soothed as soon as it arrived, chased off by the memory of Glass's eerie, cleansing voice.

That, Shaper thought, is some powerful mojo.

He wished he believed in all that crap just a little more strongly.

'They made me ring the police,' the old lady snapped, bending back to the task. 'To "get you off", they said.'

'Yeah . . . Thanks.'

'Wanted to talk to you personally, they said. Couldn't abide you in a cell.'

'Mm. Listen, Mrs S, what happened to—'

'They said it meant you owed me.'

He blinked. Her voice had gone abruptly hard.

Priorities, of course. All these quasi-criminals. All my people, all my bastards. Not bad, not scum, not evil per se, just . . .

Just very clear about what matters most.

'Yeah,' he sighed, suddenly tired. 'Absolutely. And I'll pay for all this damage, of course. But where's M—'

'And they said it meant you owed them, too.'

'Naturally.'

She got back to scraping, then sniffed across the hall at the one room that still had a door.

'She's in there. She's fine.'

Shaper nearly choked on relief.

* * *

Except that she wasn't fine.

Mary sat scrunched into the right angle between the bed and wall, arms round her shins, peering over her knees as he inspected her. She just stared.

'You OK?' he said, shutting the door behind him.

'No damage.'

No anger either, at least not of the explosive variety. In the short time Shaper had known her, Mary had responded to every trauma, every exhumed family secret, in mercurial shades of sultriness and drama. It troubled him to even see her like this, as composed as any diamond. Even so, even on emotional standby, she took his breath away.

'They said they were twins,' she mumbled. 'They don't look alike.'

'No, they don't.'

'They went through my things.' She rolled her eyes to one side, where the exploded contents of her handbag had been roughly shoved back into its innards. A tiny photo of the young Devon family – smiling mother, grinning kids – sat atop the junk.

Happy. A long, long time ago.

'I'm sorry,' Shaper said. 'It's my fault. I hope they didn't scare you.'

'They're pretty fucked off.' She glanced up for an instant. 'But not at me.'

'Yeah.'

There was a strange coldness at work here, he was realising; something deeper than fear in her eyes. He waited her out.

'They told me you'd set them on to Karl,' she said eventually.

Ah.

He sighed from his guts and creaked down on to the bed, close enough to touch her – if he dared.

'Well,' he said. 'Yeah. Yeah, I suppose I did. I thought you were in the crosshairs. Seemed sensible.'

'You sent gangsters to kill my brother . . .' She seemed to be weighing the words. 'And it seemed sensible.'

He just nodded, too calm to fuss.

'And then what? You stopped them from doing it anyway? Why?'

'I got the wrong bloke.'

He felt it dawning on her, sensing rather than seeing her head twist to face him from the side. 'So Karl's innocent?'

'Yeah. He was just . . .' He flapped a useless hand. 'Just trying to protect someone he loved.'

'None of them . . . none of them were by him? He was never out to get me?'

'No.'

'And he never hurt anyone?'

'Not as such, no.'

He could almost taste the optimism rising off her, a gathering ray of hope. He wondered how much the Corams had known when they came here, how much they'd told her, how much the police had made public in the morning's news spaff.

'So he's fine?' Mary said, reaching out for him. 'Y-you stopped the gangsters getting him? Karl's OK?'

Shaper closed his eyes. Shook his head.

And told her everything while she wilted.

He told her about a murderer with a plan. Someone so enslaved by superstition – by *faith* – that their quest towards whatever clusterfuck-crazy goal they'd assumed was a checkerboard of magic lanterns, energised chakras and ageless gurus. He told her what she'd already guessed, that her mother's tight little gang of fuckfriends and LSD lovers had, fifteen years before, focused its efforts to develop a pseudosensical treatment. He told her that each member had devoted themselves utterly to a single aspect of their psyches, each becoming a master of a single vibration, a single chakric node in the wider circuit.

'And now,' he said, 'some unstable little tit called Fossey's trawling about nicking them.'

It sounded just as ludicrous out loud as it had in his head.

Mary stared. Her fingers were still lightly touching his arm and, realising, she pulled them away, wrapping herself back round her shins and swallowing loud enough for him to hear. Then she asked the one question he was entirely incapable of answering.

'Why?'

He leaned back on his elbows and puffed his cheeks. A strange process memory told him that by now a headache should be depth-charging his forehead, but it – along with the shakes, the sweats, the pains – seemed to have got lost in transit. He almost felt guilty.

'Haven't the foggiest,' he said. 'I mean, he's insane, for a start. Doesn't exactly lend itself to sensible motives, that.' He scratched at his hair, wondering how long it had been since he last showered, how much of a shaggy scarecrow he must look. 'That's sort of the link. He's only mental in the first place because this treatment of theirs went so bloody wrong.'

'So it's revenge then?'

'Well, yeah . . . that's the sensible assumption. Except why kill Karl? He had nothing to do with any of it, and . . . *uh*.'

He realised what he'd blurted a little too late.

'So Karl's dead,' she said. Voice whisper-quiet. Looking away.

Shaper hung his head, remembering DI Canton's words from the midst of his breakdown haze. A bloke with no eyes. *Won't last the day . . .*

'No. Not quite,' he said. 'Badly hurt's all you need to know.'

Mary nodded, detached. Whispered, 'Ajna.'

'Exactly. Second sight, right?' He pinched the bridge of his nose, faking the pain of the no-show headache. It seemed the least he could do. 'You understand now why I thought you'd be next? Everything was pointing to Karl being the perp, and he'd just got his mitts on your address . . .' He coughed into a fist. 'And you did sort of spend the last few years telling everyone you had the whammyvision.'

'But it wasn't me, was it?'

'No.'

'It was Karl. Karl had the gift.'

Shaper opened his mouth with a thoughtless *if you believe in that sort of thing*, but bit down before it could escape. Mary was unravelling before his eyes.

All her life, wanting her ma's attention, bit of fucking praise. A moment's pride.

But even now, even when the old cow's dead and her twitchy little fuck of a brother's had both his eyes put out, Karl's still the special one.

He wanted to reach out to her, then. To touch her leg, grip her arm – *something*. But the bubble of concentrated emotion around her felt somehow sacrosanct; inviolable.

They sat in silence for long, slow minutes, until finally Mary shook her hair from her face, as if clearing her eyes could wipe away the rest of her miseries too.

'So what now?' she said.

Shaper breathed from his belly. 'Only one left. Number seven makes the full set.' He sat up, reluctantly motivated. 'Actually, I . . . I should be off. I need to get to him.'

'Glass.'

He nodded.

She seemed to change at that. All her fear and sadness, he guessed, being pushed aside; the clash of traumas sidelined in favour of a far worthier focus: an unshakeable concern for the one person they both felt – they both *knew* – was irreplaceable.

She took his hand. 'I want to come with you.'

Chapter Thirty-three

They were an hour down the motorway before either spoke again.

After an aeon of awkward rumination – not least on the current state of the bilateral 'we' – Shaper's confusions were swept aside by a flickered glance and a pursed lip from the passenger seat.

'You're different,' Mary said. 'Less twitchy.'

He wondered abstractly if that was different good or different bad, but shrugged his way through it with a nonchalance designed to prove her right. 'Suppose I am,' he said. 'Got some shit off my chest. Laying off the vices. That sort of thing.'

'So what happened?'

He shot her a puzzled frown. It dawned on him, gauging her expression as part way between inquisitive and afraid, that she'd detected in this new him – no longer shaking, no longer sweating and falling apart – a change in his approach to her. He realised she'd been sitting there all along, engine growling, lingering on precisely the same uncertainties as him.

Where does this leave us?

He almost blushed with the revelation. Expertly masking the happy surprise, he snapped off what he hoped was a 'you've got nothing to worry about' gesture and struggled back to her question.

What did happen, Dannyboy?

'Glass,' he shrugged, lame. 'Glass happened. He . . . he's fixed me, I think. One minute I'm all fucked up, the next he comes on the phone and—'

'No, no,' she interrupted, 'not that.' An odd look in her eye. 'I mean the first time. What happened to make you that way in the first place?'

Oh.

For a moment, just staring, he forgot the road, warping back only when a lorry bull-roared from behind to arrest his airy inter-lane drift. He could barely raise the flustered shock that seemed appropriate, focused instead fully on the enquiry. He could almost feel his muscles re-knotting at the thought of it, Glass's wyrd influence ebbing away. He could nearly even persuade himself she was cruel to be asking such things, except that when he glanced across, he saw in her eyes nothing but earnestness and care.

She was concerned for him.

This, he panicked, was adult relationship territory.

He thought back to their first real meeting, that day in Tightfisted Tony's. She'd bolshed and bullshitted then caved like a Pompeii party, baring her soul.

My turn now.

It took him a while to gather the courage.

'I worked for the Corams,' he said, mouth dry. 'I . . . I did stuff for them. Bad stuff.'

He let it hang, and could almost hear the question rustling up her spine.

'Did you kill anyone?'

'No,' he said, slow and distant. Then muttered, 'Not directly.'

Somehow it sounded worse than a simple 'yes'.

A new silence settled, until Mary shifted in her seat and blurted, 'Why? Why would you get into that?'

'Honestly?'

'Honestly.'

He steadied himself, hating the words long before they reached his tongue.

'Because it made the Corams love me.'

He kept his eyes on the road, uncomfortably aware of her silent stare, and pushed deeper into the morass of memory just to annihilate the silence.

'I didn't . . . didn't really understand that's what I was after, not at the start. But it's the truth. Structure, you know? Family. Amazing what it'll make you do.'

Mary was silent. Shaper supposed she understood the sentiment better than most.

'Anyway. I started to hate it. The job, the routine. You would, wouldn't you? Nightmares, guilty conscience, all that . . . Then one day I get this job. Bunch of Albanian bastards out of Bethnal Green, trafficking girls – fucking disgusting, the way they're treated. And Ma Coram sends me round to have a word. I mean, it's a territory thing more than a moral thing, but still . . . So it's me and a couple of lads, with the twins watching from the car, and just as we get there, there's a shipment arriving.'

Shaper saw them then, conjured through the rain and the road; in every broken drizzle speck an exhausted face, a sallow cheek, a soiled skirt.

'All but dead from the journey, poor cows, stuck in the back of a freight box all the way up Europe. And it's like I said, I was getting sick of it all by then, and these girls were in such a state . . . And one of these Albanians – the boss, y'know? – he sees me getting pissed off and he can't understand. He says they're like cattle. Products. "Just whores," he says. "Not proper people."' Shaper felt the first soft prelude to a headache invading his equilibrium, like a returning comrade. 'So instead of just putting the frighteners on the fuckers, I got the lads to kick the crap out of them. And I forced them to drop the girls' debts.' He lowered his voice, flicking Mary a courtesy glance but not seeing her at all. 'That's how it works. Charge them a fortune for the trip, make them pay it off on their backs. Four, five different johns a day. Slaves, really. "Just whores, not proper people." *Jesus.*'

He sensed her nodding. A quiet murmur, barely audible above the engine, slipped from the ether. 'Sounds like you did a good thing.'

He ignored the bad taste it brought to his mouth.

'Anyway. Just to underline the point, I get the bloke in charge and, well, and cut off one of his balls.'

Mary suddenly not nodding anymore.

'I mean, n-not personally,' he stammered, as if it mattered. 'The lads did the actual – y'know. But it was my order. And the cunt deserved it.'

The muscles in his shoulders were cramping hard now. The whites of his knuckles, stark on the wheel, hinted at the first trace of an incipient tremble. He told himself he'd imagined it – the new him, soothed and stable – and ploughed onwards.

'One of these girls . . .' (*say her name, coward*) 'Anna. She and I kind of clicked. And for a long time things got better. Didn't matter the Corams were full of shit, didn't matter the whole "family" thing was . . . was falling apart. I had her. My own little family, yeah? I tell you, if anyone was ever gonna prise me out of this . . . this world I'm in . . .' He let the sentence die before it lived, sucking in a deep breath.

'She got pregnant. Scary, but there you go. And I was on the verge of telling the Corams to go fuck themselves when . . .'

The world teetered. The rain smeared. He frowned and clenched his jaw, keeping it all together.

'The one-bollocked Albanian,' Mary interjected. He'd almost forgotten she was there. 'You mentioned it the other day.'

'Yeah. Took a shot at me in the fucking street, didn't he? Hit her.'

The images tried to ooze back, flicker flashes like needles in his brain.

He saw a petal of redness on an ivory maternity dress, smelled detergent and heard sirens. Ambulance voices snapped brusque decisions, too buried in exhaustion to seem genuine. He remembered swearing and vomit, and more fear than the world could contain, atomising everything, pissing down runnels in his soul.

'They had to operate straight away,' he said, the wobble plain in his voice. 'She was still conscious – ready to go through. And right there she looked at me . . . Sh . . . she had weird eyes, my Anna . . . She looked at me and said . . . said she'd thought for a while I'd been cheating on her. She said she was scared, you know, and . . . she didn't want to go in for surgery with this hanging over. She said whatever I'd done, she forgave me. Just wanted the truth. Clear the air.'

A toxic silence settled. The van breezed over the texture line of the hard shoulder and the brief rattle was a weird relief.

'And had you?' Mary said. 'Been cheating?'

'Yeah.' He nodded. 'Over and over. And not with anyone special either, just . . . just because. I mean I only half-understand it myself. It's like . . . Sometimes I thought I never really loved her at all, just wanted this, this situation. This family cell. Fooling myself, like. B-but I never fucking deserved it anyway – I knew that, deep down – so the second I got it, I did everything I could to bugger it up, without even knowing. That's funny, isn't it?'

No, it's not.

He sighed again. 'I always fuck it up, Mary.' With something a little like shock he realised he was thoughtlessly warning her, like a virus presenting its own inoculation. Get out while you still can.

She looked away.

Smart girl.

'You know the real irony?' he murmured, the purge achieving an irresistible momentum, impossible to arrest. 'In that hospital, before she went in, I realised I *did* love her after all. Had done all along.'

He noticed with a jolt he'd nearly missed the turn-off, and piled the van sideways harder than he'd meant. 'So, yeah . . .' he resumed, too focused on the vent to care about the rough ride, 'she asks if I've been cheating. And this is my chance. Come clean, unburden. Yes, I need to tell her. I've been cheating. But I love you, and I'll never cheat again.'

'Instead you lied.'

A cold, certain prediction.

'Course I bloody lied. And I could tell she knew. And she died half an hour later with a surgeon's hand fishing our dead baby out of her guts.' He shrugged. 'And that was that.'

The van left the main roads behind, country lanes winding like intestines. Trees clamoured overhead, and to Shaper they felt like a thousand arms, reaching down to poke and prod. Accusing.

'Something flicked in my head that day,' he said. 'I started . . . seeing thing. Things about myself and . . . people around me. Never once cried for Anna, if you want the truth, but it fucked me up, that lie. That stupid bloody betrayal. And . . . no chance to take it back, is there?'

Mary's eyes bored into him, narrow with fascination. He coughed away the tension and clung to the story.

'Anyway, there's one more exciting chapter.' He forced a bitter smirk, miming a phone. 'So I call the Corams and tell them all about it. And I'm demanding to know what the living fuck they're gonna do about this one-balled Albanian cunt who's just killed my missus. And I politely put it to them, as a personal favour, that when they catch said cunt, and have him pinned down, I be allowed to tear open his ribs and shit on his heart.'

Beside him – probably – Mary's face turned away. He didn't bother to check.

'They told me it wasn't the right time. "Couldn't make a serious power play against the Albanian cells," they said. They told me there were some interesting alliances on the table and, hey, c'mon Dan, don't let your emotions cloud your judgement.'

He glanced across at her. Her eyes, like his, wide and wine-red. She'd thoughtlessly retreated as far as she could, buttocks poised on the edge of the passenger seat, and with the certainty that she was scared of him came the thought: *good. Good for her.*

'This was my *family*,' he hissed. 'D'you understand? I threw myself at their feet and fucking begged for help.' He shook his head. 'They just offered me a pay rise.'

Mary said nothing. The van drove itself.

'I don't remember much after that. Bit of a blur. Came to my senses a few months later on my mum's sofa. Corams think I left 'em in the lurch, hence the bad blood. Walked out, got all arsey, went AWOL. It didn't help that the first thing I did when I was up and running again was get a mate to catch up with our one-bollocked friend.'

Good old DI Canton.

By the book never felt so good.

The van turned off a bosky little lane through the grand gates of Thornhill, and Shaper contemplated the long driveway with a mixture of dread and relief. The trembling in his fingers seemed to wax and wane as his breath entered and left, and – with a sudden pulse of decision – he threw a loaded look at the frightened woman beside him. And presented his filth like a gift.

'My brain didn't process things right, Mary, not after that. Not for a long time. Not till I found ways to cope.'

'You mean . . . like a sickness?'

He almost smiled. 'Maybe, yeah. Maybe like that. I even saw a few shrinks over the years; called it this or that. But . . . if you want my take on it – which ain't exactly scientific – what happened is that the whole thing fucked out the back of my skull. Like there was so much lying and shame, so much *mess*, that it sort of took over. Couldn't let me believe anything any more, least of all myself.'

He chewed at the wound inside his cheek, tearing clear moist strips. They tasted like ash.

'It's like I spent all that time deceiving, destroying . . .' He shrugged. 'Now my brain does it to me instead. Seems fair.'

The drizzle turned to rain. His voice ran out and he had the strangest sensation of segueing with himself.

Still falling.

'Why didn't you leave London?' Mary asked, voice a gentle aftershock. 'Start somewhere else?'

He tried to form the words. Tried to wrap his tongue round the diseased kernel of truth he felt sure lurked there. But the phrases wouldn't fit, the syllables seemed ugly and pompous, and no amount of articulacy could express it right.

The roof of the mansion loomed above black trees.

'You don't get to walk away from your guilt, Mary,' he said. 'You just don't.'

They drove the last minute in silence, and it was only when the van rumbled to a grateful halt that Shaper realised Mary's hand had been gripping his leg all along.

He hadn't felt a thing.

Chapter Thirty-four

Thornhill, Shaper fancied, had assumed an air of indecent smugness since his last visit, as if somehow aware the end would play out beneath its slate knuckles and relishing its own importance. He found himself fixing his gaze on the ground, as if avoiding its eyes, as he hustled Mary out of the rain.

Here. It finishes here. He shivered.

Inside, crashingly uncomfortable at the silence which had swiftly formed between Mary and Sandra, he hunted down Glass and steeled himself for interrogation. He felt he owed the old man an explanation for the mess his investigation had become, and more pertinently an apology for how events had reached this stage. Glass, after all, had doubtless met the other new arrivals already – Talvir and Tightfisted Tony, one enthusiastically playing with ultratech walkie-talkies, the other openly brandishing his ostentatiously illegal shotgun.

Vince was preparing them for a siege.

But if the old man was at all disturbed by such gung-ho displays, or irritated that his PI's efforts had culminated in such a crude last stand, then when Shaper eventually found him – reading nursery tales to Freddie – he gave no sign of it, greeting him with an unbearably decent smile and posing no tricky questions.

'Pleased you're here, m'boy,' he murmured.

When at last Glass released him from that warmest of hand

clasps, Shaper noticed with a dumb lack of surprise that his nascent shakes – semi-tangible since the confessions in the van – had faded again, and the old man's limbs had amplified their own trembling.

Like a fucking transaction, he thought, renewing the vow to protect this man. It was quite simply unthinkable – *unbearable* – to allow him any harm.

Mary's meeting with her karmic messiah was an even warmer affair: a European bout of *mwah-mwahing*, which transformed via a round of hand gestures into a chorus of 'shanti, shanti' blessings. She played the part of the fellow hippy without visible shame, and Shaper left them to it – slightly disgusted, slightly envious of their effortless connection – to inspect the troops.

Vince was busy playing drill sergeant in the grand hall.

'. . . is obviously the main target,' the brute was saying, visible exhaustion not diminishing his enthusiasm for pomp, 'so that's our primary fallback. Wherever *he* is,' he nodded at Glass, now hobbling out from Freddie's room to watch, '*you* are.'

His platoon wasn't much to look at – one puff-faced punk toting a sawn-off shooter in his sole functioning hand, one youthful campist in purple-tone camo – but they made up in straight-backed, chin-jutting attention what they lacked in everything else.

'Other non-coms too,' Vince added, pointing fingers at Freddie's room, then Mary, then Sandra as she emerged from the kitchen with fresh coffee. 'We don't know how this fucker feels about them, so let's not take any sillybollocks risks, right?'

Heads nodded, fists tightened. Vince yawned, weirdly inappropriate.

Declining a steaming mug for himself – feeling somehow that to caffeinate would be to violate his unchemical condition – Shaper turned from Sandra's proffered tray to catch, by chance,

Mary's eye. Then noticed, from a tiny angle tweak, that she'd been staring at the other woman all along. She covered it with a weak smile, helping Glass to the staircase so he could sit down and, thus settled, produced his red notebook and began to take dictation. Shaper wondered what century Glass was reliving now.

Sandra, he noted, watched the pair with barely disguised revulsion, and he remembered something she'd once said, on another cold, dark day at Thornhill, when he'd first mentioned Mary Devon.

'*No, I don't know her,*' she'd spat. '*I know of her. And if you're interested, Mr Shaper – honestly? I think she's a cunt.*'

'The problem we've got,' Vince was growling, 'is we don't want this nutcase getting away. We can't just lock up and keep him out. So when he comes we want him on a fucking plate. Now, according to Intelligence Division over there,' he hooked a sardonic thumb at Shaper, 'he's maybe got a thing for midnight, but we ain't about to take any chances. So we get the civs stashed away somewhere safe, nice and early. You two watch 'em; me and Dan are the front line. He gets past us, it's down to you.'

The two grunts all but saluted. Shaper had to give it to Vince: ten years out of uniform, he still strutted like a pro. Tony raised his crippled hand.

'Stash 'em where, then?'

Shaper stepped smartly forward, mind returning to the previous night's horror.

Vicar ensconced on the top step. Only one approach. Clever bastard.

'Top floor,' he said. 'We'll see the fucker coming a mile away, and—'

Sandra cut in with an outraged hiss, coffee tray wobbling. 'You can't drag Freddie up three flights of stairs!'

'But—'

'I won't allow it. It's too far.'

'Listen, Sandra—'

'I said no!'

'C'mon, San,' Vince tried, calming palms extended, 'it's not safe down here.' ('*San?*' Shaper silently echoed.)

'But it's just one guy!'

'Well, yeah . . .' Vince went to touch her arm then thought better of it. Shaper caught the brute's lightning glance at Talvir. 'But it's just one fucknut mentalist, who's killed a bunch of folks already. We've gotta . . . keep everyone safe.'

She looked set to fight on for a moment, then restricted herself to a surly mutter.

'It's still too far.'

'Then where?'

She javelined Shaper with a look, thick with emotions he couldn't read, and strode towards the kitchen, beckoning him to follow. 'There,' she said, aiming a finger.

He sighed, dull inevitability kneading his brain.

Warm air . . . forgotten laboratories . . . a chair made of fear.

'Fine,' he huffed. 'Put them in the sodding cellar.'

Freddie went down to the darkness. Even that short journey was enough to plunge Sandra into a mania of worries, and Shaper watched with an itching discomfort as she flapped her keys and fussed at the goons, hefting the trolley bed between them. He caught himself feeling perversely surprised at the depth of her affection – so much love and sadness and fear – for a child born in rape and ruin.

Then hated himself for even thinking it.

He's her boy. That's all it takes.

He thought back to the child he'd engendered all those years ago. A life in *potentia*, a proto-ghost frozen in time. He wondered, with all the cruelty of conjecture, what sort of father he might have made, and mentally backpedalled when it stirred in his skull a brief sensory lurch. *Don't go there.*

He rubbed his temples and pretended it hadn't happened.

At any rate, Sandra needn't have worried. Freddie seemed delighted at the attention – three quasi-criminals patiently steering him; faces cleansed with affectionate smiles – and Shaper found himself as uncomfortable with their effortless transformations as with Sandra's maternal fluster. He busied himself checking Vince's ingenious array of clatter alarms and booby traps on the ground floor – pots and pans suspended near danger doors; broken glass sown below vulnerable windows – and stood clear of the human warmth.

Besides, there were other reasons to avoid the cellars, and he caught himself pretending his reluctance to venture below was entirely due to having too much to do up here.

Not because of the dark or the heat.

The chair . . .

By the time he'd satisfied himself that any murderous intruder wouldn't be sneaking into the house unnoticed, Freddie had been successfully transferred. Shaper found Sandra filling a thermos with yet more coffee in the kitchen.

'Going to be a long night,' she explained. 'Everyone's tired.'

'They OK down there?'

'Fine.' She looked up through rising steam with a sudden sniff, fidgeting. 'Look, I'm . . . sorry if I've seemed snippy at times. I – *we* – appreciate all this. Really.'

Shaper took it with good grace, nodding gently, then seized the opportunity for a non-sequitur nuke with a guilty dribble of glee.

'Tell me everything you can about Matthew Foster.'

She almost teetered in her spot. Sandra, he'd learned, was fun to unbalance.

'Look, you were going out with the bloke. You know more about him than anyone.'

'But it was ages ago!'

'Don't care. What's he like? What are we up against here?'

Her mouth opened and closed, then sealed defiantly as a bony clicking sound began from nearby. It was Glass's cane, tapping a slow tattoo as Mary led him towards the cellar stairs.

Shaper wondered how much the old man had overheard – fascinated by Sandra's sudden poker face – and blanked his way through the guilty interruption with a nothing-to-worry-about wave and a lingering smile for Mary. She ignored it, and Glass himself simply fixed his daughter with a long gaze –

(*Liquid bronze.*)

– before clicking down into the warmth.

Sandra stood frozen until the percussion was eaten by silence, then rounded on Shaper with an urgent whisper. 'He doesn't know, all right?'

'What?'

'Dad. Doesn't know about me and Fossey. At least, doesn't *remember*. I'd like to keep it that way.'

Shaper shrugged. 'He's gone now. Spill.'

She stirred the coffee, huffing out loud.

'Fossey was . . . normal. Mostly. That's the funny thing, he wasn't this . . . this psycho you keep telling us to expect. I'm not sure I believe it.'

'"Mostly"?'

'Oh . . .' She dismissed it with a wave. 'A bit petty. Aggressive tendencies. Nothing I don't see every day.'

'You mean your work? Counselling?'

'Every relationship has a dominator and a supplicant, Mr Shaper, overtly or otherwise. Problems only arise when individuals don't know which one they are.'

Vince came clumping back from below as if invoked, rubbing

his eyes and yawning hugely. Free now from Tal's watchful gaze, he openly settled a palm on Sandra's arse, and leered at Shaper's glare.

One dominator, one supplicant. He wondered which was which.

'As a matter of fact,' Sandra said, 'he was quite caring, in a way.' She noticed Shaper's confused scowl towards Vince. 'Fossey, I mean.'

Ah.

'Clumsy, really. Awkward. I was only a kid, remember, but he wasn't much more. I don't think he knew how to play it.'

'So what happened? You weren't exactly forthcoming last time. How'd it all go wrong, Sandra?'

For one frightening second Shaper felt a clamour behind his eyes, flash-framing the woman's skull as tangled memories bubbled up inside like a lava lamp.

But the impression was lost as swiftly as it came, and took with it the momentary terror that this state of calm he'd discovered – this preternatural not-fucked-up-ness – was only temporary.

No. I'm cured.

'It gets . . . weird,' Sandra said, with an odd expression. 'The memories are sort of jumbled, you know? It was a strange time in my life. Things come back in odd places.'

'Try, yeah? I just want to know what this bastard's like.'

She crossed her arms, unhappy, and nodded once.

'We . . . were up there one night. Me and him – my bedroom. Everyone else was down here – Father and the rest.'

Shaper heard a soft sound, and turned to find Mary at the head of the cellar stairs, listening. She ignored his enquiring look, and Sandra was too lost to even notice her, hands moving across the coffee, gazing through them into the past.

'We could hear them chanting. Dad didn't even know Fossey

had got in to see me, so we were being quiet.' She risked a gentle grin towards Vince, as if sharing a silly memory, then clocked Mary at the edge of her vision. The smile died.

'Anyway,' she sniffed, suddenly flippant. 'We tried to fuck. And it didn't hurt me like he expected, so he wanted to know why.'

'You weren't a virgin,' Shaper said.

She mimed a sarcastic applause. 'So I started crying, like an idiot –'

'You were just a kid,' Vince mumbled, obscurely defending her from herself.

'– and it all came out in the open.'

Shaper gave her a moment, but it was clear she wouldn't proceed without a nudge. 'You'd been raped?' he prompted. 'Before that?'

She aimed the word at Mary. 'Yes.'

'By Karl?'

Another nod. 'A few months before, if you must know. Similar sort of night – and that's what I mean when I say it's hard to remember. Things blur together, all right?'

'All right.'

'They were all downstairs that night too. Fucking. And Karl was here because . . . oh, I don't know, his mum wanted to keep an eye, probably. Didn't trust him. We were supposed to be doing homework upstairs, him and me, but I suppose he . . . he got caught up in the sounds from down here because . . . he . . .'

Her voice cut off. For a second Shaper thought she might cry, but at the last second she jutted her chin, all false decorum. 'I don't remember it well, anyway.'

'Bollocks,' Mary cut in, voice like a scalpel. 'Karl's gay.'

Sandra looked more sympathetic than outraged. 'Gay or not, he was a jealous little sod.' She wiped an eye. 'Wanted to own

Fossey for himself. Took it out in the wrong way.' She fixed Mary with an open stare. 'It's the male condition – possess or befoul. It's a lot stronger than sexuality. I'm sorry.'

Mary almost spat, turning on her heel and stamping back downstairs. Shaper wondered, vaguely, if he should go after her.

'Anyway,' Sandra resumed, absolving his indecision and appearing to thaw. 'I told Fossey all this on the night we tried to . . . you know. I was hoping he'd be supportive. Help me. I'd missed a couple of periods and . . . and . . .'

Vince, responding to some hitherto unsuspected instinct, guided her to a seat at the kitchen table and draped an arm across her shoulder.

'But he wasn't,' she said, addressing Shaper. 'Supportive, I mean. He was angry. Shouted, screamed, got . . . possessive. I didn't understand, back then.'

'Now?'

She gave a bitter little shrug, gently – though not entirely accidentally – dislodging Vince's arm. 'Pretty typical. Territorial tree-pissing. Dominator, supplicator.'

'He got violent?'

'And then some. Did more or less what Karl had already done.' She rubbed her face, as if the pains of recollection were worsening.

For the second time Shaper felt a starburst of the unreal – a sludge-filled glot of wrongness – and instantly broke out in a sweat, pushing it away.

I'm cured, I'm cured, I'm cured.

No more delusions.

Fuck it.

It faded, but in so doing left a resonant image, like a contrail seared on his retina, of something red and many-limbed trying to unknot itself behind Sandra's eyes. A painful, squealing trauma.

'Th-this is the part I find hard to remember,' she whispered. 'I think . . . Dad came bursting in. I mean . . . It's the sort of thing that happened a lot. He'd come up to check on me. And . . . and that night he came in and found Fossey standing there.' She pointed, as if seeing the tableau in the present tense; her bedroom superimposed on the chilly tiles of the kitchen. 'Naked. And me on the floor, crying. And Dad must've . . . done something. I didn't see him move. Just . . . Fossey's nose was bleeding, and he was being . . . punched, kicked. I'd never seen Dad like that.'

Shaper sat down beside her, horrified to feel almost as sickened by the idea of George Glass in that chaotic rage as by the sexual violation that had triggered it. So profound was the old man's grip on his association with serenity that any counter-impression – the notion of him idiotic with violence – was as disturbing as the stew of horrors already circulating the case: murder, organ theft, rape and all.

'You understand now,' Sandra murmured, 'why I didn't want him to overhear? He's . . . he's better for not knowing. I never want to see him like that again.'

Shaper nodded, off balance at some deep, personal place.

'Anyway . . . Dad dragged Fossey off. There was no sound – I remember that. I remember thinking that was weird.'

'He threw him out?'

'Mm. Ran the whole length of the drive, not wearing a thread.' She blinked up abruptly, as if emerging from a dream. 'I never saw him again.'

The trio basked in a prickly silence. Shaper stared through the kitchen window, fringed with dense ivy, daring the murk to disgorge a hint of the fiend without.

'One thing . . . You said your dad didn't know Fossey had come inside to see you. But they were all downstairs that night.'

She shrugged. 'So?'

'So how did he get up there,' Shaper nodded towards the ceiling, and Sandra's distant room, 'without them knowing?'

She blinked. And slowly swivelled her head to the window and the rain slashing against it.

Chapter Thirty-five

By 11 p.m., lit only by the liquid grey of the night beyond, Shaper sat slumped on a dressing stool in Sandra's characterless bedroom and awaited the beast.

Eyes fixed immovably on the left-hand window, he fidgeted with the shotgun in his lap and wondered how Tightfisted Tony had intended to reload the thing if he ever did have to use it. Since Vince had commandeered it for a starring role up here on the front line, it was a one-handed feat he was unlikely to witness.

Glaring at the drizzle, every extra minute added weight to his growing certainty that, no matter what Sandra had said, Fossey's old access point was a dead loss.

Climbing up the bloody wall.

Buckle thy fucking swash.

Vince, opting to join him for this silent lookout – peering from on high through shoal ripples of rain, across empty lawns – had initially seemed to be demonstrating something akin to loyalty, and Shaper had thanked him for his support as they'd settled in. At which the brute had wordlessly handed over the gun, flopped on to the bed, and demonstrated that loyalty was nothing compared to the need for a comfortable lie-down. He'd nodded off three times already, the shit, and Shaper kept poking him with the gun just for the sake of it. It passed the time.

Through the window, the top few leaves of the ivy which

blanketed the mansion's flanks spun in windy gyres, jutting above the sill, and tapped softly at the pane. Vince stirred at the interruption, shooting Shaper a bleary look.

'You know what you were saying before?' he wurbled. 'Like . . . you being grateful for the support? All that?'

Shaper rolled his eyes. 'Danger bonus, is it? How much?'

'What? No, I . . . it's just, you won't be mentioning anything to Tal about . . . y'know. Will you?' He nodded into the gloom where, Shaper knew – based on a brief allowance of electric light when they'd first traipsed up here – lurked rumpled sheets, conspicuously male underpants, and a respectable heap of condom wrappers.

He sighed. 'Depends.'

'On?'

'On how long you intend to keep tupping her.' He put on his best responsible adult voice. 'I'm not sure I can condone an ongoing extra-marital.'

Even now, even half-jokey, the hypocrisy tasted like rot and shame.

'Oh, c'mon.' Vince flopped over. 'You know how these things work – contract jobs. 'Slike a holiday romance, innit? Never lasts. Stressful situations're the best fucking aphrodisiacs out.'

Shaper's mind went directly to Mary. He wondered what she was doing, packaged away in the bowels of the building, huddled with the old man whose orbit held them both. Was she thinking about him? he wondered. Gnawing at the future?

Their future?

By the time he'd hefted himself from the pointless brain spiral, Vince was snoring again, with a book he'd excavated from Sandra's shelf perched over his face. *The Gaucher's Families of Norrbotten*, Shaper read, fronted by a grainy child scowling through grotesque disfigurement. He shivered, not knowing why.

Something scampered at the window and made him jump.
Just the ivy. Settle down.

The pane on the left was the danger spot, Sandra had been very specific about that. A thick carpet of vines swarmed across the wall on both faces of the corner embrasure, but Fossey had apparently discovered, back in the day, a particular network of ledges and pipes beneath the morass, leading to one window like a god-sent ladder. Beneath its bosky shield he could scuttle up to his girlfriend's window and, providing none of the meditating morons downstairs had seen him approach the house, the ascent itself was an undetectable piece of cake.

Today the ivy was even thicker than it had been, and Shaper had thoughtfully unlatched the window, as if carelessly left, to bait his trap. He'd positioned himself close enough to keep a general eye on the grounds, but far enough back to remain undetected until the monster was at the window, poised to ooze inwards. And, with rather more foresight than the hippy squad of yesteryear, he'd placed Talvir at an unlit window downstairs, contactable via his impressive radios, specifically to watch the driveway. It was one thing to be lurking at the top of a secret magical stairway; it was quite another to be stupid enough to let anyone shimmy up unnoticed.

Not, he reminded himself, that that was likely.
Climbing the bloody wall. Too Errol Flynn.

The rain fluxed in the wind. Vince snored lower, and Shaper found himself fighting a battle between his own exhaustion and an adrenal frisson of terror, refusing to go away.
It's coming.
The monster, the killer, the crazy . . .
It ends tonight.

He shivered, and sat, and waited.

More rattling at the window, another heart-in-mouth moment. He glared at the leafy fronds and wondered how Sandra could bear such a distraction, then remembered the Serax he'd seen before.

Instant sleep. She'd hidden it away, tonight.

The sensation of wrongness crept up only slowly. Not the explosive distortion he was so used to, but a gentler insanity, a building crackle of static and fear which infected his senses one by one, and solidly pinioned his eyes to the halo of ivy ringing the glass. First came a distant whiff of rotting meat, then a metal taste and magnetic tug at the tips of his fingers, and finally a jolt of blood and fire out in the drizzle.

Something awful, his brain cooed. *Waiting* . . .

The whole thing dissipated without fuss, and left him – curiously – more depressed than disturbed. He'd been so sure (or at least so hopeful) that the delusions were done with, that the morning's eerie conversation with Glass had cleansed his psychic palette and purified the narcotic urge . . .

Fuck.

Angrily enforcing the denial, he resisted the urge to check the window, confounding every hunch of impending hazard. But it itched at him with such unignorable persistence that he huffed out loud and groped for the walkie-talkie.

Just a whim, he told himself.

'Tal?' he buzzed through. 'You down there? It's Shaper.'

Bollocks to saying 'over'.

'Yeah. Dead as a nun's knickers down here, mate. And that Sandra can't make coffee for shit.'

'Just keep watching, yeah?'

'Roger-roger.'

He laid down the radio and settled back on the stool.

And then his senses went crazy.

Faster and harder this time, as if punishing him for not acting before. His eyes sparked with a perfect storm of embers and silver, swiftly guzzled in a haze of bloody red. It coalesced like a nightmare cloud, haunting the fringes of the vine, accompanied by the stink of saffron and iron, the wail of a sitar, a tabla beat, and—

Rustling. Damp and stealthy.

A snake, slithering among leaves . . .

His whole body jerked. His hips propelled him from the stool even as his knees buckled, depositing him directly on to the carpet. He waited for the visual crackle to end, not daring to indulge his disappointment at the returning seizures, and let the fit fade like a neutron star. His eyes stayed fixed throughout on the twigs beyond the window, tapping out the time, and as soon as his feet would bear him, he leapt up to poke Vince in the spine.

'Mate.'

'*Nmf* ?'

'The window.'

'What about it?'

His voice felt alien in his mouth. 'I-is there something moving in the ivy, mate?'

Vince creaked upright, groggy, and drifted to the glass. Shaper cautiously joined him, annoyed at his own hesitance, and they peered down together.

A few feet below, sure enough, the ivy rippled. But so smooth were its movements – a soft peristalsis – that he found it impossible to judge if it was caused by something inside, some dark maggot blanketed from view, or the wash of the breeze. 'Can't be anyone,' he said, hunting reassurance. 'Tal would've seen.'

Vince tilted his head. 'Yeah. I mean. Unless.'

'What?'

'Well . . . unless the fucker's been waiting under there all evening.'

Shaper stared. 'I hate you,' he said.

Vince smirked, humourless.

Acting on some silent signal, they went to work. Vince took the gun and carefully hinged wider the window, nodding Shaper forwards.

Oh god . . .

He leant out.

The cold hit his face an instant before the rain. He held his breath for one dizzying instant – precipice dropping away, fuzzy with greenery – then tilted further still.

The gun loomed beside his head, aimed past into the womb of the vine.

Which pulsed, over and over.

He tried to ignore his heart – a painful machine, a rig pounding red oil – and hooked his fingers into the highest layer of the creeper. The leaves were cold, waxy-smooth and damp, above papery stalks. He began to pull and a cavity opened, a gulf beneath a twiggy duvet, cross-hatched by moonlight and rain spray. He squinted closer.

Is that . . .

And something exploded behind him.

Vince howled. Shattered glass spumed across Shaper's shoulders and, as he dragged himself back inside on instinct, he warded off the shards with a boneless arm.

The other window, he thought, too late. The window on the fucking right!

Something black festered there. Something atrocious, reaching from the galaxy of ice, half a brick clutched in a gloved claw.

It smacked Vince, hard, on the arm.

The gun dropped from the brute's grip, lost to the rain, and even as the big man flopped sideways, the weapon was roaring uselessly far below, firing on impact. Shaper spiralled from the sill to find Vince clutching at his elbow, on the floor. Above his head the jagged remnants of the window were kicked out in quick, efficient strikes.

And something—

IT.

– unfolded inwards like a great spider.

It snarled without sound, alive with red and gold, all angles and polished beauty. Lights popped behind Shaper's eyes, and whether the monster (*just a man just a man just a man*) pushed him or hit him or touched him at all, he felt himself stumble back, bouncing off the frame of the embrasure and collapsing to his knees, body failing.

Oh god, oh god—

Vince was upright again. Somewhere a knife flickered in the dark like a panicked fish, and the big lug was ducking with a grunt, throwing a messy punch with his left hand. It was a clumsy contact, forcing a sympathetic wince from Shaper even through the mess of his senses, but enough to send the killer staggering, screaming out loud. A wordless, bodiless howl.

Vince kept groaning, gun arm useless, and as Shaper shook his head to clear the nebulae of ghosts and monsters, the beast came on again, blade coring the air.

That, Shaper's rational brain snapped, is my fucking knife.

Vince's dodge was too slow. He screamed as the blade buried in the soft meat of his buttock – a howl of outrage as much as pain – and lashed out with his right hand, oblivious to whatever damage it had already sustained. It struck the mask with a glorious *crack* and smashed the snarling façade. Even as he hollered and spun away, clutching at his arse and the knife still lodged there, a blue segment was dropping away, revealing the killer's cheek and chin below.

Pale, pink.

Human.

And Shaper's head cleared.

It was as if the thing's rage was its truest and greatest weapon. As if its awful countenance – those coiled brows and leering lips – were enough to cripple him, and now that they were exposed as mere membranes, they were robbed of their power.

He stood up, feeling the world settle around him. And said, 'Fossey, you unspeakable little cunt.'

The killer jerked as if he'd been electrocuted. Panicking, as if his own name was enough to disarm him, he stumbled back, throwing a sideways glance at Vince, still swearing and spitting on his knees.

And the monster turned and fled.

'Hey!' Shaper screamed, indignantly certain the grand confrontation wasn't meant to go like this. The black shadow dived from the window before he could move, crazed arms grabbing matted ivy, wet handfuls tumbling, and scurried off like a gecko down the wall.

And before he could stop himself, screaming for Vince to *watch the others*, Shaper was out of the window too, clambering in pursuit.

Life's easy, he reminded himself, with something to chase.

The descent was a crude, panicked affair, a plummet indefinitely postponed. Shaper's hands seared with the friction of slick branches, snapping and shifting with every ungraceful inch, and at some uncertain stage he paused to adjust, swinging his feet below himself before his head popped with gathering blood.

Peering briefly through the ivy veil, he thought he saw something moving at the distant dog-leg in the driveway, huge and glossy, like the carapace of a gargantuan beetle. But amidst the froth of the chase, it seemed a doubtful impression – gone the instant he looked again – and at the thrashing retorts of the killer's own descent below he snapped back to the task at hand, releasing his hold and letting gravity suck him through the foliage.

(Still falling. Always falling.)

He checked an insane laugh while still in his throat, and concentrated on not breaking his neck.

At the bottom of the vine he caught sight of the tattered figure haring across the lawn, and launched in pursuit, ignoring muffled shouts from the windows at his back. Tal, screaming into his radio.

Too late, mate.

Across mud-sludged grass and the weathered drive, coat flapping like wet wings, he ran. His eyes scrunched cautiously against the barbs of rain – great whorls of cyclonic geometry surrounding him – even as his feet relentlessly slipped across smeared leaves and rabbit-hole muck.

Get him!

The figure vanished between slick bushes, branches beckoning in its wake. Shaper slapped his way through a wooded copse with his teeth gritting, cautious of an ambush but too adrenalised to decelerate.

No weapons, mate. Doesn't matter.

Slowly the light dimmed – the mansion's tungsten ochre failing to seep this far into the brush – and with it went the frenzy of his blood. In the dank blur he spent long moments hunting motion on the path, every glimpse of a trailing boot briefly resurrecting the buzz, every questionable silhouette oxygenating the embers of his excitement. And his fear.

In the branches above him, damp and surly things fluttered in disrupted sleep. Shaper ignored them, fending off the leathery gargoyles and hissing fiends they threatened to conjure, and at last stumbled to a halt in the muddy humus on the bank of a lake, abruptly and breathtakingly exposed to the sky. He felt as if its sudden vacuum had stripped off his last vestiges of anger and courage – an esoteric decompression – and the realisation lurking below them grew clearer with a lurch.

You lost him.

Panting, cursing every cigarette he'd ever called the last, he turned and trudged along the edge of the water, aiming dimly towards the mansion but adopting a wide arc, vaguely hoping he might yet intersect the killer's path.

Vaguely hoping, vaguely dreading.

As he walked, mind wandering with the gentle drip feed of fear, he became slowly aware of starker, less organic forms amidst the undergrowth. Slick and moss-speckled, each stony surface presented a hard-edged clump of pillared, pointless art. He passed pagodas beneath jealous oaks, fallen busts staring in dead-eyed indignation at the plinths that once held them, and – set behind an elm spinney – a weird dome rising from the mud, a bony scapula encrusted with dirt and rainwater slime. A rusted hatch sat like a cyborg aberration at its crown, padlocked shut. It made Shaper's flesh crawl, though he couldn't explain why, and he checked the hatch with great care, ensuring it was both locked and dry on its lipped edges, not recently opened. Thus discountable as part of the killer's disappearance, he got the fuck away from it as quickly as he could.

He stumbled upon the van almost immediately.

It was a filthy, elderly thing – not too dissimilar to his own, he thought, although even less loved. It lurked in the lee of the dome like a sleeping turtle, half submerged in the leaf litter. A few dripping branches had been clustered around it – shields against lucky glances from the driveway – but most had been torn off and dumped. Shaper's breath caught in his throat as he saw why.

The front doors hung open. The side panel was gaping wide and the cab light was still on.

He's been here.

He's been here and you didn't bring the fucking walkie-talkie, did you?

Moron.

He stole an indulgent minute pulling himself together – nerves screaming, trusting Vince and the others to hold the proverbial fort – then slowly circled the vehicle at a wide remove, goose-stepping through the brush to peer in from all angles. Only when he was certain there was no movement did he dare to creep nearer.

The cab held little of interest: a box of tissues on the dashboard and a few empty crisp packets on the floor. But if he was secretly disappointed at such prosaic findings, his first glance in the van's hold restored his flagging adrenaline, shot nails into his blood and flopped-over his stomach.

It was Tova. Blonde, buxom Tova, nurse's threads showing through the sodden folds of her coat. Her shoes were slick with mud, tucked beneath her like a coiled spring.

She was dead, and something had tried to eat her face.

'Jesus . . .' he whispered to the night.

There was little blood to see, though it was clear there had been. He supposed the side door had been left to gape for as long as she'd been inside: a smorgasbord for every fox, rat, crow . . .

At some point they'd given up gnawing at the blood in her clothes and made a start on her cheeks, lips and eyes. Even the untouched patches of her flesh were puffy and pale, threaded with a grim tracery of cold veins and young putrefaction.

She'd been strung up, that much was clear. Wrists bound in wire loops, hooked to a chassis crossbeam and left to dangle like a puppet, slowly dismembering her own hands.

Shaper hoped her throat had been cut before they'd tightened too far.

He tried not to stare at the bloodless edges of the neck wound; at the rheumy grooves round the cables on each wrist; at the thin patina of mould already forming on her coat . . . and found his mind returning, almost more painfully, to a vision of her strutting from the back door of the house, full of purpose.

'*At least wait a while!*' he'd cried out. '*We'll be going back to town after this. Give you a lift?*'

She hadn't wanted to wait. And she hadn't got far.

Tearing his eyes off the bloated vision, he peered at the space around her: three mattresses lodged with care – one on the floor, one to each vertical side – beneath the fogged covers of plastic sheeting.

Padding, he thought. No bruises.

His spine tickled him. Here, he realised, was the very vehicle that had been used to drag away and drop off each of the earliest victims – Heidi Meyer, Alice Colquhoun and Kingsley the Cocker, each composed in their spurious scene – and hot on the heels of that notion came the grim prospect that Fossey had also used it for transport over the past two days, stalking Merlin, the 'urban artist', in Limehouse, reaching Karl's home beneath the flyover . . .

If so, he wondered, had Tova been locked away like this all along – fly-wreathed and empty-eyed, body swaying on slicing cords – as the killer trundled about his business? It was a vision of casual callousness that twisted something in Shapers guts, and he squatted low at the fear of vomiting, wiping at his sweat.

Only as he straightened again, with the benefit of the lower angle, did he notice Tova's blouse pocket: not just nibbled like the rest of her clothes but entirely missing, torn free with such force that the thin material was ripped away.

Another memory arose.

'*He sent very big pay,*' she'd said, pocketing her severance cheque. '*All fine.*'

Palms prickling, trying to ignore his own actions, Shaper gingerly leaned close to scan her clothes, checking she hadn't stowed the cheque elsewhere. There was nothing, and no sign of the suitcase she'd been so valiantly struggling to carry.

He glared at the missing fabric as if personally insulted.

Why take the cheque, Fossey? It's not as if you can spend it. Another souvenir? Is that it?

As if on cue, he became abruptly convinced he was being watched, and with a slight moan spotted a tint of blue and red in the murk behind Tova's back.

The broken mask.

It had been slung into a leather holdall, he saw, and – horrifically aware of the dead forest around him – he leaned deep into the van to drag it forwards. Apart from the mask, the bag was empty, although down in the creases at its base, lodged in leathery corners, a few residual nuggets of greasy white tallow spoke volumes.

The hand.

The crazy fuck came back for the hand.

And then Shaper froze. Some ugly prescience fingered at the small of his back, raising hairs on his neck and jabbing his tongue with a metal tang. He turned as if swivelled by an invisible hand, and there to one side, gliding from the forest like some ancient god, the beast rustled forth.

Chapter Thirty-six

Fossey's entrance was deliberately theatrical. The man stepped into the clearing with all the coiled grace of a tiger, body held low but strangely rigid, legs moving to some secret, uneven pace.

Shaper forced himself to calm down, breathing deeply to slow his heart. He swiftly gauged that the man was unarmed – empty-handed but for the lumpen candle he'd come to retrieve – and tamped down the adrenal rush. The Hand of Glory was unlit, he saw, cradled like a baby against Fossey's chest, and as the killer paused to stroke and knead at it – making no attempt to approach further – Shaper could at last indulge in an inspection of the ghoul he'd been tasked with ending.

The man wore black. A shapeless hoodie was draped over dark combats and thick boots, and his leather gloves contrived to leave only the skin of his face – now liberated from its blue shield – exposed. On the cheekbone where Vince had punched him, where the broken edges of the mask had bitten in, a few jagged lines lent Fossey's expression an awkward, lopsided tilt.

Like lava, Shaper thought. Like magma showing through cracked rock.

And at that one whimsical association, fed by the silence of the forest and the rhythm of his heart, the Sickness grinned in Shaper's skull and vomited forth its poison.

Onward came the delusions. Onward came the crackling

fuzz, settling like the wings of an ill-tuned devil round Fossey's shoulders. Onward came the aura of madness and magic, eclipsing the prosaic and mutating the mundane, so that the man's whole body seemed like a field of splintering ice, reflections spewing. Onward came an arctic roar and the stink of sulphur, and Shaper found himself wallowing in the illusions – indulging the madness – to stave off a perverse disappointment at the truth below.

He's just some bloke.

Matthew Foster. Crazy Fossey. Victim of a weird treatment, driven by insane motives Shaper couldn't and wouldn't understand.

Not a supernatural terror. Not some familiar face unmasked with the crash of a cymbal. Just a dickhead in a hoodie.

Nobody would have looked at him twice in the street, this tall-ish slim-ish killer, with thinning hair and eyes so unremarkable Shaper struggled to even notice their colour. He saw now that the man bore a slick of tears on each eye and a forlorn gape to his mouth; deep sadness filtered through deeper uncertainty. Standing there in the rain, he seemed concerned only with finding the right words, and such was his air of hopeless impotence that, even with the delusions' monstrous camouflage, Shaper couldn't bring himself to feel afraid. He found himself relaxing from the fighter's stance he'd adopted – a muscle memory from the old days – anticipating nothing now from this unimpressive little man so much as a breakdown and a flood of apologies.

'All right, Fossey,' he heard himself say. 'It's all right.'

The man sniffed, failing to collect an errant trickle of snot from his trembling lip, and Shaper felt a pang of unexpected sympathy. Fossey radiated confusion.

They fucked you up, Shaper thought. They fritzed your brain, didn't they?

You poor, poor nutter.

The killer began to softly sidestep, as if warily circling round. Shaper noticed the man's eyes had dropped to the mud and leaf litter near the van, roving left and right.

'Let's just talk,' Shaper said, palms extended. 'All right, mate? No biggie. Just talk.'

Fossey ignored him and kept edging round the van, mumbling below his breath – 'Dropped it . . . dropped it . . .' and Shaper was obliged to crab to one side himself, feet squelching, just to keep him in view. It was at the edge of one such step, as he wondered if he was going to have to rush the loony after all, that Shaper's foot touched on something hard with a minuscule click.

Fossey instantly went still. Eyes latched on Shaper's shoe. The delusions fizzed around him, as if confusedly awaiting a cue, and Shaper raised his foot in silent bewilderment.

There was a cheap, pink, plastic lighter in the mud.

Fossey's eyes went huge. The hand clutching at the candle redoubled its clammy strokings, and slowly the man's gaze tilted up from the ground beneath Shaper to latch on to his face.

Want, the killer's eyes declared. *Gimme.*

Unnerved, Shaper blinked to clear the delusions before they swarmed out of control, the Sickness enervated by his bewilderment. He was on the verge of crouching to lift the lighter himself, words already forming – You want it, mate? It's yours. Let's just talk, eh? – when Fossey *changed*.

His muttered nonsense died beneath a sudden stillness. He straightened from his slouch, as if some invisible signal had activated servos along his spine, and reached a slow hand behind his back, truffling in the folds of his hoodie.

'Fossey?' Shaper breathed, tilting back into the fighter's stance with a glimmer of precognition.

Uh-oh.

Muscles bunching, fists tightening. 'C'mon, mate . . .'

And then everything was movement.

With an angry jerk Fossey withdrew something long and silver from behind his back, springing forward with a cry. Shaper had time only to rock backwards in horror—

Knife.

BIG fucking knife.

– before the distortions gobbled his reality whole and dropped curtains of nonsense across his attacker. Fossey charged him with a deranged howl, blue flames jetting from his eyes, mouth a crevice of smoke. Sparks spumed and spat, and the blade was lifted to slice at the air like a blur spot on Shaper's vision, cutting a hole in the world.

Wait! he tried to scream, hands uselessly lifting. *Stop!*

But only a gurgle emerged, and before he could spit another syllable – before he could even imagine what he *should* say – the knife was arcing wide towards his neck.

Which is when Mary Devon – lips a bloodless slash, hippy-sack handbag slapping at her side – stepped from the trees, levelled a muddy shotgun with an amateur's cringe, and shot Fossey in the back.

Afterwards, she cried.

Even caving in, even in the junkie crash of fresh shock, her anger wasn't spent. Before Shaper could pull himself together, avoiding the sight of Fossey's body, she was doing her best to offload a second shell into his head.

'It's empty,' he gently told her, when she'd pulled the useless trigger a fifth time. 'First barrel went off when Vince dropped it. It's done.'

She let the gun fall as if she'd barely realised it was there, eyes lingering on the grotesque candle in the mud. Everything seemed to dissolve around her, and she sagged into Shaper's arms with a

A Serpent Uncoiled

plaintive howl. He simply gripped her while she poured it all out, letting her shaking body resonate with his own.

'*Stressful situations,*' he remembered. '*Best aphrodisiacs out.*'

'Why'd you come out here?' he asked, finally. 'It's dangerous, Mary.'

She risked a glance at the body, inserting a croaked sentence between sobs. 'He killed Karl,' she snuffled. 'I just wanted to . . . to ask why.'

Lucky for me you're the 'shoot first' type, Shaper didn't say.

He stroked her hair and kissed her forehead, holding her until all the world went away and the Sickness simmered down.

'Vince shouldn't have let you out,' he mumbled, retrospectively protective.

'He couldn't stop me,' she whispered, and as if from nowhere an unexpected spurt of anger appeared on her face. Without warning she shoved Shaper away, eyes flashing. 'And *you*!'

'What?'

'You distrustful bastard!'

He scowled, zombie-ing back towards her, but she held him at bay with an accusing finger.

'How *could* you? After I . . . I told you everything! And then today in the van, the . . . the things you said! I thought we were . . . I thought there were no more lies!'

He felt bizarrely as though someone had yanked the world from beneath his feet without giving him notice. Worse, it was dawning on him that the intended interrogation of her brother's killer was just a sideshow for Mary's rage, and the real reason she'd come storming out here was to confront himself with . . .

With what?

'Lies?' he burbled. 'There aren't any left!'

(Right?)

Something itched at his senses, some distant impression of smoke and scent, but Mary wasn't about to surrender her hold

405

on his attention. She dug into her bag with a hiss. 'Bullshit! Mr Glass wanted me to keep something for him, so I put it in here. And *this* was down the bottom.' She produced a small black shape, pinched between finger and thumb, teeth showing. 'What's *this* then, Dan?'

His muddled perception prodded him harder – some extraneous *thing* sleazing beneath his notice – but the innocuous little shape in Mary's hand stole its thunder and demanded explanation.

It was a tracker.

No, it was *his* tracker, and she could see the recognition skyburst on his face.

'You put it there!' she hissed. 'In the brothel! Before I said I'd come along! Wanted to keep a fucking tab, did you?'

'Mary, wait, this is—'

'No!' Her eyes shuttered down, voice whisper-quiet. 'You thought it was me.'

She meant: *the killer.*

And again with the tears.

For a vivid second Shaper tasted her pain. The terrors inflicted by one awful week had struck her in shades of loneliness and self-doubt, torpedoing her career, mutilating her brother and assassinating the memory of one perfect parent. He realised in a flash that in all the world – of all the people she'd loved and trusted – *he* was now the closest.

It wasn't hard to see, in that light, how she'd presumed his betrayal. To her it was simply part of a recurring pattern.

'Mary, please,' he said, raising his hands. 'I didn't fucking *bug* you, all right? And I know you're not the mur—'

She screamed.

And something spat blood in Shaper's face.

The world ground to a halt, and as he cursed himself for not paying attention sooner, the killer rose like an ancient wyrm from the mud. Too full of hate to quit, too insane to hurt, Fossey licked bloodied teeth and scrabbled for his knife.

'Mary?' Shaper breathed. 'Get away from here.'

'But—'

'Mary!'

She vanished into the forest like a wisp of steam, and Shaper flapped his arms to keep the lunatic's eyes – snake-like – fixed on himself.

His thoughts lurched upside down. The crumbling urge to fight was overwhelmed by exhaustion, then quickly subsumed by a geyser of crazy associations. The tracker in Mary's bag screamed for consideration: an enigma which connected itself on some instinctive level to a glossy-black *thing* on the driveway; a shape he'd half-glimpsed, just minutes before, through a mat of ivy. Next, like dominoes falling through fog, he remembered a family vendetta, someone confiscating his kit with a toothy smirk; and a hand gesture through a car window. *'We'll be watching her . . .'*

Things fell together.

You fuckers.

You bugged her in Mrs Swanson's place, didn't you? You followed her.

You're already bloody here . . .

Fossey slunk forwards, reptile smile fixed.

Finish it, Shaper thought.

'Right then,' he spat, mind made up. 'Let's go.'

And he ran for it.

Heart screaming, body heavy, he was back to the fringes of the wood before he dared to glance back, checking the killer was following.

Fuck!

Fossey was barely ten steps behind. Oncoming like a frightful red train, a thing of mud and lipless sneers, wrapped in all the hellish froth of delusion. Knife glittering in one fist, unlit candle in the other, shredded hoodie flapping like a shroud. If Shaper had been disappointed before at his predator's mediocrity then here was a worthy fiend: bloodied, soiled, garlanded with the symbols of its office.

Shaper's feet touched concrete, slippery with rain, and he pelted for the blind dog-leg halfway along the drive.

Where are they? he panicked. *Where the fuck are they?*

The slapping of his feet attuned with the jackhammer in his chest, roaring so hard he was sure it would burst. Only the huffing over his shoulder pushed him on, and he decided with a spasm of abstraction that the rain was alive; not falling but circulating, every droplet a hungry fly. As his final reserves withered and his lungs howled, he shielded his face against the swarm and – at long last – glimpsed what he'd been hunting.

The beetle carapace. A shine-coated shape, lurking in the lee of a bush, opening eyes like fiery orbs.

Black Merc. Tinted windows. Subtle.

The fucking Corams.

(Finish it!)

He stumbled to a halt in the cone of the headlights and forced his body to turn away, pointing to the killer closing the distance.

'It's him!' he screamed, watching the shadows in the car. 'He's the one you want!'

Fossey stumbled to a halt nearby, hunching low, uncertain in the light. Shaper, confident it was over at last, awaited the cavalry.

Come get him.

But the car didn't move. Nobody stepped out. Beyond the halo of its light, like sharks slipping through tar, Shaper thought he could see figures moving inside. Smirking. Sneering.

Mobile phones set to record, with little red lights winking.

Enjoying the show.

'You bastards . . .' he whispered.

The world faded to silence, punctured only by the whispering drizzle. And then a strange flicking sound, like a locust trying to sing.

The lighter.

You forgot the bloody lighter.

'You know,' Fossey said, voice impossibly near and abominably gentle. 'I didn't actually kill any of them.'

Shaper turned to look – and couldn't.

What . . .

He came to a horrific stillness with all the outraged panic of a man whose body has simply stopped working, muscles mutinying at some deep hypnotic command. He watched, helpless, as backlit rain puddled in the cup of his palm, raging silently at invisible bonds, teeth grinding.

. . . the fuck?

The killer oozed into his line of sight, haloed in the headlights. Faceless.

The corpse candle was lit.

'Except for the man with the machete,' Fossey trilled. 'He *definitely* died. But then . . . he was doing things to Karl. He was a bad man, I'm certain. So that's OK.' The creature's head tilted to its side. 'Wasn't it?'

Shaper raged in his shell, hammering at the glue in his veins. The lumpen mass of the candle seeped bilious black light above his head, sputtering in the drizzle, and at first he sensed that it above all else was the agent of his restraint.

'Freezes you where you stand. Opens any door.'

Hand of Glory.

But as the Sickness wrung sweat from every pore and pissed fire through his heart, he began to imagine instead that *it* – his own disease, his own guilty self – was the true force pinning him in place.

It's you, Dannyboy. You're doing this to yourself.

He fancied he could hear his own brain laughing at him.

'*And* the nurse,' Fossey mumbled, sighing at a sudden memory. 'That was me too.' His manner brought to Shaper's roiling mind nothing so much as a kid who'd wet his bed, and was philosophically preparing for punishment.

Dave! Phyll! I know you're in there!

Help me!

Fossey fiddled with the blade, lifting it for Shaper's inspection, then hunched out a childlike shrug. 'Anyway,' he sniffed, 'I was only trying to help.'

Help me, you cunts!

Oblivious to the silent entreaties, the killer gracefully turned sideways – martyr's pout distorted by the light slicing his profile – and raised the knife towards Shaper's throat. 'Besides, she was a whore once. The nurse. Did you know that? That's like a machine for fucking.' He nodded as if convincing himself. 'Can't murder a machine. That's just obvious. Only proper people.'

Something chimed behind Shaper's eye.

A memory, dredged from hated ether, shucked off its chrysalis like a butterfly made of heat. Waiting for the knife, he remembered half-starved women clambering from a truck, streaked with their own shit, and laughing Albanians waiting with hoses. He saw a fat man – moustache wider than his face – throw up gnarled hands and say, '*Why you angry, eh? Just whores. Not proper people.*'

And the same old fury spat a grenade into his brain.

The delusions changed. Something ruby-red unknotted behind his eyes – a ghost of his old self, knuckles raw, teeth bared. It wrapped itself round the remembered rage with a righteous shiver – *those are human beings, you shit!* – and sponged up all the newer venom it could find.

Dave . . . Phyllis . . . We were a fucking family!

Stop!
Just!
Sitting there!

For a second Shaper forgot to hate the Sickness. For an instant he was *fed* by its fire, clothed in its chaos, ejecting all of its bitterness like a bullet. For a moment he stepped inside it and let it own him.

And without knowing or caring how it happened, his hand moved.

He flicked it towards the morbid candle as if it could be blasted away with a gesture alone, and almost roared in triumph when the drizzle that had collected in his palm doused it with a hiss.

His body came unstuck. He ducked below the knife, howling, and before Fossey could react was bowling forwards, fixating on the wolf he used to be, gnashing with contempt.

Don't give the audience the satisfaction, boy.
This tosspot's just a git with a cutter.
You're Dan fucking Shaper, remember?

So, a rising punch. A fist in the shithead's guts, lifting to the base of his ribs, then an elbow to catch his chin as he folded up. Next a sidestep out of range as the creep dropped and choked, lashing out blindly with the blade. Then a dart back in, an electric chop to his throat and a thrashed-out knee to smash the howling, hacking face as it rolled.

Imaginary sparks frothed around them. They felt right.

Take him apart.

Fossey scrabbled up and kept coming, blazing with ghostly fire, too angry or crazy to stop. Shaper sprang clear of a comet-like stab of the knife, already knowing there was no avoiding the follow-up punch, and resolved to simply roll with it, secretly enjoying the promise of pain. Wielded like a club, the Hand of Glory caught him on the jaw with just enough force to fritz his

411

balance, but even as he dinked downwards, he was watching the killer admire the handiwork, exulting in the knockdown.

Rookie error, mate. Never stop.

He punished the creep with a flat kick to his nearest shin and, as he tumbled with a scream, swatted the knife from his trailing hand.

Rrright.

And then followed him down, knees on chest, for the fun stuff.

Beneath him, Fossey went insane.

Bucking and screaming like a banshee, his whole body pounded. His fists made claws to tear at his attacker's face, and Shaper rode it out with a growl, alternating his arms to hold the fucker's throat and mash fists into nose, elbows into cheeks, hand-heels into eyes and lips.

At some point he realised he was laughing out loud.

Still Fossey raged. Already the killer's mouth was plastered with blood and broken skin, lips shredded, rosy spittle bubbling. One eyeball was pink with shattered tubes and his nose was swelling by the second, but still the rabid *something* behind those eyes refused to be beaten. When the man snagged enough leverage to hook an arm round Shaper's neck, it seemed rude not to go with the flow. Shaper butted him where he lay, thrilling to the *crack* of his skull on the ground, and –

Ohhh . . .

– couldn't stop himself latching teeth on to the dribbling freak's ear.

I'm a monster too, he shrieked without sound.

I'M A MONSTER TOO!

Everything seemed to explode at once – an orgasm of violence and freedom – and in its shivery hinterlands Shaper's brain could decode little but impressions of its own action, puncturing the fugue like needles into a sensory womb.

The taste of blood. Scrabbling hands going limp. A bony hammer between his hands – no, a man's skull – pounded over and over into the planet below it.

An audible crunch.

A wet retort.

A body going still.

And then just silence, and rain like neon spears crossing the light, and the dawning impression that there were people standing around him, watching.

Chapter Thirty-seven

Both twins were there.

By the time something a little like reality began to reassert itself in Shaper's mind, Phyllis had already assumed control, muttering darkly from beneath an antique umbrella. At her command a pair of fresh freelancers – hulking replacements for BeanieHat and BollockHead – slipped into the car light to lift Shaper off the ground. He hovered between them for a moment, fighting the urge to giggle drunkenly, then was deposited uncertainly on his feet.

Thus exposed, Fossey's body was left glossy with rain and ruin, slicking its dark fluids across the road. Dave bustled into the light to poke it with childlike excitement.

'Who is he, then?' he said, squirrelling away his phone. 'Gotta have a name! Who'd you kill, killer?'

Lipless and bloody, the corpse's face told a story of rage and loss, and Shaper found himself wordlessly relieved its eyes were closed. In all its sneering ugliness – vascular gunge ebbing from whatever cracked mess had met the tarmac beneath – it had come to echo the monster his flailing senses had sought to make it. He found, under those terms, it could be easily dismissed as unreal, an unconvincing waxwork to frighten children.

The delusions threatened to animate it all the same – *you did that, Dannyboy* – and he quickly looked away, sagging against the car for support.

Don't think about it.

One of the thugs stepped suddenly clear, snapping out a telescopic nightstick with a pop. 'Someone in the trees!' he snarled. 'Come out, you!'

Mary stumbled, hesitant, into the light. She looked as muddy and knackered as Shaper felt, though admittedly she suited the wet clothing look far better. He heard Dave spit a humourless *heh* as she self-consciously pulled her jacket tighter.

'Leave her out of it, guys,' Shaper sighed. 'I sincerely doubt you bugged the poor lass on account of a deep-rooted personal interest, am I right?'

Phyllis conceded a nod. 'Very insightful.'

Endearingly bedraggled, Mary had the good grace to shoot Shaper an apologetic look.

'Told you it wasn't me,' he muttered.

'We have a few issues we'd like to discuss,' Phyllis smarmed. 'And we did indeed hope the young lady would lead us your way, you being so tricksy about tails 'n' all.'

Shaper spat something pink into the rain. 'The sort of chat where you'd rather watch me get killed than step in? Thanks for that.'

Arseholes.

The woman sneered. 'The sort of chat, Danny, where pizza-face there nearly saved us a job.'

Dave blustered in from the opposite direction. 'You let us down, mate! Very important gig, and you fucked up. Got poor old Vicar killed 'n' all. Nothing to show for it.' He flashed his palms, dramatically apologetic. 'We can't have it.'

Beside him one of the freelancers began conspicuously arming a glossy little pistol. Shaper let the threat slide off like mercury, and had to tamp down the urge to laugh. None of it mattered, and he tilted back his head to enjoy the rain, gesturing vaguely at Fossey's body.

'The job's done,' he said. 'You ridiculous fucking idiots.'

The twins exchanged a blank look.

'I'm serious. You got your guy. Have a look.'

Dave nudged the monster with a foot, inspecting the shattered face. 'Don't recognise him.'

Shaper kept his own eyes carefully averted, watching Mary tremble in her spot. He ached to reach out to her, but there was something in her expression – some lingering mote of chill – that held him back.

'His name's Matthew Foster,' he sighed. 'Used to be a dealer out of Camden. The day your dad died, this twisted shit was one of the lads he and Tommy Boyle went to see. "Our territory now", all that. They roughed him up.'

The twins listened with matching expressions, interest co-mingled with doubt. Phyll, as if begrudging the unity, broke off to gesture at the troll with the gun. *Wait.*

The thug pocketed the piece and stepped back.

'Now I don't know exactly what happened,' Shaper shrugged, 'but I'm guessing Fossey here took umbrage at the kicking. He'd just been through some . . . weird shit, poor bloke. Was seeing the world in a different way.'

(*The screaming man on the chair*, he remembered. *The chanting figures, snapping his sanity . . .*)

'My guess is, he followed Tommy Boyle home. Killed him and stashed the body. Except not before hacking it up and keeping a hand for future use.'

He nodded at the mangled candle, abandoned beside the road. He felt Mary's eyes briefly leap up to watch the gesture, then slip back to a nowhere state. Phyllis, far less entranced, merely scowled, while Dave prodded the body again, as if he could test the story in the texture of its mangled flesh.

'Fossey went away for a long time, after that. Sectioned. Nothing to do with Boyle or any of it, just on account of being shit-lobbing mental. Oh, plus *her* mum,' he gestured airily at Mary, baiting her to react, 'made sure the bloke stayed tucked away as long as she could.'

'Bitch,' Mary muttered, briefly enlivened.

Progress.

The Corams spared her a semi-interested glance, shrugging in unison. 'And?'

'And then matey gets out of the loony bin, and after a few years gets up to his eyeballs in some seriously nasty nonsense. That's where we're at now.'

'This Tourist thing, like on the telly?'

'Mm-hmm.'

'*This* is your psycho?'

'Yeah. But he's *your* psycho 'n' all.'

Phyllis shook her head. 'I don't buy it. You're weaselling.'

Shaper was too tired to get arsey. 'Look, somewhere along the way Fossey told a . . . an acquaintance . . . where Tommy Boyle was buried. Coded letters from his padded cell, probably – who knows? Point is, the bloke he told,' another nod at Mary, another synchronised head twist from the twins, 'her brother, actually, took it upon himself to go dig it up and set fire to it. Along with all the letters, paperwork, Fossey's flat, *everything*. Thought he was helping, poor sod. Desperately in love with Mr Roadkill right here, and it wound up losing him both his eyes.'

'Bloke's dead, actually,' Dave grunted, tactful as a brick. He hooked a thumb towards the car. 'It was on the radio.'

Shaper darted a look at Mary. She didn't seem any more or less affected by the news than she'd been before.

On standby.

He sighed. 'Fact remains, Fossey was the last person to see Tommy Boyle alive.' He held out his palms. 'That's my job done, ain't it?'

Dave pursed his lips, abstractly impressed. Phyll, as ever, was the tougher gig.

'What,' she said, bending uncomfortably close, 'about *Dad*?'

Shaper closed his eyes, too tired to be menaced. 'Haven't the foggiest. Fossey might've done him too, for all I know. Might've had nothing to do with it.' He shuffled himself upright. 'You asked me to find out what happened to Tommy Boyle. I've *done* that. And now I'm off.'

He hooked his hand into Mary's – cold and unresponsive – and took a step away from the car, hoping she'd follow. Instead the two freelancers trundled into his path like greased boulders, and Phyllis stamped her foot in a puddle.

'Not good enough!' she snapped. 'I want to know what that dead cunt there knew about my dad, Shaper, and you're g—'

'Can I suggest you ask him?'

Everyone stopped. Heads twisted towards Mary, startled by her gentle interruption. She stared them down without obvious expression, and for a split second Shaper thought she was about to launch into the clairvoyant act: interrogation beyond the grave.

Instead she rolled her eyes and nodded calmly at the body.

Which groaned.

'He's still alive, you wankers.'

They walked back to the house together, hands clasped, and didn't even turn to see as the Merc roared away into the night. Dave had insisted the goons swaddle the killer in coats before dumping him in the boot – 'Think of the fuckin' *upholstery*' – and Shaper had propelled Mary away during the grisly operation.

'We'll be in touch,' one of the twins had called after them. Shaper wasn't sure which.

The rain stopped as they neared the mansion. He couldn't

pretend there wasn't a weird gauze of awkwardness between them, and the ghost of Mary's earlier accusation – the tracker, the suspicions, the 'you thought it was me' moment – lingered above them. In some abstract way Shaper sensed a deeper fault line had been inadvertently exposed – the impossibility of trust between liars – but in the lingering grip of the Sickness it was far easier to ignore the discomfort and focus on the light.

The killer was caught. A beautiful woman was holding his hand.

George Glass was safe.

He entered the back door like a junkie on the verge of a fix, preparing to schlep down into the basement to bask in the old man's healing presence. One of Vince's clatternukes went off as they entered – a string of pots and pans racketing against the door – and Shaper called out a pre-emptive, 'No panic! It's just us!'

Nobody came running anyway, and even that couldn't stir any anxiety in his exhausted skull.

It's over.

It's fucking over.

Mary stopped him at the head of the stairs, rummaging again in her handbag and producing Glass's leather notebook, a coy look on her face.

Almost, he dared to believe, a smile.

Flicking through its pages, she removed a small paper oblong.

'For you,' she said. 'This is what he asked me to look after. Hand it over when everything was done.'

It was a cheque. 'Fifteen thousand pounds only,' it said, a neat cursive in blue ink beside a florid, looping signature. Shaper stared at it for a long time, mentally clicking his heels. 'Why not give it to me himself?' he asked.

'Case anything happened, I suppose.'

'But then I wouldn't've earned it.'

She smiled softly. 'I suppose he wanted to reward you either way, Dan.' She squeezed his hand. 'He's like that.'

And I saved him.

That was the real reward, he thought. Not the money.

He clung to the cheque anyway, and clomped into the cellar, past the oxygen bottles, under the archway, letting the familiar tide of hot air stroke past him, with an air of unflappable victory.

Until he saw the chair.

It sat untouched in its alcove, and even at a distance could amputate Shaper's triumph and pique his senses: a cord of mist unbunching in his eyes. He averted his gaze, accelerating to get to Glass, but the nausea wouldn't pass. He found himself wondering for the first time since Vicar stole his meds, since the breakdown fugue and the old man's miraculous purification, exactly what the fuck was going on in his brain.

How, he wondered, would he move on from this? Should he still plan a detox break, in spite of the chemical clarity? Should he return to the same old routine – the same old dosage – when all was over and done with?

Could he ever, truly, kill the Sickness?

Once initiated, the worries multiplied predictably, externalising through the dingy tunnels like a stealthy tumour.

Something not right, his brain nagged.

(But it's over. For fuck's sake! Leave it alone!)

He ogled his cheque, like proof of completion, and tried to bundle away the fears. 'Lads?' he called out. 'You down here? Vince?'

There was no reply. The dark feeling wouldn't shift, and even Mary seemed uneasy, slinging uncertain glances into every side vault. They turned together at a sharp corner, and with an indrawn gasp and a flashed impression – a body – the worries found form.

Talvir!

Shaper dropped Mary's hand and rushed to the prone shape, hissing in alarm.

The little bastard was sleeping.

Shaper nudged him awake with a bubblegum burst of relief and irritation, and as the kid staggered groggily upright, yawning, did his best to restrain his urgency.

'Where is everyone, Tal?'

'Mm? Oh, they're . . . they're in there, man.' He nodded at a heavy door at the end of the corridor, retrieving a baseball bat from the floor. He seemed just as surprised at the narcoleptic skit as Shaper, checking his scalp for bruises as if convinced he'd been knocked out. There was nothing.

On the fringes of Shaper's mind the Sickness whooped for attention, hissing at the back of his brain. He ignored it, watching Mary stride to the door and knock smartly on the metal.

Shave and a haircut . . .

'V-vince came down,' Tal explained, rubbing his eyes. 'Said you'd gone after the psycho. Locked himself inside with Mr Glass. They're all in there. He said I should stay on duty out here.' He waggled the bat, lame.

I bet he did. Shaper scowled. Didn't want two fuck buddies in the same room at the same time.

'How is the big sod?'

'Bleeding a bit – his bum, y'know? But he's bound it up, says he'll be fine.' A thought crossed the youth's face. 'Look, Dan, sorry I was . . . I must've passed out.'

Behind them, Mary knocked again, brows creased. Tal fired off another bewildered yawn, wobbling in place, and Shaper inspected him with eyes narrowed, the gibbering in his mind rising to a din. 'You OK, mate?'

'Y-yeah, think so. It's weird – Vince was acting groggy too. And Tony. He thought maybe there was a gas leak down here.'

The kid held out a hand in demonstration. He couldn't stop it trembling.

The fucking shakes . . .

And without warning, like a detonation in the dark, something depth-charged Shaper's brain.

'The signature,' he whispered.

'What?'

He spun towards Mary. 'The fucking signature!'

She gave him a distracted look, busy listening at the door. 'Huh?'

Don't rock the boat. Don't question it.

It's over it's over it's ov—

'You've seen what Glass is like! The shakes! I mean, Christ, he needs you just to write his fucking memories!'

'So?'

He flapped the cheque. 'So how'd he do *this*?'

Mary seemed to relax, as if the incipient panic needed no further thought. 'Oh that . . .' She shrugged it away. 'He doesn't do money. You've seen what his memory's like – he'd forget what he'd paid for as soon as he'd done it. He hasn't looked after the cash in . . . I dunno. Best part of a decade?'

'So who's—'

Tal suddenly stumbled, baseball bat clattering to the floor. Shaper caught him on instinct, mind spinning like a buzz saw, and lowered him gently to the ground, knocking over a coffee thermos in the process.

Somewhere, through onion layers of psychic soup, Mary was knocking again at the door.

No answer.

'Tal?' he mumbled. 'Mate?'

The kid just gurgled, and in the rising flux of panic and distortion, Shaper found his eyes sucked, as if dragged by an irresistible force, to the soles of the boy's shoes, crumpled beneath him.

'Tal . . .' he heard himself say.

'Mm?'

'Tal, there's sawdust on your feet.'

'So?'

'Where's it from, Tal?'

The boy forced open groggy eyes, nodding – confused – at the metal door. 'Ice house,' he said. 'I-it's . . . it's the coolest room down here. Miss Glass said it would be best for Freddie.'

'What the fuck,' Shaper said, 'is a fucking ice house?'

'S'like a . . . a storage room. Miss Glass explained. From olden times, y'know?' The kid pushed himself upright. 'They'd bring in ice off the lake in winter, pack it down with hay and that. Stayed frozen all year.'

Alice Colquhoun, Shaper remembered, heart racing. *Sawdust and straw in her running shoes . . .*

Details rattled through his head, a tommy gun blasting his brain. Snippets of letters merged with numbers, timings, words . . . A coffee thermos backflipped through the seething image – crazy in its incongruity – propelled by a half-remembered hint of movement in warm air.

Lies sat upon lies. Linkages formed.

And a wrecking-ball of self-loathing – *you dick! You stupid dick!* – spun Shaper round to clutch Mary by her collar and all but snarl in her face, flapping his cheque like a rattle.

'Glass's money! Who handles his money, Mary?'

'Who do you think?' she stammered. 'Sandra does it.'

And through the locked door, muffled and sexless, someone screamed for a long, long time.

Chapter Thirty-eight

Up close the iron was cold. It beaded with condensation to match the salty star field on Shaper's head, and somewhere – like a code buried in the metal – he could hear the reedy whine of a sitar.

There'd been only two foil-impression picks left – the last of his supply – in the swamp of his pockets. Fighting now to restrain the shakes, he gently rocked the first back and forth in the lock, feeling the foil bite into each jagged tooth, and burned with a concentration he'd barely been able to muster, let alone sustain.

Someone, unsympathetic to his nerves, kept screaming, and Mary's up-and-down pacing was no less distracting.

'What's going on in there?' she demanded. 'Who *is* that?'

He tried not to listen – brain still rushing to solidify suspicions, sweat dripping on his hands – but she wouldn't be ignored.

'Dan!'

'*Look*,' he snapped, then instantly moderated his tone, seeing tears prickle in her eyes. 'Think about . . . think about what else Glass has paid for, yeah?'

'Like what?'

'Like . . . you remember the letter? The one your mum got from Alice Colquhoun, the accountant. About keeping the treatment quiet?'

'Y-yes.'

'It said there was enough cash in the trust fund to keep the subject out of sight six to eight years. Right?'

'So? What's that got to d—'

'Fossey was put away just after Tommy Boyle vanished – that's fifteen years ago. But it's only been three since he was released.'

She gave him a blank look. He forced himself not to shake her.

'So, altogether he was inside for twelve years, which means someone topped up the account.'

His mind spun back to the letter, tucked in the back page of Mrs Devon's freaky log.

. . . After this period it falls to Master G's discretion to provide additional monies, until such time as he deems the dangers sufficiently mitigated . . .

'I still thought Karl was the killer when I first read it,' he recalled. 'I remember thinking the numbers didn't add up, even then. Like . . . Karl said he only got released from overseas 'cos of some local trouble – army stuff, he said. As if the fund was still actively paying out. So I assumed Glass must've added to it before he went loopy, or someone was bullshitting somewhere along the line . . . or *something* . . . But the cash was nothing to do with Karl, was it? It was for keeping Fossey in the nuthouse. And that means someone decided exactly *when* to let crazy Foster out, three years ago.'

Understanding shattered across Mary's face like rain. 'And . . . and if Glass wasn't handling his own finances . . .'

Shaper bounced his eyebrows and turned back to his task. The lock pick kept trying to metamorphose in his senses, hinting at pulsing grubs, bloody organs, slippery sex toys. He stopped trusting his eyes and listened to his muscles instead, rocking, wiggling; painfully gentle.

'And that's not the only place Glass's money went,' he mumbled.

'What do you mean?'

A body, limp and damp, hanging in a van.

Neck and wrists like gums, wet and open.

A pocket – and its contents – ripped away.

A severance package.

'Nothing,' he said.

Another scream from the door, a new trail of gurgled sobs, and Mary all but stamped in frustration. A thought gripped her and she ducked back into Shaper's view.

'Sandra said Fossey beat her up,' she said. 'Tried to rape her. So why let him out at all? Why not just keep paying into the fund? Let him rot?'

'Maybe it never happened.' Shaper shrugged. 'Maybe Sandra lied. Wouldn't be the first time.'

The window, he thought, *on the fucking left*.

'So did she . . . did she *want* Fossey to do the . . .' Mary flapped a hand. 'To do what he did?'

The killings.

Shaper paused. The grisly pellet of his understanding kept growing, layers wrapping layers like mucus on a pearl, obstructing his concentration. Fossey's sad, sly voice syruped in his memories.

'*I didn't actually kill any of them,*' it said. '*I was only trying to help.*'

He recalled a dead man in the dockyard – an artist with a stupid name and his neck sliced open – and remembered being mystified, heart still pounding from the chase, that the killer could have beaten him back to finish the job . . .

He remembered poor fucked-up Karl, lying in agony with

Max Vicar bleeding out across him, as the man he loved – Fossey – clutched a flickering candle and glanced towards the stairs, whispering, '*It's not up to me . . .*' And it wasn't, Shaper realised. Oh fuck, it never was.

He focused on the lock pick and tried to keep the quaver out of his voice.

'I don't think Fossey did what we think he did,' he murmured. 'Not alone.'

The voice from inside screamed again, harder, harsher than before, shattering in a string of wordless howls and a sudden silence, and in the second it took Shaper to admit at last that it was unmistakably Glass's tone – giving out from the force of its pain – the key had snapped in his fingers and he was shouting out loud to drown the sound.

Silence settled like a tombstone drawing shut, and beneath its stony mantle Mary turned away and vanished along the corridor howling. Shaper was barely aware of it; he plucked out the shattered pick and grimly inserted his final key.

Tal, all but forgotten – leaning against a wall – piped to groggy life with the last question Shaper wanted to hear.

'What's all this about, man? Why would Miss Glass do all this?'

And *there* was the problem. There was the sick kernel that had held him back all along, obfuscating every view of the path ahead. In a world packed with credulous morons, twitchy freaks and occultist adherents, a cast-iron 'motive' need not be rational at all.

Only the patterns mattered.

Victim seven.

Sahasrara.

'She wanted to be left alone with the old man . . .' he muttered, getting it even as he spoke, wobbling with each eyeball-aching heartbeat. 'No interference, keep everyone out the way. The window on the bloody left, even getting everyone to come down here . . . *And* the fucking coffee.'

'Wh-what about the coffee?'

Shaper threw the lad an impatient look.

Realisation dawned through a demonstrative yawn. 'She . . . she *drugged* me?'

'She drugged all three of you, mate. Serax would be my guess.'

The sitar raced on through the door, joined now by a sly tabla beat. Another scream, another pickaxe to Shaper's concentration. His wobbling grew more frantic, a tiny crack forming at the key's base, growing with every movement.

The perfect man, he panicked. *The kindly, the glorious . . .*

The scream topped off in a low moan, the sitar boiling through and beyond it.

He's fucking dying in there! Do something!

You need him!

And then Mary was back, shouting and dripping with rain, and there was no time to finish the thought as she shoved in beside him, ignoring his hissed, 'Gimme some room!'

She thrust something white and gnarled at the metal, flickering in the gloom, and cried beneath her breath.

Freezes you where you stand, Shaper remembered. *Opens any door.*

Hand of Glory. She'd gone back outside to find it.

Beneath his grip, in the instant of distraction, the foil key bit a fraction harder, clattered in its runnel, and the lock snapped open.

'Coincidence,' he whispered, glancing at Mary. She just scowled.

And then the alarm started to chime in Shaper's pocket.

Out! Of! Time!

Out! Of! Time!

And even as he silenced it with a stab, Mary was pushing at the door, dropping the candle and reaching to take his hand. Tal staggered closer behind them.

The sitar swelled with the portal's swing like a bee swarm released, pulsing from a grimy ghetto blaster on a table just inside. It, like the stack of chrome dog bowls and the five jam jars beside it – lidless, fluid-filled – seemed as maddeningly out of place as Shaper felt himself.

A short corridor led to the ice house, a womb of glossy reds dimly seen along its length, obstructed by a far more prosaic – and clearly exhausted – spectre. Left hand cuffed to an iron pipe, right hand hanging ever useless at his side, Tightfisted Tony held open his eyes long enough to shoot Shaper a warning glare: *don't you say a word, fucker.*

'She was quick,' he growled, biting down on a yawn.

The cuffs, like a cruel joke, were fluffy and black.

Shaper shushed him with a finger to his lips and stepped onwards to the mouth of the chamber, only abstractly aware of Mary beside him.

They stared into the sputtering light.

'Shit,' they said, together.

The ice house was a dark, domed cavity, a cool igloo built in rock and earth.

Emerging into it, Shaper realised he was beneath the same stony scapula he'd seen in the grounds, its metal hatch sealed above. Its surfaces were masked by crumpled swathes of plastic (like drying skin, he thought, already struggling with reality) and in odd places the walls beyond could be dimly perceived, each bearing crude paintings of gambolling figures and terrible creatures, blue-skinned and red-mouthed. The scene was lit by a gnarled cluster of sputtering candles, contaminating every angle with puddles of dark and garish shades, and it took Shaper long seconds to decode the tableau from its oily first impression.

The delusions, taking their cue, danced in the shadows.

Sandra was in the centre of it all. All artifice gone, she broadcast a presence of such wanton malevolence that it slaughtered whatever mysteries had surrounded her, annihilating Shaper's last glimpse of the frightened mammalian kernel inside.

'Stay back!' she shrieked, eyes too wide. 'Stay the fuck back!'

She wore orange robes. A spot of clay marked her forehead, though the face below it took a ghastly asymmetry from a diagonal spatter of blood. Shaper's Sickness responded on tone, sketching flames and beasts around her, great crocodilian maws snapping among sapphire scales.

She held a knife.

A big, heavy, blood-slick knife.

'Stay! Fucking! *Back!*'

Her father was beside her. At the merest glimpse of him Shaper's raging mind quietened – phasing back the illusions to a spectral blur – but at the same time delivered a jolt of such fear and revulsion that its physical effects, in his guts and heart, more than outweighed the brief calm.

Glass was tied down and covered in blood.

Looped through with rubber tubes and fur-coated belts, his restraint was a thing of crossed metal struts and shaggy padding: a Z-chair pinioning him at an ugly angle. His head, affixed at a tilt by a woollen headstrap, left his neck exposed and epiglottis jutting: glossy, like everything, from a thick sheen of red. It ran in treacle-rivulets along the struts of the chair, trickling along plastic sheets to the room's borders, where it soaked into sawdust and hay.

Shaper felt his throat constrict, panic swelling like a mushroom cloud.

Don't be dead, don't be dead, don't be dead . . .

The thin foliage of the old man's hair, he saw, was lank with arterial paste, and the bald dome of his crown was lost in a mire of gristle and shine. It took Shaper a moment to work out precisely what he was seeing, eyes straying sideways to the odd scrap in Sandra's left fist: a rag of deflated *something*, like an olive-toned balloon.

Sahasrara. The crown chakra.

She'd scalped him.

Shaper felt Mary stiffen beside him – their realisations eerily synchronous – and her hand tighten around his. '*Jesus fuck* . . .'

Only when Glass's lips twitched, breaking a crusted strata of blood, did she drop Shaper's sweaty hand and lurch forward without thought, trying to get to him.

He's still alive.

Sandra's knife flickered towards the movement on instinct, and Shaper grabbed Mary by her shoulders, imagining he could hear her heart racing to attune with the gathering tabla.

'Stay back,' Sandra hissed, 'or . . . or I'll . . .'

She quit on the sentence with a breathy gasp, suddenly amused. The knife tilted backwards, flicking Shaper's gaze into the gloom beside her, where a hint of movement fleshed out the shadows just a fraction more.

It was Vince. Sprawled against the rising camber of the wall, head lolling to one side, Shaper could tell he was neither wounded nor dead, just spaced – propped up like some limp dummy. Sandra notched the blade beneath his chin and glared up, meeting Shaper's eyes, as if to test the efficacy of the threat. He tried his best to maintain a shrug-shouldered nonchalance – *fuck you, lady* – but before he could even open his mouth to begin negotiation, Tal was ramming past him, crying out.

Shaper grabbed at him too, feeling insanely as if his allotted vocation was to juggle impetuous friends. Sandra just chuckled.

'What have you done to him?' Tal shrieked. 'If you've hurt him . . .'

'Oh, he's fine – he'll sleep it off.' She arched her brows, conspicuously – and somehow unfairly – rational. 'Providing nobody does anything stupid.'

'You drugged him too? You *can't* have!' Tal's voice adopted a childish whine, petulantly insisting its expertise. 'He doesn't *drink* coffee!'

Sandra lit an indulgent smile. 'No? But he's a sucker for a beer after sex.'

Tal went quiet. Shaper felt the kid's shoulders go limp, all the fight leaving him, muscles unknotting – and softly pulled him back. He didn't want to look at the boy's face, didn't want to recognise that slow death of the heart; that icy glimmer of betrayal that had so changed his own life five years before. Instead he pushed his way in front, avoiding all focus except the one that mattered.

'Sandra,' he said. 'You don't want to do this. You . . . you don't need Vince. Let him go, eh? Give me the knife.'

Oh so Hollywood.

The woman just scowled, blade not shifting. 'Don't patronise me, Mr Shaper. You're not talking me off a cliff. I'm not some bloody lunatic.'

(Like fuck you're not.)

She must have seen some hint of his incredulity. 'There's methodology here!' she snapped, genuinely insulted. 'This isn't some . . . some psychotic kill spree, Mr Shaper. I have a job to finish and for that I require no interruptions. Consider your friend here part of the contingency.' She nodded at Vince, then again at Shaper's feet. 'One more step, I cut his throat. Two steps, the old man dies. And that goes for the fake witch there, who thinks I've forgotten her.'

Mary, inching towards Glass, shuffled back behind Shaper with an incandescent glare. Tal just moaned somewhere behind them.

'The third step?' Sandra said, warming to the authority. 'Well . . .' She glanced into the gloom at the room's rear and jutted her chin.

It was Freddie. Barely visible in the flickering light – trolley bed a tactile extension of the shadows – his rolling eyes lingered, so Shaper thought, on the scrap of flesh in his mother's fist. In the absence of the group's attention, Sandra had begun to quietly whisper to the scalp, rocking in her place.

'I'm not some bloody lunatic,' Shaper silently heard again, resisting the urge to spit, and fixed his eyes back on the boy.

Freddie's body was covered against the cold by a thin sheet, the misshapen mass of his midriff bulging beneath, and insofar as any emotion could be read on his face, Shaper found himself staggered by hints of confusion and fear, rousing inside him a protective instinct so profound it hurt. In all his life, only Glass had ever commanded an equal concern.

Innocence, his brain whispered, itching to explode. *The taste of innocence. (And you let her hurt him, you fucking failure.)*

Glass groaned on cue.

'He needs an ambulance,' Mary said, voice breaking. 'Please.'

'Shut up,' Sandra snapped, still crooning to the bloody scalp. 'I'm busy.'

Utterly. Bloody. Mental.

Shaper's senses rushed to exaggerate the impression, endlessly hunting cracks in his calm. Beneath her controlled exterior, all Sandra's pain and shame were manifested as glittering spines, each filed to a deadly point.

All her damage, he thought, *turned outwards. All her wounds become weapons.*

Holding up her grisly prize, she theatrically wrung it like a moist flannel, and when the blood had finished pattering to the floor, fixed her audience with a teacherly look.

'The seed syllable is . . . ?' she asked. 'Anyone . . . ?'

'What?'

She grinned at his confusion and held the scalp to her lips.

'*Ah,*' she whispered. 'The seed syllable is *Ah.*'

It fluttered from her mouth like a toxic insect.

Unable to rip his eyes from the vision, Shaper decided quite suddenly he'd had enough of the bullshit.

'Tova!' he spat. Sandra's head snapped round, birdlike. 'What about Tova, Sandra?'

She went still. Eyes slitting down.

'You say there's a fucking methodology, but what was *she*, Sandra?' Shaper was grasping at straws and he knew it, compelled by some primal instinct to destabilise, to undermine. 'Justifiable collateral, is that it? All she did was look after Freddie. Doesn't that matter to you?'

The woman wavered. That old force field of expression blurring, shielding her behind shame, guilt, confusion, and she stepped thoughtlessly away from Vince. Still within reach of her victims, still wired to slice at will, it seemed nonetheless that the further she shrank back, the more the knife went slack in her hand.

Keep.

Pushing.

'You didn't have to have *her* killed, Sandra – whatever "job" you're doing. You didn't have to do that . . .'

Tears appeared in the woman's eyes. Like a child, easily swayed and swiftly broken, her whole body seemed to diminish, and Shaper dared to shuffle a half-step forwards, mind spinning.

The ripped pocket . . .

The letter of dismissal . . .

The old man, forgetting he'd sacked his nurse . . .

'*You* fired her, didn't you?' he said. 'Didn't want me knowing you were getting her out of the way.' He shook his head. 'You say you're not being crazy, Sandra, but you had an innocent woman killed for the sake of a fucking signature on a fucking cheque. Does that sound rational to you?'

For a second – just a second – he thought he'd done it. The knife drooped, the tears bulged in fat globs, and Sandra seemed to teeter on tiptoes, ready to sink to her knees.

But then a blink became a slow, spreading scowl. 'You think . . . you think I had her put down for that?' The grip resumed and her head tilted to fix him with an oily smile. '*Please.*'

Back in control.

'I regret the death.' She shrugged, flippant. 'But she was a liability. Her background, her speciality . . . How could she not have guessed? And then when Father instructed her not to involve the cops . . . Yes. I'm sure she realised.'

The woman seemed to be having a conversation with herself, and Shaper blinked, lost. At his side Tal suddenly leaned close, whispering into the hairs of his neck.

'Dan . . .'

He ignored it, watching Sandra's poise return like a disease, authority restored to her fiery eyes.

Dominator; supplicant.

'That day outside the kitchen,' she whispered. 'Do you remember? That day I fired her. Fossey was waiting halfway down the drive – *ha*, you must have come straight past him. And as she left, she said she'd call you, didn't she? Said she'd be in touch. Said you needed to talk.'

'So?'

'So the little cunt would have spoiled everything. Before I had a chance to . . . to . . .'

The woman paused, staring lovingly at the crinkled skin scrap, and with a pulse of sudden venom notched the blade, hard, beneath Glass's chin. Shaper felt Mary stiffen beside him.

'To finish,' Sandra sighed.

Then went back to muttering into the grisly scalp as if nothing had happened.

Tal shuffled closer in the bewildered silence, gripping Shaper's arm. 'Dan, please, I'm wor—'

Mary exploded. 'Bitch!' she shrieked, making everyone jump. 'Fuck your fucking methodology!'

Shaper held her back again, stunned at the force of her anger. 'Mary,' he cautioned, eyes fixed on the blade. She ignored him, stabbing a finger at Glass.

'This revenge bullshit, Sandra! Whatever you think he did, he's *forgotten* it! He's ill! You can't punish him!'

Sandra simply glared, eyes hooded.

'Fossey's gone!' Mary spat. 'Whatever . . . whatever stupid fucking payback you're looking for, whatever they did to him, it won't change things!' She was coming apart now, rage unsustainable, misery percolating through the anger. 'And . . . whatever Karl did to you, however he hurt you . . .' The first sob broke the sentence. 'N-nobody deserves that . . .'

She sank into damp, broken silence.

And there in Shaper's senses, like piss from a reptile's eyes, something sickly-sweet slithered down Sandra's face.

A smile.

'You people have such a low opinion of me,' she said.

Mary was barely listening, sobbing in the darkness, and Sandra waggled the scalp officiously, catching her attention. 'Karl never raped me, dear, all right? I fibbed. Does that make you feel better?'

Freddie moaned in the gloom. Sandra shushed him softly, smile fixed on the flesh in her hand, and in the depths of that sly expression a particle began to tumble in Shaper's mind, gathering shit as it slipped and slid . . .

'It's not about revenge,' he whispered. 'Is it?'

Sandra just smirked.

'Then what?' Mary croaked, surfacing from her stoop.

Shaper nodded at the scalp. 'They're repeating the treatment,' he whispered. 'A short cut to fucking purity.'

Sandra gave him a congratulatory bow.

And then Vince coughed. Shaper's eyes darted sideways, and finally – *oh Jesus* – he saw what poor Tal had been trying to show him all along.

There was blood trickling from the brute's lips.

Shaper understood instantly that there was nothing to worry about, that the big lug had simply bitten into his tongue in the haze of narcosis – (*been there, done that*) but Talvir, betrayed, hurt, lovesick, Talvir had only fear.

'She's fucking OD'd him!' the boy yelped, shaking off Shaper's fumbled grip and darting forward, breaking into the space Sandra had dominated so utterly. Reaching for his lover.

Everything happened at once.

Sandra blurred. Slack puppet strings abruptly strained, muscle memory ignited in outrage. Tal stumbled downwards, oblivious, hands grasping for Vince's face—

And something silver flashed.

And the youth's cry became an empty rasp.

And then there was blood and gravity, and a shattered voice gurgling through honey, and the whites of Talvir's eyes rolling in confusion.

'I said stay back!' Sandra shrieked, a knee-jerk defence to some cosmic jury. 'I *told* him!'

The knife was still outstretched, her arm locked straight to one side. She blinked, as if finally aware of what had happened, then turned her back to the crumpling youth and stalked back to her father and son.

Tal rested on his knees. Upright – for now. His throat gaped open.

The wound seemed to burp at one edge, spraying with a

violence utterly incongruous to the confusion of the body's gaze, then bubbled at the other with thick, deoxygenated slime. Shaper saw in horror that Vince's eyes – below the boy – were open, fluttering but aware, focused through rheumy exhaustion on the youth pouring out across him. The big man tried to lift his hands, tried to address his lover before the puzzlement went out of his eyes and his slow collapse ended. But Vince's body wouldn't work – Shaper could see the frustration of his empty effort – and his lips were too slack to form words. And so he stared, helpless, as Talvir vented out his life liquid then pitched forward, head striking the wall, to flounder sideways into his lap.

Gurgling, twitching, and finally lying still.

There was silence for a long, long time.

Chapter Thirty-nine

Eventually Shaper became aware of the need to breathe. He wondered how long he'd been holding it in.

Mary's hands, beside him, were cupped over her mouth – an elegant vision of silent trauma – and he could feel the weight of his Sickness building with the same impulse: a pustule ready to pop. He watched Glass's chest rise and fall, forming each frail sign of life into an extra layer of armour, swaddling the storm.

If he dies . . .

Oh god, don't let him die . . .

'I warned you,' Sandra murmured, eyes stroking across Tal's form. 'I warned you.'

Like, not my fault.

She replaced the blade at Glass's throat and rebuilt her composure, and just like that – without warning or segue – something snapped in Shaper's brain.

Enough.

'Fuck you!' he screamed. 'You can't . . . you can't cleanse *this*. Look what you did! Look!'

'But I *said*.'

Careless with rage, he strode another two paces, separated from Sandra only by Glass's bloody form. His senses tingled like dying cells, desperate to get crazy, to bathe the scene in the madness it deserved, but he tore his way through it and focused on the woman.

'You put that knife down. You fucking do it! Enough's enough!'

She rallied for a second, petulant in defence – 'I haven't *finished* yet!' – but Freddie let out a moan of such palpable fear that the anger hissed out of her, and she bent to whisper to him, soothing.

'I don't have the mask, my darling . . . I'm sorry. You can imagine, can't you?' She spoke in such soft tones that for a second all Shaper's rage was disarmed. 'You can make-believe old Asitanga-Shiva, yes? Old blue-face Bhairava, angel, come to steal you from mean Vishnu . . .'

(*Vishnu*, Shaper distantly remembered, a coil of memory delivered in Vince's voice. '*Brahmā the creator, Vishnu the maintainer, Shiva the destroyer.*')

Through it all, through the caring gaze and the sugar-sweet voice, Sandra's knife didn't move from her father's throat, holding Shaper back like a terrible promise – an invisible curtain of causality – effective even through his anger.

'Sandra!' he barked. 'Fossey's gone! Fossey's gone and there's too much blood on your hands! Your fucking treatment's not going to clean this!' He leaned further forwards, basking in the old man's presence, and lowered his voice like a spear for the charge. 'It *clings*, Sandra,' he whispered. 'You can't wash it away.'

But the woman wasn't listening. Instead she peered at him through narrowed eyes, as if fixated on a detail rather than the whole, and tilted her head until it was almost horizontal.

'Me?' she said.

'Put the knife down. I'm not joking!'

'You think . . . You think we did this for *ourselves*? Fossey and me?'

'Sandra!'

And she smiled, the creeping rictus of one who knows the initiative is theirs.

'You don't understand,' she said. 'Do you? Even after everything.'

'Just put the knife down.'

She turned to the side, blade never shifting, and with a theatrical flourish drew back the sheet that covered her son.

And finally – at long last – Shaper realised precisely how insane she was.

Mary, somewhere behind him, hissed like a snake.

Freddie was naked. Misshapen and shivering, he was held tight by fabric straps to both sides of the gurney . . . And he'd been prepared.

The souvenirs.

The missing parts . . .

They were laid across his body like some awful diagram, nuggets of drying flesh and bone. Each was held in place with a coloured ribbon and a pair of long needles, a vile acupuncture that looked as painful as it was precise.

Fucking meat butterflies.

Below the bulge of the boy's testes a tiny knuckle of polished ivory, looped through a red cord, was pinioned between his lumpen legs. The boy's privates were smothered by a ragged hood of crinkled flesh, held by an orange thong and more pins. Higher, above the mass of his lopsided belly, a formless bead of gristle was notched in place – its sling a bright sunlit yellow – and higher still a more recognisable trophy, shrunken though it was: a human heart, lassoed in a green satin sheath. In the dip of his collar, where the sheet had been drawn before, a prism of rubbery cartilage was fixed to a sky-blue choker, and even as Shaper watched, crippled with awe, Sandra deftly scooped a white band from a pocket and settled it across the boy's eyes. Sewn into the fabric, a pair of lumpy shapes spread inner moisture across the weave of the blindfold, and Shaper couldn't help but flick a glance at Mary.

Karl's eyes.

She was too busy gagging to notice.

His senses rebelled again, haunting the grisly scene like a djinn in a bottle, rattling to be free, and he physically clenched himself around them, as if cramping in his belly. Sandra spared him only a vague glance, uninterested in his spasm, and got on with her muttered mantras, flapping the scalp like a rag doll.

Sweating openly, feeding energy into what little remained of his rational brain, Shaper felt something wretched stir in the oil of his imagination. It slithered towards the jigsaw he'd built in his skull and *smeared* itself across every piece, changing them, darkening them, soaking in like alcohol . . .

What did Tova know? he thought, mind straining at its anchors. *What did Sandra mean, 'her background'? What 'speciality'?*

What secret could she have exposed?

As if in a dream, Sandra appeared to become aware of his flailing thoughts. She paused, watching him with a spreading smile. Waiting, he thought.

Waiting for me to get it.

He craned closer to Glass – a parasite suckling on calm – and forced himself to believe it made a difference.

'*In Norrbotten,*' he heard Tova say, voice coiling up from that first day on the job, sunlit in Freddie's room, '*many small communities. Insular. Small . . . what is the word?*'

(The Sickness viciously conjured a contemporary vision – Tova as she now was – like a counterpoint to the memory: bloodless, face gnawed, cold like the soil.)

'*Pond for genes, yes?*' he heard her say. '*High incidence of Type Three Gaucher.*'

Wait.

Oh Jesus, wait . . .

She was talking about . . .

Mary, somewhere off in the distant dark, was recovering from the retching fit, craning to see the ghastly game board arranged across Freddie. 'What the *fuck* . . . ?' she hissed.

Shaper ignored her, casting forwards through the murk of recollection, and heard Sandra speaking of muddled pasts and old confusions. '*The memories are sort of jumbled, you know?*' she'd said. '*It was an odd time in my life . . .*'

A kid, he thought, struck by a shitty disease.

A genetic joke.

Hints of a vile act.

And there, back in the ice house, he saw the hatred in her eyes for the bloody, bare-skulled, broken old man under her power, this perfect, holy, Unascended Master, and the idea *heaved* through Shaper's soul.

The world turned to treacle.

'It was him,' he said out loud. 'It was Glass who raped you.'

And time came back in a whinge of sitars and a pound of drums, and Shaper found himself recoiling from the old man as if from a lit fuse. Opposite him, Sandra seemed to sag, as if simply speaking the truth had robbed it of its dark potency. For a moment Shaper's growing disgust, commingled with fury at his own idiocy, and a slash of heartbroken idolism, paused in its muster, and he wobbled on his axis to leap forward, ready to knock away the knife before Sandra could recover.

But.

But at last the delusions rolled in fully, unrestrained, bellowing in the eye of his disgust. The truth had robbed him of his last medication – that final spooky salve, a perfect person's kindly regard – as surely as if Sandra had shifted the blade and killed the old man already. The seizure hit him like a sledgehammer to the soul, locking his bones and crippling his muscles, and he groaned through an indrawn breath – fighting for life – and staggered in his spot.

Glass.

Not you . . .

It rang out from the caves of his mind.

I was supposed to save you! I was supposed to do something good!

Across the room, Sandra seemed more animated with every second, liberated by the shared secret. 'The first time,' she said, oblivious to Shaper's paralysis, 'was after one of their . . . sessions, downstairs. He was all fired up, you understand. Tripping, too. Giggling.'

She lifted her eyes. Even dissipated – even diffused like a vented toxin – the hate still burned, a white-hot pilot.

'He was just . . . being silly, I thought. Cuddling. Tickling.' She sneered, ghastly. 'Kissing.'

Shaper's distortions painted her with an unexpected sympathy, a hint of innocence, a glimmer of childish joy, all of it soured – contaminated – by oceans of shit and blood. The muck drew flies – hallucinated or not – and they whirlpooled round the chamber like a great angry cloud, buzzing beyond sound, stinking beyond smell, settling on the sticky skin of George Glass like a robe.

Shaper wrestled his own body, every muscle electrolysed. Nothing worked.

'He drugged me, too,' Sandra went on. 'A glass of wine, the first time. 'You're old enough now, he said. Tasted funny – I remember that. And it made everything . . . like a dream. Lights and shapes and . . . sounds.' She blinked. The times after that he just dripped it on to my tongue. He had this little eye-dropper bottle – liquid LSD. "Magic potion," he called it. It made the whole thing . . . not real. Do you see? So I didn't have to know. So I could bear it.'

She coughed to clear her throat, the ugly sound appearing to lift her from her own trance, and fixed her eyes back on to Shaper. 'And so he could say I'd just imagined it.'

Bastard.

Beside him blood still snotted from the old man's ruined head – *tappety-tapping* to the sitar – and Shaper found himself thinking, *good. Hope it hurts.*

'And then a few months later,' Sandra said, suddenly arch, flapping the sodden scalp at Mary, '*her* mum started putting together the big idea, didn't she? The big treatment. Wanted to purify poor crazy Karl, and you can't blame her for that. Looking for a guinea pig.'

'Your dad caught you with Fossey,' Shaper cut in, mouth spared the physical lockdown, final connections meshing.

'Yes. He heard shouting. Fossey was angry – I'd just told him about . . . about . . .'

'About being pregnant.'

She looked away, nodding just once.

'*Small pond for genes,*' Shaper heard, a ghost among ghosts. '*High incidence of Type Three Gaucher . . .*'

That's incest, love.

His heart suddenly boiled in its cage, as if punishing him for his slowness; dropping him to one knee and making him cry out, a clattering succession of pains along every artery. Sweat clogged his eyes and mouth now, the effort of moving – of overcoming this inertia – too much to bear.

His own brain, killing him at last.

Nearby, the shimmering demigod that was George Glass was utterly transformed. Gone was the purifying aura, that cleansing radiance that had becalmed Shaper's psyche again and again. In some quiet, cynical corner of his mind a soft voice dared to wonder if – *whisper it* – the frail old man had ever had anything to do with it at all.

Psychic placebos.

For fuckssakes.

He pulled himself back on to his feet – an automatic shift

beyond any conscious defeat of the stasis – and tried to focus on the woman at the heart of the maelstrom. He found her simply staring into space, lost in another universe.

'Dad said . . . l-later-on, I mean, when I asked . . . He said Fossey was naked when he came in. Said Fossey was . . . was going to do things to me.' She shut her eyes and shook her head. 'It wasn't like that!'

'But you weren't sure?'

Keep her talking. You can beat this!

'I was confused. I think . . . I think I would've believed anything Dad said, then.' Her eyes opened, brimming with tears, even as a new layer of bitterness incised her voice. 'He was George Glass. The Great. The Special. How could *he* lie?' Her lip wobbled. 'Everyone believed him, so I did too.'

Shaper realised, distantly, that Mary was weeping behind him. He ignored it – another betrayal, another nail in the coffin of her trust – and fixed his gaze on the killer.

Keep.

The nutter.

Talking.

'S-so the group got its guinea pig,' he said. 'Right? Except the treatment didn't work like they wanted.'

Sandra stared at him for a long time. Eyes shuttered down to a reptilian slash, lip curling, as if she couldn't believe anyone could be so dumb.

And then she laughed. A sudden three-note volley, empty of humour, which retched out of her with such brutal discord that her whole body shook. For a second Shaper thought she might have slipped the knife across Glass's throat without even meaning it, but no, the grip was as steady as ever.

He wasn't sure if he was pleased or disappointed.

On cue the old man groaned, a bubble of fevered pain through slack lips, and to Shaper his fluttering eyes became coals, flaring through a dense mat of mayflies and maggots.

'Do you seriously think,' Sandra said, 'that this wasn't what he wanted?'

What?

'You seriously think the treatment went wrong *by accident*?'

Staggering again, Shaper flashed to an innocuous memory: the look he'd seen on the old man's face the day before, when Vince flirted with Sandra on the stairs. That stay-away-from-my-daughter glare, so incongruous in a man so genial.

He couldn't stand her being with anyone except himself. So he deliberately fucked it up. Deliberately short-circuited Fossey's ... what?

His chi-energy circuit? His chakra grid? Is that it?

You believe that crap now, do you?

'He broke Fossey's brain,' Sandra snarled, as if to settle the matter. 'Just to get him out of the way.'

Behind his back, Shaper sensed Mary sink to the floor. He tried to turn but couldn't, detecting her only at the far edge of his pinioned gaze shuffling to prop herself against the wall. Sobbing and retching across her knees.

Broken.

Sandra's anger finally bubbled over, a nova of green light which rippled through every brick of the ice house, drawing forth the shrieking paintings from beneath their plastic veils.

'You see?' she shouted, waving at Mary. 'You see how he affects people? They love him! They can't help it! They don't know what he's like!'

The figures danced. Sleazy, tribal gestures, great breasts swinging, blue skin slick with spittle. A sudden coldness clenched at Shaper, and he realised he recognised faces on each swaying body.

Anna ...

The Corams ...

Bloody, broken, beaten men and women . . .

He dropped back to the floor with a moan. The very earth seemed alive with weirdness – the ghosts of his past crowding around – and Sandra moved through it all like a conductor, waggling the knife at her gurgling father.

'It's not fair!' she wailed. 'He just . . . forgot it! A fucking stroke, "meditation", *whatever*! That's not *fair*. That's not *forgiveness*.'

'I . . . I know,' Shaper managed. 'I *know*, Sandra.'

'He just *put it away*. Tattooed a fucking reminder to keep him from the police and, and . . .'

'I know.'

'It took me ten years!' She was screaming now, losing control. 'Ten years just to remember! Even then there are gaps. All the . . . the acid, the trauma . . .' She sniffed violently. 'You said it yourself, it *clings*.'

You don't get to walk away from your guilt. Shaper's own words, back to taunt him.

He felt the memories seethe along his back, each old victim twisting his spine, each ghastly action tainting his soul. He saw men crying as he beat them to paste, women howling as thugs crippled husbands and brothers, one-bollocked Albanians bleeding round rubber-band tourniquets, and too many faceless faces, menaced by remote. They fingered and dragged at him, wobbling the world on its head, slurping him into the same pestilent mire as Glass and his daughter. He felt himself infected by the same ruddy taint, and heard the buzzing of flies become unbearable, a great invisible dynamo, building to detonation.

He tried one last time, gritting his teeth through the storm.

'I agree! All right, Sandra? I fucking *agree*. I've done . . . Th-there's baggage, OK? I understand! But this chakra bollocks, this treatment stuff. It's not the answer! There's no quick fix! It's gotta be hard, or it's not worth shit! You've gotta *work at it*!'

The woman went animal-still. The world seemed to pause, listening close.

'But my son, Mr Shaper. My son can't do that.'

Such was the simplicity of the statement, so plain in its love and devotion, that he found his self-restraints weakening, the Sickness quietened by the sentiment. He found he could heave himself upright once more, and slugged forward in a single, Herculean step.

The woman snapped back round before he could take another.

'I *will* kill him,' she said, businesslike, knife at Glass's throat.

Shaper stared, fresh shivers climbing from his feet.

'I don't think I care any more,' he said.

Sandra almost smiled. 'You're quite right. Let's cut the shit, shall we?'

And she turned in one graceful arc, impossibly serene, and positioned the knife vertically above Freddie's heart.

'No!' he shouted, visions boiling with a new urgency. Her voice reached him through the hurricane walls.

'Evil,' she whispered. 'Do you understand? A child conceived in . . . in violence and disgust. He's corrupted in the flesh, Mr Shaper. A living sin, through no fault of his own. Don't you see that?'

She bent to kiss the boy's head, whispering strange secrets in his ear – 'Lam, Vam, Ram, Yam, Ham, Aum . . .' – and each syllable rustled upwards in Shaper's eyes as a tattered, bruise-toned moth. Around Freddie the distortion was even stronger, an irresistible vacuum of light and loss. Even as Shaper watched, it seemed to crystallise, and one by one a grid of lights appeared along its flank, a runway strip, spread along the boy's flexing spine.

A spirit engine, chugging to life.

Magic.

(Shutupshutupshutup!)

Somewhere, in some sideways world beyond his sight, Tightfisted Tony moaned between distant snores, afflicted by nightmares. Nearer to the heart of the darkness – as if gripped by some communal mania – Mary was vomiting noisily across the floor, and Vince—

Wait.

Vince was moving his arm.

Inspired, Shaper tried one last time to shift, to shatter his restraints and end the insanity. But the Sickness was too strong – exultant in its liberation, free from all chemical bond and spiritual salve – and he realised at last that he couldn't fight it any more. It was too much, too great a burden of memories, too rich a soup of bygone sins.

He supposed, in some quiet lagoon of self-knowledge, that he'd always known it would beat him eventually.

The string of lights along Freddie's body began to pulse. Like some slow thrum – a mechanical cycle, brightening and dimming – it sent a lazy ripple from the child's hips to his head. The sitar snagged itself in the vibration – a shark in a barbed net – and thrashed along the strip.

'He deserves better,' Sandra said. 'He deserves to escape.'

And something awoke. Shaper could see it.

Something that was bunched and coiled – a spiral of muddy, base energy – writhed to life at the tip of Freddie's tailbone.

Kundalini.

The soul serpent.

Sandra reached out to her son and softly spread her father's scalp across his hair, sniffing back a tear.

'*Ah,*' she intoned.

Sahasrara. The word boomed through the world.

Above Freddie's head, aching in Shaper's eyes, a new light appeared. Stronger, brighter, clearer than the rest, a thick violet maelstrom, which somehow drew the others into it, and pounded in his muscles with each pulsation.

In the shadows, he saw, Vince was wrestling himself too, fighting exhaustion, struggling beneath the weight of his dead, dripping lover. A tear had slicked itself down the brute's cheek, and Shaper noticed with a sudden thrill that the man was staring at him, eyes focused and clear.

Look, they said. *See!*

His hand, glacier-slow, creeping into his jacket pocket.

Shaper felt the world stop spinning. He felt the sitar shrug off all pretension of musicality and the tabla break all rudiment of rhythm, and together become mere chaos, a basal vibration in the rocks of reality. The room fluttered and spumed with unspeakable power, and – beaten, overwhelmed, helpless – Shaper sagged like a puppet.

And surrendered to his disease.

Somewhere, Sandra said, 'Be free, my son,' and raised the knife for the killing blow. 'Enter Samadhi and be free.'

The worm in the boy's spine untangled with a hiss, and in another universe Vince's hand crept free from its pocket.

Shaper heard Freddie blurt a single *oom* of fear, and the serpent pulsed like a star being born – like the death of everything, like a world torn to shreds – and then raced, *rocketed*, along the string of stolen lights. Straight for his skull.

Sandra's arm, Shaper saw, went tense.

Vince was growling in his throat, blood flecking his chin, and with a gasp of impossible effort – gaugeless fury – he skittered something bright across the plastic floor. Directly towards Shaper.

And as if impregnated by his friend's anger, in that endless instant of resignation, Shaper stopped trying to block the Sickness and let it swallow him whole. As he did so, he remembered another time, a confrontation just minutes before, which felt like another life. A moment when he'd broken free from Fossey's spell and escaped the stasis of a corpse candle, just by letting his own rage have its day.

By refusing to fight himself.

Let go.

He let the shivers consume him so utterly that they burned themselves out, silenced like competing wave forms.

He let the horrors of the past stain themselves so deeply on to his vision that they transmuted from shadow to shade, a secret render to inform and deepen every shape, without first obscuring it.

He let the sensory tangles build to their mightiest crescendo, no longer caring that he could see sounds and taste sights, content that each crackling impression was important – was *honest* – irrespective of its sanity.

He let his heart groan and palpitate, and learned to love it.

You don't get to walk away from your guilt, he thought.

So walk to-fucking-wards it.

And his arms came unstuck.

And Sandra lurched for the killing blow.

And he moved faster than he'd ever moved, scooping up the flick knife his friend had thrown – *mine!* – and snapping open the blade.

And he threw it.

All of it one perfect, continuous motion, a golden blur which gurgled its poetry and beauty into his capsized psyche, then—

Then killed the delusions dead.

The blade hit Sandra in the face. It gouged open her cheek and knocked her back, her own knife dropping away unused. She screamed and shook and boiled, smashing into Glass's chair, upsetting the candles, howling like an animal. Even as the shakes slurped clear like sludge down a drain, Shaper watched in fading tones as lightning and lava vomited from her body, hosing from the slash of her face.

Little by little she came to stillness. Little by little Shaper's eyes cleared, and even as he sensed Mary strangling a sob and Vince finally slumping in a heartbroken faint, still he watched her, silent, glowering into nothing as blood soaked her robes.

Slowly, she reached for the knife she'd dropped.

And before Shaper could even tense himself to react, she slid it – with something a little like a smile – into her own chest.

And then there was nothing but stillness and dark, and the lingering patters of liquid on the floor.

Chapter Forty

Time did what it does.

December rolled in with a shell-shocked furtivity – *don't mind me, just passing through* – and among the gathering vultures of premature decoration and garish advertising, the weather mutated, a fierce coldness tilting the balance from relentless drizzle to crisper, clearer days. Pigeons still huddled in chilly squares, but now grew fat on the leavings of charitable lunatics and late-night snackers, while smokers – still lurking outside pubs – grumbled not at soggy smokes but lighter-singed gloves. Night settled earlier with an obese comfort, mornings arrived later, and the parakeets . . .

The fucking parakeets truculently refused to bugger off south.

They – in their small, window-bothering way – explained at least in part why, one cloudless morning a week before Christmas, Dan Shaper haunted a table in Tony's Grill'n'Sizzler, fixating on the slimy remainder of his coffee. He was trying to imagine how a particle of caffeine might appear to the eye if studied up close, what journey it might take if he tilted the mug for one last slurp, and what secret chambers it might visit in his brain, to execute its sense-tightening purpose.

There'd been no meds in three weeks. No twitchy calls to semi-hostile men in hospital overalls and sunglasses; no surreptitious rebuilding of the long-lost pill file. Coffee, he'd concluded, wasn't much of a substitute, even when ably backed by Tightfisted Tony's greasiest bacon bomb, but it was all he had.

This time, he'd promised himself. This time for good.

It wasn't as if he needed them any more.

(Keep telling yourself that, fucko.)

The door jangled as it opened, and he straightened with a conspicuous lack of cool, excited. Then slumped, grouchy, and drained the coffee.

'Oh,' he mumbled. 'It's *you*.'

DI Canton settled himself at the seat opposite and remained blissfully unaware of the green-and-orange spikes of out-of-place awkwardness surrounding him. His imperious glance across at the counter tasted of ash and authority, and Tony – making a rare front-of-house appearance – gave a sheepish nod and babbled instructions at his staff, before fleeing into the office, famously allergic to cops. Shaper filed each impression away and, as was his habit these days, glanced at his own hands.

Not a tremor.

The two men sat in silence until an apron jockey deposited a groaning carb nuke in front of Canton, and whipped away Shaper's egg-encrusted plate, administering fresh coffee all round. He ignored Shaper's unconvincing protests – *I'll be pissing all day, ho ho ho* – then left them in peace.

At least, semi peace.

At a nearby table sat a boy – no older than sixteen, swaddled in an enormous coat – who'd been nursing his tea for hours and focusing intently on playing a card game with himself. To Shaper's senses he smelled of hair and hostility, and a weird little bubble of concentration – creamy-yellow – was glowing round his hands.

Homeless, Shaper supposed. Poor little fuck.

Sympathetic or not, the *fnap*, *fnap* of cards on tabletop had achieved a parakeet level of annoying, and in spite of the cop's fussy little chewing sounds, Canton presented his best hope of distraction.

'So,' said Shaper, at exactly the moment the cop did the same.

They stared some more, each gesturing the other to begin – an instant politeness duel – until Canton flashed his palms and snapped, 'Right, bollocks, *I'll* start.'

Shaper felt quietly victorious.

'What it is,' the cop began, 'is I've got a closed case. So-called. And I've no fucking idea what happened.'

The man levelled an expectant look across the table, all silver needles and herby scents. Shaper ignored it and waited him out. There somehow didn't seem such a rush to the world, these days.

Canton sighed and lumbered on alone, counting on his fingers. 'I've got a dead woman, right? Self-inflicted – that's fine. I've got a half-eaten Swede in the stately fucking grounds. I've got an Indian lad with his throat cut, I've got evidence of shotgun damage, and I've got two witnesses who'll swear blind this little cow – the one who stabbed herself – did all of it on her tod. *And* that she confessed to the Tourist shit right before.'

'I see,' said Shaper, unable to resist a quantum smile. 'Golly.'

Canton dialled up his acidic Look. 'That's "witnesses", by the way, with all the credibility of a rotten bollock.' He shook his head. 'One's a scally with a record longer'n his solitary functioning arm – who, frankly, should be shot for crimes against sausage –' he picked revoltedly at his teeth – 'and the other's not only been selling herself as a fucking spirit medium for years, but now merrily admits it was all toss.' He swirled his coffee, glum. 'Couldn't you have found more reliable people, mate?'

'Don't know what you mean.' Shaper shrugged, playing the game.

Canton harpooned a concrete yolk with another sigh and changed tack, voice softening through floral tones to an intimate paisley.

(*Off the record*, Shaper understood. *Mates, not allies.*)

'You seen her?' the cop said. 'Miss Devon?'

'Seeing her today,' he chirruped – too fast. 'Be along any minute.' Even he could hear the overstrained jauntiness in his voice.

Canton *mm*ed politely – smart enough not to push – and resumed the business tone as if the intermission had never happened.

'So anyway, all those . . . bits, you know? The stolen organs. They were there too, true enough, so that helps. Tash s— That is, *forensics* say . . .' Canton coughed away the slip, 'there were some jam jars down there, recently used for pickling. Storage, they think. And Sandra's prints are on those, so the star witnesses aren't exactly key, thank god.'

Shaper was still gently smirking – '*Tash*', *is it? Not* '*Natasha*'? – but wiped it clear before Canton noticed, forgoing the right to piss-take. It was enough to know, somehow, that *something* good had come of all this.

Canton thanked him – *ungrateful bastard* – by suddenly going sly, a distinct eel-like sheen rendering his body.

'Haven't found the weapon, mind,' he dangled. 'The one she did herself in with.'

And nor will you, mate, on account of it's in my pocket.

Shaper straight-faced a non-committal, 'Ah,' and got back to his coffee.

At the next table the kid's grubby hands turned over the deck and started again.

Fnap, fnap.

For fuckssakes.

Canton gave up on the official line with a huff and tilted forward, all enthused conspiracy.

'What happened, Shaper?'

'How on earth should I know, officer?' *Butter wouldn't melt.* 'I wasn't there.'

The cop wadded his tongue into a cheek, the first fuzzy glimmers of impatience like a second skin, minutely defracting the light. 'Oh really?'

'Really.'

'Well, *fine*, but see, here's the thing. We've also got a traumatised old git with no scalp up at the hospital. I'm wondering if he might have something to say about that.'

Shaper sipped his coffee, deliberately slow. 'You mean, if he ever wakes up from his coma? Long enough to stop screaming, like.'

Canton just glared.

'And anyway, the way I understand it,' Shaper waved a tremble-free hand, 'and this is just what I've heard, you'd also have to take into account some weird DNA results from a certain paternity test, on a certain special needs kiddie.'

'All right, smartarse, but—'

'And given the age of the mother – when she got knocked up, I mean – that'd be, what? Statutory rape?'

Canton looked away, glowing harmless blue. Disarmed. 'You've made your point.'

'Too fucking right.' Shaper's turn, now, to lean forward – joining the cop in the Venn overlap of secrecy and honesty above the table's centre. 'If he ever does recover, starts making sense . . .'

'Yeah?'

'You fucking *throw away the key*, Canton.'

They sat back in their seats. Shaper peered into his mug and tried not to hear the *fnap*ping of the kid's cards, trying to let the wraparound muddle of sensory weirdness swaddle rather than terrify. It was getting a little easier every day.

Even so, he couldn't help glancing up, electrified, when the door swung open with an imagined fanfare and a burst of gold.

Just a tourist. Fuck.

The cop was too canny to miss it. 'So when's she supposed to arrive?' he asked, faux innocent.

'Sometime.' *Move on, fucko.*

Canton took the hint.

'As for the Tommy Boyle angle,' the cop mumbled, 'they've dismissed it. A "random intersection of disconnected cases" – that's how my super put it.'

'Right then.'

A strange intensity slipped across the cop's face, annihilating the flippant façade in tones of gun metal and greasy gas. 'That *is* right, isn't it Dan? There's nothing else you want to tell me?'

He needs to know, Shaper saw.

Not for his career. Not for promotions or closed cases. Canton needed to know simply because he hated the Corams too; because they fascinated and obsessed him, and because the only way he'd ever be free – free from that one stupid decision he made, back when he took their money – was to bring the fuckers down in flames.

'They called me,' Shaper said.

'And?'

'They had a . . . conversation. With Fossey. About old times.'

Canton had stopped breathing. Shaper sighed, itchy at the unblinking stare.

'It's pretty much like I thought, mate. Foster had a bee in his bonnet about the once-over he got from Tommy Boyle. Followed him home that night, got even. End of.'

'And the boss? Sam Coram?'

'Fossey never went near him.'

'They're sure? How do they know he's not lying?'

'Mate, they're *persuasive*. Whatever happened to the twins' dad, it's nothing to do with Sandra, Glass, Fossey, all that. "Random intersection", like you said.' He decanted an apologetic tone into his voice. 'You did everything you could, mate, you're just . . . you're not going to get the sods this time. Not through Boyle, and not through crazy Foster.'

The Corams don't get their hands dirty, mate.

'I'm sorry.'

Canton slumped in his seat. Not for the first time Shaper caught himself feeling desperately intertwined with this prim, vengeful little man: just another fuck-up, another hopeless case trying to tidy the shit stains of the past.

Me, but in a suit.

'Look, don't worry, all right?' He deliberately brightened his voice. 'You'll get 'em.'

You've got to. For my sake.

The twins' call, when it had come, had seared itself with unpleasant vividity on to Shaper's brain. The moment Dave had finished enthusiastically expounding the outcome of their 'chat' with Fossey – in rather gorier detail, *the fucks*, than the version he'd just served Canton – there'd been a strange and sudden lull, then the clanking of a new hand on the phone. And then—

Her. Like nerve gas hissing from the earpiece.

'Hello, Daniel,' she'd said. 'The twins tell me you did some good work.'

Since the basement at Thornhill – since he stopped fighting his own brain – Shaper's acceptance of the Sickness had progressed in leaps. It was never easy, never comfortable, but in absorption and acceptance he'd found an end to the horrors, the palpitations, the chemical urge. He was finding his way.

Only when he'd heard her voice – *Maude, you evil puff-pastry bitch* – had the resolve faltered.

'Such a pity we didn't get the result we wanted,' she'd said, as the phone started to shake in his hand, 'but then . . . that's not your fault, I suppose.'

Fuck off, fuck off, fuck off.

'Still, there's such a lot going on, these days. We can use all the help we can get. I'd like to . . . have a chat about the future. Would you think about that?'

Die, die, die.

'We miss you, Daniel.'

He'd hung up without saying a word.

(I miss you too.)

Canton dragged him back to the present with an appraising grunt. 'What?'

'Nothing.' *Wave it away. Again and again and again.* 'Doesn't matter.'

'Suit yourself.'

'Listen, how's the boy?'

'Freddie?' Canton puffed out his cheeks. 'He's . . . Actually, he's not great. They've got him in a home, you know? Nice place, all very professional. But . . . he just won't eat, mate. I had a word with the doctors. He's weak. Cries a lot. Pukes up whatever they put down him. They're not expecting much.'

'I see.'

Somehow the gloomy news tugged Shaper's eyes back to the boy in the corner, laying out his cards. Annoying or not, he found himself abruptly robbed of his anger, his petty little hatreds, and could almost imagine a radiant aura – a peaceful, perfect ghost of innocence – around the child.

But then he noticed each card bore a squiggly picture and more bright colours than a paintpocalypse, and thought: *tarot.*

Oh, you little twerp.

He'd had quite enough of magic.

'Your lass, Mary,' Canton blurted, following some spooky thematic cue. 'She goes to visit him now and then, the doctors said.'

'Yeah. I expect she would.'

His eyes went back to the door, determinedly unmoving. *Damn it, Mary.*

She'd said, last time they spoke, she needed time to think. A lot of weird stuff, she'd said, has been going on.

He couldn't argue with that, anyway.

'Maybe I'll study for something,' she'd said, and Shaper had known without thought – in the depths of her baleful look, as thoroughly absorbing as only an abstract future could be – that whatever carelessly woven thread of shared lies and wallowed uncleanliness had connected them was already frayed beyond repair. 'I think . . . I think it might be sort of good to become a therapist.' Then she'd blinked and added a cautious, 'Or something. Something to help people, anyway.'

Well, yeah, he'd thought, one last pulse of selfish indignation, *that's what I try and do as w—*

'*Really* help them,' she'd said, before he could open his mouth. 'You know?'

Like, *not just scrabbling about in the shit. Not like you, Dannyboy. Not this bullshit underworld life, endlessly polishing turds.*

'Uh,' he'd managed.

'See you in Tony's some time. OK?'

Yeah. Sometime.

He sucked back more coffee and listened to the past, no longer afraid of it.

'*Stressful situations,*' Vince had said, not long ago. '*Best fucking aphrodisiac out.*'

Shaper stared at the cafe door and admitted – *fuck it* – he felt pretty unstressed these days.

'What about Vince?' Canton said, cursed by coincidence. 'How's he? I heard there were . . . tensions.'

Shaper fidgeted. 'He's . . .'

Well.

He's shit.

He's shit because his lover died right in front of him, and burning in the poor little queen's eyes when he croaked was the clear and certain knowledge the big lug had been less than faithful.

He's shit because, not long after, I tried to tell him I knew how he felt – that I could help if he'd let me, that the last thing he should do is try to bottle it away – and he just shot me a look like he'd found me squirming in his fucking food and said, 'This is your fault.'

'He'll come round,' Shaper said.

Maybe.

One day.

Canton wiped his mouth with an initialled handkerchief and gave a none-of-my-business-anyway nod. More time passed.

More tarots flapped.

More people who weren't Mary shuffled in.

'Better be off,' Canton finally grunted, shrugging on his jacket. 'You be all right?'

'Course. Why not?'

'Yeah. Why not?'

'And you take care too, officer. Rumour going round it's a jungle out there.'

'Cheers, mate. And thanks for breakfast.'

Shaper had already nodded a thoughtless *no problem*, watching the cop leave amidst smug purples and plinkity pianos, before realising he'd been cheerfully diddled out of four pounds fifty without having offered. *Bloody cops.*

In fact, money was going to be a problem. Even after Glass's cheque cleared, even after Vince told him to stick his fee up his shitter, there was still Tony to pay off, Mrs Swanson to appease, bills to settle.

Back to the gutter, ratboy, a sly brain voice giggled. *'Twas ever thus.*

But then such curmudgeonly thoughts – money, living, day-to-day crap – required a fevered ability to inspect one's own future, something in which Shaper had entirely no interest. So he pushed it all away, resigned himself to buying Canton's breakfast without grudge, and went back to . . .

To sitting alone.

To watching the door.

To *fnap, fnap, fnap.*

Sooner or later his phone rang. He managed to avoid the breathless '*Mary?*' that shot up in his throat – Unknown Number, after all – but couldn't disguise the excitement of his, 'Hello?'

'Mr Shaper?'

A man's voice. Damn.

'Mr Shaper, my name's Alfie Werner. I've . . . I've met you a couple times down the Mutt's Nut. I work the bar there, odd nights.'

'OK?'

'It's . . . the thing is, Mr Shaper, I'm in sort of a . . . a bit of bother, and a few folks've said you might be the feller to help. And I can pay, after all, and . . . and . . .'

And so on.

He talked for a while.

'On my way,' Shaper said, hanging up. And then didn't move.

He sat and stared at his coffee, and when that was gone he sat and stared at his hand. It seemed to him to be not only *steady* – free from tremor – but to be also somehow imbued with a new *solidity*, as if before there'd been some surreal uncertainty as to whether it, or the rest of his body, was really anything to do with him at all.

You're going mad, his brain told him, filling the room with fluttering gulls and gently tolling bells. He told it, *What d'you mean, 'going'?* and smiled despite himself.

He tried to imagine that same old delusion – the lesions marking his flesh, the mould within, the pustules and pestilence splitting the skin – but it wouldn't clarify. Even when he dared to leaf through his memory, to scratch at the past with a cavalier nonchalance, still he could draw up only the faintest echo, like a botched exposure from a cheap camera.

Progress, he thought.

And then, almost straight away: *she's not coming, mate.*

So he stood and paid at the till. And as he crossed back to the door, fully intending to go help Alfie Werner with whateverthefuck was the problem – assuming the guy wasn't a scumbag or rapist or child-molesting Unascended Master, or just plain annoying – he paused by the homeless kid with the tarot cards and considered saying something.

Mate, you do know it's all bollocks, don't you?

But he bottled it.

Instead he gave the boy the change from his pockets, felt slightly stupid, and went out into London.

Contract

Simon Spurrier

Michael Point doesn't seem anything special. He dresses conservatively, is thoughtful, methodical and well spoken. He also happens to kill people for a living. But there's no personal agenda here, it's not about revenge; for Michael it's much simpler than that:

IT'S ALL ABOUT THE MONEY.

But things are starting to get strange: his hits are coming back to life and trying to kill him. That's not right – not right at all – and Michael hasn't a clue what's going on. Is his conscience caving in? Is he losing his grip? Or could it be that the things he sees are hints of a divine conflict: a heavenly war, sucking him in . . . ?

'Spurrier is very, very good . . . exceptionally vivid'
SFX

978 0 7553 3590 9

headline